A Buddhist Manual of Psychological Ethics

Pali Text Society
Translation Series, No. 41

A BUDDHIST MANUAL OF PSYCHOLOGICAL ETHICS

Translation of the first book *Abhidhammapiṭaka*
entitled *Dhammasaṅgaṇī*
Compendium of States or Phenomena

With introductory essay and notes by

MRS. RHYS DAVIDS

MOTILAL BANARSIDASS PUBLISHERS
PRIVATE LIMITED • DELHI

First Indian Edition : **Delhi, 2016**
Third Edition : 1974 (1993, 2012)
Second Edition : 1923
First Published : 1900

ISBN: 978-81-208-4041-6

MOTILAL BANARSIDASS

41 U.A. Bungalow Road, Jawahar Nagar, Delhi 110 007
8 Mahalaxmi Chamber, 22 Bhulabhai Desai Road, Mumbai 400 026
203 Royapettah High Road, Mylapore, Chennai 600 004
236, 9th Main III Block, Jayanagar, Bangaluru 560 011
8 Camac Street, Kolkata 700 017
Ashok Rajpath, Patna 800 004
Chowk, Varanasi 221 001

MLBD *Cataloging-in-Publication Data*
A Buddhist Manual of Psychological Ethics
Translated by MRS. RHYS DAVIDS
in *MLBD Sacred Books of the Buddhist Series*
ISBN : 978-81-208-4041-6
Includes Translation of the first book in the *Abhidhammapiṭaka* entitled *Dhammasaṅgaṇī*, Appendix and Index
I. Buddhism II. Psychology III. Ethics
IV. Abhidhammapiṭaka V. Dhammasaṅgaṇī
VI. Davids, A.F. Rhys

Published by
Motilal Banarsidass Publishers Private Limited
www.mlbd.com • mlbd@mlbd.com
Printed by Replika Press Pvt. Ltd.

To

EDWARD T. STURDY,

BY

WHOSE GENEROUS ASSISTANCE

THE EDITION OF THE COMMENTARY

HAS BEEN RENDERED ACCESSIBLE TO SCHOLARS,

AND

A TRANSLATION OF THE TEXT TO READER GENERALLY,

THIS VOLUME IS DEDICATED

WITH THE CORDIAL REGARD OF HIS FRIEND,

THE TRANSLATOR.

PREFACE TO THE THIRD EDITION

The original edition of A Buddhist Manual of Psychological Ethics was published in 1900 by the Royal Asiatic Society as vol. XII in the Oriental Translation Fund, New Series. Before this date neither Dhammasaṅgaṇi nor any of the other six Abhidhamma works had been translated into English. The R.A.S. therefore must command the respect and gratitude of everyone interested in this area of Pali canonical literature for its pioneer venture in publishing Mrs Rhys Davids's translation, and thus not only opening up a field at that time virtually untrodden and unexplored by westerners, but also making more widely known both her name and her considerable powers. That this venture was well justified may be judged by the publication of a 2nd edn. in 1923, also by the R.A.S., and of this 3rd edn. produced by the Pali Text Society with the gracious approval and assent of the R.A.S.

The 2nd edn., slightly revised by Mrs Rhys Davids, was re-set in a smaller type than that used in the original edn. Consequently the pagination differed. It is hoped, however, that all inconsistencies in the numbering of the page-references have now been removed. In addition, it must be stated that as this 3rd edn. is a photocopy of the 2nd it retains its pagination except in one particular now to be explained:

Between 1900 and 1923 Mrs Rhys Davids came to realize that the 2nd edn. must begin " as the 1st edn. should have begun, with the real beginning of the Abhidhamma-Piṭaka, i.e. with the Mātikā or Table of Contents " (2nd edn. p. ix). Unfortunately, however, though this integral part of Dhammasaṅgaṇi was included in the 2nd edn., it was paginated in roman figures (p. cv–cxiii) thus running on from the end of the Introductory Essay as though it were part of that. In order to rectify this anomaly without re-paginating the 364 pages of translation and indexes that follow, we have ventured to call these Mātikā pages M1–M9.

Moreover, it has seemed advisable to replace Mrs Rhys Davids's Preface to the Second Edition by this brief biographical sketch of the book together with the few paragraphs that follow. She was always in favour of advance, not of standing still, and since the publication of the 2nd edn., just over 50 years ago, great strides have been made in Abhidhamma studies. To keep pace with these developments we have decided to utilize the space at our disposal for a rather more precise and instructive analysis of the significance of Dhammasaṅgaṇi than could be presented half a century ago.

I. B. Horner.

London, 1973.

In any consideration of Abhidhamma studies the term to be examined before all others is " mātikā ". The reason for this lies in the method adopted throughout the Abhidhamma-Piṭaka of examining the nature and behaviour of the many states, mental and material, which in accord with the fundamental principles of anicca, dukkha and anatta are shown to arise and pass away throughout the whole continuity of process which existence is demonstrated to be. The method is above all analytical, and in order that the system of analysis may be searching and precise it is confined to operating within the terms of reference of individual and pre-stated plans. These plans, or matrices, are the points of growth from which complete structural arguments concerning particular states, or conditioned things, are developed in absolute terms. Consequently mātikā, although frequently rendered in translation as table of contents, should not be considered only in that sense ; its more cogent purpose is to declare the nucleus, or to indicate the course upon which a subsequent analytical structure is to be developed. Moreover, in their ancient and traditional role as specific passages for recitation, the mātikās provide the learner with a stable source of essential material on which to exercise practice and gain understanding.

Each of the seven books of the Abhidhamma Piṭaka is considered to have its own mātikā, and these have been commented upon at some length in Mohavicchedanī (P.T.S. edition 1961).

This work is considered to have been compiled by a certain Kassapa Thera at the request of his pupils. The text, classified in Burma as one of the nine "little-finger" manuals, was probably written in the early thirteenth century at the Nāgānana Vihāra in the Coḷa country of southern India. It is a most valuable work in that it summarizes the whole of the Abhidhamma Piṭaka, book by book, from Dhammasaṅgaṇī to Paṭṭhāna. The mātikās concerned are in this instance, however, viewed mainly as tables of contents and should in certain cases be considered as standing outside the fundamental texts in so far as in only four works can there be shown to be sections specifically entitled " mātikā ", existing internally as part of the text, though there are many uddesas also which are indeed lists of contents. These internal mātikās are: (1) that of Dhammasaṅgaṇī, which commences that volume; (2) a short mātikā following the uddesa of Rūpakkhandha in the same work; (3) one following immediately on the sixteenfold classification of the nidānas in the Abhidhammabhājanīya section of Paṭiccasamuppāda in Vibhaṅga; (4) a series of five short mātikās at the beginning of Dhātukathā, and (5) a rather more lengthy mātikā at the beginning of Puggalapaññatti. Of these five the first, i.e. the initial section of Dhammasaṅgaṇī, is by far the most important, its influence being felt strongly throughout the whole of the Abhidhamma-Piṭaka. Not only are the definitions and expansions of the classifications of this mātikā the material used in the detailed analysis of states in Dhammasaṅgaṇī itself, but they form the basis on which a large proportion of subsequent discussion is built in the remaining books of the Piṭaka.

The mātikā of Dhammasaṅgaṇī consists of two main sections. The first of these is the tikamātikā, which comprises twenty-two groups of threefold designations. The second is the dukamātikā comprising one hundred groups of twofold designations; this is followed by a subsidiary section known as the suttantadukamātikā, consisting of forty-two groups of twofold designations. Although all one hundred and sixty-four groups are important, it is the twenty-two tikas and one hundred dukas which form the dominant basis of Abhidhamma analysis.

In examining the Dhammasaṅgaṇī mātikā the main feature to be recognized in what might at first sight appear to be a bewildering and almost random system of classification is that each individual tika and duka is to be regarded as a quite separate and unique standpoint from which every mental state or material quality that is cognizable in any way may be examined in terms of detailed analysis. Thus each of the one hundred and twenty-two groups represents a discrete mode by which those states or qualities on the occasions of their arising present themselves and can be recognized by virtue of the duty they perform, the qualities they exhibit, the effects they produce, their nature, origins, etc. Once, however, the mātikā has been stated, and thereby the terms of reference for future discussion established, it becomes the purpose of Dhammasaṅgaṇī to elucidate fully, in the greatest possible detail, the structure and content of those states and qualities in the absolute caregories of Abhidhamma argument. Examples of some of the categories concerned are: consciousness (citta), mental concomitants (cetasikā), aggregates (khandhā), bases (āyatanā), elements (dhātū), the four great material essentials (mahābhūtā), etc.

Within the framework of these categories, and strictly in accord with the terms of reference provided by the individual components of each tika or duka, analysis is conducted. In consequence of the entire range of possible mental states and material qualities capable of being expressed under the heading of any one group of tikas or dukas, Dhammasaṅgaṇī accordingly confines itself initially to the fullest possible analysis, in the terms summarized above, of the first tika, viz. states that are good, bad, indeterminate (i.e. cannot be classified as either good or bad), and this it does with great deliberation in the opening 983 sections of the present translation. Because of the particular tika adopted for this initial examination it establishes in the course of the process of expansion and analysis the formal group designations by which the now fully analysed states may be recognized: e.g. good states concerning the sensuous universe (kāmāvacara), the universe of form (rūpāvacara), the formless universe (arūpāvacara), the higher ideal (lokuttara), greedy, hateful and ignorant states, resultant conditions, material form, etc. As a result of this it is possible in the following 312 sections to classify clearly and comprehensively in the terms of those group designations the distribution of all mental states and material qualities within the internal subdivisions of the remaining twenty-one tikas and one hundred dukas.

So far as Abhidhamma as a whole is concerned the analysis of states conducted by Dhammasaṅgaṇī is but the beginning of a process, for although it establishes the terminology by which the states it isolates may be identified, their extent and limitation are continued in subsequent volumes. It is not the purpose here to discuss these works in detail, but in order to emphasize the importance of the tikas and dukas it might be well to show something of what occurs in some of the volumes. In Vibhaṅga, for example, fourteen of the eighteen divisions include a section entitled " Interrogation " (pañhāpucchaka) where the subject of each vibhaṅga—the subjects also being drawn from Dhammasaṅgaṇī—is assessed in terms of the twenty-two tikas and one hundred dukas. Thus in Khandhavibhaṅga each of the five aggregates: matter, feeling, perception, mental concomitants and consciousness, is expressed in terms of the tikas and dukas, whereas in Dhammasaṅgaṇī the tikas and dukas are used to isolate and establish the make-up of the khandhas. The same process obtains with regard to such other vibhaṅgas as bases, elements, truths, controlling faculties, stations of mindfulness, etc. The purpose of this is to make clear that not only can the individual tikas and dukas be shown to express the presentation and modes of action of the many states comprising the khandhas, etc., but that those same states can themselves be expressed separately in terms of tikas and dukas in order to show their behaviour, suitability, unsuitability, their association with good or bad roots, ability to produce desirable or undesirable resultant, whether they are helpful or unhelpful to progress, whether they are defilements, fetters, ties, bonds, floods, etc.

In Dhātukathā the purpose is a detailed elucidation of the bases (āyatanā), and here again it is carried out on the same basis as Dhammasaṅgaṇī and Vibhaṅga, making the tikas and dukas a most important feature of the method. The most elaborate use, however, of the Dhammasaṅgaṇī mātikā occurs in the massive final work of the Abhidhamma Piṭaka. This is Paṭṭhāna, where the whole structure of the relationship between states in their arising and passing away is displayed not merely in terms of the individual tikas and dukas but coupled with the combinations and permutations of the twenty-four paccayas (hetu—avigata). In this manner then the mātikā of Dhammasaṅgaṇī operates first as a means of exploring fully all those states and qualities inherent in experience, mental and material. Secondly it acts as a series of focal points at which the ultimate value of any state may be assessed. Thirdly it provides the structure upon which the relationship between states may be realized, not statically as isolated factors, but in their normal process of coming to be and passing away.

Thus to those observant practisers concerned seriously with matters relevant to progress towards ultimate perfection and penetrative wisdom, to whom "seeing danger in the slightest fault" refers not only to moral practice but to the building up of rightness of view, the mātikā of Dhammasaṅgaṇī and its full development therein, and in succeeding works, is of paramount importance. If the teaching of Enlightened Ones is that there should be an abandoning of evil states, a practising of good states and a purification of the mind, then it is evident that in the final analysis a proper knowledge of the qualities and behaviour of all relevant states must be known, in order that purity of mind in its fullest sense of attaining to rightness of view may be achieved. This the mātikās of Dhammasaṅgaṇī and the succeeding works are designed to provide.

R. E. Iggleden.

Waltham St. Lawrence, 1973.

"Yaṃ kiñci dhammaṃ abhijaññā
ajjhattaṃ athavāpi bahiddhā."

SUTTA NIPĀTA, 917.

"Api khvāham āvuso imasmiṃ yeva vyāmamatte kaḷevare saññimhi samanake lokaṃ paññāpemi . . ."

SAṂYUTTA-NIKĀYA, i, 62; = A., ii, 48.

"Kullūpamaṃ vo bhikkhave ājānantehi dhammā pi vo pahātabbā, pag-eva adhammā."

MAJJHIMA-NIKĀYA, i, 135.

"We shall find that every important philosophical reformation, after a time of too highly strained metaphysical dogmatism or unsatisfying scepticism, has been begun by some man who saw *the necessity of looking deeper into the mental constitution.*"

G. CROOM ROBERTSON.

CONTENTS.

BOOK I.

THE UPRISING OF MIND (C i t t u p p ā d a - k a ṇ ḍ a ṃ).

Part I.

GOOD STATES OF CONSCIOUSNESS.

ABBREVIATIONS.

1. BUDDHIST CANONICAL BOOKS.

A.—Anguttara-Nikāya.
C.—Cullavagga.
D.—Dīgha-Nikāya.
Dhp.—Dhammapada.
Dh.K.—Dhātu-Kathā.
Dh.S.—Dhamma-Sangaṇi.
Jāt.—Jātaka.
K.—Siamese (Kambodian) edition of the text.
KV.—Kathā Vatthu, trs. Points of Controversy.
M.—Majjhima-Nikāya.
PP.—Puggala-Paññatti.
Pṭs.—Paṭisambhidāmagga.
S.—Saṃyutta-Nikāya.
SN.—Sutta-Nipāta.
Vin.—Vinaya.

2. OTHER BOOKS.

Abh.S.—Abhidhammattha-Sangaha.
Asl.—Atthasālinī, trs. The Expositor.
Compendium of Philosophy, trs. of Abh.S.
Div.—Divyāvadāna.
JPTS.—Journal of the Pali Text Society.
JRAS.—Journal of the Royal Asiatic Society.
MBV.—Mahā-Bodhi-Vaṇsa.
Mah.—Mahā-Vaṃsa.
Mil.—Milinda-Pañha.
Npk.—Nettipakaraṇa.
Pss.B.—Psalms of the Brethren, trs. Theragāthā.
SBE.—Sacred Books of the East.
Sum.—Sumangala-Vilāsinī.
Vis.M.—Visuddhi Magga.

[By "printed text", or simply "text", is always meant, unless otherwise stated, the edition of the Dhamma-Sangaṇi, published in 1885 by the Pali Text Society.]

INTRODUCTORY ESSAY.

I.

The Manual and the History of Psychology.

If the sands of Egypt or the ruins of Greece itself were to give up, among their buried things that are now and again being restored to us, a copy of some manual with which the young Socrates was put through the mill of current academic doctrine, the discovery would be hailed, especially by scholars of historical insight, as a contribution of peculiar interest. The contents would no doubt yield no new matter of philosophic tradition. But they would certainly teach something respecting such points as pre-Aristotelian logical methods, and the procedure followed in one or more schools for rendering students conversant with the concepts in psychology, ethics and metaphysic accepted or debated by the culture of the age.

Readers whose sympathies are not confined to the shores of the Mediterranean and Ægean seas will feel a stir of interest, similar in kind if fainter in degree, on becoming more closely acquainted with the Buddhist textbook entitled Dhamma-Sangaṇi. The edition of the Pali text, prepared for the Pali Text Society by Professor Dr. Ed. Müller, and published in 1885, has so far failed to elicit any critical discussion among Pali scholars. A cursory inspection may have revealed little but what seemed dry, prolix and sterile, Such was, at least, the verdict of a younger worker, now, alas! no more among us.[1] Closer study of the work will, I believe, prove less ungrateful, more especially if the conception of it as a student's manual be kept well in view. The method of the book is explicative, deductive; its object

---

[1] H. C. Warren, *Buddhism in Translations,* xviii. Cf. Kern, *Indian Buddhism*, p. 3.

was, not to add to the Dhamma, but to unfold the orthodox import of terms in use among the body of the faithful, and, by organizing and systematizing the aggregate of doctrinal concepts, to render the learner's intellect both clear and efficient.

Even a superficial inspection of the Manual should yield great promise to anyone interested in the history of psychology. When in the year 1893 my attention was first drawn to it, and the desirability of a translation pointed out by Professor Rhys Davids, I was at once attracted by the amount of psychological material embedded in its pages. Buddhist philosophy is ethical first and last. This is beyond dispute. But among ethical systems there is a world of difference in the degree of importance attached to the psychological prolegomena of ethics. In ethical problems we are on a basis of psychology of conation or will,[1] with its co-efficients of feeling and intelligence. And in the history of human ideas, in so far as it clusters about those problems, we find this dependence is sometimes made prominent, sometimes slurred over. Treated superficially, if suggestively and picturesquely, in Plato, the nature and functions of that faculty in man, whereby he is constituted an ethical and political " animal ", are by Aristotle analyzed at length. But the Buddhists were, in a way, more advanced in the psychology of their ethics than Aristotle—in a way, that is, which would now be called scientific. Rejecting the assumption of a psyche and of its higher manifestations or noûs, they were content to resolve the consciousness of the Ethical Man, *as they found it*, into a complex continuum of subjective phenomena. They analyzed this continuum, as

---

[1] Cf. G. C. Robertson, *Elements of General Philosophy*, pp. 191, 197; *Philosophical Remains*, p. 3; A. Bain, *Moral Science—The Psychological Data of Ethics*. " Every ethical system involves a psychology of conduct, and depends for its development upon its idea of what conduct actually is " (C. Douglas, *The Philosophy of J. S. Mill*, p. 251).

we might, exposing it, as it were, by transverse section. But their treatment was genetic. The distinguishable groups of d h a m m ā—approximately, states or mental psychoses—"arise" in every case in consciousness, in obedience to certain laws of causation, psychical and moral [1]—that is, ultimately, as the outcome of antecedent states of consciousness. There is no exact equivalent in Pali, any more than there is in Aristotle, for the relatively modern term "consciousness", yet is the psychological standpoint of the Buddhist philosophy virtually as thoroughgoing in its perceptual basis as that of Berkeley. It was not solipsism any more than Berkeley's immaterialism was solipsistic. It postulated other percipients [2] as Berkeley did, together with, not a Divine cause or source of percepts, but the implicit Monism of early thought veiled by a deliberate Agnosticism. And just as Berkeley, approaching philosophical questions through psychology, "was the first man to begin a perfectly scientific doctrine of sense-perception as a psychologist," [3] so Buddhism, from a quite early stage of its development, set itself to analyze and classify mental processes with remarkable insight and sagacity. And on the results of that psychological analysis it sought to base the whole rationale of its practical doctrine and discipline. From studying the processes of attention, and the nature of sensation, the range and depth of feeling and the plasticity of the will in desire and in control, it organized its system of personal self-culture.

Germany has already a history of psychology half completed on the old lines of the assumed monopoly of ancient thought by a small area of the inhabited world. England has not yet got so far. Is it too much to hope that, when such a work is put forth, the greater labour of a wider and juster initiative will have been undertaken, and the

---

[1] Called by Commentators the c i t t a - n i y a m a and k a m m ạ - n i y a m a.

[2] Cf. e.g. below, p. 250[1045].

[3] G. C. Robertson, op. cit., p. 154.

development of early psychological thought in the East have been assigned its due place in this branch of historical research ?

II.

The Date of the Manual.

We can fortunately fix the date of the Dhamma-Sangaṇi within a limit that, for an Indian book, may be considered narrow. Its aim is to systematize or formulate certain doctrines, or at least to enumerate and define a number of scattered terms or categories of terms, occurring in the great books of dialogues and sundry discourse entitled the Nikāyas of the Sutta Piṭaka. The whole point of view, psychological and philosophical, adopted in them is, in our Manual, taken for granted. The technical terms used in them are used in it as if its hearers, subsequently its readers, would at once recognize them. No one acquainted with those books, and with the Dhamma-Sangaṇi, will hesitate in placing the latter, in point of time, after the Nikāyas.

On the other hand, the kind of questions raised in our Manual are on a different plane altogether from those raised in the fifth book in the Abhidhamma-Piṭaka, viz. the Kathā-Vatthu, which we know to have been composed by Tissa at Patna, in the middle of the third century B.C.[1] The Dhamma-Sangaṇi does not attempt to deal with any such advanced opinions and highly-elaborated points of doctrine as are put forward by those supposed opponents of the orthodox philosophy who are the interlocutors in the Kathā-Vatthu. It remains altogether, or almost altogether, at the old standpoint of the Nikāyas as regards doctrine, differing only in method of treatment. The Kathā-Vatthu raises new questions belonging to a later stage in the development of the faith.

The Dhamma-Sangaṇi is therefore younger than the

---

[1] Atthasālinī, p. 3; Mahā-Bodhi-Vaṃsa, p. 110; KV. Cy., *Points of Controversy*, p. 7.

Nikāyas, and older than the Kathā-Vatthu. If we date it half-way between the two, that is, during the first third of the fourth century B.C. (contemporary, therefore, with the childhood of Aristotle, b. 384), we shall be on the safe side. But I am disposed to think that the interval between the completion of the Nikāyas and the compilation of the Dhamma-Sangaṇi is less than that between the latter work and the Kathā Vatthu; and that our manual should therefore be dated rather at the middle than at the end of the fourth century B.C., or even earlier. However that may be, it is important for the historian of psychology to remember that the ideas it systematizes are, of course, older. Practically all of them go back to the time of the Sangha's early editorial work. Some of them are older still.

The history of the text of our Manual belongs to that of the canonical texts taken collectively. There are, however, two interesting references to it, apart from the general narrative, in the Mahā Vaṃsa, which show, at least, that the Dhamma-Sangaṇi was by no means laid on the shelf among later Buddhists. King Kassapa V. of Ceylon (A.D. 929–39) had a copy of it engraved on gold plates studded with jewels, and took it in procession with great honour to a vihāra he had built, and there offered flowers before it.[1] Another King of Ceylon, Vijaya Bāhu I. (A.D. 1065–1120), shut himself up every morning for a time against his people in the Hall of Exhortation, and there made a translation of the Dhamma-Sangaṇi, no doubt from Pali into Siṇhalese.[2]

I can testify to the seriousness of the task, and feel a keen sympathy with my royal predecessor, and envy withal for his proximity in time and place to the seat of orthodox tradition. Nothing, unfortunately, is now known, so far as I have been able to ascertain, of his work, in which the translator was very likely aided by the best scholarship of

---

[1] Mah., chap. l, vv. 50, 51, 56.
[2] Ibid., chap. lxx, v. 17.

the day, and which might have saved me from many a doubt and difficulty.

III.

On the Commentaries and the Importance of the Atthasālinī.

It will be seen from Appendix I. that the last part of the text of our Manual is a supplement added to it by way of commentary, or rather of interpretation and digest. It is, perhaps, not surprising that so much of this kind of material has survived within the four corners of the Piṭakas. We have the old Commentary embedded in the Vinaya, and the Parivāra added as a sort of supplementary examination paper to it. Then there is the Niddesa, a whole book of commentary, on texts now included in the Sutta Nipāta, and there are passages clearly of a commentarial nature scattered through the Nikāyas. Lastly, there are the interesting fragments of commentaries tacked the one on to the Dhamma-Sangaṇi itself (below, p. 331), the other on to the Vibhanga. As these older incorporated commentaries are varied both in form and in method, it is evident that commentary of different kinds had a very early beginning. And the probability is very great that the tradition is not so far wrong when it tells us that commentaries on all the principal canonical books were handed down in schools of the Order *along with* the texts themselves.

This is not to maintain that all of the Commentaries were so handed down in all the schools, nor that each of them was exactly the same in each of the schools where it was taught. But wherever Commentaries were so handed down, tradition tells us that they were compiled, and subsequently written, in the dialect of the district where the school was situated. From two places, one in India and the other in Ceylon, we have works purporting to give in Pali the substance of such ancient traditional comment as had been handed down in the local vernacular. One of these is the Atthasālinī,

Buddhaghosa's reconstruction, in Pali, of the Commentary on our present work, as handed down in Siṇhalese at the school of the Great Monastery, the Mahā-Vihāra at Anurādhapura in Ceylon.

The Mahā-Vaṃsa, indeed, says (p. 251) that he wrote this work at Gayā, in North India, before he came to Anurādhapura. This, however, must be a mistake, if it refers to the work as we have it. For in that work he frequently quotes from and refers to another work which he certainly wrote after his arrival in Ceylon, namely, the Visuddhi-Magga, and once or twice he refers to the Samanta-Pāsādikā, which he also wrote in Ceylon.

The Saddhamma-Sangaha [1] has two apparently inconsistent statements which suggest a solution. The first is that he wrote, at the Vihāra at Gayā, a work called the *Uprising of Knowledge* (Ñāṇodaya), and a Commentary on the Dhamma-Sangaṇi, called the Atthasālinī, and began to write one on the Parittas. Then it was that he was urged to go, and actually did go, to Ceylon to obtain better materials for his work. The second is that, after he had arrived there and had written seven other works, he then wrote the Atthasālinī. When the same author makes two such statements as these, and in close conjunction, he may well mean to say that a work already written in the one place was revised or rewritten in the other.

Dhammakitti, the author of the Saddhamma-Sangaha, adds the interesting fact that Buddhaghosa, in revising his Atthasālinī, relied, not on the Mahā-Atthakathā in Siṇhalese, but on another Commentary in that language called the Mahā-Paccari.

We know, namely, that at the time when Buddhaghosa wrote—that is, in the early part of the fifth century A.D.—the Commentaries handed down in the schools had been, at various times and places, already put together into treatises

---

[1] *Journal of the Pali Text Society*, 1888, pp. 53, 56.

and written books in the native dialects. And we know the names of several of those then existing. These are :

1. The Commentary of the dwellers in the "North Minster"—the Uttara Vihāra—at Anurādhapura.[1]

2. The Mūla-, or Mahā-Atthakathā, or simply "The Atthakathā", of the dwellers in the "Great Minster"—the Mahā-Vihāra—also at Anurādhapura.[2]

3. The Andha-Atthakathā, handed down at Kāñcipura (Congevaram), in South India.

4. The Mahā-Paccari, or Great Raft, said to be so called from its having been composed on a raft somewhere in Ceylon.[3]

5. The Kurundī Atthakathā, so called because it was composed at the Kurundaveḷu Vihāra in Ceylon.[4]

6. The Sankhepa-Atthakathā or Short Commentary, which, as being mentioned together with the Andha Commentary,[5] may possibly be also South Indian.

Buddhaghosa himself says in the introductory verses to the Atthasālinī : [6]

"I will set forth, rejoicing in what I reveal, the explanation of the meaning of that Abhidhamma as it was chanted forth by Mahā-Kassapa and the rest (at the first Council), and re-chanted later (at the second Council) by the Arahats, and by Mahinda brought to this wondrous isle and turned into the language of the dwellers therein. Rejecting now the tongue of the men of Tambapaṇṇi [7] and turning it into that pure tongue which harmonizes with the texts [I will set it forth] showing the opinion of the dwellers in the Great Minster, undefiled by and unmixed with the views of the

---

[1] JPTS., 1882, pp. 115, 116. English in Turnour's Mahā-Vaṃsa, pp. xxxvii, xxxviii.

[2] Sum. 180, 182 ; Saddhamma-Sangaha, 55 ; MBV. 134–6.

[3] Papañca Sūdanī on M. ii, 13 ; Saddhamma-Sangaha, 55.

[4] Saddhamma-Sangaha, 55.

[5] Vijesinha in the JRAS., 1870 (vol. v, N.S.), p. 298 : "Origin of the Buddhist Arthakathās."

[6] Asl., p. 1, v. 13 *et seq.*

[7] Taprobane = Ceylon.

sects, and adducing also what ought to be adduced from the Nikāyas and the Commentaries." [1]

It would be most interesting if the book as we have it had been written at Gayā in North India, or even if we could discriminate between the portion there written and the additions and alterations made in Ceylon. But this we can no longer hope to do. The numerous stories of Ceylon Theras occurring in the book are almost certainly due to the author's residence in Ceylon. And we cannot be certain that these and the reference to his own book, written in Ceylon, are the only additions. We cannot, therefore, take the opinions expressed in the book as evidence of Buddhist opinion as held in Gayā. That may, in great part, be so. But we cannot tell in which part.

In the course of his work Buddhaghosa quotes often from the Nikāyas without mentioning the source of his quotations; and also from the Vibhanga [2] and the Mahā-Pakaraṇa [3] (that is the Paṭṭhāna), giving their names. Besides these Piṭaka texts, he quotes or refers to the following authorities:—

1. His own Samanta-Pāsādikā, e.g. pp. 97–8.
2. His own Visuddhi-Magga, pp. 168, 183, 186, 187 (twice), 190, 198.[4]
3. The Mahā-Atthakathā, pp. 80, 86, 107.
4. The Atthakathācariyā, pp. 85, 123, 217.
5. The Atthakathā, pp. 108, 113, 188, 267, 313.
6. The Atthakathā's, pp. 99, 188.
7. The Āgamatthakathā's, p. 86.[5]

---

[1] Āgamatthakathāsu, perhaps "from the commentaries on the Nikāyas". See note 5 below; cf. *Expositor*, 3. See its index for list of references to commentaries.

[2] For instance, pp. 165–70, 176, 178.

[3] For instance, pp. 7, 9, 87, 212, 409.

[4] The apparent references at pp. 195, 196 are not to the book.

[5] The reading in the printed text is āgamanatthakathāsu. But this is not intelligible. And as we have āgamatthakathāsu at p. 2, v. 17, it is probable we

8. Ācariyānaṃ samānaṭṭhakathā, p. 90.
9. Porāṇā, pp. 84, 111, 291, 299, 313.
10. The Thera (that is Nāgasena), pp. 112, 121, 122.
11. Nāgasenatthera, p. 114.
12. Āyasmā Nāgasena, p. 119.
13. Ayasmā Nāgasenatthera, p. 142.
14. Thera Nāgasena, p. 120.
15. Dīgha-bhāṇakā, pp. 151, 399 (cf. p. 407).
16. Majjhima-bhāṇakā, p. 420.
17. Vitaṇḍa-vādī, pp. 3, 90, 92, 241.
18. Peṭaka, Peṭakopadesa, p. 165.

I do not claim to have exhausted the passages in the Atthasālinī quoted from these authorities, or to be able to define precisely each work—what, for instance, is the distinction between 5 and 6, and whether 4 was not identical with either. Nor is it clear who were Porāṇā or Ancients, though it seems likely, from the passages quoted, that they were Buddhist thinkers of an earlier age but of a later date than that of our Manual, inasmuch as one of the citations shows that the "Door-theory" of cognition was already developed (see below, p. lxi, etc.). From the distinct references to 3 and to 7, it seems possible that the so-called "Great Commentary" (3) dealt not so much with any particular book, or group of books, as with the doctrines of the Piṭakas in general.

The foregoing notes may prove useful when the times are ready for a full inquiry into the history of the Buddhist Commentaries.[1] With respect to the extent to which the Atthasālinī itself has been quoted in the following pages, it may be judged that the scholastic teaching of eight centuries

---

must so read also here, where the meaning clearly is "in the commentaries on the Nikāyas".

[1] I may add that a Ṭīkā, or sub-commentary on the Atthasālinī, written by a Siamese scholar, Ñāṇakitti, of unknown date, was edited in Siṇhalese characters by Koḍagoḍa Paññāsekhara of Kalutara, in Ceylon, and published there in 1890.

later is a very fallacious guide in the interpretation of original doctrines, and that we should but darken counsel if we sought light on Aristotle from mediaeval exegesis of the age of Duns Scotus.

Without admitting that the course of Buddhist and that of Western culture coincide sufficiently to warrant such a parallel, it may readily be granted that Buddhaghosa must not be accepted *en bloc*. The distance between the constructive genius of Gotama and his apostles as compared with the succeeding ages of epigoni needs no depreciatory criticism on the labours of the exegesists to make itself felt forcibly enough. Buddhaghosa's philology is doubtless crude, and he is apt to leave cruces unexplained, concerning which an Occidental is most in the dark.[1] Nevertheless, to me his work is not only highly suggestive, but also a mine of historic interest. To put it aside is to lose the historical perspective of the course of Buddhist philosophy. It is to regard the age of Gotama and of his early Church as constituting a wondrous "freak" in the evolution of human ideas, instead of watching to see how the philosophical tradition implanted in that Church (itself based on earlier culture) had in the lapse of centuries been carefully handed down by the schools of Theras, the while the folklore that did duty for natural science had more or less fossilized, and the study of the conscious processes of the mind (and of atheistic doctrine) had been elaborated.

This is, however, a point of view that demands a fuller examination than can here be given it. I will now only maintain that it is even more suggestive to have at hand the best tradition of the Buddhist schools at the fullness of their maturity for the understanding of a work like the Dhamma-Sangaṇi than for the study of the Dialogues. Our Manual is itself a book of reference to earlier books, and presents us with many terms and formulæ taken out of that setting of occasion and of discourse enshrined in which we meet them

[1] Cf. Dr. Neumann in *Die Reden Gotamo Buddhos*, p. xv *et seq.*

in the Nikāyas. The great scholar who comments on them had those Nikāyas, both as to letter and spirit, well pigeon-holed in memory, and cherished both with the most reverent loyalty. That this is so, as well as the fact that we are bred on a culture so different in mould and methods (let alone the circumstances of its development) from that inherited by him, must lend his interpretations an importance and a suggestiveness far greater than that which the writings of any Christian commentator on the Greek philosophy can possess for us.

IV.

On the Method and Argument of the Manual.

The title given to my translation is not in any way a faithful rendering of the canonical name of the Manual. This is admitted on my title-page. There is nothing very intelligible for us in the expression "Compendium of States", or "Compendium of Phenomena". Whether the Buddhist might find it so or not, there is for him at all events a strong and ancient association of ideas attaching to the title Dhamma-Saṅgaṇi which for us is entirely non-existent. I have, therefore, let go the letter, in order to indicate what appears to me the real import of the work. Namely, that it is, in the first place, a manual or textbook, and not a treatise or disquisition, elaborated and rendered attractive and edifying after the manner of most of the Sutta Piṭaka. And then, that its subject is ethics, but that the inquiry is conducted from a psychological standpoint, and, indeed, is in great part an analysis of the psychological and psycho-physical data of ethics.

I do not mean to assert that the work was compiled solely for academic use. No such specialized function is assigned it in the Commentary. Buddhaghosa only maintains that, together with the rest of the Abhidhamma,[1] it was the

[1] But including the Mātikā only of the later Kathā Vatthu. Cf. *Dialogues of the Buddha*, p. xi; Asl., p. 1.

ipsissima verba of the Buddha not attempting to upset the mythical tradition that it was the special mode he adopted in teaching the doctrine to the "hosts of devas come from all parts of the sixteen world-systems, he having placed his mother (reincarnate as a devī) at their head because of the glory of her wisdom".[1] Whether this myth had grown up to account for the formal, unpicturesque style of the Abhidhamma, on the ground that the devas were above the need of illustration and rhetoric of an earthly kind, I do not know. The Commentary frequently refers to the peculiar difference in style from that employed in the Suttanta as consisting in the Abhidhamma being nippariyāya-desanā—teaching which is not accompanied by explanation or disquisition.[2] And the definition it gives, at the outset, of the term Abhidhamma shows that this Piṭaka, and *a fortiori* the Dhamma-Sangaṇi, was considered as a subject of study more advanced than the other Piṭakas, and intended to serve as the complement and crown of the learner's earlier courses.[3] Acquaintance with the doctrine is, as I have said, taken for granted. The object is not so much to extend knowledge as to ensure mutual consistency in the *in*tension of ethical notions, and to systematize and formulate the theories and practical mechanism of intellectual and moral progress scattered in profusion throughout the Suttas.[4]

---

[1] Asl., p. 1.

[2] e.g. Asl. 403. The meaning of this expression is illustrated by its use on p. 317 of the Cy.: na nippariyāyena dīghaṃ rūpāyatanaṃ; i.e. "that which is long is only figuratively a visual object" (is really tactile object).

[3] Asl., p. 2. Translated by Mr. A. C. Taylor, JRAS. 1894. Cf. *Expositor*, 24*f*.

[4] Professor Edmund Hardy, in his Introduction to the fifth volume of the Anguttara Nikāya, expresses the belief that the Dhamma-Sangaṇi is "entirely dependent upon the Anguttara". For my part, I have found no reason to limit the Manual's dependence on the Suttantas to any one book. Buddhaghosa does not specially connect the two works.

It is interesting to note the methods adopted to carry out this object. The work was in the first instance inculcated by way of oral teaching respecting a quantity of matter which had been already learnt in the same way. And the memory, no longer borne along by the interest of narrative or by the thread of an argument, had to be assisted by other devices. First of these is the catechetical method. Questions, according to Buddhist analysis, are put on five several grounds :[1]

To throw light on what is not known ;
To discuss what is known ;
To clear up doubts ;
To get assent (i.e. the premises in an argument granted) ;[2]
To (give a starting-point from which to) set out the content of a statement.

The last is selected as the special motive of the catechizing here resorted to. It is literally the wish to discourse or expound (k a t h e t u k a m y a t ā), but the meaning is more clearly brought out by the familiar formula quoted, viz. : " Four in number, brethren, are these stations in mindfulness. Now which are the four ? " Thus it was held that the questions in the Manual are analytic or explicative, having the object of unfolding and thereby of deliminating the implications of a mass of notions which a study of the Suttas, if unaided, might leave insufficiently co-ordinated in the mind.

And the memory, helped by the interrogative stimulus, was yet further assisted by the symmetrical *form* of both question and answer, as well as by the generic uniformity in the *matter* of the questions. Throughout Book I, in the case of each inquiry which opens up a new subject, the answer is set out on a definite plan called u d d e s a , or "argument", and is rounded off invariably by the a p p a n ā ,

---

[1] Asl. 55, 56 ; cf. Sum. V, i, 68 ; cf. the different grounds in A. iii, 191, and the four ways of answering, D. iii, 221 ; A. i, 197 ; ii, 46.

[2] A favourite method in the Dialogues. The Cy. quotes as an instance M. i, 232.

or emphatic summing up: "all these (whatever they may stand for on other occasions or in other systems) on this occasion = x." The u d d e s a is succeeded by the n i d - d e s a or exposition, i.e. analytical question and answer on the details of the opening argument. This is indicated formally by the initial adverb t a t t h a—what *here* (in this connexion) is *a* . . . *b* . . . *c* ? Again, the work is in great part planned with careful regard to logical relation. The Buddhists had not elaborated the intellectual vehicle of genus and species as the Greeks did, hence they had not the convenience of a logic of Definition. There is scarcely an answer in any of these Niddesas but may perhaps be judged to suffer in precision and lucidity from lack of it. They substitute for definition proper what J. S. Mill might have called predication of æquipollent terms—in other words, the method of the dictionary. In this way precision of meaning is not to be expected, since nearly all so-called synonyms do but mutually overlap in meaning without coinciding; and hence the only way to ensure no part of the connotation being left out is to lump together a number of approximate equivalents, and gather that the term in question is defined by such properties as the aggregate possesses in common. If this is the rationale of the Buddhist method, the inclusion, in the answer, of the very term which is to be defined becomes no longer the fallacy it is in Western logic. Indeed, where there is no pursuit of exact science, nor of sciences involving "physical division", but only a system of research into the intangible products and processes of mind and character, involving aspects and phases, i.e. *logical* division, I am not sure that a good case might not be made out for Buddhist method. It is less rigid, and lends itself better, perhaps, to a field of thought where "a difference in aspects *is* a difference in things".[1]

However that may be, the absence of a development of

---

[1] Professor J. Ward, *Ency. Brit.*, 9th ed., "Psychology."

the relation of Particular and Universal, of One and All, is met by a great attention to degree of Plurality. Number plays a great part in Buddhist classes and categories.[1] Whether this was inherited from a more ancient lore, such as Pythagoras is said to have drawn from, or whether this feature was artificially developed for mnemonic purposes, I do not know. Probably there is truth in both alternatives.

But of all numbers none plays so great a part in aiding methodological coherency and logical consistency as that of duality. I refer, of course, especially to its application in the case of the correlatives, Positive and Negative.

Throughout most of Book II the learner is greatly aided by being questioned on positive terms and their opposites, taken simply and also in combination with other similarly dichotomized pairs. The opposite is not always a contradictory. Room is then left in the "universe of discourse" for a third class, which in its turn comes into question. Thus the whole of Book I is a development of the triplet of questions with which Book III begins (a-kusalaṃ being really the contrary of kusalaṃ, though formally its contradictory): What is *A*? What is *B*? What is (*ab*), i.e. non-*A* and non-*B*? (The other Indian alternative: What is *AB*? finds here no special treatment.) In Book III there is no obvious ground of logic or method for the serial order or limits observed in the "Clusters" or Groups, and the interpolated sets of "Pairs" of miscellaneous questions. Nevertheless, a uniform method of catechizing characterizes the former.

Finally, there is, in the way of mnemonic and intellectual aid, the simplifying and unifying effect attained by causing all the questions (exclusive of sub-inquiries) to refer to the one category of dhammā.

There is, it is true, a whole Book of questions referring to rūpaṃ, but this constitutes a very much elaborated sub-

[1] Cf. especially not only Book II of this work, but also the whole of the Anguttara.

inquiry on material "form" as one sub-species of a species of d h a m m ā—r ū p i n o d h a m m ā, as distinguished from all the rest, which are a - r ū p i n o d h a m m ā. This will appear more clearly if the argument of the work is very concisely stated.

It will be seen that the M ā t i k ā, or table of subjects of all the questions, refers in detail only to Book III. Book III, in fact, contains the entire work considered as an inquiry (not necessarily exhaustive) into the concrete, or, as one might say, the applied ethics of Buddhism. In it many, if not all, fundamental concepts are taken as already defined and granted. Hence Books I and II are introductory and, as it were, of the nature of inquiry into data. Book II is psycho-physical; Book I is psychological. Together they constitute a very elaborate development, and, again, a sub-development of the first triplet of questions in Book III, viz. d h a m m ā which are good, i.e. make good karma, those which are bad, and those which make no karma (the indeterminates). Now, of these last some are simply and solely results[1] of good or bad d h a m m ā, and some are not so, but are states of mind and expressions of mind entailing no moral result (on the agent).[2] Some, again, while making no karma, are of neither of these two species, but are d h a m m ā which might be called either unmoral (r ū p a ṃ)[3] or else *super*-moral (unconditioned element or Nirvana).[4] These are held to constitute a third and fourth species of the third class of dhammā called indeterminate. But the former of the two alone receives detailed and systematic treatment.

Hence the whole Manual is shown to be, as it professes to be, a compendium, or, more literally, a co-enumeration of d h a m m ā.

The method of treatment or procedure termed Abhidhamma (for Abhidhamma is treatment rather than matter) is,

---

[1] Book I, Pt. III, Chap. I.
[2] Ibid., Chap. II.
[3] Book II.
[4] Appendix II.

according to the Mātikā, held to end at the end of the chapter entitled P i ṭ ṭ h i - d u k a ṃ or Supplementary Set of Pairs. The last thirty-seven pairs of questions [1] and answers, on the other hand, are entitled S u t t a n t i k a - d u k a ṃ. They are of a miscellaneous character, and are in many cases not logically opposed. Buddhaghosa has nothing to say by way of explaining their inclusion, nor the principle determining their choice or number. Nor is it easy to deduce any explanation from the nature or the treatment of them. The name S u t t a n t i k a means that they are pairs of terms met with in the Suttas. This is true and verifiable. But I, for one, cannot venture to predicate anything further respecting them.

V

On the Chief Subject of Inquiry—D h a m m ā.

If I have called Buddhist ethics psychological, especially as the subject is treated in this work, it is much in the same way in which I should call Plato's psychology ethical. Neither the founders of Buddhism nor of Platonic Socratism had elaborated any organic system of psychology or of ethics respectively. Yet it is hardly overstating the case for either school of thought to say that, whereas the latter psychologized from an ethical standpoint, the former built their ethical doctrine on a basis of psychological principles. For, whatever the far-reaching term d h a m m o may in our Manual have precisely signified to the early Buddhists, it invariably elicits, throughout Book I, a reply *in terms of subjective consciousness.* The discussion in the Commentary, which I have reproduced below, p. 2, n. 3, on d h a m m ā r a m m a ṇ a ṃ, leaves it practically beyond doubt that d h a m m o, when thus related to m a n o, is as a visual object to visual perception—is, namely, mental object in general. It thus is shown to be equivalent to Herbart's *Vorstellung*, to Locke's idea—"whatsoever is the

[1] §§ 1296–1366.

immediate object of perception, thought, or understanding"—and to Professor Ward's "presentation".[1]

The dhammā in question always prove to be, whatever their ethical value, factors of cittaṃ used evidently in its widest sense, i.e. concrete mental process or state. Again, the analysis of rūpaṃ in Book II, as a species of "indeterminate" dhammā, is almost wholly a study in the phenomena of sensation and of the human organism as sentient. Finally, in Book III the questions on various dhammā are for the most part answered in terms of the four mental skandhas, of the cittāni dealt with in Book I, and of the springs of action as shown in their effect on will. Thus the whole inquiry in its most generalized expression comes practically to this: Given man as a moral being, what do we find to be the content of his consciousness?

Now this term dhammo is, as readers are already aware, susceptible of more than one interpretation. Even when used for the body of ethical doctrine it was applied with varying extension, i.e. either to the whole doctrine, or to the Suttanta as opposed to Vinaya and Abhidhamma, or to such doctrines as the Four Truths and the Causal Formula. But whatever in this connexion is the denotation, the connotation is easy to fix. That this is not the case where the term has, so to speak, a secular or "profane" meaning is seen in the various renderings and discussions of it.[2] The late H. C. Warren, in particular, has described the difficulties, first of determining what the word, in this or that connexion, was intended to convey, and then of discovering any word or words adequate to serve as equivalent to it. One step towards a solution may be made if we can get at a Buddhist survey of the meanings of dhammo from the Buddhists'

---

[1] *Ency. Brit.*, 9th ed., art. "Psychology".

[2] Cf. e.g. Oldenberg, *Buddha*, etc., 6th ed., p. 288; Warren, *Buddhism in Translations*, pp. 116, 364; Kern, *Ind. Buddhism*, p. 51, n. 3; Neumann, *Reden des Gotamo*, pp. 13, 23, 91; Gogerly, *Ceylon Friend*, 1874, p. 21; M. & W. Geiger, *Pāli Dhamma*, p. 35 f.

own philosophical point of view. And this we are now enabled to do in consequence of the editing of the Atthasālinī. In it we read Buddhaghosa's analysis of the term, the various meanings it conveyed to Buddhists of the fifth century A.D., and his judgment, which would be held as authoritative, of the special significance it possessed in the questions of the Dhamma-saṅgaṇi. "The word dhammo," runs the passage (p. 38), "is met with [as meaning] doctrine (pariyatti), condition or cause (hetu), virtue or good quality (guṇo), absence of essence or of living soul (nissatta-nijjīvatā)," etc. Illustrative texts are then given of each meaning, those referring to the last being the beginning of the answer in our Manual numbered [121]: "Now at that time there are states"; and, further, the passage from the Satipaṭṭhānasutta [1]: "Concerning dhammas he abides watchful over dhammas." And it is with the fourth and last-named meaning of dhammo that the term is said to be used in the questions of the Manual. Again, a little later (p. 40), he gives a more positive expression to this particular meaning by saying that dhammo, so employed, signifies "that which has the mark of bearing its own nature" (or character or condition—sabhāva-dhāraṇo); i.e. that which is not dependent on any more ultimate nature.[2] This, to us, somewhat obscure characterization may very likely, in view of the context, mean that dhammo as phenomenon is without substratum, is not a quality cohering in a substance. "Phenomenon" is certainly our nearest equivalent to the negative definition of nissatta-nijjīvaṃ, and this is actually the rendering given to dhammo (when employed in this sense in the Sutta just quoted) by Dr. Neumann: "Da wacht ein Mönch bei den Erscheinungen . . ." If I have used states, or states of consciousness, instead of phenomena, it is merely

---

[1] D. (suttanta 22); M. i, 61.

[2] Cf. Pap. Sūd. i, p. 17; attano lakkhaṇaṃ dhārentī ti dhammā. Herein dhammo = dhātu, *Compendium*, 255.

because, in the modern tradition of British psychology, "states of consciousness" is exactly equivalent to such phenomena as are mental, or, at least, conscious. And, further, because this use of "states" has been taken up into that psychological tradition on the very same grounds as prompted this Buddhist interpretation of d h a m m ā—the ground of non-committal, not to say negation, with respect to any psychical substance or entity.

That we have, in this country pre-eminently, gone to work after the manner of electrical science with respect to *its* subject-matter, and psychologized without a psyche, is, of course, due to the influence of Hume. In selecting a term so characteristic of the British tradition as "states" of mind or consciousness, I am not concerned to justify its use in the face of a tendency to substitute terms more expressive of a dynamic conception of mental operations, or of otherwise altered standpoints. The Buddhists seem to have held, as our psychology has held, that for purposes of analysis it was justifiable to break up the mental continuum of the moral individuality into this or that congeries of states or mental phenomena. In and through these they sought to trace the working of moral causation. To look beneath or behind them for a "thing in itself" they held to be a dangerous superstition. With Goethe they said: "Suche nichts hinter den Phänomenen; sie selbst sind die Lehre!" And, in view of this coincidence of implication and emphasis, "states of mind" or "of consciousness" seemed best to fit d h a m m ā when the reply was made in terms of mental phenomena.

In the book on Material Form, the standpoint is no doubt shifted to a relatively more objective consideration of the moral being and his contact with a world considered as external. But then the word d h a m m ā (and my rendering of it) is also superseded by r ū p a ṃ.

It is only when we come to the more synthetic matter of Book III that d h a m m ā strains the scope of the term

I have selected if " states " be taken as strictly states of mind or of consciousness. It is true that the Buddhist view of things so far resembles the Berkeleian that all phenomena, or things or sequences or elements, or however else we may render dhammā, may be *regarded* as in the last resort " states of mind ", albeit they were not held as being, all of them, such and no more. This in its turn may seem a straining of the significance which the term possessed for early Buddhists in a more general inquiry such as that of Book III. Yet consider the definitions of dhammā, worthy of Berkeley himself, in §§ 1044–5.

The difficulty lay in the choice of another term, and none being satisfactory, I retained, for want of a better, the same rendering, which is, after all, indefinite enough to admit of its connoting other congeries of things or aspects beside consciousness.

The fundamental importance in Buddhist philosophy of this Phenomenalism or Non-substantialism as a protest against the prevailing Animism, which, beginning with projecting the self into objects, saw in that projected self a noumenal quasi-divine substance, has by this time been more or less admitted. The testimony of the canonical books leaves no doubt on the matter, from Gotama's second sermon to his first converts, and his first Dialogue in the " Long Collection ", to the first book of the Kathā Vatthu.[1] There are other episodes in the books where the belief in a permanent spiritual essence is, together with a number of other speculations, waived aside as subjects calculated to waste time and energy. But in the portions referred to the doctrine of repudiation is more positive, and may be summed up in one of the refrains of the Majjhima Nikāya: Suññaṃ idaṃ attena vā attaniyena vā ti—Void is this of soul or of aught of the nature of soul![2] The force of the often repeated

[1] Cf. Rhys Davids' *American Lectures*, pp. 39, 40.

[2] Or " self " or " spirit " (attena). M. i, 297; ii, 263 (*lege* suññaṃ); cf. S. iv, 54; and KV. 67, 579. Cf. the " Emptiness-concept ", below, p. 30, n. 1.

"This is not mine, this is not I, this is not my Self", is not intended to make directly for goodness but for truth and insight. "And since neither self nor aught belonging to self, brethren, can really and truly be accepted, is not the heretical position which holds: This is the world and this is the self, and I shall continue to be in the future, permanent, immutable, eternal, of a nature that knows no change, yea, I shall abide to eternity!—is not this simply and entirely a doctrine of fools?"[1]

And now that the later or scholastic doctrine, as shown in the writings of the greatest of the Buddhist scholastics, becomes accessible, it is seen how carefully and conscientiously this anti-substantialist position had been cherished and upheld. Half-way to the age of the Commentators, the Milinda-pañho places the question of soul-theory at the head of the problems discussed. Then turning to Buddhaghosa we find the *much more emphatic negation* of the Sumangala Vilāsinī (p. 194): "Of aught within called self which looks forward or looks around, etc., there is none!" matched in the Atthasālinī, not only by the above-given definition of dhamma's, but also by the equally or even more emphatic affirmation respecting them, given in my n. 1 to p. 33: "There is no permanent entity or self which acquires the states . . . these are to be understood as ultimates (sabhāvaṭṭhena). There is no other essence or existence or personality or individual whatever." Again, attention is drawn in the notes to his often-reiterated comment that when a disposition or emotion is referred to cittaṃ, e.g. nandīrāgo cittassa,[2] the repudiation of an ego is thereby implied. Once more, the thoughts and acts which are tainted with "Āsavas" or with corruptions are said to be so in virtue of their being centred in the soul

[1] M. i, 138.

[2] p. 255, n. 2; also pp. 119, n. 3; 275, n. 2, etc.; and cf. p. 159, n. 3. See also on dhātu, p. lxxxv.

or self,[1] and those which have attained that "ideal Better" and have no "beyond" (a n - u t t a r ā) are interpreted as having transcended or rejected the soul or self.[2]

To appreciate the relative consistency with which the Buddhists tried to govern their philosophy, both in subject and in treatment, in accordance with this fundamental principle, we must open a book of Western psychology, more or less contemporary, such as the *De Animâ*, and note the sharply contrasted position taken up at the outset.

"The object of our inquiry," Aristotle says in his opening sentences, "is to study and ascertain the nature and essence of the Psyche, as well as its accidents . . . It may be well to distinguish . . . the genus to which the Psyche belongs, and determine what it is . . . whether it is a something and an essence, or quantity or quality . . . whether it is among entities in potentiality, or whether rather it is a reality . . . Now, the knowledge of anything in itself seems to be useful towards a right conception of the causes of the accidents in substances . . . But the knowledge of the accidents contributes largely in its turn towards knowing what the thing essentially is . . . Thus the essence is the proper beginning for every demonstration . . ."

The whole standpoint which the Buddhists brought into question, and decided to be untenable as a basis of sound doctrine, is here accepted and taken as granted. A phenomenon, or series of phenomena, is, on being held up for investigation, immediately and unhesitatingly looked upon under one of two aspects: *either* it must be a substance, essence, reality, *or* it belongs to one of those nine other "Categories"—quantity, quality, etc.—which constitute the phenomenon an attribute or group of attributes cohering in a substance.

It is true that Aristotle was too progressive and original a thinker to stop here. In his theory of mind as εἶδος or "form", in itself mere potentiality, but becoming actuality

[1] p. 271, n.4 ; p. 303, n. 1. [2] p. 312, n. 2.

as implicate in, and as energizing body, he endeavoured to transform the animism of current standpoints into a more rational conception. And in applying his theory he goes far virtually to resolve mind into phenomenal process (*De An.*, III, chaps. vii, viii). But he did not, or would not, wrench himself radically out of the primitive soil and plant his thought on a fresh basis, as the Buddhist dared to do. Hence Greek thought abode, for all his rationalizing, saturated with substantialist methods, till it was found acceptable by and was brought up into an ecclesiastical philosophy which, from its Patristic stage, had inherited a tradition steeped in animistic standpoints.

Modern science, however, has been gradually training the popular mind to a phenomenalistic point of view, and joining hands in psychology with the anti-substantialist tradition of Hume. So that the way is being paved for a more general appreciation of the earnest effort made by Buddhism—an effort stupendous and astonishing if we consider its date and the forces against it—to sever the growth of philosophic and religious thought from its ancestral stem and rear it in a purely rational soil.

But the philosophic elaboration of soul-theory into Substantialism is complicated and strengthened by a deeply important factor, on which I have already touched. This factor is the exploitation by philosophy, not of a primitive *Weltanschauung*, but of a fundamental fact in intellectual procedure and intellectual economy. I refer to the process of assimilating an indefinite number of particular impressions, on the ground of a common resemblance, into a "generic idea" or general notion, and of referring to each assimilated product by means of a common name. Every act of cognition, of coming-to-know anything, is reducible to this compound function of discerning the particular and of assimilating it into something relatively general. And this process, in its most abstract terms, is cognizing Unity in Diversity, the One through and beneath the Many.

Now no one, even slightly conversant with the history of philosophy, can have failed to note the connexion there has ever been set up between the concept of substratum and phenomena on the one hand, and that of the One and the Many on the other. They have become blended together, though they spring from distinct roots. And so essential, in every advance made by the intellect to extend knowledge and to reorganize its acquisitions, is the co-ordinating and economizing efficacy of this faculty of generalizing, that its alliance with any other deep-rooted traditional product of mind must prove a mighty stay. A fact in the growth of religious and of philosophic thought which so springs out of the very working and growth of thought in general as this tendency to unify must seem to rest on unshakeable foundations.

And when this implicit logic of intellectual procedure, this subsuming the particular under the general, has been rendered explicit in a formal system of definition and predication and syllogism, such as was worked out by the Greeks, the breach of alliance becomes much harder. For the progress in positive knowledge, as organized by the logical methods, is brought into harmony with progress in religious and philosophic thought.

This advance in the West is still in force, except in so far as psychological advance, and scientific progress generally, tell on the traditional logic and philosophy. Psychological analysis, for instance, shows that we may confuse the effective registration of our knowledge with the actual disposition of the originals. That is to say, this perceiving and judging, by way of generalizing and unifying, is the only way by which we are able to master the infinite diversities and approximate uniformities of phenomena. And it is true that through such procedure great results are attained. Conceptions are widened and deepened. Laws are discovered and then taken up under more general laws. Knowledge groups all phenomena under a few aspects of all but supreme generality. Unification of knowledge is everywhere considered as the ideal aim of intellect.

But, after all, this is only the ideal *method* and *economy* of intellect. The stenographer's ideal is to compress recorded matter into the fewest symbols by which he can reproduce faithfully. Limitations of time and faculty constrain us to become mental stenographers. We simplify concrete reality by abstractions, we compress it by generalizations. And the abstract and general terms become symbols which perhaps are not adequately the mirrors of the real and the true.

Now whatever be our view as to the reality of an external world outside our perception of it, psychology teaches us to distinguish our fetches of abstraction and generalization for what they are *psychologically*—i.e. for effective mental shorthand—whatever they may represent besides. The logical form of Universal in term and in proposition is as much a token of our weakness in realizing the Particular as of our strength in constructing what is at best an abstract and hypothetical whole. The philosophical concept of the One is pregnant with powerful associations. To what extent is it simply as a mathematical symbol in a hypothetical cosmos of carefully selected data, whence the infinite concrete is eliminated lest it "should flow in over us" [1] and overwhelm us?

Now, the Buddhistic phenomenalism had also both the one and the other member of this great alliance of Noumenon and Unity to contend with. But the alliance had, so far at least as we know or can infer, not yet been welded together by a logical organon, or by any development in inductive science. Gotama and his apostles were, to some extent, conversant with the best culture of their age, yet when they shape their discourse according to anything

[1] Infra, § 1345: "Yam . . . pāpakā akusalā dhammā anvāssaveyyuṃ." Cf. Maudsley, *Body and Will*, p. 225.

we should call logic, they fall into it rather than wield it after the conscious fashion of Plato or Aristotle. Nor is there, in the books, any clear method practised of definition according to genus and species, or of mutual exclusion among concepts. Thus freer in harness, the Buddhist revolutionary philosophy may be said to have attempted a relatively less impracticable task. The development of a science and art of logic in India, as we know it, was later in time; and though Buddhist thinkers helped in that development,[1] it coincided precisely with the decline of Buddhistic non-substantialism, with the renascence of Pantheistic thought.

VI.

On the Inquiry into R ū p a ṃ (Form), and the Buddhist Theory of Sense.

Taking d h a m m ā, then, to mean *phenomena considered as knowledge*—in other words, as actually or potentially states of consciousness—we may next look more closely into that which the catechism brings out respecting r ū p a ṃ (Book II and § 583) considered as a *species* of d h a m m ā. By this procedure we shall best place ourselves at the threshold, so to speak, of the Buddhist position, both as to its psychology and its view of things in general, and be thus better led up to the ethical import of the questions in the first part.

The entire universe of d h a m m ā is classed with respect to r ū p a ṃ in questions 1091, 1092 (Book III). They are there shown to be either r ū p i n o, having form, or a - r ū p i n o, not having form. The positive category comprises "the four great phenomena (four elements) and all their derivatives". The negative term refers to what we should call modes or phases of consciousness, or subjective experience—that is, to "the skandhas of feeling, perception,

[1] Cf. the writer's art. "Logic" (Buddhist): *Ency. Religion and Ethics*.

synergies, and cognition"—as well as to "unconditioned element". (The skandhas are also "elements"—that is, irreducible but phenomenal factors (see p. 119, n. 3), real although phenomenal.[1] R ū p a ṃ would thus appear at first sight to be a name for the external world, or for the extended universe, as contrasted with the unextended, mental, psychical, or subjective universe. Personally, I do not find, so far, that the Eastern and Western concepts can be so easily made to coincide. It will be better before, and indeed without, as yet, arriving at any such conclusive judgment to inquire into the application made of the term in the Manual generally.

We find r ū p a ṃ used in three, at least, of the various meanings assigned to it in the lexicons. It occurs first, and very frequently, as the general name for the objects of the sense of sight. It may then stand as simply r ū p a ṃ (§ 617, "this which is visible object", as opposed to § 621, etc., "this which is 'sound', 'odour'," etc.). More usually it is spoken of as r ū p ā r a m m a ṇ a ṃ, object of sight (p. 1), or as r ū p ā y a t a n a ṃ, sphere (province, *Gebiet*) of sights or things seen (pp. 158, 167 *et seq.*). It includes both sensations of colour and lustre and the complex sensations of form. Used in this connexion, it is nearest to its popular meaning of "shape", "visible likeness", and its specialization is, of course, only due to the psychological fact that sight is the spokesman and interpreter of all the senses, so that "I see" often stands for "I perceive or discern through two or more modes of sensation".

On this point it is worth while pointing out an interesting flash of psychological discrimination in the Commentary. It will be noticed in the various kinds of r ū p ā y a t a n a ṃ enumerated in § 617 (p. 168, n. 1) that, after pure visual sensations have been instanced, different magnitudes and forms are added, such as "long", "short",

[1] Cf. *Compendium of Philosophy*, p. 255.

etc. On these Buddhaghosa remarks: "Here, inasmuch as we are able to tell 'long', 'short', etc., by touch, while we cannot so discern 'blue', etc., therefore 'long', 'short', and the rest are *not* objects of vision except figuratively (literally, not without explanation, cf. p. xxxiii, n. 2). *A*, *B*, placed in such a relation to *C*, *D*, is only by customary usage spoken of as something seen" (Asl. 316).[1] This may not bring us up to Berkeley, but it is a farther step in that direction than Aristotle's mere hint—"There is a movement which is perceptible both by Touch and Sight"—when he is alluding to magnitudes, etc., being "common sensibles", i.e. perceptible by more than one sense.[2]

To resume: R ū p a ṃ, in its wider sense (as "all form"), may be due to the popular generalization and representative function of the sense of sight, expressed in Tennyson's line:—

"For knowledge is of things we see. . . ."

And thus, even as a philosophical concept, it may, loosely speaking, have stood for "things seen", as contrasted with the unseen world of d h a m m ā a r ū p i n o. But this is by no means an adequate rendering of the term in its more careful and technical use in the second Book of our Manual. For, as may there be seen, much of the content of "form" is explicitly declared to be invisible.[3]

R ū p a ṃ occurs next, and, with almost equal frequency, together with its opposite, a r ū p a ṃ, to signify those two other worlds, realms or planes [4] of temporal existence,

---

[1] The symbols are my own adaptation, not a literal rendering. In the account of the "external senses" or Indriyas given in the (later) Sānkhya textbooks, Professor Garbe points out that the objects of sight are limited to colour (r ū p a), exclusive of form (Garbe, *Die Sāṃkhya-Philosophie*, p. 258).

[2] *De Animâ*, II, vi.

[3] Cf. §§ 597 *et seq.*, 657, 658, 751, 752, etc.

[4] To the employment of "universe" for a v a c a r a ṃ exception may be taken, since the latter term means only a

which Buddhism accepted along with other current mythology, and which, taken together with the lowest, or sensuous plane of existence, exhaust the possible modes of rebirth. These a v a c a r a s , or loci of form and non-form, are described in terms of vague localization (§§ 1280–5), but it is not easy to realize how far existence of either sort was conceived with anything like precision. Including the "upper" grades of the world of sensuous existence, they were more popularly known as heaven or s a g g a (s v a r g a), i.e. the Bright. Their inhabitants were devas, distinguished into hosts variously named. Like the heaven of the West or the Near East, they were located "above", "upari", i.e. above each next lower world (cf. below, § 1281, n. 4).[1] Unlike that heaven, life in them was temporal, not eternal.

But the Dhamma-sangaṇi throws no new light on the kind of states they were supposed to be. Nor does Buddhaghosa here figure as an Eastern Dante, essaying to body out more fully, either dogmatically or as in a dream, such ineffable oracles as were hinted at by a Paul "caught up to the third heaven . . . whether in the body or out of the body I cannot tell—God knoweth", or the ecstatic visions of a John in lonely exile. The Atthasālinī is not free from

---

part of the Oriental cosmos. I admit it calls for apology. If I have used it throughout Book I, it was because there the term a v a c a r a ṃ seemed more suggestive of the logician's term "universe of discourse", or "of thought", than of any physically conceived actuality. It seemed to fit De Morgan's definition of "the universe of a proposition"—"a collection of all objects which are contemplated as objects about which assertion or denial may take place", the universe of form, for instance, either as a vague, vast concept "in" time and effort, or as a state of mind, a rapt abstraction—in either case a "universe of thought" for the time being.

[1] The simplest (possibly the oldest) Sutta-statement of the four whereabouts of rebirth other than human is in M. i, 73. Cf. the writer's "Buddhist Theory of Rebirth": *Quest Review*, Jan., 1922.

divagations on matters of equally secondary importance to the earnest Buddhist.[1] Yet it has nothing to tell of a mode of being endowed with r ū p a , yet without the k ā m ā , or sensuous impulses held to be bound up with r ū p a , when the term is used in its wider sense.[2] Nor does it enlighten us on the more impalpable denizens of a plane of being where r ū p a itself is not, and for which no terms seem held appropriate save such as express high fetches of abstract thought.[3] We must go back, after all, to the Nikāyas for such brief hints as we can find. We do hear, at least, in the Dīgha Nikāya, of beings in one of the middle circles of the Form heavens termed Radiant (Ābhassara) as " made of mind, feeding on joy, radiating light, traversing the firmament, continuing in beauty ".[4] Were it not that we miss here the unending melody sounding through each circle of the Western poet's Paradise[5] we might well apply this description to Dante's " anime liete ", who, like incandescent spheres :—

" Fiammando forte a guisa di comete,
E come cerchi in tempra d' oriuoli
Si giran." . . .

---

[1] Cf. e.g. on a similar subject, Sum.V. i, 110. Buddhaghosa tells us, it is true (see Asl., p. 332), that the food of the devas who inhabited the highest sphere of the *sensuous* world was of the maximum degree of refinement, leading perhaps to the inference that in the two superior planes it was not required.

[2] See § 595: " All form is that which is . . . related, or which belongs to the universe of sense, *not* to that of form, or to that of the formless."

[3] See the four Āruppas, pp. 65–8.

[4] D. i, 17. Again we read (D. i, 195), that of the three possible " personalities " of current tradition, one was made of mind, having form, and a complete organism, and one was without form and made of consciousness, or perception (a r ū p ī s a ñ ñ ā m a y o). In M. i, 410 f., devā rūpino manomayā are distinguished from devā arūpino saññāmayā.

[5] There is no lack of music in some of the lower Indian heavens. Cf. e.g. M. i, 252, on Sakka the god enjoying the music in his sensuous paradise. And see Vimāna Vatthu, *passim*.

Liker to those brilliant visions the heavens of Form seem to have been than to the "quiet air" and "the meadow of fresh verdure" on that slope of Limbo where

"Genti v' eran con occhi tardi e gravi",

who

"Parlavan rado, con voci soavi".

Yet the rare, sweet utterances of these devas of Europe, discoursing with "the Master of those who know", may better have accorded with the Buddhist conception of the remotest worlds as inhabited by "beings made of mind" than the choric dances of the spheres above.

Among these shadowy beings, however, we are far from the fully bodied out idea of the "all form" and the "skandha of form" of the second and third Books of the Manual. It may be that the worlds of rūpa and arūpa were so called in popular tradition because in the former, visible, and in the latter, invisible beings resided.[1] But there is no lack of information concerning the attributes of form in the "sensuous universe" of kāmāvacaraṃ. If the list given of these in the first chapter of Book II be consulted, it will be seen that I have not followed the reading of the PTS. edition when it states that all form is kāmāvacaram eva, rūpāvacaram eva, that is, is both related to the universe of sense and also to that of form. The Siamese edition reads kāmāvacaram eva, na rūpāvacaram eva. It may seem at first sight illogical to say that form is not related to the universe of form. But the better logic is really on the side of the Siamese. In §§ 1281–4 of my translation

[1] The Suttas leave us in no doubt as to the presence of material conditions in the Brahma sphere of the Rūpa world and its devas. Cf. *Kindred Sayings*, i, 173: The shoulder, knee, arms of its ruler and his robe. He assumed a relatively grosser body to enable him to visit the "lower" heavens. *Dialogues*, ii, 244, 264. Whether a yet grosser one was needed for earth-visits is not stated. Because of this glimpse of sublimated matter in the Rūpa world I called it, in Maung Tin's *Expositor*, the realm of attenuated matter. But no good term is forthcoming. Cf. note, p. ciii.

it is seen that the avacaras were mutually exclusive as to their contents. To belong to the universe of form involved exclusion from that of sense. But in the inquiry into "all form" we are clearly occupied with facts about this present world and about women and men as we know them—in a word, with the world of sense. Hence the "all form" of Book II is clearly *not* the form of the rūpāvacaraṃ. It is not used with the same implications.

Further than this, further than the vague avacara-geography gathered already from other sources, the Manual does not bring us, nor the Commentary either.

We come, then, to rūpaṃ in the sensuous plane of being, or at least to such portion of that plane as is concerned with human beings; to sabbaṃ rūpaṃ and to its distribution in each human economy, termed rūpakkhandho. Under it are comprised four ultimate primary, or underivable, constituents and twenty-three secondary, dependent, or derived modes. Thus:—

Rūpaṃ

No upādā	Upādā
= (*a*) The Tangible (i.e. earthy or solid, lambent or fiery, gaseous or aerial elements, or great phenomena),	= (*a*) The Five Senses,
(*b*) The Fluid (or moist) element.	(*b*) The Four Objects of Sense (excluding Tangibles),
	(*c*) The Three Organic Faculties,
	(*d*) The Two Modes of Intimation,
	(*e*) The Element of Space,
	(*f*) Three Qualities of Form,
	(*g*) Three Phases in the Evolution of Form,
	(*h*) Impermanence of Form,
	(*i*) Nutriment.

To enter with any fullness of discussion into this

classification, so rich in interesting suggestions, would occupy itself a volume. In an introduction of mere notes I will offer only a few general considerations.

We are probably first impressed by the *psychological* aspect taken of a subject that might seem to lend itself to purely objective consideration. The main constituents of the material world, classified in the East as we know them to have been classified, contemporaneously, in the West, are set down in terms of subjective or conscious experience. The ā p o - d h ā t u is not called explicitly the Intangible; virtually, however, it and the other three "Great Phenomena", or literally "Great things that have Become",[1] are regarded from the point of view of how they affect us by way of sense. We might add, how they affect us most fundamentally by way of sense. In the selection of Touch among the senses the Indian tradition joins hands with Demokritus. But of this no more at present.

Again, in the second table, or secondary forms, the same standpoint is predominant. We have the action and reaction of sense-object and sense, the distinctive expressions of sex and of personality generally, and the phenomena of organic life, as "sensed" or inferred, comprehended under the

---

[1] Better in Greek *τὰ γιγνόμενα*, or in German *die vier grossen Gewordenen*. In the *Compendium* (1910), S. Z. Aung and I agree to use the term "Great essential". P. M. Tin, in the *Expositor*, follows suit. How the Buddhist logic exactly reconciled the anomaly of ā p o d h ā t u as underived and yet as inaccessible to that sense which comes into contact with the underived is not, in the Manual, clearly made out. In *hot* water, as the Cy. says, there is heat, gas, and *solid*, and hence we feel it. Yet by the definition there must be in fluid a something underived from these three elements.

The Buddhist Sensationalism was opposed to the view taken in the Upanishad, where the senses are derived from p r a j ñ ā (rendered by Professor Deussen "consciousness"), and again from the World Soul. In the Garbha Up., however, sight is spoken of as *fire*. The Buddhist view was subsequently again opposed by the Sānkhya philosophy, but not by the Nyāya.

most general terms. Two modes of form alone are treated objectively: space and food. And of these, too, the aspect taken has close reference to the conscious personality. Ā k ā s o is really o k ā s o, room, or opportunity, for life and movement. Food, though described as to its varieties in objective terms, is referred to rather in the abstract sense of nutrition and nutriment than as nutritive *matter*. (Cf. p. 186, n. 3.)

Or we may be more especially struck by the curious selection and classification exercised in regard to the items of the catalogue of form.

Now, the compilers of this or of any of the canonical books were not interested in r ū p a ṃ on psychological grounds as such. Their object was not what we should term scientific. They were not inquiring into forms, either as objective existences or as mental constructions, with any curiosity respecting the macrocosm, its parts, or its order. They were not concerned with problems of primordial ὕλη, of first causes, or of organic evolution, in the spirit which has been operative in Western thought from Thales (claimed by Europe) to Darwin. For them, as for the leaders of that other rival movement in our own culture, the tradition of Socrates and Plato, man was, first and last, the subject supremely worth thinking about. And man was worth thinking about as a moral being. The physical universe was the background and accessory, the support and the "fuel" (u p ā d ā n a ṃ), of the evolution of the moral life. That universe was necessary to man (at least during his sojourn on the physical plane), but it was only in so far as it affected his ethical life that he could profitably study it. The Buddhist, like the Socratic view, was that of primitive man—"What is the *good* of it?"—transformed and sublimated by the evolution of the moral ideal. The early questioning: Is such and such good for life-preservation, for race-preservation, for fun? or is it bad? or is it indeterminate? becomes, in evolved ethics: Does it make for my perfection, for others' perfection, for noblest enjoyment? does it make for the contrary? does it make for neither?

And the advance in moral evolution which was attempted by Buddhist philosophy, coming as it did in an age of metaphysical dogmatism and withal of scepticism, brought with it the felt need of looking deeper into those data of mental procedure on which dogmatic speculation and ethical convictions were alike founded.[1]

Viewed in this light, the category of r ū p a ṃ or of r ū p a k k h a n d h o becomes fairly intelligible, both as to the selection and classification of subject matter and as to the standpoint from which it is regarded. As a learner of ethical doctrine pursuing either the lower or the higher ideal, the Buddhist was concerned with the external world just as far as it directly and inevitably affected his moral welfare and that of other moral beings, that is to say, of all conscious animate beings. To this extent did he receive instruction concerning it.

In the first place, the great ultimate phenomena of his physical world were one and the same as the basis of his own physical being. That had form; so had this. That was built up of the four elements; so was this. That came into being, persisted, then dissolved; this was his destiny, too, as a temporary collocation or body, "subject to erasion, abrasion, dissolution, and disintegration."[2] And all that side of life which we call mind or consciousness, similarly conceived as collocations or aggregates, was bound up therein and on that did it depend.

Here, then, was a vital kinship, a common basis of physical being which it behoved the student of man to recognize and take into account, so as to hold an intelligent and consistent attitude towards it. The b h i k k h u s e k h o[3]

---

[1] G. Croom Robertson, *Philosophical Remains*, p. 3.
[2] D. i, 76, e.g.
[3] The brother in orders undergoing training. M. i, 4.

"who has not attained, who is aspiring after, the unsurpassable goal", has to know, *inter alia*, earth, water, fire, air, each for what it is, both as external and as part of himself [1]—must know "unity" (e k a t t a ṃ) for what it is; must indulge in no conceits of fancy (m ā m a ñ ñ i) about it or them, and must so regard them that of him it may one day be said by the wise: p a r i ñ ñ ā t a ṃ t a s s a !—"he knows it thoroughly."

To this point we shall return. That the elements are considered under the aspect of their tangibility involves for the Buddhist the further inquiry into the sensitive agency by which they affect him as tangibles, and so into the problem of sensation and sense-perception in general. On this subject the Dhamma-sangaṇi yields a positive and valuable contribution to our knowledge of the history of psychology in India in the fourth century B.C. It may contain no matter additional to that which is reproduced in Hardy's *Manual of Budhism* (pp. 399–404, 419–23). But Hardy drew *directly* from relatively modern sources, and though it is interesting to see how far and how faithfully the original tradition has been kept intact in these exegetical works, we turn gladly to the stronger attractions of the *first academic formulation* of a theory of sense which ancient India has hitherto preserved for us. There is no such analysis of sensation—full, sober, positive, so far as it goes—put forward in any Indian book of an equally early date. The pre-Buddhistic Upanishads (and those, too, of later date) yield only poetic adumbrations, sporadic aphorisms on the work of the senses. The Nyāya doctrine of p r a t y a k s h a or perception, the Jaina Sūtras, the elaboration of the Vedânta and Sānkhya doctrines are, of course, of far later date. It may not, therefore, be uncalled for if I digress at some length on the Buddhist position in this matter and look for parallel theories in the West rather than in India itself.

---

[1] M. i, pp. 185 *et seq.*; pp. 421 *et seq.*

The theory of action and reaction between the five special[1] senses and their several objects is given in pp. 172–90 and 197–200 of my translation. It may be summarized as follows:

A. The Senses.

First, a general statement relating each sense in turn (*a*) to the four elements, i.e. to "Nature", (*b*) to the individual organism, and affirming its invisibility and its power of impact.

Secondly, an analysis of the sensory process, in each case, into

(*a*) A personal agency or apparatus capable of reacting to an impact not itself;

(*b*) An impingeing "form", or form producing a reaction of one specific kind;

(*c*) Impact between (*a*) and (*b*), with reference to the time-dimension[2];

(*d*) Resultant modification of the mental continuum, viz. in the first place, contact (of a specific sort); then hedonistic result, or intellectual result, or, presumably both. The modification is twice stated in each case, emphasis being laid on the mutual impact, first as causing the modification, then as constituting the object of attention in the modified consciousness of the person affected.

B. The Sense-objects.

First, a general statement, relating each kind of sense-object in turn to nature, describing some of the typical varieties, and affirming its invisibility, except in the case of visual objects,[3] and its power of producing impact.[4]

---

[1] They are called "special" in modern psychology to distinguish them from organic, general, or systemic sense, which works without specially adapted peripheral organs.

[2] Not as in any way constructing space-percepts, but as pertinent to the question of karma and rebirth.

[3] This insistence on the invisibility of all the senses, as well as on that of all sense-objects except sights or visual forms, is to me only explicable on the ground that r ū p a ṃ recurring in each question and each answer, and signifying, whatever else

Secondly, an analysis of the sensory process in each case as under A, but, as it were, from the side of the sense-object, thus :—

(*a*) A mode of form or sense-object, capable of producing impact on a special apparatus of the individual organism;

(*b*) The impact of that apparatus ;

(*c*) The reaction or complementary impact of the sense-object;

(*d*) Resultant modification of the mental continuum, viz. in the first place contact (of a specific sort) ; then hedonistic result, or intellectual result, or, presumably, both. The modification is twice stated, in each case emphasis being laid on the mutual impact, first as causing the modification, then as constituting the object of attention in the modified consciousness thus affected.

If we, for purposes of comparison, consult Greek views on sense-perception before Aristotle—say, down to 350 B.C.—we shall find nothing to equal this for sobriety, consistency, and thoroughness. The surviving fragments of Empedoklean writings on the subject read beside it like airy fancies ; nor do the intact utterances of Plato bring us anything more scientific. Very possibly in Demokritus we might have found its match, had we more of him than a few quotations. And there is reason to surmise as much, or even more, in the case of Alkmæon.

Let me not, however, be understood to be reading into the Buddhist theory more than is actually there. In its sober, analytical prose, it is no less archaic, naïve, and inadequate as explanation than any pre-Aristotelian theory of the Greeks. The comment of Dr. Siebeck on Empedokles applies equally

---

it meant, in popular idiom, things *seen*, it was necessary, in philosophic usage, to indicate that the term, though referring to sense, did *not*, with one exception, connote things seen. Thus, even solid and fiery objects were, *quâ* tangibles, not visible. They were not visible to the k ā y o, or skin-sensibility. They spelt visible only to the eye.

[4] See n. 1 to § 617.

to it:[1] "It sufficed him to have indicated the possibility of the external world penetrating the sense-organs, as though this were tantamount to an explanation of sensation. The whole working out of his theory is an attempt to translate in terms of a detailed and consecutive physiological process the primitive, naïve view of cognition." Theory of this calibre was, in Greece, divided between *impact* (Alkmæon, Empedokles, with respect to *sight*, Demokritus, Plato, who, to impact, adds a *commingling* of sense and object) and *access* (efflux and pore theory of Empedokles) as the essential part of the process. The Buddhist explanation confines itself to *impact*.[2] But neither East nor West, with the possible exception of Alkmæon, had yet gripped the notion of a conducting medium. In Aristotle all is changed. "Eidôla" which collide, and "aporrhoæ" which penetrate, have been thrown aside for an examination into "metaxu". And we find the point of view similarly shifted in Buddhaghosa's time, though how long before him this advance had been made we do not know. Because of the eye and the visible shape, eye-consciousness arises; the collision (sangati) of the three is contact (phasso, or, as we should say, sensation).[3] So the early Sutta. According to the commentator, the eye itself (and each sense-organ) does not touch the object; it is phasso that touches it, *quâ* ārammaṇaṃ, that is, mental object.[4] Hence phasso appears as pure psychic medium or process, working psycho-physically through the active sense-organ. Nor was there, in the earlier thought of East and West, any clear dualistic distinction drawn between mind and matter, between physical (and physiological) motion or stimulus on the one hand, and consequent or concomitant mental modification on the other, in an act of sense-perception.

---

[1] *Geschichte der Psychologie*, i, 107.

[2] *Access* comes later into prominence with the development of the "Door-theory". See following section.

[3] M. i, 111.

[4] Sum. V. i, 124.

The Greek explanations are what would now be called materialistic. The Buddhist description may be interpreted either way. It is true that in the Milinda-pañho, written some three or four centuries later than our Manual, the action and reaction of sense and sense-object are compared in realistic metaphor to the clash of two cymbals and the butting of two goats.[1] But, being metaphorical, this account brings us really no further. The West, while it retained the phraseology characterizing the earlier theory of sense, ceased to imply any direct physical impact or contact when speaking of being "struck" by sights, sounds, or ideas. How far, and how early, was this also the case in the East?

The Buddhist theory, with an unconscious parallelism, discerned, in the word for a material sensation: "touch," or "contact", a psychical complement getting at and transforming the external object, making it a mental presentation. If dhammā are conceived, as in the Manual, as actual or potential states of consciousness, and rūpaṃ is conceived as a species of dhammā, it follows that both the rūpaṃ, which is "external" and comes into contact with the rūpaṃ which is "of the self", and also this latter rūpaṃ are regarded in the light of the two *mental* factors necessary to constitute the third factor, viz. an act of sensory consciousness, actual or potential.

Such may have been the psychological aspect adumbrated, groped after—not to go further—in the Dhamma-sangaṇi itself. That the traditional interpretation of this impact-theory grew psychological with the progress of culture in the schools of Buddhism seems to be indicated by such a comment in the Atthasālinī as: "*strikes* (impinges) *on form* is a term for the eye (i.e. the visual sense) being receptive of the object of consciousness."[2] This seems to be a clear attempt to resolve

---

[1] *Milindapañho*, p. 60. SBE., vol. xxxv, pp. 92, 93. Cf. below, p.4, n.2.

[2] Asl. 309. Cakkhuṃ ārammaṇaṃ sampaṭicchayamānam eva rūpamhi paṭihaññati nāma.

the old metaphor, or, it may be, the old physical concept, into terms of subjective experience. Again, when alluding to the simile of the cymbals and the rams, we are told by Buddhaghosa to interpret "eye" by "visual cognition", and to take the "concussion" in the sense of *function*.[1] Once more he tells us that when feeling arises through contact the real causal antecedent is mental, though apparently external.[2]

Without pursuing this problem further, we cannot leave the subject of sense and sensation without a word of comment and comparison on the prominence given in the Buddhist theory to the notion of "contact" and the sense of touch. As with us, both terms are from the same stem. But p h a s s o (contact), on the one hand, is generalized to include all *receptive* experience, sensory as well as ideational,[3] and to represent the essential antecedent and condition of all feeling (or sensation = v e d a n ā). On the other hand, p h u s a t i, p h o ṭ ṭ h a b b a ṃ (to touch, the tangible) are specialized to express the activity of one of the senses. Now, the functioning of the tactile sense (termed body-sensibility or simply body, k ā y o , pp. 166, 167) is described in precisely the same terms as each of the other four senses. Nevertheless, it is plain, from the significant application of the term tangible, or object of touch, alluded to already—let alone the use of "contact" in a wider sense—that the Buddhists regarded Touch as giving us knowledge of things "without" in a more fundamental way than the other senses could. By the table of the contents of r ū p a ṃ given above, we have seen that it is only through Touch that a knowledge of the *underived elements* of the world of sense could be obtained, the fluid or moist element alone excepted. This interesting point in the psychology of early Buddhism may possibly be formulated somewhere in the Abhidhamma

---

[1] Ibid. 108: "k i c c a ṭ ṭ h e n" eva.

[2] See below, p. 4, n. 2.

[3] See below, p. 6, n. 3.

Piṭaka. I should feel more hopeful in this respect had the compilers been, in the first instance, not ethical thinkers, but impelled by the scientific curiosity of a Demokritus. The latter, as is well known, regarded all sensation as either bare touch or developments of touch—a view borne out to a great extent by modern biological research. This was, perhaps, a corollary of his atomistic philosophy. Yet that Demokritus was no mere deductive system-spinner, but an inductive observer, is shown in the surviving quotation of his dictum, that we should proceed, in our inferences, "from phenomena to that which is not manifest." Now, as the Buddhist view of r ū p a ṃ calls three of the four elements "underived" and "the tangible", while it calls the senses and all other sense-objects "derived from that tangible" and from fluid, one might almost claim that their position with respect to Touch was in effect parallel to that of Demokritus. The Commentary does not assist us to any clear conclusion on this matter. But, in addition to the remark quoted above, in which visual magnitudes are pronounced to be really tactile sensations, it has one interesting illustration of our proverb, "Seeing is believing, but Touch is the real thing." It likens the four senses, excluding touch, to the striking of four balls of cotton-wool on anvils by other lumps of cotton. But in Touch, as it were, a hammer smites through the wool, getting at the bare anvil.[1]

Further considerations on the Buddhist theory of sense, taking us beyond bare sensation to the working up of such material into concrete acts of perception, I propose to consider briefly in the following section. The remaining heads of the rūpa-skandha are very concisely treated in the Niddesa-answers (pp. 190–7), and, save in the significance of their selection, call for no special treatment.

---

[1] Asl. 263; below, n. 1 to § 443. I have corrected this passage in accordance with S. Z. Aung's criticism. *Compendium*, 232.

C. The Three Organic Faculties.

It is not quite clear why senses and sense-objects should be followed by three indriyas—by three only and just these three. The senses themselves are often termed indriyas, and not only in Buddhism. In the indriyas of sex, however, and the phenomena of nutrition, the rūpa-skandha, in both the self and other selves, is certainly catalogued under two aspects as general and as impressive as that of sense. In fact, the whole organism as modifiable by the "sabbaṃ rūpaṃ" without, may be said to be summed up under these three aspects. They fit fairly well into our division of the receptive side of the organism, considered, psycho-physically, as *general* and *special* sensibility. From his ethical standpoint the learner did well to take the life in which he shared into account under its impressive aspects of sense, sex and nutrition. And this not only in so far as he was receptive. The very term indriyaṃ, which is best paralleled by the Greek δύναμις, or faculty—i.e. "powers in us, and in all other things, by which we do as we do"[1]—and which is interpreted to this effect by Buddhaghosa,[2] points to the active, self-expressive side of existence. And there is in later exegesis a felt awareness of the importance of faculties as controllers and preservers of the organism.[3] Both as recipient, then, and as agent, the learner of the Dharma had to acquire and maintain a certain attitude with respect to these aspects of the rūpa-skandha.

D, E. Intimation and Space.

The same considerations apply to the next two kinds of rūpaṃ, with which we may bracket the next after them. The two modes of "intimation" or self-expression exhaust the active side of life as such, constituting, as one might say, a world of sub-derivative or tertiary form, and calling

[1] Republic, v. 477.
[2] Asl., p. 119 and *passim*.
[3] *Compendium*, 228.

quite especially for modification by theory and practice (dassanena ca bhāvanāya ca). And the element of space, strange as it looks, at first sight, to find it listed just here, was of account for the Buddhist only as a necessary datum or postulate for his sentient and active life. The vacua of the body, as well as its *plena*, had to be reckoned in with the rūpa-skandha; likewise the space without by which bodies were delimitated, and which, yielding room for movement, afforded us the three dimensions.[1]

The grounds for excluding space from the four elements and for calling it "derived" remain in obscurity. In the Mahā Rāhulovāda-Sutta (cited below) it is ranked immediately after, and apparently as co-ordinate with, the other four. And it was so ranked, oftener than not, by Indian thought generally. Yet in another Sutta of the same Nikāya—the Mahā Hatthipadopama - Sutta — Sāriputta describes four elements, leaving out ākāso. Eliminated for some reason from the Underived, when the Dhamma-saṅgaṇi was compiled, it was logically necessary to include it under Derived Rūpaṃ. That it was so included because it was held to be a mental construction or a "pure form of intuition", is scarcely tenable.

F, G, H. Qualities of Form.

And yet the next seven items of derived form are apparently to be accepted rather as concepts or aspects of form than as objective properties or "primary qualities" of it. Be that as it may, all the seven are so many common

[1] See below, n. 1 to § 638; also M. i, 423. In the former passage space is described as if external to the organism; in the latter Gotama admonishes his son respecting the internal ākāso. On the interesting point put forward by von Schroeder of a connexion between ākāça and the Pythagorean ὄλκας, see Professor Garbe in the *Vienna Oriental Journal*, xiii, Nro. 4, 1899. The former scholar refers to the ranking of space as a fifth element, as a *schwankend uberlieferte Bezeichnung*. It was so for Buddhism (D. iii, 247; M. iii, 239, 240).

facts about r ū p a ṃ, both as "s a b b a ṃ" and as skandha. The Three Qualities[1] indicated the ideal efficiency for moral ends to which the rūpa-skandha, or any form serving such an end, should be brought. The Three Phases in the organic evolution of form and the great fact of Impermanence applied everywhere and always to all form. And as such all had to be borne in mind, all had to co-operate in shaping theory and practice.

I. Nutriment.

Concerning, lastly, the ā h ā r o, or support, of the rūpa-skandha, the hygiene and ethics of diet are held worthy of rational discussion in the Sutta Piṭaka.[2]

We have now gone with more or less details into the divisions of r ū p a ṃ in the "sensuous universe", with a view of seeing how far it coincided with any general philosophical concept in use among ourselves. For me it does not fit well with any, and the vague term "form", implicated as it is, like r ū p a ṃ, with "things we see", is perhaps the most serviceable. Its inclusion of faculties and abstract notions as integral factors prevent its coinciding with "matter", or "the Extended", or "the External World". If we turn to the list of attributes given in Chapter I of Book II, r ū p a ṃ appears as pre-eminently the *unmoral* (as to both cause and effect) and the *non-mental*. It was "favourable" to *im*moral states, as the chief constituent of a world that had to be mastered and transcended by moral culture, but the immoral states exploiting it were of the other four skandhas. It included the phenomena of sense, but rather on their physical pre-mental side than as full-fledged facts of consciousness. And it was sharply distinguished, as a constituent "collocation" or "aggregate" (skandha, rāsi), in the total

[1] Lightness, plasticity, wieldiness, §§ 639–41.

[2] Cf. e.g. M. i, Suttas 54, 55, 65, 66, 70. There was also the philosophical aspect of āhāro as cause, or basis. See my *Buddhist Psychology*, 1914, p. 61 f.

aggregate of the individual organism from the three collocations called c e t a s i k ā (feelings, perceptions, conformations, or synergies), and from that called c i t t a (consciousness, thought, cognition). The a t t a b h ā v o, or personality, *minus* all mental and moral characteristics, is r ū p a ṃ.

As such it is one with all r ū p a ṃ not of its own composition. It is "in touch" with the general impersonal r ū p a ṃ, as well as with the mental and moral constituents of other personalities by way of *their* r ū p a ṃ. That this intercommunication was held to be possible on the basis, and in virtue of, this common structure was probably as implicit in the Buddhist doctrine as it was explicit in many of the early Greek philosophers. There are no open allusions to "like being known by like" in the Piṭakas as a consciously held and deliberately stated principle or ground of the impressibility of the sentient organism. *A fortiori* no such statement occurs in our Manual. But the phrase, recurring in the case of each of the special senses, "derived from the four Great Phenomena," may not have been inserted without this implication. Without further evidence, however, I should not be inclined to attach philosophical significance in this direction to it. But, on the one hand, we have an interesting hint in the Commentary that such a principle *was* held by Buddhist scholars. "Where there is difference of kind (or creature), we read,[1] there is no sensory stimulus. According to the Ancients, 'Sensory stimulus is of similar kinds, not of different kinds.'"

And again: "The solid, both within and without, becomes the condition of the sense of touch in the laying hold of the object of perception—in discerning the tangible."[2] It is

---

[1] Asl. 313. Bhūta visese hi sati pasādo va na uppajjati. "Samānānaṃ bhūtanaṃ hi pasādo, na visamānānan ti" Porāṇā.

[2] Ibid. 315. Ajjhattika-bāhirā paṭhavī etassa kāyapasādassa ārammaṇagahaṇe . . . phoṭṭhabbajānane paccayo hoti.

true that Buddhaghosa is discoursing, not on this question, but on what would now be called the specific energy, or specialized functioning, of nerve. Nevertheless, it seems inferable from the quotations that the principle was established. And we know, also, how widely accepted (and also contested)[1] this same principle—'*Η* γνῶσις τοῦ ὁμοίου τῷ ὁμοίῳ was in Greece, from Empedokles to Plato and to Plotinus,[2] thinkers, all of them, who were affected, through Pythagorism or elsewise, by the East. The vivid description by Buddhaghosa (cf. below, pp. 173–4) of the presence in the seat of vision of tl our elements is very suggestive of Plato's account of sight in the "Timæus", where the principle is admitted.

Whether as a principle, or merely as an empirical fact, the oneness of man's rūpaskandha with the s a b b a ṃ r ū p a ṃ without was thoroughly admitted, and carefully taught as orthodox doctrine. And with regard to this kinship, I repeat, a certain philosophical attitude, both theoretical and practical, was inculcated as generally binding. That attitude is, in one of the Majjhima discourses,[3] led up to and defined as follows: All good states (d h a m m ā) whatever are included in the Four Noble Truths concerning Ill.[4] Now the First Noble Truth unfolds the nature of Ill: that it lies in using the five skandhas for Grasping.[5] And the first of

---

[1] Cf. Aristotle's discussion, *De An.*, i, 2, 5.

[2] Cf. the passage, Enn. i, 6, 9, reproduced by Goethe: οὐ γὰρ ἂν πώποτε εἶδεν ὀφθαλμὸς ἥλιον ἡλιοειδὴς μὴ γεγενημένος.

[3] M. i, 184, *et seq.*

[4] See below, § 1057.

[5] Ibid., p. 323. I have retained the meaning of "Grasping" as dictated by Buddhaghosa for the group of the Four Kinds of Grasping. Dr. Neumann renders u p ā d ā n a k k h a n d h o by "element of the impulse to live" (L e b e n s t r i e b; an expression doubtlessly prompted by Schopenhauer's philosophy). It would be very desirable to learn from the Papañca-sūdanī (Buddhaghosa's "Commentary on the Majjhima Nikāya"), whether the Commentator interprets the term to the same effect in both passages. He adheres to it

the five is that of r ū p a ṃ. Now r ū p a ṃ comprises the four Great Phenomena and all their derivatives. And the first of the four is Earth (the solid element). Then the solid *within*, or "belonging to the self", is catalogued, with the injunction that *it is to be regarded as it really is with right wisdom* (y a t h ā b h ū t a ṃ s a m m ā p a ñ ñ ā y a d a ṭ ṭ h a b b a ṃ).[1] And this means that—while recognizing his kinship with the element to the full—the good student should not identify himself with it so as to see in it a permanent unchanging substance *as which* he should persist amid transient phenomena. He was to reflect, "This is not mine, it is not *I*, it is not the soul of me!" "It is void of a Self."[2] And so for the other three elements. In their mightiest manifestations—in the earthquake as in the flood, in conflagration as in tempest—they are but temporal, phenomenal; subject to change and decay. Much more is this true of them when collocated in the human organism. So far from losing himself in his meditation in the All, in Nature, in "cosmic emotion" of any kind, he had to realize that the r ū p a ṃ in which he participated was but one of the five factors of that life which, in so far as it engulfed and mastered him and bore him drifting along, was the great Ill, the source of pain and delusion. From each of those five factors he had to detach himself in thought, and attain that position of mastery and emancipation whereby alone a better ideal self could emerge—temporary as a phenomenal collocation, yet aiming at the eternal. And the practical result of cultivating "this earth-culture" and the rest, as Gotama called it in teaching his son, was that "the mind was no longer entranced by the consideration of things as affecting

in *Vis. Magga*, p. 569. Dhammadinnā, the woman-apostle, explains u p ā d ā n a ṃ, used with a similar context, as meaning "passionate desire in the five skandhas-of-grasping" (M. i, 300).

[1] M. iii, 272 f.

[2] See above, p. xlii f., where the context leaves no doubt as to what the reflection is meant to emphasize.

him pleasantly or disagreeably ",[1] but " the equanimity which is based on that which is good was established ".[2] And he thereat is glad—and rightly so—" for thus far he has wrought a great work ! " [3]

These seem to me some of the more essential features in the Buddhist Dhamma concerning Rūpa.

VII.

On the Buddhist Philosophy of Mind and Theory of Intellection.

It would have been the greatest possible gain to our knowledge of the extent to which Buddhism has developed any clear psychological data from its ethics, had it occurred to the compilers of the Dhamma-Sangaṇi to introduce an analysis of the other four skandhas parallel to that of the skandha of form. It is true that the whole work, except the book on rūpaṃ, is an inquiry into arūpino dhammā, i.e. incorporeal, immaterial phenomena, but there is no separate treatment of them divided up as such. Some glimpses we obtain incidentally, most of which have been pointed out in the footnotes to the translation. And it may prove useful to summarize briefly such contribution as may lie therein to the psychology of Buddhism.

And, first, it is very difficult to say to what extent, if at all, such psychological matter as we find is distinctively and originally Buddhist, or how much was merely adopted from contemporary culture and incorporated with the Dhamma. Into this problem I do not here propose to inquire farther. If there be any originality, any new departure in the psychology scattered about the Nikāyas, it is more likely to be in aspect and treatment than in new matter. Buddhism preached a doctrine of regenerate personality, to be sought after and developed by and out of the personal resources of the individual. This development, in the case of the

---

[1] M. i, 423, 424. [2] M. i, 186. [3] Ibid. 191.

religieux, was to be largely effected through a system of intellectual self-culture. Thrown back upon himself, he developed introspection, the study of consciousness. But, again, his doctrine imposed on him the study of psychical states without the psyche. Nature without and nature within met, he was taught, acted and reacted, and the result told on the organism in a natural, orderly, necessary way.[1] But there was no one adjusting the machinery.[2] The Buddhist might have approved of Leibniz's amendment of Locke's "Nihil est in intellectu quod non prius fuerit in sensu" in the additional phrase "nisi ipse intellectus". But he would not thereby have exalted viññāṇaṃ, cittaṃ, or mano to any hypostatic permanence as prior or as immanent. He would only admit the arising of consciousness as a potential reaction to stimuli of sense or "ideas" (*dhammā*).

Psychological earnestness, then, and psychological inquiry into mental phenomena, coexisting apart from and in opposition to, the usual assumption of a psychical entity: such are the only distinctively Buddhist features which may, in the absence of more positive evidence than we yet possess, be claimed in such analysis of mind as appears in Buddhist ethics.

Of the results of this earnest spirit of inquiry into mental phenomena, in so far as they may be detached from ethical doctrine, and assigned their due place in the history of human ideas, it will be impossible, for several years, to prepare any adequate treatment. Much of the Abhidhamma Piṭaka, and even some of the Sutta Piṭaka, still remains unedited.[3]

Of the former collection nothing has been translated with the exception of the attempt in this volume. And, since Buddhist psychology has an evolution to show covering nearly a thousand years, we have to await fresh materials

[1] Cf. Mil. 57–61. [2] Sum. V. i, 194.

[3] This is happily now (1923) no longer the case, with the sole exception of most of the metrical legends of the Apadāna.

from the yet unedited works of Buddhaghosa, the Buddhist Sanskrit texts, and such works as the Netti-pakaraṇa, Professor Hardy's edition of which is now in the press.[1] Meanwhile there is an increasing store of accessible material which might be sifted by the historical investigator.

There are, for instance, in the Dhamma-Sangaṇi several passages suggesting that Buddhist scholars, in contemplating the consciousness or personality as affected by phenomena considered as external, were keenly alive to the distinction between the happening of the expected and the happening of the unexpected, between instinctive reaction of the mind and the organism generally, on occasion of sense, and the deliberate confronting of external phenomena with a carefully adjusted intelligence. Modern psychology has largely occupied itself with this distinction, and with the problems of consciousness and subconsciousness, of volition and of memory, involved in it. The subject of attention, involuntary and voluntary, figures prominently in the psychological literature of the last two decades. But it is not till the centuries of post-Aristotelian and of neo-Platonic thought that we see the distinction emerging in Western psychology contemporaneously with the development of the notion of consciousness.[2]

In the history of Buddhist thought, too, the distinction does not appear to have become explicitly and consciously made till the age of the writing of the Pali editions of the Commentaries (fifth century). A corresponding explicitness in the notion of consciousness and self-consciousness, or at least in the use of some equivalent terms, has yet to be traced.[3] Buddhism is so emphatically a philosophy, both in theory and practice, of the conscious will, with all that

---

[1] Published by the PTS. in 1901.

[2] Cf. Siebeck, op. cit., ii, pp. 200, 353, 388.

[3] In the Mahā Nidāna Sutta Gotama discourses on *sibi conscire* by way of n ā m a - r ū p a. See in Grimblot's "Sept Suttas", p. 255.

this involves of attention and concentration, that we hardly look to find terms discriminating such notions from among other mental characteristics. We are reminded instead of Matthew Arnold's well-known remark that as, at Soli, no one spoke *of* solecisms, so in England we had to import the term Philistine.

But, whereas it is the Atthasālinī, written from the standpoint of a later elaboration of thought, that makes explicit what it holds to be the intention of the classic manual, the latter work lends itself without straining to such interpretation. I pass over Buddhaghosa's comments on the limitations and the movements of attention, reproduced below (pp. 198, n. 2; 200, n. 1), as derived very possibly from thought nearer to his own times. Again, with respect to the residual unspecified factors in good and bad thoughts—the "or-whatever-other states"[1]—among which the Commentator names, as a constant, manasikāra, or attention—this specifying may be considered as later elaboration.[2] But when the Commentary refers the curious alternative emphasis in the description of the sensory act[3] to just this distinction between a percipient who is prepared or unprepared for the stimulus, it seems possible that he is indeed giving

---

[1] See below, p. 4, n. 2; also Asl., pp. 168, 250, etc. The definition given of manasikāra in the "ye-vā-panaka" passage of the Commentary (p. 133) is difficult to grasp fully, partly because, here and there, the reading seems doubtful in accuracy, partly because of the terms of the later Buddhist psychology employed, which it would first be necessary to discuss. But I gather that manasikāra may be set going in the first, middle, or last stage of an act of cognition—i.e. on the ārammaṇaṃ or initial presentation, the vīthi (or āvajjanaṃ), and the javanaṃ; that in this connexion it is concerned with the first of the three; that it involves memory, association of the presentation with [mental] "associates", and confronting the presentation. And that it is a constructive and directing activity of mind, being compared to a charioteer. Cf. *Compendium*, pp. 95, 282.

[2] See preface to 2nd ed. above. [3] Below, § 599, nn. 1, 2.

us the original interpretation. Again, the remarkable distinction drawn, in the case of every type of good or bad thoughts, "relating to the sensuous universe," i.e. to the average moral consciousness, between thoughts which are prompted by a conscious motive,[1] and such as are not, seems to me to indicate a groping after the distinction between instinctive or spontaneous intellection, on the one hand, and deliberate, purposive, or motivated thought on the other.

Taken in isolation, there is insufficient material here to establish this alternative state of mind as a dominant feature in Buddhist psychology. Taken in conjunction with the general mental attitude and intellectual culture involved in Buddhist ethical doctrine and continually inculcated in the canonical books, and emphasized as it is by later writings, the position gains in significance. The doctrine of karma, inherited and adopted from earlier and contemporary thought, never made the Buddhist fatalistic. He recognized the tremendous *vis a tergo* expressed in Watts's doggerel :—

"For 'tis their *nature* to."

But he had unlimited faith in the saving power of *nurture*. He faced the grim realities of life with candour, and tolerated no mask. This honesty, to which we usually add a mistaken view of the course of thought and action he prescribed in consequence of the honesty, gains him the name of Pessimist. But the hope that was in him of what might be done to better nature through nurture, even in this present life, by human effort and goodwill, reveals him as a strong Optimist with an unshaken ideal of the joy springing from things made perfect. He even tried to "pitchfork nature" in one or two respects, though opposed to asceticism generally—simply to make the Joy more easily attainable by those who dared to "come out".

---

[1] Cf. below, p. 32, n. 1. The thoughts which are not called sasankhārena are by the Cy. ruled as being a-sankhārena, though not explicitly said to be so (Asl. 71).

And this regenerating nurture resolves itself, theoretically, into a power of discrimination; practically, into an exercise of selection. The individual learner, pervious by way of his "fivefold door" to an inflooding tide of impressions penetrating to the sixth "door", i.e. the co-ordinating "mind", was to regulate the natural alertness of reception and perception by the special kind of attention termed yoniso manasikāra, or thorough attention, and by the clear-eyed insight referred to already as yathābhūtaṃ sammappaññāya daṭṭhabbaṃ, or the higher wisdom of regarding "things as in themselves they really are"—to adopt Matthew Arnold's term. The stream of phenomena, whether of social life, of nature, or of his own social and organic growth, was not so much to be ignored by him as to be marked, measured and classed according to the criteria of one who has chosen to "follow his own uttermost",[1] and has recognized the power of that stream to imperil his enterprise, and its lack of power to give an equivalent satisfaction.[2] The often-recurring subject of sati-sampajaññaṃ, or that "mindful and aware" attitude, which evokes satire in robust, if superficial criticism, is the expansion and ethical application of this psychological state of prepared and pre-adjusted sense or voluntary attention.[3] The student was not to be taken by surprise —"evil states of covetousness and repining flowing in over him dwelling unprepared"—until he had

"... The nobler mastery learned
Where inward vision over impulse reigns."[4]

Then indeed he might dwell at ease, strong in his emancipation.

---

[1] Seṭṭhaṃ upanamaṃ udeti . . . attano uttariṃ bhajetha (A. i, 126).

[2] Cf. M. i, 85–90, on kāmānaṃ assādañ ca ādīnavañ ca nissaraṇañ ca . . . yathābhūtaṃ pajānitvā.

[3] See below on guarding the door of the senses, §§ 1345–8. Also note on D. i, 70, in *Dialogues of the Buddha*, p. 81.

[4] George Eliot, *Brother and Sister*.

Step by step with his progress in the cultivation of attention, he was also practising himself in that faculty of selection which it were perhaps more accurate not to distinguish from attention. Alertness is never long, and, indeed, never strictly, attending to anything and everything at once. We are reminded of Condillac's definition of attention as only an "exclusive sensation". From the multitude of excitations flowing in upon us, one of them is, more or less frequently, selected,[1] the rest being, for a time, either wholly excluded or perceived subconsciously. And this selective instinct, varying in strength, appears not only in connexion with sense-impressions, but also in our more persisting tendencies and interests, as well as in a general disposition to concentration or to distraction.

Buddhism, in its earnest and hopeful system of self-culture, set itself strenuously against a distrait habit of mind, calling it tatra-tatrābhinandinī[2]—"the there-and-there dalliance", as it were of the butterfly. And it adopted and adapted that discipline in the concentration (samādhi), both physical and psychical, both perceptual and conceptual, for which India is unsurpassed. It appreciated the special practice of rapt, absorbed, concentrated thought called Dhyāna or Jhāna, not as an end in itself, but as a symbol and vehicle of that habit of selection and single-minded effort which governed "life according to the Higher Ideal". It did not hold with the robust creed, which gropes, it may be, after a yet stronger ideal :—

> "Greift nur hinein ins volle Menschenleben,
> Und wo ihr's packt, da ist es interessant."

"Full life" of the actual sort, viewed from the Buddhist standpoint, was too much compact of Vanity Fair, shambles and cemetery, to be worth the plunge. It had, on the other hand, great faith in experimenting on nature by a

---

[1] Cf. Höffding's criticism of Condillac in *Outlines of Psychology*, London, 1891, p. 120.

[2] M. i, 299, and in many other suttas.

judicious pruning of everything it judged might wreck or hinder the evolution of a life of finer, higher *quality*. If we, admitting this intention, look on the frequent injunctions respecting what "was to be put away" (p a h ā t a b b a ṃ)[1] from the life of each disciple, whether by insight or by culture, whether by gentle or by forcible restraint,[2] not as so much mere self-mortification and crippling of energy, but as expressions of selective culture for the better "forcing" of somewhat tender growths, we may, if we still would criticize, appraise more sympathetically.

If I have dwelt at some length on a side of Buddhist psychological ethics which is not thrown into obvious relief in our Manual, it was because I wished to connect that side with the specially characteristic feature in Buddhist psychology where it approximates to the trend of our own modern tradition. There, on the one hand, we have a philosophy manifestly looking deeper into the mental constitution than any other in the East, and giving especial heed to just those mental activities—attention and feeling, conation and choice—which seem most to imply a subject, or subjective unity *who* attends, feels, wills, and chooses. And yet this same philosophy is emphatically one that attempts to "extrude the Ego". If, on the other hand, we leap over upwards of 2,000 years and consider one of the most notable contributions to our national psychology, we find that its two most salient features are a revival of the admission of an Ego or Subject of mental states, which had been practically extruded, and a theory of the ultimate nature of mental procedure set out entirely in terms of attention and feeling.[3]

And yet the divergence between the two conclusions,

---

[1] See e.g. below, § 1002 *et seq*.

[2] Cf. the Sabbāsava Sutta and *passim*, M. i, especially the Vitakkasanthāna Sutta.

[3] I refer to Professor Ward's "Psychology": *Ency. Brit.*, 9th ed.

widely removed though they are by time and space, is not so sharp as at first appears. The modern thinker, while he finds it more honest not to suppress the fact that all psychologists, not excepting Hume, do, implicitly or explicitly, assume the conception of "a mind" or conscious subject, is careful to "extrude" metaphysical dogma. That everything mental is referred to a Self or Subject is, for him, a psychological conception which may be kept as free from the metaphysical conception of a soul, mind-atom, or mind-stuff as is that of the individual organism in biology. In much the same way the Buddhists were content to adopt the term attabhāvo (self-hood or personality—for which Buddhaghosa half apologizes [1])—ajjhattikaṃ (belonging to the self, subjective [2]) and the like, as well as to speak of cittaṃ, mano and viññānaṃ where we might say "the mind". It is true that by the two former terms they meant the totality of the five skandhas; that is to say, both mind and body, but this is not the case with the three last named. And if there was one thing which moved the Master to quit his wonted serenity and wield the lash of scorn and upbraiding, and his followers to use emphatic repudiation, it was just the reading into this convenient generalization of mind or personality that "metaphysical conception of a soul, mind-atom, or mind-stuff" which is put aside by the modern psychologist.

And I believe that the jealous way in which the Buddhists guarded their doctrine in this matter arose, not from the wish to assimilate mind to matter, or the whole personality to a machine, but from the too great danger that lay in the unchecked use of attā,[3] ahankāra, attabhāvo, *even as* a mere psychological datum, in that it afforded a

---

[1] See below, p. 159, n. 3.

[2] Ibid., p. 189, n. 1.

[3] Svayaṃ (this one) is nearly always substituted for attā as a nominative, the latter term usually appearing in oblique cases.

foothold to the prevailing animism. They were as Protestants in regard to the crucifix. They remembered with Ste. Beuve: "La sauvagerie est toujours là à deux pas, et, dès qu'on lâche pied, elle recommence."

What, then, was their view of mind, as merely phenomenal, in relation to the rūpa-skandha or non-mental part of the human individual? We have considered their doctrine of external phenomena impingeing on and modifying the internal or personal r ū p a ṃ by way of sense. Have we any clue to their theory of the propagation of the modifications, alleged in their statement[1] to take place in relation to those factors of personality which were a r ū p i n o, and not derived from material elements—the elements (d h ā t u ' s), namely, or skandhas of feeling, perception, synergies, and cognition? How did they regard that process of co-ordination by which, taking sensuous experience as the more obvious *starting-point* in mental experience, sensations are classed and made to cohere into groups or percepts, and are revived as memories, and are further co-ordinated into concepts or abstract ideas? And finally, and at back of all this, *who* feels, or attends, or wills?

Now the Dhamma-Sangaṇi does not place questions of this kind in the mouth of the catechist. In so far as it is psychological (not psycho-physical or ethical), it is so strictly *phenomenological* that its treatment is restricted to the analysis of certain broadly defined states of mind, felt or inferred to have arisen in consequence of certain other mental states as conditions. There is no reference anywhere to a "subjective factor" or agent *who has* the c i t t a ṃ or thought, with all its associated factors of attention, feeling, conception, and volition. Even in the case of Jhāna, where the book is dealing with more active modes of regulated attention, involving a maximum of constructive thought with a minimum of receptive sense, the agent, *as conscious subject*, is kept in

[1] See answers in §§ 600, 604, etc.

the background. It was claimed by leading disciples to be perfectly practised Jhāna when self-reference was eliminated; cf. e.g. S. iii, 235–7. The inflexion of the verb [1] alone implies a given personal agent, and the Commentary even feels it incumbent to point him out. It is this psychologizing without a psyche that impressed me from the first, and seemed to bring the work, for all its remoteness in other respects, nearer to our own Experiential school of, and since, Locke than anything we find in Greek traditions.

It is true that each of the four formless skandhas is defined or described, and this is done in connexion with the very first question of the book. But the answers are given, not in terms of respective function or of mutual relation, but of either synonyms or of modes or constituent parts. For instance, feeling (v e d a n ā) is resolved into three modes,[2] perceptiom (s a ñ ñ ā) is taken as practically self-evident and not really described at all,[3] the complexes or synergies (s a n k h ā r ā) are resolved into modes or factors, cognition (v i ñ ñ ā ṇ a ṃ) is described by synonyms.

Again, whereas the skandhas are enumerated in the order in which, I believe, they are unvaryingly met with, there is nothing, in text or Commentary, from which we can infer that this order corresponds to any theory of genetic procedure in an act of cognition. In other words, we are not shown that feeling calls up perception or that the sankhāras are a necessary link in the evolution of perception into conception or reasoning.[4] If we can infer anything in the nature of

---

[1] B h ā v e t i, v i h a r a t i (cultivates, abides); p. 43 *et seq.*

[2] See pp. 3–9, 25-7. An attempt to define each skandha is given in S. iii, 86 f.

[3] Described with some fullness in the Cy. See my note s.v.

[4] Cf. the argument by Dr. Neumann, "Buddhistische Anthologie", xxiii, xxiv. If I have rendered s a n k h ā r ā by "syntheses", it is not because I see any coincidence between the Buddhist notion and the Kantian *Synthesis der Wahrnehmungen.* Still less am I persuaded that *Unterscheidungen* is a virtually equivalent term. Like the "confections" of

causal succession at all, it is such that the order of the skandhas as enumerated is upset. Thus, taking the first answer (and that is typical for the whole of Book I when new ground is broken into): a certain sense-impression evokes, through "contact", a complex state of mind or psychosis called a thought or c i t t a ṃ. *Born of this contact and the "appropriate"* c i t t a ṃ, now (i.e. in answer 3) called, in terms of its synonym, representative intellection (m a n o v i ñ ñ ā ṇ a-d h ā t u), feeling, we are told, is engendered. Perception is called up likewise and, apparently, simultaneously. So is volition (c e t a n ā)—of the sankhāra-skandha. And "associated with" the c i t t aṃ come all the rest of the constituent dhammas, both sankhāras, as well as specific *modes* [1] or different *aspects* [2] of the feeling and the thought already specified. In a word, we get contact evoking the *fifth* skandha, and, as the common co-ordinate resultant, the genesis or excitement of the other three. This is entirely in keeping with the many passages in the Nikāyas, where the concussion of sense and object are said to result in v i ñ ñ ā ṇ a ṃ = cittaṃ = the fifth skandha. "Eye", for instance, and "form", in mutual "contact", result in "visual cognition".

In the causal chain of that ancient formula, the P a t i c c a - s a m u p p ā d a,[3] on the other hand, we find quite another order of genesis, sankhāras inducing consciousness, and contact alone inducing feeling. This mysterious old rune must not further complicate our problem. I merely allude to it as not in the least supporting the view that the order of statement,

---

Rhys Davids and the *Gestaltungen* of Professor Oldenberg, I used syntheses simply as, more or less, an etymological equivalent, and waited for more light. The new rendering "synergies" is etymologically as literal (saṃ-skṛ) as confections. I may here add that I have used intellection consciousness, cognition interchangeably as comprehending the whole process of knowing or coming to know.

1 e.g. ease.

2 e.g. the "faculties" of mind (ideation) and of pleasure.

3 Given below on p. **323** [1336].

in the skandhas, implies order of happening. What we may more surely gather from the canon is that, as our own psychological thought has now conceived it,[1] the, let us say, given individual "*attends* to or cognizes (v i j ā n ā t i) changes in the sensory continuum, and, in consequence, co-efficients of consciousness arise, emotional, volitional, intellectual". All this is in our Manual called a c i t t u p p ā d o— a genesis, an uprising of mind.

Of mind or of thinking. There seems to be a breadth and looseness of implication about c i t t a ṃ fairly parallel to the popular vagueness of the English term. It is true that the Commentary does not sanction the interpretation of contact and all the rest (I refer to the type given in the first answer) as so many attributes of the thought which "has arisen". The sun rising, it says, is not different from its fiery glory, etc., arising. But the c i t t a ṃ arising is a mere expression to fix the occasion for the induction of the whole concrete psychosis, and connotes no more and no less than it does as a particular constituent of that complex.[2]

This is a useful hint. On the other hand, when we consider the synonymous terms for c i t t a ṃ, given in answer 6, and compare the various characteristics of these terms scattered through the Commentary, we find a considerable wealth of content and an inclusion of process and product similar to that of our "thought". For example, "c i t t a ṃ means mental object or presentation (ā r a m m a ṇ a ṃ);

---

[1] Professor Ward, op. cit.

[2] Asl. 113. *I gather, however, that the adjective c e t a s i k a ṃ had a wider and a narrower denotation. As wider, it meant "not bodily", as on p. 6. In the latter it served to distinguish three of the incorporeal skandhas from the fourth, i.e. c i t t a m, as on pp. 265, 318—c i t t a c e t a s i k ā d h a m m ā. Or are we to take the Commentator's use of k ā y i k a ṃ here to refer to those three skandhas, as is often the case (p. 43, n. 3)? Hardly, since this makes the two meanings of c e t a s i k a ṃ self-contradictory. In later Abhidhamma the cetasikas came to be used for the sankhāras. Cf. *Compendium*, pt. ii; also pp. 124, 193.

that is to say, he thinks; that is to say, he attends to a thought."[1] Hence my translation might well have run: When a good thought . . . has arisen . . . *as* the object of this or that sense, etc. Again, c i t t a ṃ is defined as a process of connecting (s a n d h ā n a ṃ) the last (things) as they keep arising in consciousness with that which preceded them.[2] Further, it is a co-ordinating, relating, or synthesizing (s a n d a h a n a ṃ);[3] and, again, it has the property of initiative action (p u r e c ā r i k a ṃ). For, when the sense-impression gets to the "door" of the senses, c i t t a ṃ confronts it before the rest of the mental congeries.[4] The sensations are, by c i t t a ṃ, wrought up into that concrete stream of consciousness which they evoke.

Here we have c i t t a ṃ covering both thinking and thought or idea. When we turn to its synonym or quasi-synonym m a n o we find, so far as I can discover, that only activity, or else spring, source or *nidus* of activity, is the aspect taken. The faculty of ideation (m a n i n d r i y a ṃ), for instance,[5] while expressly declared to be an equivalent (v e v a c a n a ṃ) of c i t t a ṃ, and, like it, to be that which attends or cognizes (v i j ā n ā t i), is also called a *measuring* the mental object—declared above to *be* c i t t a ṃ.[6] In a later passage (ibid. 129) it is assigned the function of accepting, receiving, analogous, perhaps, to our technical expression "assimilating" (s a m p a ṭ i c c h a n a ṃ). In thus apprais-ing or approving, it has all sensory objects for its field, as well as its more especial province of dhammas.[7] These, when thus

---

[1] Ibid. 63.

[2] Asl., pp. 112, 113.

[3] Cf. the characteristic—s a m v i d a h a n a ṃ—of c e t a n ā in my note, p. 8.

[4] The figure of the city-guardian, given in Mil. 62, is quoted by the Cy.

[5] See below, p. 16, and Asl. 123.

[6] It is at the same time said to result in (establishing) fact or conformity (t a t h ā b h ā v o), and to succeed sense-perception as such.

[7] See p. 2, n.2.

distinguished, I take to mean ideas, including images and general notions. And it is probably only in order to distinguish between mind in this abstract functioning and mind as cognition in its most comprehensive sense that we see the two terms held apart in the sentence: "C i t t a ṃ cognizes the dhammas which are the objects of m a n o, just as it cognizes the visual forms, etc., which are the objects of the senses." [1]

When c i t t a ṃ is thus occupied with the abstract functioning of m a n o [2]—when, that is, we are reflecting on past experience, in memory or ratiocination—then the more specific term is, I gather, *not* c i t t a ṃ, but m a n o v i ñ-ñ ā ṇ a ṃ (corresponding to c a k k h u v i ñ ñ ā ṇ a ṃ, etc.). This, in the Commentarial psychology, certainly stands for a further stage, a higher "power" of intellection, for "representative cognition", its specific activity being distinguished as investigating (s a n t ī r a ṇ a ṃ), and as fixing or determining (v o t t h a p p a n a ṃ).

The affix d h ā t u, whether appended to m a n o or to m a n o v i ñ ñ ā ṇ a ṃ, probably stands for a slight distinction in *aspect* of the intellectual process. It may be intended to indicate either of these two stages as an irreducible element, a psychological ultimate, an activity regarded as its own spring or source or basis. Adopted from without by Buddhism, it seems to have been jealously guarded from noumenal implications by the orthodox. Buddhaghosa, indeed, seems to substitute the warning against its abuse for the reason why it had come to be used. According to him, the various lists of dhammas (e.g. in the first answer), when considered under the aspect of phenomena, of "emptiness", of non-essence, may be grouped as together forming two classes of d h ā t u.[3] Moreover, each special

[1] Asl., p. 112.

[2] Cf. the expression s u d d h a - m a n o d v ā r o in my note, p. 3. And on what follows, cf. pp. 129, 132, nn.

[3] Viz. m a n o v i ñ ñ ā ṇ a-d h ā t u and d h a m m a-d h ā t u see Asl. 153, and below, p. 24 n. 1. The term "element" is similarly used in our owh psychology.

sense can be so considered (cakkhu-dhātu, etc.; see pp. 214, 215), and so may each kind of sense-object. For, with respect to sense, or the apprehension of form, they are so many phenomenal ultimates—the two terms, so to speak, in each sensory relation.

How far dhātu corresponds to vatthu—how far the one is a psychological, the other a physical, conception[1] of source or base—is not easily determined. But it is interesting to note that the Commentator only alludes to a basis of thought (cittassa vatthu), that is to the heart (hadaya-vatthu), when the catechizing is in terms of mano-dhātu.[2] His only comment on "heart", when it is included in the description of cittaṃ (answer [6]), is to say that, whereas it stands for cittaṃ, it simply represents the inwardness (*intimité*) of thought.[3] But in the subsequent comment he has a remark of great interest, namely, that the "heart-basis" is the place whither all the "door-objects" come, and where they are assimilated, or received.[4] In this matter the Buddhist philosophy carries on the old Upanishad lore about the heart, just as Aristotle

---

[1] Cf. below, pp. 214, 215, with 209–211.

[2] Asl. 264; below, p. 129, n.

[3] Asl. 140: "Heart = thought (hadayan ti cittaṃ). In the passage (S. i, 207)—'I will either tear out your mind or break your heart'—the heart in the breast is spoken of. In the passage (M. i, 32)—'Methinks he planes with a heart that knows heart' (like an expert)!—the mind is meant. In the passage—'The vakkaṃ is the heart'—heart is meant as basis. But *here* cittaṃ is spoken of as heart in the sense of inwardness (abbhantaraṃ)." It is interesting to note that, in enumerating the rupaskandha in the Visuddhi Magga, Buddhaghosa's sole departure from conformity with the Dhamma-Sangaṇi is the *inclusion of* hadaya-vatthu *after* "life". On the reticence of the canon to recognize heart as seat of mind, see S. Z. Aung, *Compendium*, 278.

The other term, "that which is clear" (paṇḍaram), is an ethical metaphor. The mind is said to be naturally pure, but defiled by incoming corruptions. (Cf. A. i, p. 10.)

[4] Cf. Kaushītakī Up. 3, 2; Praś. Up. 3, 1, 5; samaṃ nayati.

elaborated the dictum of Empedokles that perception and reasoning were carried on in "the blood round the heart".

It is possible that this ancient and widely received tradition of the heart (rather than the brain, for instance) as the seat of the soul or the mind is latent in the question put by Mahākoṭṭhita, a member of the Order, to Sāriputta, the leading apostle:[1] "Inasmuch as these five indriyas (senses) are, in province and in gratification, mutually independent, what process of reference is there,[2] and who is it that is gratified by them in common?" So apparently thinks Dr. Neumann, who renders Sāriputta's answer—"The mind (m a n o)"—by *Herz*. This association must, however, not be pressed. For in another version of this dialogue more recently edited, Gotama himself being the person consulted, his interlocutor goes on to ask (S. v, 217 f.): What is the p a ṭ i s a r a ṇ a ṃ of m a n o—of recollection (s a t i)—of emancipation—of Nirvana?[3] So that the meaning of the first question may simply be that as emancipation *looks to*, or *makes for*, Nirvana, and recollection or mindfulness for emancipation, and ideation or thinking refers or looks to

---

[1] M. i, 295.

[2] K i m p a ṭ i s a r a ṇ a ṃ. The word is a crux, and may bear more than one meaning. Cf. Vinaya Texts (SBE. xvii), ii, p. 364, n.; *Dialogues of the Buddha*, i, p. 122, n. Dr. Neumann renders it by *Hort*, following Childers. Cf. the light thrown by the Commentaries, *Bud. Psychology*, 1914, 69.

It is worthy of note that, in connexion with the heresy of identifying the self with the physical organism generally (below, p. 259), the Cy. makes no allusion to heart, or other part of the r ū p a m, in connexion with views (2) or (4). These apparently resembled Augustine's belief: the soul is wholly present both in the entire body and in each part of it. With regard to view (3), is it possible that Plotinus heard it at Alexandria, or on his Eastern trip? For he, too, held that the body was "in the soul", permeated by it as air is by fire (Enn. iv). Buddhaghosa's illustrative metaphor, in Pṭs. i, 143 f., is "as a flower being 'in' its own perfume". I regret that space fails me to reproduce his analysis of these twenty soul-hypotheses.

[3] S. v, p. 218. In the replies m a n o is referred to s a t i, s a t i to v i m u t t i, and this to Nirvana.

memory,[1] so sensation depends on thinking, on mental construction (to become effective as knowledge).

It is, indeed, far more likely that Buddhist teaching made little of and passed lightly over this question of a physical basis of thought or mind. It was too closely involved with the animistic point of view—how closely we may see, for instance, in the Bṛihadāraṇyaka Upanishad. When King Milinda puts a similar question respecting the subject of sensations,[2] he does so from so obviously animistic a standpoint that the sage, instead of discussing mano, or heart, with him, argues against any one central subjective factor whatever, and resolves the process of cognition into a number of " connate " activities. The method itself of ranking mental activity as though it were a sixth kind of sense seems to point in the same direction, and reminds us of Hume's contention, that when he tried to " catch himself " he always " tumbled on some particular perception ". Indeed, it was, in words attributed to Gotama himself, the lesser blunder in the average man to call " this four-elementish body " his soul than to identify the self with " what is called cittaṃ, that is mano, that is viññāṇaṃ ". For, whereas the body was a collocation that might hold together for many years, " mind by day and by night is ever arising as one thing, ceasing as another ! " [3]

Impermanence of conscious phenomena was one of the two grounds of the Buddhist attack. So far it was on all fours with Hume. The other ground was the presence of law, or necessary sequence in mental procedure. The Soul was conceived as an entity, not only *above change*, an absolute constant, but also as an *entirely free agent*. Both grounds, be it noted, are laid down on psychological evidence—on

---

[1] Cf. the interesting inquiry into the various modes of *association in remembering*, given in Mil., pp. 78, 79, and 77, 78.

[2] Mil. 54. He calls it vedagū (knower), and, when cross-examined, abbhantare jīvo (the living principle within).

[3] S. ii, pp. 94–6.

the testimony of consciousness. And both grounds were put forward by Gotama in his second sermon.[1] The standard formula for the latter only—that of an entirely free (and therefore God-like) agency—is reproduced in our Manual.[2] And it is interesting to see the same argument clothed in fresh dress in the dialogue with Milinda referred to above. The point made is this: that if any one of the skandhas could be identified with a self or soul it would, as not subject to the conditions of phenomena, act through any other faculty it chose. It would be a principle, not only of the nature of what *we* should call will, but also of genuine free will.[3] Soul and Free Will, for the Buddhist, stand or fall together. But, he said, what we actually find is no such free agency. We only find certain organs (doors), with definite functions, natural sequence, the line of least resistance and association.[4] Hence we conclude there is no transcendent "knower" about us.

Here I must leave the Buddhist philosophy of mind and theory of intellection. We are only at the threshold of its problems, and it is hence not strange if we find them as baffling as, let us say, our own confused usage of many psychological terms—feeling, will, mind—about which we ourselves greatly differ, would prove to an inquiring Buddhist. If I have not attempted to go into the crux of the sankhāra-skandha, it is because neither the Manual nor its Commentary brings us any nearer to a satisfactory hypothesis. For future discussion, however, the frequent enumerations of that skandha's content, varying with ever changing mood, should prove pertinent. In every direction there is very much to be done. And each addition to the texts edited brings new light. Nor can philosophic interest fail in the long run to accumulate about a system of thought which at that early time of day

---

[1] Vin. i, 14 = M. i, 138, 300; S. iii, 66; cf. iv, 34.

[2] p. 257 *et seq.*

[3] Cf. the writer's article on the Vedalla Suttas, JRAS., April, 1894.

[4] Mil., loc. cit.

took up a task requiring such vigour and audacity—the task, namely, of opposing the prevailing metaphysic, not because problems of mind did not appeal to the founders of that system, but because further analysis of mind seemed to reveal a realm of law-governed phenomenal sequence, for which the ready hypothesis of an unconditioned permanent Self *super grammaticam* was too cheap a solution.

VIII.

On the Buddhist Notions of "Good, Bad, and Indeterminate".

By way of dhammā, rūpaṃ and cittaṃ, by way of Buddhist phenomenology and psychology, we come at last to the ethical purport of the questions in the Manual. Given a human being known to us by way of these phenomenal states, what is implied when we say that some of them are good, some bad, others neither ?

The Dhamma-Sangaṇi does not, to our loss be it said, define any one of these concepts. All it does is to show us the content of a number of "thoughts" known as one or the other of these three species of dhammā. In a subsequent passage (pp. 345–8) it uses the substantival form of "good" (kusalatā; another form is kosallaṃ) in the sense of skill or proficiency as applied to various kinds of insight, theoretical or practical.

Now if we turn to the later expression of old tradition in the Commentaries, we find, on the one hand, an analysis of the meaning of "good"; on the other, the rejection of precisely that sense of skill, and of that alone out of four possible meanings, with respect to "good" *as used in Book I.* Kusalaṃ, we read,[1] may mean (*a*) wholesome, (*b*) virtuous, (*c*) skilful, (*d*) felicific, or productive of happy result. The illustrations make these clear statements clearer. E.g. of (*a*): "Is it good for you, sir, is it wholesome ?"[2] Of (*b*)

[1] Asl. 38.

[2] The two adjectives are kusalaṃ, anāmayaṃ. Childers Dict. s.v. Kacci, refers this question to the Dasaratha Jātaka, in Fausböll's *Ten Jātakas.* It is not in his edition of the complete Jātaka.

"What, sir, is good behaviour in act? Sire, it is conduct that is blameless (a n a v a j j o)".[1] Of (*c*) "You are good at knowing all about the make of a chariot".[2] Again: "The four girl-pupils are good at singing and dancing."[3] Of (*d*) "Good states, brethren, are acquired through good karma having been wrought and stored up."[4]

Of these four, (*c*) is alone ruled out as not applicable to the eight types of good thoughts constituting d h a m m ā k u s a l ā. In so far, then, as we suffer the Buddhist culture of the fifth century to interpret the canon for us, "good," in the earlier ethics, meant that which ensures soundness, physical and moral, as well as that which is felicific.

The further question immediately suggests itself, whether Buddhism held that these two attributes were at bottom identical. Are certain "states" intrinsically good, i.e. virtuous and right, independently of their results? Or is "good", in the long-run at least, felicitous result, and only on that account so called? Are Buddhists, in a word, Intuitionists, or are they Utilitarians? Or is not a decidedly eclectic standpoint revealed in the comprehensive interpretation given of k u s a l a ṃ?

These are, however, somewhat modern—I am tempted to say, somewhat British—distinctions to seek in an ancient theory of morals. They do not appear to have troubled Buddhism, early or late. The Buddhist might possibly have replied that he could not conceive of any thought, word, or deed as being intrinsically good and yet bad in its results, and that the distinction drawn by the Commentator was simply one of aspects.

If pressed, however, we can almost imagine the Buddhist well content with the relative or dependent good of Utilitarianism, so closely is his ethics bound up with cause and effect. Good, for him, is good with respect to karma—that is, to pleasurable effect or *eudæmonia*.

---

[1] M. ii, 115.
[2] Cf. M. ii, 94.
[3] Jāt. vi, 25.
[4] Cf. D. iii, 58.

With respect to the supremely good effect, that is, to arahatship or Nirvana, he might, it is true, have admitted a difference, namely, that this state was absolutely good, and not good because of its results. It *was* the supreme Result or Fruit, and there was "no beyond". But then he did not rank Nirvana exactly in the category of good, and precisely for this reason, that in it moral causation culminated and ceased. He spoke of it as Indeterminate, as without result—as a Freedom, rather than as a Good.

He would not then have fallen in with Aristotle's definition of Good in terms of *aim*, viz. as "that at which everything aims". Good was rather the *means by and with which we aim*. But that at which we aim is, in all lower quests, Sukhaṃ, in the one high quest, Vimutti (emancipation) or Nirvana.

Nor must the substitution of these two last terms for that well-being, that well-ness, "τὸ εὐ ζῆν," which is the etymological equivalent of sukhaṃ,[1] be taken as indicating the limit of the consistent Hedonism or Eudæmonism of the Buddhist. For he did not scruple to speak of these two also (Emancipation and Nirvana) in terms of pleasurable feeling. Gotama, attaining his supreme enlightenment beneath the Bo-tree, is said to have "experienced Emancipation-bliss" (vimutti-sukha-paṭisaṃvedī).[2] And Nirvana is emphatically declared to be "absolute (or entire) happiness" (ekanta-sukhaṃ).[3] And we know, too, that Buddhism defined all right conduct and the sufficient motive for it in terms of escape from ill (dukkhaṃ, the antithesis of sukhaṃ) or suffering. Here then again their psychological proclivity is manifested. They analyzed feeling, or subjective experience, into three modes: sukhaṃ, dukkhaṃ, adukkhaṃ-asukham. And in Good and Bad they saw, not ends or positions of attainment, but the vehicles or

[1] Cf. p. 10, n. 3.
[2] Vin. i, 2, 3, quoted Jāt. i, 77.
[3] M. ii . . .; Mil. 313.

agencies, or, to speak less in abstractions, the characteristic quality of those kinds of conduct, by which well-being or ill-being might respectively be entailed.

The Buddhist, then, was a Hedonist, and hence, whether he himself would have admitted it or not, his morality was dependent or, in the phrase of British ethics, utilitarian, and not intuitionist. Hedonist, let us say, rather than eudæmonist, because of the more subjective (psychological) import of the former term. And he found the word s u k h a ṃ good enough to cover the whole ground of desirability, from satisfaction in connexion with sense—compare Buddhaghosa's traveller refreshed obtaining both joy and ease [1]—up to the ineffable "Content" of Nirvana.[2] He did not find in it the inadequacy that some moral philosophers have found in our "Pleasure". His ethical system was so emphatically a study of *consequences*—of karma and v i p ā k a (effect of karma)—of seeing in every phenomenon a *reaping* of some previous sowing—that the notion of good became for him inevitably bound up with result. As my late master used to say (*ex cathedrâ*): "If you bring forward consequences—how acts by way of result affect self and others—you *must* come to feeling. Thence pleasure becomes prominent. And did not folk suffer loose, lower associations to affect their judgment, there would be no objection to Hedonism. For pleasures are of all ranks, up to that of a good conscience."

A reflection may here suggest itself to readers in this country who have, at the feet of Spencer, Bain, and Leslie Stephen, learnt to see, behind Nature's device of Pleasurable Feeling, the conservation of the species—"quantity of life, measured in breadth as well as in length"—as the more fundamental determinant of that which, in the long run, becomes the end of conduct. Namely, that there seems a strange contradiction in a philosophic position which is content to find its fundamental spring of moral action in the

---

[1] Below, p. 10, n. 3.
[2] S a n t u ṭ ṭ h i. See p. 332, n. 3.

avoidance of pain and the quest of pleasurable feeling, while, at the same time, it says of life—apart from which would admit no feeling to be possible—that the attainment of its *last phase* is the one supremely happy span. Pleasurable feeling, from the evolutionist's standpoint, means, and is in order to, the increase, "intensive and extensive," of life. Yet to the Hedonistic Buddhist, the dissolution of the conditions of renewed existence is a happy event, i.e. an event that causes pleasurable feeling in the thoughtful spectator.

I believe that the modern ethics of evolution would have profoundly interested the early Buddhists, who, after their sort and their age, were themselves evolutionists. And I believe, too, that they would have arisen from a discussion with our thinkers on this subject as stanch Buddhists and as stanch Hedonists as they had sat down. I admit that with respect to the desirableness of life taken quantitatively, and in two dimensions, they were frankly pessimistic. As I have already suggested,[1] and have put forward elsewhere,[2] to prize mere *quantity* of living stood by Gotama condemned as ignoble, as stupid, as a mortal bondage, as one of the four Āsavas or Intoxicants.[3] The weary, heartrending tragedies immanent in the life of the world he recognized and accepted as honestly and fully as the deepest pessimist. The complexities, the distractions, the burdens, the dogging sorrow, the haunting fear of its approaching tread, inevitable for life lived in participation of all that the human organism naturally calls for and human society puts forward as desirable—all this he judged too heavy to be borne, not, indeed, by lay followers, but by those who should devote themselves to the higher life. To these he looked to

---

[1] See above, pp. lxxvii *et seq.*

[2] In an article "On the Will in Buddhism": JRAS., January, 1898; also "On the Value of Life in Buddhism": *Buddhism*, Rangoon, 1908; *Buddhism*, Home Univ. Library, London, 1912, pp. 165 f.

[3] Cf. below, p. 268 *et seq.*

exemplify and propagate and transmit his doctrine. Theirs it was to lift the world to higher standpoints and nobler issues. Life in its fullness they at least could not afford to cultivate.

But if we take life of a certain *quality* where selective economy, making for a certain object, cuts off some lines of growth but forces others on—then Buddhism, so far from "negating the will to live" that kind of life, pronounced it fair and lovely beyond all non-being, beyond all after-being. If final death, as it believed, followed inevitably on the fullest fruition of it, it was not this that made such life desirable. Final dissolution was accepted as welcome, not for its own sake, but as a corollary, so to speak, of the solved problem of emancipation. It merely signified that unhealthy moral conditions had wholly passed away.

Keeping in view, then, the notion of Good in thought, word, and deed, as a means entailing various kinds of felicific result, we may see in Book I of our Manual, first, the kind of conscious experience arising apart from systematic effort to obtain any such specific result, but which was bound, none the less, to lead to hedonistic consequences, pleasant or unpleasant (pp. 1–42). Next, we see a certain felicific result deliberately aimed at through self-cultivation in modes of consciousness called Good (pp. 43–97). And, incidentally, we learn something of the procedure adopted in that systematic culture.

The Commentary leaves us no room to doubt whether or not the phase rūpūpapattiyā maggaṃ bhāveti ("that he may attain to the heavens of Form he cultivates the way thereto") refers to a flight of imaginative power merely. "Form = the rūpa-bhavo," or mode of existence so called. "Attainment = nibbatti, jāti, sañjāti"—all being terms for birth and re-birth.[1] So for the attaining

[1] Asl. 162. See below, pp. 40 *et seq.*, 65 *et seq.*

to the Formless heavens. Through the mighty engine of "good states", induced and sustained, directed and developed by intelligence and self-control, it was held that the student might modify his own destiny beyond this life, and insure, or at least promote, his chances of a happy future. The special culture or exercise required in either case was that called Jhāna, or rapt contemplation, the psychology of which, when adequately investigated, will one day evoke considerable interest. There was first intense attention by way of "an exclusive sensation",[1] to be entered upon only when all other activity was relaxed to the utmost, short of checking in any way the higher mental functions. After a time the sensation practically ceases. The wearied sense gives out. Change, indispensable to consciousness, has been eliminated; and we have realized, at all events since Hobbes wrote, how *idem semper sentire et non sentire ad idem recidunt.* Then comes the play of the "after-image", and then the emergence of the mental image, of purely ideational or representative construction. This will be, not of the sense-object first considered, but some attenuated abstraction of one of its qualities. And this serves as a background and a barrier against all further invasion of sense-impressions for the time being. To him thus purged and prepared there comes, through subconscious persistence, a *reinstatement* of some concept, associated with feeling and conation (i.e. with desire or aspiration), which he had selected for preliminary meditation.[2] And this conception he now proceeds by a sort of psychical involution to raise to a higher power, realizing it more fully, deepening its import, expanding its application.

Such seems to have been the Kasiṇa method according to the description in the Visuddhi Magga, chap. iv.,[3] but

[1] See above, p. lxxvii. [2] Cf. *Vibhanga*, 1904, xvii f.

[3] Translated in Warren's "Buddhism in Translations", p. 293 *et seq.* Cf. below, Book I, Pt. I, Chap. II. Cf. also Rhys Davids' *Yogāvacara's Manual*, Introduction.

there were several methods, some of which, the method e.g. of respiration, are not given in our Manual. Of the thoughts for meditation, only a few occur in the Dhamma-Sangaṇi, such as the "Divine States" of thought—love, pity, etc.[1] But in the former work we find numerous lists for exercise in the contemplative life, with or without the rapt musing called Jhāna.

In the exercises calculated to bring out re-birth in the world of Form, it was chiefly necessary to ponder on things of this life in such a way as to get rid of all appetite and impulse in connexion with them, and to cultivate an attitude of the purest disinterestedness towards all worldly attractions. If the Formless sphere were the object of aspiration, it was then necessary, by the severest fetches of abstraction, to eliminate not only all sense-impression, but also all sensory images whatever, and to endeavour to realize conditions and relations other than those obtaining in actual experience.[2] Thus, in either method, a foretaste of the mode of re-becoming aspired after was attempted.

But besides and beyond the sort of moral consciousness characterizing these exercises which were calculated to promote a virtuous and happy existence in any one of the three worlds, there were the special conditions of intellect and emotion termed lok'uttaraṃ cittaṃ.[3] Those exercises were open to the lay pupil and the bhikkhu alike. There was nothing especially "holy", nothing esoteric, about the practice of Jhāna. The diligent upāsaka or

---

[1] See below, p. 65.

[2] In translating the formula of the Third Āruppa or meditation on Nothingness, I might have drawn attention to Kant's development of the concept of None or Nothing, in the *Kritik der reinen Vernunft* (end of Div. i of Transc. Logic). Some great adepts were credited with the power of actually partaking in other existences while yet in this, notably Mahā Moggallāna (e.g. M. i). Gotama tells of another in the Kevaddha Sutta (D. i, 215), but tells it as a "story".

[3] P. 74 *et seq.* Cf. n. 2 on p. 74, and M. i, 455.

upāsikā, pursuing a temporary course of such religous and philosophic discipline as the rising schools of Buddhism afforded, might be expected to avail himself or herself of it more or less. But those "good" dhammas alluded to were those which characterized the Four Paths, or Four Stages, of the way, to the full "emancipation" of Nirvana. If I have rendered l o k u t t a r a ṃ c i t t a ṃ by "thought engaged upon the higher ideal" instead of selecting a term more literally accurate, it is because there is, in a way, less of the "supramundane" or "transcendent", as we usually understand these expressions, about this c i t t a ṃ than about the aspiring moods described above. For this sort of consciousness was that of the man or woman who regarded not heaven nor re-birth, but one thing only as "needful": the full and perfect efflorescence of mind and character to be brought about, if it might be, here and now.

The Dhamma-Sangaṇi never quits its severely dry and formal style to descant on the characteristics and methods of that progress to the Ideal, every step in which is elsewhere said to be more wonderful and excellent than the last,[1] with a wealth of eulogy besides. Edifying discourse it left to the Suttanta Books. But no rhetoric could more effectively describe the separateness and uncompromising other-ness of that higher quest than the one word A - p a r i y ā p a n n a ṃ —Unincluded—by which reference is made to it in Book III.

Yet for all this world of difference in the *quo vadis* of aspiration, there is a great deal of common ground covered by the moral consciousness in each case, as the respective expositions show. That of the Arahat *in spe* differs only in two sets of additional features conferring greater richness of content, and in the loftier quality of other features not in themselves additional.

This quality is due to mental awakening or enlightenment (s a m b o d h i). And the added factors are three constituents of the Noble Eightfold Path of conduct (which are,

---

[1] S. iv, 225 f.

more obviously, modes of overt activity than of consciousness) and the progressive stages in the attainment of the sublime knowledge or insight termed a ñ ñ ā.[1] Our Western languages are scarcely rich enough to ring the changes on the words signifying "to know" as those of India did on j ñ ā and v i d, d ṛ ś, and p a ś. Our religious ideals have tended to be emotional in excess of our intellectual enthusiasm. "Absence of dullness" has not ranked with us as a cardinal virtue or fundamental cause of good. Hence it is difficult to reproduce the Pali so as to give impressiveness to a term like a ñ ñ ā as compared with the more general term ñ ā ṇ a ṃ,[2] (which usually, though not always, implies less advanced insight), with which the "first type of good thought" is said to be associated.

But I must pass on. As a compilation dealing with positive culture, undertaken for a positive end, it is only consistent that the Manual should deal briefly with the subject of bad states of consciousness. It is true that a k u s a l a ṃ, as a means leading to unhappy result, was not conceived as negatively as its logical form might lead us to suppose. Bad karma was a "piling up", no less than its opposite. Nevertheless, to a great extent, the difference between bad types of thought and good is described in terms of the contradictories of the factors in the one kind and in the other. Nor are the negatives always on the side of evil. The three cardinal sources of misery are positive in form. And the five "Path-factors" go to constitute what was called the Base Eightfold Path.[2]

We come, finally, to the third ethical category of a - v y ā k a t a ṃ, the Inexplicit or Indeterminate. The subject is difficult, if interesting, bringing us as it does within closer range of the Buddhist view of moral causation. The

---

[1] Viz. A n a ñ ñ ā t'a ñ ñ a s s ā m ī t i n d r i y a ṃ, a ñ ñ i n-d r i y a ṃ, a ñ ñ ā t ā v i n d r i y a ṃ, pp. 78, 88, 89, 140. Cf. Dh.K. 53.

[2] S. ii, 168; iii, 109; v, i; 15–18; 23; 334; A. ii, 220, etc.

hall-mark of Indeterminate thought is said to be "absence of result"[1]—that is, of pleasant or painful result. And there are said to be four species of such thought: (1) v i p ā k o, or thought which *is* a result; (2) k i r i y ā, or consciousness leading to no result; (3) form, as outside moral causation; (4) unconditioned element (or, in later records, Nirvana), as above or beyond the further efficacy of moral causation.

Of these four, the third has been dealt with already; the fourth I cannot discuss here and now.[2] It is conceivable that the earlier Buddhists considered their *summum bonum* a subject too ineffably sublime and mysterious for logical and analytical discussion. Two instances, at least, occur to me in the Nikāyas[3] where the talk was cut short, in the one case by Gotama himself, in the other by the woman-apostle Dhammadinnā, when the interlocutor brought up Nirvana for discussion of this sort. This is possibly the reason why, in a work like our Manual, the concept is presented—in all but the commentarial appendixes—under the quasi-metaphysical term "unconditioned element". It is classed here as a species of Indeterminate, because, although it was the outcome of the utmost carrying power of good karma, it could, as a state of mind and character, itself work no good effect *for that individual* mind and character. *These* represented pure effect. The Arahat could afford to live wholly on withdrawn capital and to use it up. His conduct, speech, and thought are, of course, necessarily "good", but good with no "heaping-up" potency.

Of the other two Indeterminates, it is not easy to say whether they represent *aspects* only of states considered with respect to moral efficacy, or whether they represent *divisions* in a more rigid and artificial view of moral causation than we should, at the present day, be prepared to maintain. To explain: every thought, word, and deed (morally considered)

---

[1] Asl. 39.
[2] See Appendix II.
[3] S. v, 218; M. i, 304.

is for us at once the effect of certain antecedents and the cause, or part of the cause, of subsequent manifestations of character. It is a link, both held and holding. But in vipāko we have dhammas considered, with respect to cause, *merely* as effects; in kiriyā[1] we have dhammas considered, with respect to effect, as having *none*. And the fact that both are divided off from Good and Bad—that is to say, from conduct or consciousness considered as *causally effective*—and are called Indeterminate, seems to point, not to aspects only, but to that artificial view alluded to. Yet in this matter I confess to the greater wisdom of "fearing to tread" with the angels, rather than of rushing in with the fools. Life presented itself to the Buddhist much as the Surrey heath appeared to the watchful eye of a Darwin—as a teeming soil, a khettaṃ,[2] where swarmed the seeds of previous karmas waiting for "room", for opportunity to come to effect. And in considering the seed as itself an effect, they were not, to that extent, concerned with *that* seed as a cause, [capable of producing not only its own flower and fruit, but other seed] in its turn.

However that may have been, one thing is clear, and for us suggestive. Moral experience *as result* pure and simple was not in itself uninteresting to the Buddhists. In dealing with good and bad dhammas they show us a field of the struggle for moral life, the sowing of potential well-being or of ill. But in the Avyākatas either we are outside the struggle and concerned with the unmoral Rūpaṃ, or we walk among the sheaves of harvest. From the Western standpoint the struggle covers the whole field of temporal life. Good and

---

[1] Inoperative consciousness (S.Z. Aung). I am indebted to the Rev. Sumangala, of Ceylon, for information very kindly given concerning the term kiriyā or kriyā. He defines it as "action ineffective as to result", and kiriyā-cittaṃ as "mind in relation to action ineffective as to result". He adds a full analysis of the various modes of kiriyā taught by Buddhists at the present day.

[2] *Origin of Species*, p. 56. A. i, 223 224. Cf. Asl. 360.

bad " war in the members " even of its Arahants. The ideal of the Buddhist, held as realizable under temporal conditions, was to walk among his sheaves " beyond the Good and the Bad ".[1] The Good consisted in giving hostages to the future. His realized ideal was to be releasing them,[2] and, in a span of final, but glorious existence, to be tasting of the finest fruit of living—the peace of insight, the joy of emancipation. This was life supremely worth living, for

" leben heisst
In Freiheit leben und mit freiem Geist ! " [3]

The Good, to take his own metaphor, was as a raft bearing him across the stream of danger. After that he was to leave it and go on. " And ye, brethren, learn by the parable of the raft that ye must put away good conditions, let alone bad." [4]

It is not easy for us, who have learnt from Plato to call our Absolute the Good and our Ideal a *summum bonum*, to sympathize readily with this moral standpoint. Critics see in it an aspiration towards moral stultification and self-complacent egoism. Yet there is little fear but that in the long run fuller knowledge will bring deeper insight into what in Buddhism is really worthy of admiration for all time. If it is now accused of weakening the concept of individuality by rejecting soul, and, at the same time, of fostering egoistic morality, it is just possible that criticism is here at fault. On the ruins of the animistic view, Buddhism had to reconstruct a new personality, wholly phenomenal, impermanent, law-determined, yet none the less able, and alone able, by indomitable faith and will, to work out a personal salvation, a personal perfection. Bearing this in mind and surveying the history of its altruistic missionary labours, we cannot

---

[1] Cf. Nietzsche on Buddhism in " Der Antichrist ".

[2] C. A. i, 108.

[3] A. Pfungst, " An Giordano Bruno."

[4] See the third quotation above, p. vii, and " puññañ ca pāpañ ca bahitvā . . . bhikkhu vuccati ", S. i, 182; Dhp., ver. 267.

rashly cast egoistic morality at it to much effect. Nor has it much to fear from charges of stultification, quietism, pessimism, and the like. We are misled to a certain extent by the very thoroughness of its methods of getting at the moral life by way of psychical training. We see, as in our Manual and other canonical records, elaborate systems for analyzing and cultivating the intellectual faculties, the will, and feeling, and we take these as substitutes for overt moral activity, as ends when they are but means. And if the Dhamma-Sangaṇi seems to some calculated to foster introspective thought to a morbid extent, it must not be forgotten that it is not Buddhist philosophy alone which teaches that, for all the natural tendency to spend and be spent in efforts to cope, by thought and achievement, with the world without, "it is in this little fathom-long mortal frame with its thinkings and its notions that the world"[1] itself and the whole problem of its misery and of the victory over it lies hid.

If I have succeeded to any extent in connecting the contents of this Manual with the rest of the Buddhist Piṭakas, it is because I had at my disposal the mass of material accumulated in my husband's MS. Pali dictionary. Besides this, the selection of material for Sections II and III of my Introduction in his work. Besides this, I owe him a debt of gratitude indefinitely great for advice and criticism generally.

---

[1] See second quotation above, p. xiii.

Note to p. liii.—Professor Sthcherbatzky has given from later Buddhist sources this solution of the Rūpaloka crux: In an older dual division of worlds into Rūpa (corporeal mental life) and Arūpa (incorporeal mental life), the Kāmaloka (life where sense-desires are operative) was a sub-division of Rūpaloka. This subdivision came to be raised to a main division. Hence the three divisions. This seems to me a plausible hypothesis. Ancient eschatology was vague and careless enough (we are no better even now) to let this disorderly division stand.

MĀTIKĀ

(THE TABLE OF CONTENTS)

A. ABHIDHAMMA.

M2

Sections.		
1028–30.	15.	States that are of a wrongfulness fixed as to consequences; that are of a righteousness fixed as to consequences; that do not entail fixed consequences.
1031–4.	16.	States that have the Path as object; whose moral root is the Path; whose dominant influence is the Path.
1035–7.	17.	States that have arisen; that have not arisen; that are bound to arise.
1038–40.	18.	States that are past; present; future.
1041–3.	19.	States that have the past as their object; the present . . .; the future as their object.
1044–6.	20.	States that belong to one's self; are external to one's self; are belonging or external to one's self.
1047–9.	21.	States that have for an object one's self; an object external to one's self; an object that is both.
1050–2.	22.	States that are visible and reacting; invisible and reacting; neither.
		Here end the triplets.
1053–72.		States that are moral roots; not moral roots.
1073, 1074.		States concomitant with a moral root; not so concomitant.
1075, 1076.		States associated with a moral root; dissociated from a moral root.
1077, 1078.		States that are both moral roots and concomitant with a moral root; states of mind that are the latter but not the former.
1079, 1080.		States that are both moral roots and associated with moral roots; states of mind that are the latter but not the former.

Sections.

1081, 1082. States that are not moral roots, b
either concomitant with moral ro
not.

This is the moral root group.

1083, 1084. States that are causally related;
causally related.

1085, 1086. States that are conditioned; unconditione

1087, 1088. States that are visible; invisible.

1089, 1090. States that are reactions; not reactions.

1091, 1092. States that have material form; that are immaterial.

1093, 1094. States that are mundane; supramundane.

1095. States that may be cognized in a given way; that may not be cognized in that given way.

This is the short intermediate set of pairs.

1096–1102. States that are āsavas; are not āsavas.

1103, 1104. States that have āsavas, have not āsavas.

1105, 1106. States that are associated with āsavas; dissociated from āsavas.

1107, 1108. States that both are and have āsavas; that have āsavas but are not āsavas.

1109, 1110. States that are both āsavas and associated with āsavas; that are associated with āsavas but are not āsavas.

1111, 1112. States that are dissociated from āsavas, but may have or may not have āsavas.

This is the Āsava group.

1113–24. States that are fetters; are not fetters.

1125, 1126. States that are favourable to fetters; are not so.

1127, 1128. States that are associated with fetters; are dissociated from fetters.

ons.

1130. States that are both fetters and favourable to fetters; that are the latter but not the former.

1131, 1132. States that are both fetters and associated with fetters; that are the latter but not the former.

1133, 1134. States that are dissociated from fetters, but may be favourable to fetters or unfavourable.

This is the Fetter Group.

1135–40. States that are ties; are not ties.

1141, 1142. States that are favourable to ties; are not so.

1143, 1144. States that are associated with ties; dissociated from ties.

1145, 1146. States that are both ties and favourable to ties; that are the latter but not the former.

1147, 1148. States that are both ties and associated with ties; are the latter but not the former.

1149, 1150. States that are dissociated from ties; but may or may not be favourable to ties.

This is the Ties group.

1151, 1151*a*. 1152–73. Here follow the Floods group, the Yokes group, the Hindrances group. Each follows the same order of treatment as the three preceding groups.

1174–6. States that are perversions; are not perversions.

1177, 1178. States that are perverted; unperverted.

1179, 1180. States that are associated with perversion; dissociated from perversion.

1181, 1182. States that are both perversions and perverted; are the latter but not the former.

Sections.

1183, 1184. States that are dissociated from perversion, but are either perverted or unperverted.

This is the Perversion group.

1185, 1186. States that have objects of thought; have not such.

1187, 1188. States that have thought; have not thought.

1189, 1190. States that are mental properties; are not such.

1191, 1192. States that are associated with thought; dissociated from thought.

1193, 1194. States that are conjoined with thought; detached from thought.

1195, 1196. States that are sprung from thought; are not so.

1197, 1198. States that come into being together with thought; do not so come into being.

1199, 1200. States that are consecutive to thought; are not so.

1201, 1202. States that are conjoined with and sprung from thought; are not so.

1203, 1204. States that are conjoined with, sprung from, come into being together with thought; are not so.

1205, 1206. States that are conjoined with, sprung from, consecutive to, thought; are not so.

1207, 1208. States that are one's own; are external.

1209, 1210. States that are derived; are not derived.

1211, 1212. States that are grasped at; are not grasped at.

This is the Great Intermediate Set of Pairs.

1213–18. States that are graspings; are not graspings.

1219, 1220. States that are favourable to grasping; not favourable.

1221, 1222. States that are associated with grasping; dissociated from grasping.

Sections.

1223, 1224. States that are both graspings and favourable to grasping; are the latter but not the former.

1225, 1226. States that are both graspings and associated with grasping; are the latter but not the former.

1227, 1228. States that are dissociated from grasping, but may be either favourable or unfavourable to grasping.

This is the Graspings group.

1229–40. States that are vices; are not vices.

1241, 1242. States that are vicious; are not vicious.

1243, 1243a. States that are vitiated; are not vitiated.

1244, 1245. States that are associated with vice; are dissociated from vice.

1246, 1247. States that are both vices and vicious; are vicious but not vices.

1248, 1249. States that are both vices and vitiated; are vitiated but not vices.

1250, 1251. States that are both vices and associated with vice; are the latter but not the former.

1252, 1253. States that are dissociated from vice, but may be either vicious or not.

This is the Vices group.

1254–8. States that may be put away by vision; not so put away.

1259, 1260. States that may be put away by culture; not so put away.

1261–5. States the moral root of which may be put away by vision; may not be so put away.

1266, 1267. States the moral root of which may be put away by culture; may not be so put away.

Sections.

1268, 1269. States having applied thinking ; not having applied thinking.

1270, 1271. States having sustained thinking ; not having sustained thinking.

1272, 1273. States concomitant with zest ; not concomitant with zest.

1274, 1275. States accompanied by zest ; unaccompanied by zest.

1276, 1277. States accompanied by ease ; unaccompanied by ease.

1278, 1279. States accompanied by indifference ; unaccompanied by indifference.

1280-7. States of the universe of sense ; not of that universe.
States of the universe of form ; not of that universe.
States of the formless universe ; not of that universe.
States that are included ; unincluded.

1288, 1289. States that lead onward ; do not lead onward.

1290, 1291. States that are fixed ; are not fixed.

1292, 1293. States that have a beyond ; have no beyond.

1294, 1295. States that are harmful ; are harmless.

This is the Supplementary Set of Pairs.

B. Suttanta.

1296, 1297. States that partake of wisdom ; do not partake of wisdom.

1298, 1299. States that resemble lightning ; are comparable to the thunderbolt.

1300, 1301. States that are foolish ; discreet.

1302, 1303. States that are dark ; bright.

1304, 1305. States that conduce to remorse ; that do not.

1306. States that are equivalent terms ; processes of such.

Here ends the Table of Contents.

[BOOK I.

THE UPRISING OF THOUGHTS
(Cittuppāḍa-kaṇḍaṃ).

PART I.—GOOD STATES OF CONSCIOUSNESS.

CHAPTER I.]

The Eight Main Types of Thought relating to the Sensuous Universe (kāmāvacara-aṭṭha-mahācittāni).][1]

I.

[1] Which are the states[2] that are good?

When a good thought concerning the sensuous universe[3] has risen, which is accompanied by gladness and associated with knowledge,[4] and has as its object a sight,[5] a sound,

---

[1] The brackets enclosing this and all other headings indicate that the latter have been transposed from the position they occupy in the text. There each heading stands at the end of its section.

[2] On this rendering, see Introduction, pt. v.

[3] See pp. 1 f., ciii (note).

[4] Ñāṇa-sampayuttaṃ. According to the Cy., a good thought deserves to be thus distinguished on four grounds: it has arisen through good karma, through present favourable conditions, through maturity of faculties, and from the remoteness or mental and moral infirmity which it implies (Asl. 76). Sampayuttaṃ—lit., con-yoked—is, in the Kathāvatthu quoted by the Cy. (p. 42), described as including the following relations (between one "state" and another): concomitant (sahagatā), co-existent (sahajātā), contiguous (saṃsaṭṭhā), having a common origin (ekuppādā), a common cessation (ekanirodhā), a common basis or embodiment (ekuvatthukā), a common object of attention (ekārammaṇā). In the present work the term is subsequently rendered by "connected", e.g. in § 1007, etc. The preceding adjectival phrase, somanassa-sahagataṃ, which I have rendered "accompanied by gladness", is

a smell, a taste, a touch,[1] a [mental] state,[2] or what not,[3] then there is

---

virtually declared by the Cy. (69 f.) to be here equivalent to somanassa-sampayuttaṃ, inasmuch as it is to be interpreted in its fullest intension. Of its five distinguishable shades of meaning, the one here selected is that of "conjoined" (saṃsaṭṭhaṃ). And of the four distinguishable connotations of "conjoined" the one here selected is that of "co-existent". Thus far, the intricate Buddhaghosa. But I have yet to discover any attempt to analyse the laws governing the process of association between mental states, such as we first find in Aristotle. On "gladness", see §§ 10, 18.

[5] Rūpārammaṇam, saddārammaṇaṃ, etc., i.e. either as a present sensation or as a representative image relating to the past or future; in the language of Hume, as an impression or as an idea; in the more comprehensive German term, as *Vorstellung* (Asl. 71). See above, xlix.

[1] Literally, a tangible object—the standard Pali term.

[2] Dhammārammaṇaṃ—the "object", that is, of perception, imagination, or ideation (mano, cittaṃ, Asl. 71), just as a thing seen is the object of sight. Buddhaghosa rejects the opinion that a dhammārammaṇaṃ is something outside the range of the senses, and cites M. i, 295, where Sāriputta declares that, whereas each sense has its specific field, the mano has all these five fields as its scope. At the moment when an object enters "the door of the eye" or other sense it enters also the door of the ideating faculty, causing the potential consciousness, or one's being, to vibrate (bhavangacalanassa paccayo hoti), just as the alighting bird, at the same moment, strikes the bough and casts a shadow (ibid. 72). As we might say, presentative cognition is invariably accompanied by representative cognition. Then, in the course of the mental undulations arising through this disturbance by way of sense impact, one of these eight psychoses termed Mahācittāni may emerge. "But in bare representative cognition (suddha-manodvāre) there is no process of sensory stimulation," as when we recall past sense-experience. The process of representation is illustrated in detail, and completes an interesting essay in ancient psychology. In the case of seeing, hearing, and smell, past pleasant sensations are described as being simply revived during a subsequent state of repose. In the case of taste and touch, it is present disagreeable sensations which suggest certain contrasted experience in the past. But the commentator is not here interested in "association by contrast" as such.

(i) contact (§ 2),
(ii) feeling (§ 3),
(iii) perception (§ 4),
(iv) volition (§ 5),
(v) thought (§ 6),
(vi) application (§ 7),
(vii) sustained thinking (§ 8),
(viii) zest (§ 9),
(ix) ease (§ 10),
(x) self-collectedness (§ 11),
(xi) the faculty of faith (§ 12),
(xii) the faculty of energy (§ 13),
(xiii) the faculty of mindfulness (§ 14),
(xiv) the faculty of concentration (§ 15),
(xv) the faculty of insight (§ 16),
(xvi) the faculty of ideation (§ 17),
(xvii) the faculty of gladness (§ 18),
(xviii) the faculty of life (§ 19) ;
(xix) right views (§ 20),
(xx) right intention (§ 21),
(xxi) right endeavour (§ 22),
(xxii) right mindfulness (§ 23),
(xxiii) right concentration (§ 24) ;
(xxiv) the power of faith (§ 25),
(xxv) the power of energy (§ 26),
(xxvi) the power of mindfulness (§ 27),
(xxvii) the power of concentration (§ 28),
(xxviii) the power of insight (§ 29),
(xxix) the power of conscientiousness (§ 30),
(xxx) the power of the fear of blame (§ 31) ;
(xxxi) absence of greed (§ 32),

---

[3] Lit., "or whatever [object the thought] is about." The gist of the comment is that, while no new class of objects is here to be understood over and above those of present or past sensations as specified, there is no serial or numerical order in which these become material for thought (ib. 106 f.).

(xxxii) absence of hate (§ 33),
(xxxiii) absence of dullness (§ 34) ;
(xxxiv) absence of covetousness (§ 35),
(xxxv) absence of malice (§ 36),
(xxxvi) right views [1] (§ 37) ;
(xxxvii) conscientiousness (§ 38),
(xxxviii) fear of blame (§ 39) ;
(xxxix, xl) serenity in mind and mental factors (§§ 40, 41),
(xli, xlii) lightness in mind and mental factors (§§ 42, 43),
(xliii, xliv) plasticity in mind and mental factors (§§ 44, 45),
(xlv, xlvi) facility in mind and mental factors (§§ 46, 47),
(xlvii, xlviii) fitness in mind and mental factors (§§ 48, 49),
(xlix, l) directness in mind and mental factors (§§ 50, 51),
(li) mindfulness (§ 52),
(lii) intelligence (§ 53),
(liii) quiet (§ 54)
(liv) intuition (§ 55),
(lv) grasp (§ 56),
(lvi) balance (§ 57).

Now these—or whatever other incorporeal, causally induced states [2] there are on that occasion—these are states that are good.

---

[1] According to Buddhaghosa the " states " numbered xxxiv-vi are considered as equivalents of those numbered xxxi-iii respectively, but as taken under another aspect. In the prior enumeration the threefold " root of good " is set out ; in the latter, reference to the " path of karma " is understood (Asl. 129).

[2] This clause has given opportunity to later psychology to intrude. Nine other states, according to the Cy., are here implied as factors in this psychosis, viz. desire (or conation, or intention, c h a n d o), resolve (a d h i m o k k h o), attention (m a n a s i k ā r o), equanimity (t a t r a m a j j h a t t a t ā), pity

[2] What on that occasion is contact (p h a s s o)?[1]

The contact which on that occasion is touching, the being brought into contact, the state of having been brought into touch with—this is the contact that there then is.

(k a r u ṇ ā), sympathy (m u d i t ā), abstinence from evil conduct in act, speech, and mode of livelihood. And the opening words of this and similar supplementary clauses in the text are coined into a technical term—y e - v a - p a n a k ā, "the or-whatever" [states],—to signify such groups.

The Cy. then "defines" the nine: desire, qualified as orthodox desire (d h a m m a c h a n d o), to distinguish it from ethically undesirable desire (cf. § 1097, etc.), is the wish to act, the stretching forth the hand of the mind (cf. ὄρεξις) to grasp the object in idea. Resolve is steadfastness, decision, the being unshaken as a pillar. Attention is movement, direction of the mind, confronting the object. Equanimity—lit., the mean (medium) state—is the being borne along evenly, without defect or excess, without partiality. Pity and sympathy are described in § 258 *et seq.* The last three give those three factors of the Eightfold Path unrepresented in the analysis of the thought (Asl. 132, 133).

It is not without interest to note that in this later supplementary category all the purely psychological states are wholly, or at least mainly, volitional or emotional, as if it had come to be felt that the older analysis had imperfectly represented this side.

[1] Touch or contact must be understood in a very general sense, as the outcome of three conditions: an impingeing or reacting sentient organ, an impingeing or reacting agency conceived as external to the sentient organ, and impact or collision (M. i, 111; iii, 281; S. ii, 72; iv, 32, etc.). The similes in Mil. 60 of the rams and the cymbals are quoted in the Cy. The eye and its object are the usual illustration, but the representative imagination (m a n o or c i t t a ṃ) and its object are included as proceeding by way of contact, only without impact (s a n g h a ṭ ṭ a n a ṃ). The real causal connexion in every case is mental, even though we speak of an external agency, just as when lac melts with heat we speak of hot coals as the cause, though the heat is in the lac's own tissue (Asl. 109).

"Contact" is given priority of place, as standing for the inception of thought and as being the *sine quâ non* of all the allied states, conditioning them much as the roof-tree of a storied house supports all the other combinations of material (ibid. 107).

[3] What on that occasion is feeling (vedanā)?[1]

The mental pleasure, the mental ease, which, on that occasion, is born of contact with the appropriate element of representative intellection;[2] the pleasurable, easeful sensation which is born of contact with thought;[3] the pleasurable, easeful feeling which is born of contact with thought—this is the feeling that there then is.

[4] What on that occasion is perception (saññā)?[4]

---

[1] Vedanā is a term of very general import, meaning sentience or reaction, bodily or mental, on contact or impression. Sensation is scarcely so loyal a rendering as feeling, for though vedanā is often qualified as "born of the contact" in sense-activity, it is always defined generally as consisting of the three species—pleasure (happiness), pain (ill), and neutral feeling—a hedonistic aspect to which the term "feeling" is alone adequate. Moreover, it covers representative feeling.

This general psychical aspect of vedanā, as distinct from sensations localized bodily—e.g. toothache—is probably emphasized by the term "mental" (cetasikaṃ) in the answer. The Cy. points out that by this "mind-dependence (= cittanissitattaṃ) bodily pleasure is eliminated" (Asl. 139). It also illustrates the general scope of vedanā by the simile of a cook who, after preparing soups and currys for his lord, tastes each critically to test them, the lord partaking of whichever he pleases. The cook represents all the associated states in the thought-complex, each functioning in one specific way. Vedanā, the master, "enjoys the essence (taste) of the object" as a whole.

[2] Tajjā-manoviññāṇadhātu. Tajjā is paraphrased by anucchavikā, sarūpā. Cf. A. i, 207; S. iv, 215; M. i, 190, 191; Mil. 53. On the remainder of the compound term, see § 6. And on the hedonistic expressions in the answer, see § 10.

[3] Ceto-samphassajaṃ . . . vedayitaṃ. The latter term (experience) is, more literally, that which is felt, *das Empfundene*. Ceto, cittaṃ are used interchangeably in the Cy. on these terms (see § 6). The "contact" is that between idea or object and thought, or the ideating agency, conceived as analogous to the impact between sense-organ and sense-object. In consequence of this contact or presentation, emotional affection arises in consciousness.

[4] The apparently capricious way in which the intension of the term saññā is varied in the Piṭakas makes it difficult

The perception, the perceiving, the state of having perceived which on that occasion is born of contact with the appropriate element of representative intellection—this is the perception that there then is.

[5] What on that occasion is volition (c e t a n ā)?[1]

---

to assign any one adequate English rendering. In the Mahāvedalla Sutta (M. i, 293) and elsewhere (cf. Mil. 61) it is explained as the relatively simple form of intellection or cognition which consists in the discernment, recognition, assimilation of sensations—e.g. of colours, as "blue", etc. Such is the process termed in modern English psychology sense-perception, except that it is not quite clear that, in Buddhist psychology, as in English, the perception is made only *on occasion of sense-stimulation*. Cf. also below, p. 72, n. 2. Hence some experts in mediaeval Buddhist metaphysic (Stcherbatzky, MacGovern) prefer the rendering "conception".

Here, if we follow the Cy. (Asl. 110), s a ñ ñ ā means simply that perception which discerns, recognizes and gives class-reference to (u p a ṭ ṭ h i t a - v i s a y a), the impressions of sense. Its procedure is likened to the carpenter's recognition of certain woods by the mark he had made on each; to the treasurer's specifying certain articles of jewelry by the ticket on each; to the wild animal's discernment in the scarecrow of the work of man. The essence of s a ñ ñ ā is said to be recognition by way of a mark. In this notion of mark and marking lies such continuity of thought as may be claimed for the various uses of the term. The bare fact of consciousness means ability to discriminate—that is, to mark. To mark is to perceive.

[1] It is unfortunate that Buddhaghosa does not give a comparative analysis of the two forms, c i t t a ṃ, c e t a n ā, as he does in the case of v i t a k k a - v i c ā r a and p ī t i - s u k h a ṃ. Under c e t a n ā he expatiates in forcible similes, describing it as a process of activity and toil, and as a co-ordinating, ordering function. He likens it to an energetic farmer, bustling about his fifty-five labourers (the fifty-five co-constituents in the thought-complex) to get in the harvest; to a senior apprentice at the carpenter's, working himself and supervising the tasks of others; to the leader of a warrior band, fighting and inciting. To these notions the definition of Nāgasena (Mil. 61) only adds that of preparing (a b h i s a n k h a r a ṇ a ṃ), the other qualifying term being merely a denominative form (as if we should say "thinkifying").

C i t t a ṃ, together with the terms in which it is described, is discussed in Pt. VII of the Introduction.

The volition, purpose, purposefulness, which is born of contact with the appropriate element of representative intellection—this is the volition that there then is.

[6] What on that occasion is thought (c i t t a ṃ)?

The thought which on that occasion is ideation, mind, heart, that which is clear, ideation as the sphere of mind, the faculty of mind, intellection, the s k a n d h a of intellection, the appropriate element of representative intellection—this is the thought that there then is.

[7] What on that occasion is application of mind (v i t a k k o)?[1]

The discrimination, the application, which on that occasion

---

[1] V i t a k k o and v i c ā r o is a pair of terms which it is hard to fit with any one pair of English words. It is very possible that academic teaching came to attach a more pregnant and specialized import to them than was conveyed in popular and purely ethical usage. Cf. M. i, Suttas xix and xx, where v i t a k k ā would be adequately rendered by ideas, notions, or thoughts. In Asl. 114, 115, on the other hand (cf. Mil. 62, 63), the relation of the two to c i t t a ṃ and to each other is set out with much metaphor, if with too little psychological grasp. V i t a k k o is distinctively mental procedure at the inception of a train of thought, the deliberate movement of voluntary attention. As a king ascends to his palace leaning on the arm of favourite or relative, so mind, or consciousness, ascends to its object depending upon the apprehensive act (v i t a k k o; Asl. 114). Other metaphorical attributes are its impingeing upon, circum-impingeing upon (p a r y ā h a n a ṃ), the object, and, again, bringing it near. Hence in selecting "application" in preference to "reasoning", by which v i t a k k o has often been translated, I wished to bring out this grasping, apprehending, reaching-out act of the mind, this incipient fetch of the consciousness elaborated in the Buddhist scholastic analysis of the term. Yet, just as applied thinking may include "reasoning" or "ratiocination", so v i t a k k o is, in the reply, described by t a k k o, the term used for ratiocinative procedure, argument, or logic (cf. D. i, 12, 21). "What," asks the Cy., "does one reason about (t a k k e s i)? About a pot, a cart, the distance of anything. Well, v i t a k k o is a stronger reasoning."

is the disposing,[1] the fixing, the focussing,[2] the superposing of the mind,[3] right disposing—this is the application that there then is.

[8] What on that occasion is sustained thought (v i c ā r o)? [4]

The process, the sustained procedure (v i c ā r o), the progress and access [of the mind] which on that occasion is the [continuous] adjusting and focussing of thought[5]—this is the sustained thought that there then is.

[9] What on that occasion is zest (p ī t i)? [6]

---

[1] On "disposing" see § 21.

[2] A p p a n ā v y a p p a n ā, the latter an intensive form of the former (Asl. 142, 143). In the "Yogāvacara's Manual" (p. xi and *passim*) a p p a n ā denotes the dawn of the desired concept during the practice of regulated meditation. Buddhaghosa defines it thus: e k a g g a ṃ c i t t a ṃ ā r a m m a ṇ e a p p e n t i.

[3] C e t a s o a b h i n i r o p a n ā = ā r a m m a ṇ e c i t t a m . . . p a t i ṭ ṭ h a p e t i (ibid.).

[4] V i c ā r o, as compared with v i t a k k o, was used to express the movement and maintenance of the voluntary thought-continuum, as distinguished from the initiative grappling with the subject of reflection. Examining in detail, as compared with grasping the whole, is also read into it by commentators (Asl. 114). It is a pounding up (a n u m a j j a n a ṃ), as well as a linking together. Metaphors are multiplied, to show its relation to v i t a k k o. It is as the reverberation of the beaten drum or bell is to the beating; as the planing movement of the bird's wings after the initial upsoaring; as the buzzing of the bee when it has alighted on the lotus; as the scouring of the dirty bowl when clutched; as the manipulating hand of the potter, v i t a k k o being represented by the hand which holds the clay to the wheel, and so on. "Investigation" would well represent the sustained activity; "analysis" the cogitation in details; "discursive thought" gives some of the import of both.

[5] Like the adjusting of bow and arrow. "Focussing" is a n u p e k k h a m ā n o.

[6] P ī t i, as distinguished from s u k h a ṃ, is explicitly excluded from the skandha of feeling, considered as the irreducible hedonic constituent, and referred to the composite psychoses of the s a n k h ā r a skandha. It connotes emotion, as distinct from bare feeling; that is to say, p ī t i is a complex

The zest which on that occasion is joy, rejoicing at, rejoicing over, mirth and merriment, felicity,[1] exultation, transport of mind [2]—this is the zest that there then is.

[10] What on that occasion is ease (s u k h a ṃ)? [3]

---

psychical phenomenon, implying a "central psycho-physical origin" and a widely diffused "somatic resonance" (cf. Sully, *The Human Mind*, ii, 56). It arises out of a present idea, and suffuses the whole being. By Buddhaghosa's day it was divided into five species: the thrill of joy, just causing "the flesh to creep"; the flash of joy, like lightning; the flood of joy, like the breakers on a seashore; ecstasy or transport, in which the subject could float in the air; and overwhelming suffusing joy (Asl. 115, 116). Instances are related of the fourth species (u b b e g a - p ī t i), the inspiring idea being "B u d d h ā r a m m a ṇ a ṃ" (see also Visuddhi Magga, chap. iv; "Yogāvacara's Manual," vii; *Bud. Psy.*, 1914, 187 f.). The same word (u b b e g o) is used to describe the anguish or trembling over guilt discovered. See below, § 30, n.

[1] V i t t i, meaning literally, as the Cy. points out, prosperity, wealth, and used here by analogy as a state conditioned by a source of pleasure. "Happiness arises to him who is joyful through his zest, as it arises to the wealthy through his rice-possessions." (Asl. 143.)

[2] A t t a m a n a t ā c i t t a s s a. Buddhaghosa, who did not know the true etymology of this term (cf. Vedic ātta), is ready as ever with a guess—a wrong one: a t t a n o m a n a t ā, or mentality of one's self, not of another, subjective experience. If I am pained or pleased, that is peculiarly my affair (ibid.). Psychologically it is interesting to note that he is prepared to find this intimate, subjective reference in a state of intense feeling. "Feeling is subjective experience *par excellence* . . . our feelings . . . are all our own" (Sully, *The Human Mind*, ii, 2; G. C. Robertson, *Elements of Psychology*, 185–8).

[3] To contrast p ī t i with s u k h a ṃ, Buddhaghosa draws a charming picture of the traveller who, fordone with journeying through a desert, hears with rapture of a pool in a grove, and with joy comes upon it, and who, on drinking, bathing, and resting in the shade is filled with ease. S u k h a m, it is true, is not bare quiescence; it is positive, pleasurable feeling, and may have active concomitants; its "essence" is expansion or increase (u p a b r ū h a ṇ a ṃ). But just as d u k k h a ṃ means, not so much pain as ill-being or misery, so does s u k h a ṃ mean well-being or sane and sound cænæsthesis. And as "zest" lies in the satisfaction of gaining

The mental pleasure, the mental ease, which on that occasion is the pleasant, easeful experience born of contact with thought—this is the ease that there then is.

[11] What on that occasion is self-collectedness (cittass' ekaggatā)?[1]

The stability, solidity, absorbed steadfastness of thought[2] which on that occasion is the absence of distraction,

---

(potentially or actually) what we desire, so is "ease" the enjoyment of the flavour (French *savourer*) of what we have gained (Asl. 117). See further § 60. "Mental ease" (cetasikaṃ sukhaṃ) is perhaps more correctly somanassam, rendered (§ 1, etc.) by "gladness", sukhaṃ being sometimes distinguished as bodily (kāyikam) only. See S. v, 209; *contra*, A. i, 81; *pro*, Npk. 12.

[1] "Citt', or cittass'," ekaggatā, the one-peaked condition of mind, is a name for concentration (samādhi)," says the Cy. (p. 118). And accordingly, whereas under § 15 it gives no further description of samādhi, it here applies to citt' ekaggatā the metaphors used in Mil. 38 to illustrate samādhi, viz. the centre part of a tent-shaped hut, and a chieftain leading his army. It then adds that "this samādhi, which is called self-collectedness, has, as its characteristic mark, the absence of wandering, of distraction; as its essence, the binding together of the states of mind that arise with it, as water binds the lather of soap; and as its concomitants, calmness, or wisdom—for it is said, 'he who is at peace he understands, he sees things as they really are'—and ease. The steadfastness of thought is likened to the steadiness of a lamp-flame in a windless place". See "Yogāvacara's Manual", p. xxvi.

[2] These three cognate terms are in the text cittassa ṭhiti saṇṭhiti avaṭṭhiti. According to the Cy. (p. 143), the standing unshaken in or on the object (ārammaṇe) connoted by ṭhiti is modified by the prefix saṃ to imply kneading together (sampiṇḍetvā) the associated states in the object, and by the prefix ava to imply the being immersed in the object. The last metaphor is in Buddhist doctrine held applicable to four good and three bad states—faith, mindfulness, concentration (= self-collectedness), and wisdom; craving, speculation, and ignorance, but most of all to self-collectedness.

balance,[1] unperturbed mental procedure, quiet,[2] the faculty and the power of concentration, right concentration—this is the self-collectedness that there then is.

[12] What on that occasion is the faculty of faith (s a d d h i n d r i y a ṃ)?[3]

The faith which on that occasion is a trusting in, the professing confidence in,[4] the sense of assurance, faith,[5]

---

[1] A v i s a h ā r o, a v i k k h e p o (v, § 57). Distraction and loss of equilibrium are attributed to the presence of "excitement and perplexity" (§§ 425, 429; Asl. 144).

[2] S a m a t h o. Distinguished as of three species: mental calm (so used here); legal pacification, or settlement; calm in all the sanskāras, by which, according to the Cy. (144), is meant the peace of Nirvana.

[3] On "faculty", see p. lxv.

Faith is characterized and illustrated in the same terms and approximately the same similes as are used in Mil., pp. 34–60. That is to say, it is shown to be a state of mind where the absence of perplexity sets free aspiration and energy. It is described as trust in the Buddha and his system. There is, however, no dwelling just here on any terminus *ad quem*, as St. Paul did in speaking of "the prize for the mark of the high calling", etc., towards which he pressed in ardent faith. There is, rather, an insistence on that self-confidence born of conviction of the soundness of one's basis and methods which is, as it were, an aspect of faith as a *vis a tergo*. In the simile of the stream, the Cy. differs from Trenckner's version of the Milinda to the extent of making the folk afraid to cross because of alligators and other monsters till the hero takes his sword and plunges in. See the note on "faith" in the translation of Mil. i, 56.

[4] i.e. in the Buddha, the Doctrine and the Order. Buddhaghosa is only interested in making the etymology bear on ethics, and compares the "downward plunge" of confidence (o - k a p p a n ā) in the attitude of faith to the "sinking" in "mindfulness", the "grounded stand" in "concentration", and the "sounding" penetration of "wisdom" (Asl. 144, 145).

[5] The Cy. puts forward an alternative explanation of the repetition in the description of this and following compounds of the first term of the compound, viz. "faith". According to the former it is the method of Abhidamma to set out in isolation the adjectival part of a compound on which the substantial part depends: faith-faculty = faith (faculty of). According to the latter, the identity between the two abstractions, faith and

faith as a faculty and as a power—this is the faith that there then is.

[13] What on that occasion is the faculty of energy (viriyindriyaṃ)?[1]

The mental inception[2] of energy which there is on that occasion, the striving and the onward effort, the exertion and endeavour, the zeal and ardour,[3] the vigour and fortitude, the state of unfaltering effort, the state of sustained desire, the state of unflinching endurance and solid grip of the burden, energy, energy as faculty and as power, right endeavour—this is the energy that there then is.

---

faith-faculty, is brought out. The case of woman and attribute of femininity, it remarks, is different. (This may be a groping after the distinction between concrete and abstract.)

[1] Viriyaṃ is by Buddhaghosa connected with (*a*) vīra, the dynamic effectiveness which is the essence of the genus "hero" (vīro); (*b*) īriya, vibrating movement. He characterizes it by the two notions, "supporting" and "grasping at", or "stretching forward" (paggaho), and, again, by "exerting" (ussāhanaṃ). Cf. Mil. 36; Sum. Vil. 63. And he cites the same similes as appear in the Milinda. He seems to have wished, as modern psychologists have done, to account for the two modes of conscious effort: resistance and free energy. But he also emphasizes the fact that the energy in question is mental, not bodily (pp. 120 *et seq.*, 145).

[2] Ārambho (cf. ārammaṇaṃ), overt action as distinguished from inaction, hence action at its inception, is distinguished by the Cy. as having six different implications, according as there is reference to karma, to a fault committed, to slaying or injury, or to action as such (kiriyā) or energy as such.

I do not pretend that the four following pairs of words fit those in the text exactly. They are mere approximations. "Endeavour" is vāyāmo, the term representing "energy" in the Noble Eightfold Path. "Unfaltering" effort (asithila-parakkamatā) is the attitude of one who has made the characteristic Buddhist vow: Verily may skin and nerve and bone dry up and wither, or ever I stay my energy, so long as I have attained whatsoever by human vigour, energy, and effort is attainable! (M. i, 480). The desire sustained—lit., not cast down—is that felt on an occasion for making good karma.

[3] Cf. A. ii, 195.

[14] What on that occasion is the faculty of mindfulness (s a t i n d r i y a ṃ)?[1]

The mindfulness which on that occasion is recollecting, calling back to mind; the mindfulness[2] which is remembering, bearing in mind, the opposite of superficiality[3] and of obliviousness; mindfulness as faculty, mindfulness as power, right mindfulness—this is the faculty of mindfulness that there then is.

[15] What on that occasion is the faculty of concentration (s a m ā d h i n d r i y a ṃ)?[4]

---

[1] Buddhaghosa's comment on s a t i, in which he closely follows and enlarges on the account in Mil. 37, 38, shows that the traditional conception of that aspect of consciousness had much in common with the Western modern theory of conscience or moral sense. S a t i (Sk.: smṛti, memory) is in Buddhism not merely memory, but is lucid retention of both the past and the present. It appears under the metaphor of an inward mentor, discriminating between good and bad and prompting choice. Hardy went so far as to render it by "conscience", but this slurs over the interesting divergencies between Eastern and Western thought. The former is quite unmystical on the subject of s a t i. It takes the psychological process of representative functioning (without bringing out the distinction between bare memory and judgment), and presents the same under an ethical aspect. See also under h i r i, § 30; and the notion as described in *Questions of Milinda*, 38, n. 2.

[2] The *three*fold mention of s a t i in the reply (cf. § 12) agrees with K., but not with Puggala Paññatti (p. 25). It is not noticed by the Cy.

[3] A p i l ā p a n a t ā. The Atthasālinī solves the problem presented by this term (see Milinda (SBE.), vol. i, p. 58, n. 2) by deriving it from p i l a v a t i, to float, and interprets: "not floating on the surface like pumpkins and pots on the water," s a t i entering into and plunging down into the object of thought. Cf. § 11, n. 2; § 12, n. 2, in which connexion the term is again used. The positive form occurs *infra*, § 1349. PP. has (*a*) v i l ā p a n a t ā (21, 25). (Asl. 147; cf. 405). I should have rendered the word by "profundity", had I not preferred to bring out the negative form of the original.

[4] Buddhaghosa's etymology—"ā r a m m a ṇ e c i t t a ṃ s a m m ā a d h ī y a t i, ṭ h a p e t ī t i"—is no doubt incorrect, s a m - ā - d h ā being the sounder analysis; nevertheless, he

Answer as for "self-collectedness", § 11.

[16] What on that occasion is the faculty of insight (paññindriyaṃ)? [1]

---

brings out that voluntary and deliberate adjustment of the attention with a view to sustained mental effort which is connoted by samādhi (Asl. 122).

[1] To fit the term paññā with its approximate European equivalent is one of the cruces of Buddhist philosophy. I have tried in turn wisdom, reason, intellect, insight, science, understanding, and knowledge. All of these have been, and are, used in the literature of philosophy with varying shades of connotation, according as the sense to be conveyed is popular and vague, psychological and precise, or transcendental and—*passez-moi le mot*—having precise vagueness. And each of them might, with one implication or another, represent paññā. The main difficulty in choice lay in determining whether, to the Buddhist, paññā stood for a mental function or for the aggregate product of certain mental functioning, or for both. When all the allusions to paññā in the Sutta Piṭaka have been collated, a final translation may become possible. Here it must suffice to quote two. In M. i, 292, he who has paññā (paññavā) is declared in virtue thereof to understand (pajānāti) the nature of the phenomenon of pain or ill (the Four Noble Truths). In D. i, 124, Gotama asks: What is this paññā? and himself sets out its content as consisting in certain intellectual attainments, viz. the Jhānas, insight into the nature of impermanence, the mental image of one's self, the power of Iddhi, clairaudience, insight into other minds, into one's own past lives, clairvoyance, and the elimination of all vitiating tendencies. Buddhaghosa also (Vis.M., chap. xiv) distinguishes paññā from saññā and viññāṇa. He describes it as adequate to discern not only what these can, viz. sense-objects and the Three Marks (impermanence, pain, and non-substantiality) respectively, but *also* the Path. For him, then, it might be called intellect "at a higher power". And in Gotama's reply, all those attainments are described in terms of *intellectual process*. Nevertheless, it is clear that the term did not stand for *bare mental process of a certain degree of complexity*, but that it also implied mental process as cultivated in accordance with a *certain system of concepts objectively valid* for all Buddhist adepts. Hence, I think it best to reject such terms as reason, intellect, and understanding, and to choose wisdom, or science, or knowledge, or insight. Only they must be understood in this connexion as implying the body of learning

The insight which there is on that occasion is understanding, search, research, searching the Doctrine,[1] discernment, discrimination, differentiation, erudition, proficiency, subtlety, criticism, reflection, analysis, breadth,[2] sagacity,[3] a "guide",[4] intuition,[5] intelligence, a "goad"; wisdom as faculty, wisdom as power, wisdom as a sword, wisdom as a height,[6] wisdom as light,[7] wisdom as glory,[8] wisdom as splendour,[9] wisdom as a precious stone; the absence of dullness, searching the Truth,[10] right views—this is the wisdom that there then is.

[17] What on that occasion is the faculty of mind (representative imagination, m a n i n d r i y a ṃ)?

Answer as for "thought" (c i t t a ṃ), § 6.

[18] What on that occasion is the faculty of pleasure (s o m a n a s s i n d r i y a ṃ)?

Answer as for "ease" (s u k h a ṃ), § 10.

[19] What on that occasion is the faculty of life (j ī v i t i n d r i y a ṃ)?

The persistence of these incorporeal states, their subsistence, going on, their being kept going on, their progress, continuance,

---

as assimilated and applied by the intellect of a given individual. See further under s a ñ ñ ā (§ 4) and v i j j ā (§ 1296).

[1] i.e. the doctrines of the "Four Truths" (Asl. 147). Cf. Mil. 83

[2] Insight compared to the breadth and amplitude of the earth (Asl. 147, 148).

[3] Or acuteness, m e d h ā. The Cy. explains the specific wisdom of this term to lie in "slaying" vice, or else in "grasping and bearing" (148).

[4] P a r i ṇ ā y i k ā.

[5] "For the slaying of vices" (Asl. 148; cf. Therag. ver. 1095; Jāt. iv, 174).

[6] "In the sense of something lofty" (ibid.; cf. Dhp. v 28 = Mil. 387).

[7] Ang. ii, 139.

[8] Ibid.

[9] Ibid.

[10] Repeated by way of antithesis to "dullness" (Asl. 148).

preservation, life, life as faculty [1]—this is the faculty of life that there then is.[2]

[20] What on that occasion are right views (sammā-diṭṭhi)?[3]

Answer as for the "faculty of insight", § 16.

[21] What on that occasion is right intention (sammā-sankappo)?[4]

Answer as for "application of mind", § 7.

[22] What on that occasion is right endeavour (sammā-vāyāmo)?

Answer as for the "faculty of energy", § 13.

[23] What on that occasion is right mindfulness (sammāsati)?

Answer as for the "faculty of mindfulness", § 14.

[24] What on that occasion is right concentration (sammāsamādhi)?

Answer as for "self-collectedness", § 11.

[25] What on that occasion is the power of faith (saddhābalaṃ)?

Answer as for the "faculty of faith", § 12.

[26] What on that occasion is the power of energy (viriyabalaṃ)?

Answer as for the "faculty of energy", § 13.

---

[1] In the text, hoti before idaṃ is probably an error; K. omits it. Cf. § 441 in text.

[2] This answer is exceptional in the omission of tasmiṃ samaye ("on that occasion") at the beginning of the sentence. Cf. §§ 82, 295, 441. The reason of its omission is possibly that in the presence of life, by which the complex of dhammas is sustained as lotuses by water or as an infant by its nurse (Asl. 124), there is nothing contingent on the *ethical* quality (good, bad, or indeterminate) of the given complex.

[3] For a discussion of the term diṭṭhi see § 1003. On these five factors of the Path see Introduction.

[4] Sankappo is by the Cy. especially identified with the expression cetaso abhiniropanā, superposing of the mind, the disposition or adjustment of attention, that on which the heart is set, hence aspiration, intention, purpose, design. In M. ii, 27 f., it is said to arise out of saññā (perception).

[27] What on that occasion is the power of mindfulness (s a t i b a l a ṃ)?

Answer as for the "faculty of mindfulness", § 14.

[28] What on that occasion is the power of concentration (s a m ā d h i b a l a ṃ)?

Answer as for "self-collectedness", § 11.

[29] What on that occasion is the power of insight (p a ñ ñ ā b a l a ṃ)?

Answer as for the "faculty of wisdom", § 16.

[30] What on that occasion is the power of conscientiousness (h i r i b a l a ṃ)? [1]

The feeling of conscientious scruple [2] which there is on that

---

[1] H i r i and o t t a p p a ṃ, as analysed by Buddhaghosa, present points of considerable ethical interest. Taken together, they give us the emotional and conative aspect of the modern notion of conscience, just as s a t i represents it on its intellectual side. The former term "is equivalent to shame" (l a j j ā), the latter to "anguish (u b b e g o) over evil-doing". H i r i has its source within; o t t a p p a ṃ springs from without. H i r i is autonomous (a t t ā d h i p a t i); o t t a p p a ṃ, heteronomous, influenced by society (l o k ā d h i p a t i). The former is established on shame; the latter on dread. The former is marked by consistency; the latter by discernment of the danger and fearsomeness of error. The subjective source of h i r i is fourfold, viz. the idea of what is due to one's birth, age, worth, and education. Thus, one having h i r i will think, "Only mean folk (fishers, etc.), children, poor wretches, the blind and ignorant, would do such an act," and he refrains. The external source of o t t a p p a ṃ is the idea that "the body of the faithful will blame you", and hence one refrains. If a man have h i r i, he is, as said the Buddha, his own best master. To one who is sensitive by way of o t t a p p a ṃ, the masters of the faith are the best guides (Asl. 126).

In a supplementary paragraph (p. 127) the "marks" (consistency, etc.) are thus explained: In h i r i one reflects on the worth of one's birth, one's teacher, one's estate, and one's fellow-students. In o t t a p p a ṃ one feels dread at self-reproach, the blame of others, chastisement, and retribution in another life.

[2] H i r i y a t i, paraphrased by j i g u c c h a t i (Asl. 149; D. i, 174; M. i, 78).

occasion when scruples ought to be felt, conscientious scruple at attaining to bad and evil states—this is the power of conscientiousness that there then is.

[31] What on that occasion is the power of the fear of blame (ottappabalaṃ)?

The sense of guilt [1] which there is on that occasion, where a sense of guilt ought to be felt, a sense of guilt at attaining to bad and evil states—this is the fear of blame that there then is.

[32] What on that occasion is disinterestedness (alobho)?

The absence of greed, of being greedy, of greediness, which there is on that occasion, the absence of infatuation, the feeling and being infatuated, the absence of covetousness, that absence of greed which is the root of good [2]—this is the absence of greed that there then is.

[33] What on that occasion is the absence of hate (adoso)?

The absence of hate, of hating,[3] of hatred, which there

---

[1] Ottappati, paraphrased by ubbego (Asl. 124).

[2] i.e. the fundamental condition, the cause of goodness. On "covetousness" and "infatuation", see §§ 35, 1059. Alobho and its two co-ordinate virtues, the threefold "root" of goodness, lose all their force in English negatives, but to a Buddhist may convey as much impressiveness, as much of positive import, as the negative "immortality" does to the Christian. Alobho, e.g. clears the way for active altruism; adoso, for active sympathy; amoho, for a life of culture (see § 34, n.). I do not know any positive terms meet to represent them, but "disinterestedness" is a fair equivalent of alobho.

The "mark" of the first is absence of adhesion, as a drop of water runs off a lotus leaf. Its essence is independence, like that of the emancipated bhikshu (Asl. 127).

[3] K. reads adūsanā, adūsitattaṃ. The "mark" of adoso is said to be absence of churlishness and crossness (see § 1060); its essence the suppression of annoyance and fever; its immediate result is loveliness—like the full moon (Asl. 127).

is on that occasion, the absence of malice, of spleen,[1] the absence of hate, which is the root of good—this is the absence of hate that there then is.

[34] What on that occasion is the absence of dullness (a m o h o)?

Answer as for the "faculty of insight", § 16.[2]

[35] What on that occasion is the absence of covetousness (a n a b h i j j h ā)?

Answer as for "disinterestedness", § 32.[3]

[36] What on that occasion is the absence of malice (a v y ā p ā d o)?[4]

Answer as for the "absence of hate", § 33.

[37] What on that occasion are right views (s a m-m ā d i t t h i)?[5]

Answer as for the "faculty of insight", § 16.

[38] What on that occasion is conscientiousness (h i r i)?

Answer as for the "power of conscientiousness", § 30.

[39] What on that occasion is the fear of blame (o t t a p p a ṃ)?

Answer as for the "power of the fear of blame", § 31.

---

[1] "The opposite of the pain felt when one is angry" (Asl. 150).

[2] Buddhaghosa expatiates at some length on the excellencies of the fundamental trinity of Buddhist virtue. To take a few only: a l o b h o (1) involves health, a d o s o (2) youth (hate ages quickly), a m o h o (3) long life (through prudence). (1) tends to material good through generosity (cf. "he that soweth plenteously", etc.); (2) to the acquisition of friends, won and held by love; (3) to self-development. (1) leads to life in the devaloka, (2) to life in the Brahmaloka, (3) to Arahantship. (1) gives insight into impermanence, and, conversely, (2) and (3) into the other two marks ("pain" and "non-substantiality", respectively).

[3] A b h i j j h ā and l o b h o are synonymous. See §§ 1059 and 1136, where a b h i j j h ā stands for l o b h o.

[4] Described (Asl. 129) as the being void of any wish to destroy the welfare of others, bodily or mental, their advantages in this or other worlds, or their good reputation.

[5] Cf. § 1 (xxxvi), footnote.

[40] What on that occasion is repose of mental factors (k ā y a p p a s s a d d h i)?[1]

The serenity,[2] the composure which there is on that occasion, the calming, the tranquillizing, the tranquillity of the skandhas of feeling, perception and synergies—this is the serenity of mental factors that there then is.

[41] What on that occasion is serenity of mind (c i t t a p a s s a d d h i)?

The serenity, the composure which there is on that occasion, the calming, the tranquillizing, the tranquillity of the skandha of mind—this is the serenity of mind that there then is.

[42] What on that occasion is buoyancy[3] of mental factors (k ā y a l a h u t ā)?

The buoyancy which there is on that occasion, the alertness in varying,[4] the absence of sluggishness[5] and inertia, in the skandhas of feeling, perception, and synergies—this is the buoyancy of mental factors that there then is.

[43] What on that occasion is buoyancy of mind (c i t t a l a h u t ā)?

The buoyancy, etc. (*as in* § 42), in the skandha of consciousness—this is the buoyancy of mind that there then is.

[44] What on that occasion is pliancy of mental factors (k ā y a m u d u t ā)?[6]

---

[1] On the meaning of k ā y o here (k ā y o is lit. "group"); cf. Comp. 96, n. 3.

[2] P a s s a d d h i is described as a state free from pain—where pain is allayed and suppressed; where tremor or unquiet is replaced by "coolness"—the opposite to the states called k i l e s a s, especially excitement (§ 1229). Cf. D. i, 73; M. 1, 37.

[3] Literally, lightness, described as the opposite of heaviness, sluggishness, and the rigidity of stolidity and stupor (§ 1185).

[4] "The capacity of changing quickly" (Asl. 150). Cf. Childers' Dictionary, s.v. p a r i v a t t i.

[5] Read a d a n d h a n a t ā. K. reads a d a n d h a t ā, but a d a n d h a n a t ā in § 43 and § 639.

[6] The suppression of stiffness and resistance, or oppugnancy; the attitude antithetical to that belonging to the kilesas of opinionativeness and conceit.

The pliancy which there is on that occasion, the suavity, smoothness, absence of rigidity, in the skandhas of feeling, perception, and synergies—this is the pliancy of mental factors that there then is.

[45] What on that occasion is pliancy of mind (c i t t a m u d u t ā)?

The plasticity which, etc. (*as in* § 44), in the skandha of consciousness—this is the pliancy of mind that there then is.

[46] What on that occasion is wieldiness [1] of mental factors (k ā y a k a m m a ñ ñ a t ā)?

The wieldiness which there is on that occasion, the tractableness, the workableness, of the skandhas of feeling, perception, and synergies—this is the wieldiness of mental factors that there then is.

[47] What on that occasion is wieldiness of mind (c i t t a k a m m a ñ ñ a t ā)?

The wieldiness, etc. (*as in* § 46), of the skandha of consciousness—this is the wieldiness of mind that there then is.

[48] What on that occasion is fitness [2] of mental factors (k ā y a p ā g u ñ ñ a t ā)?

The fitness which there is on that occasion, the competence, the efficient state of the skandhas of feeling, perception, and synergies—this is the fitness of mental factors that there then is.

[49] What on that occasion is fitness of mind (c i t t a - p ā g u ñ ñ a t ā)?

The fitness, etc. (*as in* § 48), of the skandha of consciousness—this is the fitness of mind that there then is.

[50] What on that occasion is rectitude [3] of mental factors (k ā y u j j u k a t ā)?

---

[1] K a m m a ñ ñ a t ā, literally workableness, or serviceableness—for good action (Asl. 151), by which one "succeeds in constructing objects of thought" (ibid. 130).

[2] The antithesis to illness and diffidence (ibid. 131).

[3] Defined as the antithesis of crookedness, deception (m ā y ā), and craftiness (Asl. 131).

The straightness which there is on that occasion, the rectitude, without deflection, twist or crookedness, of the skandhas of feeling, perception, and synergies—this is the directness of mental factors that there then is.

[51] What on that occasion is rectitude of mind (c i t t u j j u k a t ā)?

The straightness, etc. (*as in* § 50), of the skandha of consciousness—this is the rectitude of mind that there then is.

[52] What on that occasion is mindfulness (s a t i)?

Answer as for the "faculty of mindfulness", § 14.

[53] What on that occasion is intelligence (s a m - p a j a ñ ñ a ṃ)?[1]

Answer as for "insight", § 16.

[54] What on that occasion is quiet (s a m a t h o)?

Answer as for "self-collectedness", § 11.

[55] What on that occasion is intuition (v i p a s s a n ā)?

Answer as for "insight", § 16.

[56] What on that occasion is grasp (p a g g ā h o)?

Answer as for the "faculty of energy", § 13.

[57] What on that occasion is balance (a v i k k h e p o)?[2]

Answer as for "self-collectedness", § 11.

These, or whatever other[3] incorporeal, causally induced states there are on that occasion—these are states that are good.

Here ends the analysis of terms (P a d a - b h ā j a n i - y a ṃ).

End of the First Portion for Recitation.

---

[1] Or comprehension; to know anything according to its usefulness, its expediency, its scope, and to know it clearly. Named as approximately equivalent to "wisdom", the Cy. assigns to it as well the characteristics of mindfulness (ibid.). Cf. the frequent twin qualification of s a t i - s a m p a j ā n o (e.g. M. i, 274), which = self-awareness.

[2] "The opposite of excitement or fluster" (Asl. ibid.). Literally, "the absence of wavering" (or vacillation or unsteadiness).

[3] See above, p. 4.

[Summary of the constituents of the First Type of Thought (sangahavāraṃ or koṭṭhāsavāraṃ).][1]

[58] Now, on that occasion

the skandhas are four,
the spheres (āyatanāni) are two,
the elements (dhātuyo) are two,
the nutriments (āhārā) are three,
the faculties (indriyāni) are eight,
the Jhāna is fivefold,
the Path is fivefold,
the powers (balāni) are seven,
the moral roots (hetu) are three;

contact,
feeling,
perception,
volition,
thought,
} are each single [factors];

the skandhas of
feeling,
perception,
synergies,
consciousness,
} are each single [factors];

---

[1] The constituent dhammas of the first of the eight schemata of "good thoughts" (cittangāni) are now rehearsed with reference to class and number. The motive probably was to aid the student either to a conspectus of the psychosis in question, or mnemonically. Thus, if the constituent factors of the thought be regarded under the aspect of classified aggregates (rāsaṭṭhena, or khandhaṭṭhena), they all fall under four heads. All that do not belong to the skandhas of feeling, perception, or consciousness, come under the sanskāra-skandha. Regarded under the aspect of collocation or conjuncture (āyatanaṃ), they all fall under two heads, corresponding to the fourth, and to the first, second, and third, of those four skandhas respectively. Regarded under the aspect of phenomena, of *non-noümena* (sabhāvaṭṭhena, suññataṭṭhena, nissattaṭṭhena), they all fall under two heads, corresponding to the two preceding. We then come to partial aspects.

the sphere of ideation (manāyatanaṃ), the faculty of ideation, the element of intellection (manoviññāṇadhatu), the sphere of a [purely] mental state, the element of a [purely] mental state,	are each single [factors].

These, or whatever other incorporeal, causally induced states there are on that occasion—these are states that are good.

[59] What on that occasion are the four skandhas ?

The skandhas of feeling, perception, synergies, and consciousness.

[60] (i) What on that occasion is the skandha of feeling ?

The mental pleasure, the mental ease, which there is on that occasion,[1] the pleasurable, easeful sensation which is born of contact with thought, the pleasant, easeful feeling born of contact with thought—this is the skandha of feeling that there then is (§§ 3, 10, 18).

[61] (ii) What on that occasion is the skandha of perception ?

The perception, the perceiving, the state of having perceived, which there is on that occasion—this is the skandha of perception that there then is (§ 4).

[62] (iii) What on that occasion is the skandha of synergies ?

(i) Contact,
(ii) volition,

---

[1] The omission in both this and the next answer of the phrase, used in §§ 3 and 4—"born of contact with the appropriate element of representative intellection"—is not noticed in the Cy. K. draws attention to it in a footnote, not at this passage, but at §§ 108–10. The omission is probably accidental.

(iii) application of mind,
(iv) sustained application,
(v) zest,
(vi) self-collectedness,
(vii) the faculty of faith,
(viii) the faculty of energy,
(ix) the faculty of mindfulness,
(x) the faculty of concentration,
(xi) the faculty of insight,
(xii) the faculty of life,
(xiii) right views,
(xiv) right intention,
(xv) right endeavour,
(xvi) right mindfulness,
(xvii) right concentration,
(xviii) the power of faith,
(xix) the power of energy,
(xx) the power of mindfulness,
(xxi) the power of concentration,
(xxii) the power of insight,
(xxiii) the power of conscientiousness,
(xxiv) the power of the fear of blame,
(xxv) disinterestedness,
(xxvi) absence of hate,
(xxvii) absence of dullness,
(xxviii) absence of covetousness,
(xxix) absence of malice,
(xxx) right views,
(xxxi) conscientiousness,
xxxii) the fear of blame,
(xxxiii) serenity of mental factors,
(xxxiv) serenity of mind,
(xxxv) buoyancy of mental factors,
(xxxvi) buoyancy of mind,
(xxxvii) plasticity of mental factors,
(xxxviii) plasticity of mind,

(xxxix) wieldiness of mental factors,
(xl) wieldiness of mind,
(xli) fitness of mental factors,
(xli) fitness of mind,
(xliii) rectitude of mental factors,
(xliv) rectitude of mind,
(xlv) mindfulness,
(xlvi) intelligence,
(xlvii) quiet,
xlviii) intuition,
(xlix) grasp,
(l) balance.

These, or whatever other incorporeal causally induced states there are on that occasion, exclusive of the skandhas of feeling, perception, and consciousness—these are the skandha of synergies.

[63] (iv) What on that occasion is the skandha of consciousness ?

The thought which on that occasion is ideation, mind, the heart, that which is clear, ideation as the sphere of mind, as the faculty of mind, the skandha of consciousness, the appropriate element of representative intellection—this is the skandha of consciousness that there then is (§ 6).

These on that occasion are the four skandhas.

[64] What on that occasion are the two spheres ?

The sphere of mind, the sphere of [mental] states.

[65] What on that occasion is the sphere of mind (m a n ā y a t a n a ṃ) ?

Answer as for " thought ", § 6, *and for the* " skandha of consciousness ", § 63.

[66] What on that occasion is the sphere of [mental] states (d h a m m ā y a t a n a ṃ) ?

The skandhas of feeling, perception, synergies—this is on that occasion the sphere of [mental] states.

These are on that occasion the two spheres.

[67] What on that occasion are the two elements?

The element of representative intellection, the element of [mental] states.

[68] What on that occasion is the element of [purely] mental consciousness (m a n o v i ñ ñ ā ṇ a d h ā t u)?

Answer as for "thought", § 6; cf. §§ 63, 65.

[69] What on that occasion is the element of [mental] states (d h a m m a d h ā t u)?

The skandhas of feeling, of perception, of synergies, these are on that occasion the element of [mental] states.

These are on that occasion the two elements.

[70] What on that occasion are the three nutriments? [1]

The nutriment of contact, the nutriment of volition, the nutriment of consciousness.

[71] What on that occasion is the nutriment which is contact (p h a s s ā h a r o)?

Answer as for "contact", § 2.

[72] What on that occasion is the nutriment which is volition (m a n o s a ñ c e t a n ā h ā r o)?

The volition, the willing, the purposiveness which there is on that occasion—this is the representative cogitation that there then is.

[73] What on that occasion is the nutriment which is consciousness (v i ñ ñ ā n ā h ā r o)?

---

[1] These three incorporeal nutriments or foods, together with the fourth or corporeal food, are given in the Sutta Piṭaka: M. i, 261; S. ii, 11. In the A. they are not classified under the Catukka Nipāta; but in the Dasaka Nipāta (A. v, 136) ten species of ā h ā r o are named, which have no reference to the four. e.g. "appropriate action is the ā h ā r o of health". Buddhaghosa, dwelling on the etymology, calls them not so much conditions as supplementary causal "adducts" (ā - h ā r). Given e.g. a living individual, adduce contact, and you get feeling; adduce will, and you get the three "becomings" (in the universe of sense, etc.); adduce consciousness, and you get thinking and name-and-shape (Asl. 153).

Answer as for the " skandha of consciousness ", § 63.

These on that occasion are the three nutriments.

[74] What on that occasion are the eight faculties ?

The faculties of faith, energy, mindfulness, concentration, insight, ideation, happiness, life.

[75–82] What on that occasion is the faculty of faith . . life ?

Answers as in §§ 12–19 *respectively.*

These on that occasion are the eight faculties.

[83] What on that occasion is the fivefold Jhāna (pañcangikaṃ jhānaṃ)?

Applied and sustained thought, zest, ease, self-collectedness.

[84–8] What on that occasion is applied thought . . . self-collectedness ?

Answers as in §§ 7–11 *respectively.*

This on that occasion is the fivefold Jhāna.

[89] What on that occasion is the fivefold Path (pañcangiko maggo)?

Right views, right intention, right endeavour, right mindfulness, right concentration.

[90–4] What on that occasion are right views . . . is . . . right concentration ?

Answers as in §§ 20–4 *respectively.*

This on that occasion is the fivefold Path.

[95] What on that occasion are the seven powers ?

The power of faith, energy, mindfulness, concentration, insight, conscientiousness, the fear of blame.

[96–102] What on that occasion is the power of faith . . . the fear of blame ?

Answers as in §§ 25–31 *respectively.*

These on that occasion are the seven powers.

[103] What on that occasion are the three moral roots (tayo hetū)?

The absence of lust, of hate, and of dullness.

[104–6] What on that occasion is disinterestedness, . . . absence of dullness ?

Answers as in §§ 32–4 *respectively.*

These are on that occasion the three causes.

[107] What on that occasion is contact . . .
[108] feeling . . .
[109] perception . . .
[110] volition . . .
[111] thought . . .
[112] the skandha of feeling . . .
[113] the skandha of perception . . .
[114] the skandha of synergies . . .
[115] the skandha of consciousness . . .
[116] the sphere of mind . . .
[117] the faculty of mind . . .
[118] the element of (purely) mental consciousness . . .
[119] the sphere of (mental) states . . .
[120] the element of (mental) states, . . .
regarded as a single factor ?

Answers as in §§ 2–6, 60–3, 65, 65, 65, 66, 66, *respectively.*

These, or whatever other incorporeal, causally induced states there are on that occasion—these are states that are good.

[Here ends] the Summary [of the constituents of the First Main Type of Good Thoughts].

[The " Emptiness " Section (s u ñ ñ a t a v ā r o)].[1]

---

[1] On the significance of the term " emptiness ", see Introduction; cf. § 344. The significance of this section in the student's course of study seems to have consisted simply in this: That the interest being withdrawn from the nature and numbers of the particular constituents in each of the species of mental activity to which the thought-complex is reducible, emphasis is laid on the principle that this same thought-complex is an aggregate or combination of such phenomenal factors,

[121] Now, at that time there are
states (distinguishable constituents of the "thought"),

skandhas,	powers,
spheres,	causes,
elements,	contact,
nutriments,	feeling,
faculties,	perception,
Jhāna,	volition,
the Path,	thought,

the skandha of feeling,
the skandha of perception,
the skandha of synergies,
the skandha of consciousness,
the sphere of mind,
the faculty of mind,
the element of [purely] mental consciousness,
the sphere of [mental] states,
the element of [mental] states.

These, or whatever other incorporeal, causally induced states there are on that occasion—these are states that are good.

[122] What on that occasion are states ?

The skandhas of feeling, of perception, of synergies, of consciousness.

[123] What on that occasion are skandhas ?

Answer as in § 59.

[124–145] *Similar questions are then put respecting* "spheres", "elements", *and so on through the list of constituent species. The answers are identical with those given to similar*

---

and nothing more. "There are states of consciousness" (dhammā honti); that is (Asl. 155), "there is no permanent entity or self which acquires the states." "The states are to be understood phenomenally. There is no other being or existence or person or individual whatever."

questions in the previous "Summary", *viz. in* §§ 64, 67, 70, 74, 83, 89, 95, 103, *and* 107–20.

[Here ends] the "Emptiness" Section.

[Here ends] the First Main Type of Good Thoughts.

II.

[146] Which are the states that are good?

When a good thought concerning the sensuous universe has arisen by instigation,[1] a thought which is accompanied by gladness, associated with knowledge, and having, as its object, a sight, a sound, a smell, a taste, a touch, a [mental]

---

[1] S a s a n k h ā r e n a. Buddhaghosa's explanation of the term is terse and explicit. S a = co-; s a n k h ā r o = plan, instigation, grasping of means, or a cause (u s s ā h o, p a y o g o, u p ā y o, p a c c a y o - g a h a ṇ a ṃ). For instance, a bhikshu dwelling in the neighbourhood of a vihāra is inclined, when duty calls him to sweep the terrace round the sthūpa, wait on the elders, or listen to the Dhamma, to find the way too far, and shirk attendance. Second thoughts, as to the impropriety of not going, induce him to go. These are either self-prompted (a t t a n o v ā p a y o g e n a), or are due to the exhortation of another who, showing the disadvantage in shirking, and the profit in attending, says, "Come, do it!" And the "good thought", i.e. of course, the resolve to go, is said "to have arisen by way of a concomitant motive, by way of the taking hold of a cause". Asl. 156. Cf. the vaguer use in A. ii, 155, of the term sa- and a-sankhāraparinibbāyi.

This explanation is not discrepant with that of s a s a n - k h ā r i k o, given to Childers by Vijesinha Mudliar. He was not, I take it, so bad a Buddhist as to mean that an a s a n k h ā r i k a ṃ c i t t a ṃ was a thought in and for itself spontaneous, i.e. uncaused. He would mean only that the subject of the thought experienced it without being conscious of its mental antecedent *as such*, without p a c c a y a - g a h a ṇ a ṃ. In a c i t t a ṃ s a s a n k h ā r e n a, on the other hand, the thought presents itself in consciousness together with its mental conditions. In the Abhidhammattha-Sangaha the terms used in a similar connexion are a s a n k h ā r i k a ṃ and s a s a n k h ā r i k a ṃ. JPTS., 1884, p. 1 *et seq.*

state, or what not, then there is contact, feeling, etc.[1] [*here follows the list of "states" dealt with in* §§ 1–145 *and constituting the First Thought*]—these, or whatever other incorporeal, causally induced states there are on that occasion—these are states that are good . . .

[Here ends] the Second Thought.[2]

III.

[147] Which are the states that are good ?

When a good thought concerning the sensuous universe has arisen accompanied by gladness, disconnected with knowledge, and having as its object a sight, a sound, a smell, a taste, a touch, a [mental] state, or what not, then there is

contact, application,
feeling, sustained application,
perception, zest,
volition, ease,
thought, self-collectedness ;

the faculty of
faith, concentration,
energy, mind,
mindfulness, happiness,
life ;

right intention,[3] right mindfulness,

---

[1] In the text (§ 146), at the omitted repetitions indicated by ". . . pe . . ." reference is made to § 147. More correctly reference should be made to § 1. The second type-thought is in all respects (including Summary and "Emptiness" Section) identical with the first (Asl. 156), with the sole exception of the additional implication "by the prompting of a conscious motive". With the same exception the fourth, sixth, and eighth type-thoughts are identical with the third, fifth, and seventh respectively. Hence the reference in § 159 of the text should have been to § 157.

[2] K. reads Dutiyaṃ Cittaṃ, and so on for the eight.

[3] Sammādiṭṭhi should have been here omitted in the text, just as it is rightly omitted at the place of its second

right endeavour, right concentration;

the power of

faith, concentration,
energy, conscientiousness,
mindfulness, the fear of blame;

disinterestedness,
absence of hate,
absence of covetousness,
absence of malice;
conscientiousness,
fear of blame;

serenity, wieldiness,
buoyancy, fitness,
plasticity, rectitude,

both of mental factors and mind;

mindfulness, grasp,
quiet, balance.

These, or whatever other incorporeal, causally induced states there are on that occasion—these are states that are good.

[Summary, cf. § 58 *et seq.*]

[147*a*] Now, on that occasion

the skandhas are four,
the spheres are two,
the elements are two,
the nutriments are three,
the faculties are seven,[1]
the Jhāna is fivefold,
the Path is fourfold,
the powers are six,[2]

---

mention between a v y ā p ā d o and h i r i. Its absence from the third type of thought is involved in the qualifying phrase "disconnected with knowledge", just as "insight", "absence of dullness", etc., are. Cf. K. In 147*a* the Path is said to be *fourfold* only.

[1] That of "insight" being omitted.

[2] See preceding note.

the causes are two,[1]
contact, etc.

[*Continue as in* § 58.]

*   *   *   *

[148] What on that occasion is the skandha of synergies ?

The content of the sanskāra-skandha is the same as in the First Type of Thought, § 62,[2] *with the following omissions :*

" The faculty of insight,"
" right views,"
" the power of insight,"
" the absence of dullness,"
" intelligence,"
" intuition."

These are omitted as incompatible with the quality " disconnected with knowledge."

*   *   *   *

These, or whatever other incorporeal, etc.

*   *   *   *

[Here ends] the Third Type of Thought.[3]

IV.

[149] Which are the states that are good ?

When a good thought concerning the sensuous universe has arisen by instigation, a thought which is accompanied by gladness, disconnected with knowledge, and having as its object a sight, a sound, a smell, a taste, a touch, a [mental] state, or what not, then there is contact, etc. [*continue as in* § 147]—these, or whatever other incorporeal, causally

---

[1] " Absence of dullness " being omitted.

[2] In the text the reader is referred to § 62 without reservation, and is thereby landed in inconsistencies. K. enumerates the content of the skandha in full, omitting all those factors which are incompatible with a thought divorced from knowledge. I have thought it sufficient to name only these excluded factors.

[3] Placed erroneously in the text after § 147.

induced states there are on that occasion—these are states that are good. . . .[1]

* * * *

[Here ends] the Fourth Thought.

V.

[150] Which are the states that are good?

When a good thought concerning the sensuous universe has arisen, accompanied by indifference,[2] associated with knowledge, and having as its object a sight, a sound, a smell, a taste, a touch, a [mental] state, or what not, then there is contact, etc. [*continue as in* § 1, *but for* "zest" *and* "gladness" *substitute* "indifference" (u p e k k h ā), *and for* "the faculty of gladness" *substitute* "the faculty of indifference"].[3]

[151] What on that occasion is contact?

Answer as in § 2.

---

[1] So K. The text, by omitting not only the repetitions, but also the essentially distinctive factor s a s a n k h ā r e n a, renders the insertion of the "Fourth Thought" quite unintelligible.

Buddhaghosa gives a different illustration of this type of thought in harmony with its resemblance to and difference from the former c i t t a ṃ s a s a n k h ā r e n a, viz.: in its involving a pleasurable state of mind, but not any great understanding or discernment. Such is the thought of little boys, who, when their parents duck their heads to make them worship at a cetiya, willingly comply, though doing so without intelligent conviction. Asl. 156.

[2] U p e k k h ā. "This is impartiality (lit., middleness) in connexion with the object of thought, and implies a discriminative knowledge" (Asl. 157). Cf. its significance in the cultivation of Jhāna, § 165. In the Jhāna that may arise in connexion with the first type of thought, which is concomitant with "zest" and "ease", it is replaced by "self-collectedness". See § 83.

[3] Here, again, the excision, in the text, of practically the whole answer, and the reference to § 156, where the sixth thought is differentiated from this, the fifth thought, by the quality s a s a n k h ā r e n a, quite obscures the classification adopted in the original.

[152] What on that occasion is feeling?

The mental [condition] neither pleasant nor unpleasant, which, on that occasion, is born of contact with the appropriate element of [purely] mental consciousness; the sensation, born of contact with thought, which is neither easeful nor painful; the feeling, born of contact with thought, which is neither easeful nor painful—this is the feeling that there then is.

*　　*　　*　　*

[*Continue as in* §§ 4–8.]

[153] What on that occasion is indifference? [1]

Answer as in preceding reply, omitting the phrase "born of contact with the appropriate element of purely mental consciousness".

*　　*　　*　　*

[*Continue as in* §§ 11–17.]

[154] What on that occasion is the faculty of indifference?

Answer as in preceding reply. Continue as in §§ 19–57.

[Summary.]

[154*a*] Now, on that occasion

the skandhas are four,
the spheres are two,
the elements are two,
the nutriments are three,
the faculties are eight,
the Jhāna is fourfold,[2]
the Path is fivefold,
the powers are seven,
the causes are three,

---

[1] Substituted for "zest" and "ease", §§ 9, 10.

[2] Consisting presumably in "applied and sustained thought, indifference" (superseding "zest" and "ease") and "self-collectedness". Cf. § 83. The last-named attitude of mind does not usually figure in the Piṭakas as the culminating (or other) stage of Jhāna (cf. § 160 *et seq.*). In the Abhidhammattha-Sangaha, however, it does occur as such, and side by side also with "indifference". JPTS., 1884, p. 3; *Compendium*, p. 89: "individualization."

contact,

etc., etc. [cf. § 58],

the sphere of mental states is a single factor,

the element of mental states is a single factor.

These, or whatever other incorporeal, causally induced states there are on that occasion—these are states that are good. . . .

[*Continue as in* §§ 59–61.]

[155] What on that occasion is the skandha of synergies ? *Answer as in* § 62, *omitting* " joy ".[1]

*   *   *   *

[*Continue as in the Summary and* " Emptiness " *Section of the First Type of Thought.*]

[Here ends] the Fifth Type of Thought.

VI.

[156] Which are the states that are good ?

When a good thought concerning the sensuous universe has arisen, accompanied by indifference, associated with knowledge, by instigation, and having, as its object, a sight, a sound, a smell, a taste, a touch, a [mental] state, or what not, then there is contact, etc.

*   *   *   *

[*Continue as in the Fifth Type of Thought.*]

*   *   *   *

[Here ends] the Sixth Type of Thought.

VII.

[157] Which are the states that are good ?

When a good thought concerning the sensuous universe has arisen, accompanied by indifference, disconnected with knowledge, and having, as its object, a sight, a sound, a smell, a taste, a touch, a [mental] state, or what not, then there is contact, etc. . . .

*   *   *   *

---

[1] K. gives the skandha in full, omitting " zest ", zest and indifference being mutually exclusive.

[*Continue as in the Third Type of Thought, substituting* "indifference" *for* "zest" *and* "ease", *the* "faculty of disinterestedness" *for that of* "gladness", *and* "fourfold" *for* "fivefold Jhāna".[1]]

* * * *

[Summary.]

[157*a*] Now, on that occasion
the skandhas are four,
etc., etc.

[*Continue as in the Third Type of Thought, substituting* "fourfold" *for* "fivefold Jhāna."]

* * * *

[158] What on that occasion is the skandha of synergies? *The content of this skandha is the same as in the Third Type of Thought* (see § 148), *with the further omission of* "zest".

* * * *

[*Continue as in the First Type of Thought.*]

* * * *

[Here ends] the Seventh Type of Thought.

VIII.

[159] Which are the states that are good?

When a good thought concerning the sensuous universe has arisen, accompanied by indifference, disconnected with knowledge, by instigation, and having, as its object, a sight, a sound, a smell, a taste, a touch, a [mental] state, or what not, then there is contact, etc.

* * * * * *

[*Continue as in the Seventh Type of Thought.*]

* * * * * *

[Here ends] the Eighth Type of Thought.

[End of Chapter I on] the Eight Main Types of Thought concerning the Sensuous Universe.

(Here ends the Second Portion for Recitation.)

---

[1] Ñāṇindriyaṃ in the text should be manindriyaṃ.

CHAPTER II.

[Good in relation to the Universe of Form (r ū p ā - v a c a r a - k u s a l a ṃ).

Methods for inducing Jhāna.

I.

The Eight Artifices (a ṭ ṭ h a k a s i ṇ a ṃ).

1. The Earth Artifice p a ṭ h a v ī k a s i ṇ a ṃ).

(*a*) *The Fourfold System of Jhāna* c a t u k k a n a y o).]

[160] Which are the states that are good?

When, that he may attain to the heavens of Form,[1] he[2] cultivates the way [thereto], aloof from sensuous desires, aloof from evil ideas,[3] and so, by earth-gazing, enters[4] into

---

[1] See Introduction, pt. vi; also p. x.

[2] The subject of these states of consciousness.

[3] V i v i c c' e v a k ā m e h i, v i v i c c a a k u s a l e h i d h a m m e h i. Lit., "having separated one's self, having become without, having departed from" (Asl. 164). That is to say—again according to the Cy. (ibid.)—from the objects of sensual desires, and from corrupt desires themselves, respectively (v a t t h u k ā m ā, k i l e s a k ā m ā. Childers' Dictionary, s.v. k ā m o). The former phrase (v i v i c c' e v a k ā m e h i) includes the whole psychological realm of sense-presentation (k ā y o, or the three skandhas of feeling, perception, and synergies); the latter, d h a m m e h i, referring to the realm of ideation (c i t t a ṃ) only.

The Cy. repudiates the idea that the emphatic enclitic e v a, occurring only in the former of the two phrases, renders the latter less important, and quotes, in support, the opening words of the Cūla-sīhanāda Discourse (M. i, 63).

[4] P a ṭ h a v ī k a s i n a ṃ. The first of the Karmasṭhāna methods, or quasi-hypnotic devices for attaining to temporary rapt oblivion of the outer world. The percept of the circle of mould induces the vivid image (n i m i t t a ṃ), and therefore Jhāna supervenes.

and abides in[1] the First Jhāna (the first rapt meditation), wherein is thinking applied and sustained,[2] which is born of solitude,[3] and full of zest[4] and ease—then the contact, the feeling . . . the grasp, the balance, which arise in him, or whatever other[5] incorporeal, causally induced states that there are on that occasion—these are states that are good.

* * * * * *

Continue as in the First Type of Thought relating to the sensuous universe, including the Summary and "Emptiness" *divisions.*[6]

---

[1] i.e. sustains the mood indefinitely. The Cy. quotes the Vibhanga as paraphrasing the term by the same expressions, "going on," etc., as are used to describe above (§ 19) the "faculty of life".

[2] Savitakkaṃ savicāraṃ. Leaving the negative essential conditions of Jhāna, we pass to the positive features (Asl. 166). The meditation progresses by means of these two in particular, as a tree does by its flowers and fruit. According to the Vibhanga, they reveal the determined resolves of the individual student (puggalādhiṭṭhānā). (Ibid.)

[3] According to the Cy., the solitude is rather moral than physical, and means "born in the seclusion which the student creates by thrusting from his heart the five hindrances (ibid.; *infra*, § 1152). According as it is said in the Peṭaka (Peṭakopadesa), concentration opposes sensual desire; zest opposes malice; the onset of intellect opposes stolidity and torpor; ease opposes excitement and worry; sustained thought opposes perplexity or doubt (Asl. 165). See D. i, 73, where the hindrances are explicitly mentioned in connexion with Jhāna; also the notes in Rhys Davids's *Dialogues of the Buddha*, i, p. 84.

[4] i.e. zest of the fourth species, pharaṇa-pīti (Asl. 166), § 9; also compare the passage just referred to, D. i, 73. See above, so imam eva kāyaṃ . . . abhisandeti . . . parippharati.

[5] These are said to be the four first—desire, etc.—of the nine named above, p. 5, n. 1 (Asl. 168).

[6] So the Cy. (ibid.). In the text, therefore, the reader should have been referred, not to (147), but to (1). K. indicates the elision simply by a . . . pe . . . at the point corresponding to the comma before "or whatever . . ." in my translation, followed by "ime dhammā kusalā".

I am inclined, however, to think that the detailed catechism as to the nature of the various dhammas, such as

[161] Which are the states that are good?

When, that he may attain to the heavens of Form, he cultivates the way [thereto], suppressing the working of applied and sustained thinking, and so, by earth-gazing, enters into and abides in the Second Jhāna (the second rapt meditation), which is self-evolved,[1] born of concentration, full of zest and ease, in that, set free from the working of applied and sustained thinking, the mind grows calm and sure,[2] dwelling on high [3]—then the contact, the feeling, the

---

occurs at §§ 2–57, is not to be understood as included in the passage elided, either here or in the remaining Jhānas. K. does not repeat the . . . p e . . . cited above at the corresponding point in the three remaining Jhānas, where the Summary is not elided, but given. Nor does it give the . . . p e . . . which stands in the text, in §§ 163, 165, before T a s m i ṃ k h o p a n a s a m a y e. Similarly it omits the . . . p e . . . given in the text at the corresponding points in the formulæ for the "five-fold Jhāna", § 168 *et seq.*

[1] A j j h a t t a ṃ, i.e. according to the Cy. (169), a t t a n o j ā t a ṃ, a t t a s a n t ā n e n i b b a t t a ṃ; according to the Vibhanga, p a c c a t t a ṃ. It is not quite clear to me what is the special force of the term in just this Jhāna, unless it be that the "earth-gazing" is not now continued—the individual becoming more rapt from external determinants of consciousness, more susceptible to purely subjective conditions.

[2] S a m p a s ā d a n a ṃ, tranquillizing, paraphrased in the Cy. (ibid.) by s a d d h ā, assurance or faith (above, § 12). It is a term for Jhāna itself, blent as it is with the whole contemplative discipline, "just as cloth steeped in purple is 'purple'"—to adapt the commentator's simile to our idiom. The following word c e t a s o, "of the mind," may be taken either with this term, or with that next after it, e k o d i b h ā v a ṃ (ibid.).

[3] In the text read e k o d i b h ā v a ṃ. Buddhaghosa's comments on this expression contain the original of the Thera Subhūti's quotation given in Childers. The substance of them is that the c e t o (intellect, mind, heart), no longer overwhelmed or encumbered by v i t a k k o and v i c ā r o, rises up slowly pre-eminent (e k o = s e ṭ ṭ h o or a s a h ā y o) in its meditative concentration, or s a m ā d h i, this term being synonymous with e k o d i b h ā v a ṃ (s a m ā d h i s s' e t a ṃ a d h i v a c a n a ṃ). The discursive intellection of the First Jhāna, troubling the c e t o, as waves rendering water turgid,

perception, the volition, the thought, the joy, the ease, the self-collectedness, the faculties of faith, energy, mindfulness, concentration, insight, mind, happiness, and life, the right views,[1] right endeavour, . . .[2] the grasp, the balance that arises—these, or whatever other incorporeal, causally induced states that there are on that occasion—these are states that are good.

[Summary.]

[161*a*] Now, on that occasion
the skandhas are four,
the spheres are two,
the elements are two,
the nutriments are three,
the faculties are eight,
the Jhāna is threefold,[3]
the Path is fourfold,[4]
the powers are seven,
the causes are three,
contact counts as a single factor,
etc., etc.

[*Continue as in* § 58 *et seq.*]

*　　*　　*　　*

---

has in the Second Jhāna sunk to rest. And this uplifting is said (the commentator emphasizes) of ceto, and not of an individual entity, nor of a living soul (na sattassa na jīvassa). See Morris's note, JPTS., 1885, p. 32.

[1] Sammāsankappo is here, its usual order of place, omitted. It involves vitakko; see § 7.

[2] The reference in the text to § 157 cannot be right. The subject has not yet banished pleasurable emotion, and attained to the calm of indifference ; nor is his state of mind " disconnected with knowledge ". The type of thought, as to its remaining components, is still the first, i.e. that of § 1.

[3] Cf. § 83. " Applied " and " sustained thought " are now suppressed.

[4] Cf. § 89. " Right intention," as involving " applied thought ", is now suppressed. The mind is no longer occupied with overt activities concerned with this life.

[162] What on that occasion is the skandha of synergies?

Contact,	zest,
volition,	self-collectedness;
the faculties of	
faith,	concentration,
energy,	insight,
mindfulness,	life;

right views,
right endeavour,
etc., etc.

[*Continue as in* § 62 *et seq.*[1]]

[163] Which are the states that are good?

When, that he may attain to the heavens of Form, he cultivates the way [thereto], and further, through the waning of all passion for zest,[2] holds himself indifferent,[3] the while, mindful and self-aware,[4] he experiences in his sense-consciousness[5] that ease whereof the Noble Ones[6] declare: "He that is indifferent and watchful dwelleth at ease"—and so, by earth-gazing, enters into and abides in the Third Jhāna —then the contact, the feeling, the perception, the volition, the thought, the ease, the self-collectedness, the faculties of faith, energy, mindfulness,[7] concentration, insight, mind,

---

[1] Including, presumably, the "Emptiness" Section, as in the case of the First Jhāna.

[2] Pītiyā ca virāgā, "meaning either distaste for zest or the transcending of it." The ca indicates the progressive continuity from the preceding to the present Jhāna (Asl. 171).

[3] Upekkhako. He looks on from the standpoint of one who has arrived, says the Cy. (172). As we might say:—

"E terra magnum alterius spectare laborem."

Buddhaghosa expatiates here on the ten kinds of upekkhā (enumerated in Hardy, *Man. Budhism*, 505).

[4] Sampajāno.

[5] Kāyena.

[6] See *infra*, § 1003, n. 6.

[7] Omitted in the text, but not so in K. The context requires its insertion.

happiness, and life, the right views, right endeavour,[1] etc. . . . the grasp, the balance that arises [2]—these, or whatever other incorporeal, causally induced states that there are on that occasion—these are states that are good.

[Summary.]

[163*a*] Now, on that occasion
the skandhas are four,
the spheres are two,
the elements are two,
the nutriments are three,
the faculties are eight,
the Jhāna is twofold,[3]
the Path is fourfold,[4]
the powers are seven,
the causes are three,
contact counts as a single factor,
etc., etc.
[*Continue as in* § 58.]

* * * *

[164] What on that occasion is the skandha of synergies ?
Contact,
volition,
self-collectedness ;
the faculties of
faith, concentration,
energy, insight,
mindfulness, life ;
right views, right endeavour,
etc., etc.
[*Continue as in* § 62.]

* * * *

---

[1] Sammāsati, inserted in the text, but not in the right order, is of course required by the context, but is, here and in K., assumed in the " etc."

[2] § 157, to which the reader is referred in the text, is obviously wrong. § 1 would be nearer the mark.

[3] " Ease " remains and " self-collectedness ".

[4] Cf. § 161*a*, n. 2.

[165] Which are the states that are good?

When, that he may attain to the heavens of Form, he cultivates the way [thereto], and, by the putting away of ease and by the putting away of ill, by the passing away of (any) gladness or sorrow [1] he was feeling, he thus, by earth-gazing, enters into and abides in the Fourth Jhāna (the fourth rapt meditation) of that utter purity of mindfulness which comes of indifference,[2] where no ease is felt nor any ill—then the contact, the feeling, the perception, the volition, the thought, the indifference, the self-collectedness, the faculties of faith, energy, mindfulness, concentration, insight, mind, indifference, and life, the right views, the right endeavour, etc. . . .

[*Continue as in* § 163.]

* * * *

---

[1] "Ease" and "ill", according to the Cy., are k ā y i k a ṃ, or relating to the three skandhas of feeling, etc.—relating to the mental factors. "Gladness" and "sorrow" (s o m a n-a s s a ṃ, d o m a n a s s a ṃ) relate to consciousness in general. "Gladness" is the last of these to be transcended; the others have been expelled in the course of the previous stages of Jhāna (Asl. 175, 176). But all four are here enumerated, as if all were only in this Fourth Jhāna transcended, in order to show more clearly, by the method of exhaustive elimination, what is the subtle and elusive nature of that third species of feeling termed "neutral" (a d u k k h a m - a s u k h ā), or "disinterested" (u p e k k h ā)—the zero point, or line, as we should say, of hedonic quantity. The Cy. then gives the simile of selecting heads of cattle by elimination of the rest of the herd, which Hardy cites (ibid. 177; *East. Monachism*, 270; Asl. 175–7).

[2] U p e k k h ā - s a t i p a r i s u d d h i ṃ. According to the Vibhanga, the mindfulness that is made pure stands for all the other elements present in consciousness, which have also been brought into clear relief, as it were, by the calm medium of equanimity. The simile is then adduced, given also in Hardy (op. cit. 271), of the moon by day and by night. U p e k k h ā is latent in consciousness in the other stages of Jhāna, but rendered colourless by the radiance of intellectual and emotional exercise, as the crescent moon during the day, though present in the sky, is dimmed by the sun's splendour (Asl. 178).

[Summary.

[165*a*] Now, on that occasion
the skandhas are four,
the spheres are two,
the elements are two,
the nutriments are three,
the faculties are eight,
the Jhāna is twofold,[1]
the Path is fourfold,
the powers are seven,
the causes are three,
contact counts as a single factor,
etc., etc.
[*Continue as in* § 58, *etc.*]

* * * *

[166] What on that occasion is the skandha of synergies? *Answer as in* § 164.[2]

* * * *

[Here ends] the Fourfold System of Jhāna.

(*b*) The Fivefold System of Jhāna (pañcakanayo).][3]

[167] *The First Jhāna. Question and answer as in the fourfold course,* § 160.

---

[1] Namely, "indifference" and "self-collectedness" (Asl. 179). Else one would have looked to find ekangikaṃ jhānaṃ.

[2] The printed text omits satindriyaṃ, though it is explicitly required by the context. K. gives it.

[3] Jhāna is usually alluded to in the Piṭakas in the fourfold order. The fivefold division is obtained by the successive, instead of simultaneous, elimination of vitakko and vicāro. According to the Cy., it was optional to the teacher, after the example of the Buddha, to use either at his discretion, adapting himself to the particular mental state of his pupils, or having a view to the effective flow of his discourse. A passage is quoted from the Piṭakas (A. iv, 310 f.; cf. S. iv, 360; D. iii, 219; M. iii, 162), where samādhi is distinguished as (1) having vitakko and vicāro, (2) having only the latter, (3) having neither.

[168] Which are the states that are good?

When, that he may attain to the heavens of Form, he cultivates the way [thereto], and so, by earth-gazing, enters into and abides in the Second Jhāna (the second rapt meditation) wherein is no application of mind, but only of sustained thinking—which is born of concentration, and is full of zest and ease—then the contact, the feeling, the perception, the volition, the thought, the sustained thinking, the zest, the ease, the self-collectedness, etc. . . .

[*Continue as for the Second Jhāna in* § 161.]

[Summary.]

[168*a*] Now, on that occasion
the skandhas are four,
the spheres are two,
the elements are two,
the nutriments are three,
the faculties are eight,
the Jhāna is fourfold,
the Path is fourfold,
etc., etc.

[*Continue as in* § 58.]

*   *   *   *

[169] What on that occasion is the skandha of synergies? Contact, volition, sustained thinking, zest, etc. . . .

[*Continue as in* § 162.]

*   *   *   *

[170–5] The Third, Fourth, and Fifth Jhānas.

[*These are identical in formulation with the Second, Third, and Fourth Jhānas of the Fourfold System. Questions and answers as in* §§ 161–6.]

[Here ends] the Fivefold System of Jhāna.

[(*c*) The Four Modes of Progress (catasso paṭipadā).][1]

[176] Which are the states that are good?

When, that he may attain to the heavens of Form, he cultivates the way [thereto], aloof from sensuous desires, aloof from evil ideas, and so, by earth-gazing, enters into and abides in the First Jhāna . . . progress being painful and intuition sluggish—then the contact[2] . . . the balance that arises—these . . . are states that are good.

[177][3] . . . [*or*] when . . . he . . . so enters into and

[1] A. ii, 149 f.; v, 63. It has been seen that, before the several stages of Jhāna could be attained to, the student had to purge and discipline himself in specific ways—elimination of all attention to mundane matters, elimination of reflection on these, and so on. The special stage of Jhāna supervened after each act of self-control and intensified abstraction. In these processes there was an earlier and a subsequent stage called—at least in the later books—upacāra and appanā respectively. The effective cognition linking these two was an exercise of paññā which, in the text, is known as abhiññā ("intuition"), probably the intuitive or subconscious fetch of the mind to compass the desired appanā, or conception. Now, whether the preparatory abstraction was easy or difficult, and whether the constructive generalizing effort was sluggish or vigorous, depended on the moral temperament and the mental ability respectively of the individual student (Asl. 182–4). See the double explanation in A. ii, 149–52, where the swiftness or sluggishness of intuition in both accounts depends on the acuteness or flabbiness of the five faculties of faith, energy, mindfulness, concentration, insight. The ease or difficulty in self-abstraction depends, in the first explanation, on whether the student is by nature passionate, malignant, dull, or the reverse of these three. In the second account progress is painful if he have filled his consciousness with the disciplinary concepts of the Foul Things (*vide* below, § 263), Disgust with the World, Impermanence and Death; easy if he simply work out the Four Jhānas.

On the varying import of abhiññā, lit. super-knowledge (which occurs in no other connexion in the present work), see *Dialogues of the Buddha*, iii, 257. On upacāra and appanā, see *Yogāvacara's Manual*, p. xi; Visuddhi Magga, 137 f.; *Comp.* 55, 129.

[2] Cf. § 1.

[3] The same question is to be understood as repeated in each section.

abides in the First Jhāna . . . progress being painful, but intuition quick . . .

[178] . . . [*or*] when . . . he . . . so enters into and abides in the First Jhāna . . . progress being easy, but intuition sluggish . . .

[179] . . . [*or*] when . . . he . . . so enters into and abides in the First Jhāna . . . progress being easy and intuition quick—then the contact, etc. . . the balance that arises—these . . . are states that are good.

[180] *These four combinations are repeated in the case of the 2nd to the 4th Jhānas on the Fourfold System, and of the 2nd to the 5th on the Fivefold System.*

[Here end] the Four Modes of Progress.

[(*d*) The Four Objects of Thought (c a t t ā r i ā r a m m a ṇ ā n i).] [1]

[181] Which are the states that are good?

When, that he may attain to the heavens of Form, he cultivates the way [thereto], and so, aloof from sensuous desires, aloof from evil ideas, by earth-gazing, enters into and abides in the First Jhāna (the first rapt meditation), wherein is application and sustaining of thought, which is born of solitude, and is full of zest and ease, but which is limited, and has a limited object of thought—then the contact [2] . . . the balance that arises—these . . . are states that are good.

[182] . . . [*or*] when . . . the First Jhāna [3] . . . is limited, but has an object of thought capable of infinite extension . . .

---

[1] That is to say, the percepts or concepts on which the student, in seeking to induce Jhāna, fixes his attention are here classified as having the potentiality to induce a weak or a lofty mood of rapt contemplation. Buddhaghosa describes the former kind of object as having the shallowness of a little sieve, or pot-cover (Asl. 184). See also below, §§ 1019–24.

[2] Cf. § 1.

[3] In the following condensed passages the question and answer in the text respectively coincides with, and commences like, the precedent given in § 181.

[183] . . . [*or*] when . . . the First Jhāna . . . is capable of infinite extension, but has a limited object of thought . . .

[184] . . . [*or*] when . . . the First Jhāna . . . is capable of infinite extension, and has an object of thought capable of infinite extension—then the contact, etc. . . . the balance that arises, these . . . are states that are good.

[185] *These four combinations are repeated in the case of the 2nd to the 4th Jhānas on the Fourfold System, and of the 1st to the 5th*[1] *Jhānas on the Fivefold System.*

[Here end] the Four Objects of Thought.

[(*e*) (= *c* and *d*) The Sixteenfold Combination (soḷasakkhattukaṃ).]

[186] Which are the states that are good?

When, that he may attain to the heavens of Form, he cultivates the way [thereto], aloof from sensuous desires, aloof from evil ideas, and so, by earth-gazing, enters into and abides in the first Jhāna . . .

where progress is painful and intuition sluggish,

which is limited, and has a limited object of thought . . .

[187] . . . [*or*] which is limited, but has an object of thought capable of infinite extension . . .

[188] . . . [*or*] which is capable of infinite extension, but has a limited object of thought . . .

[189] . . . [*or*] which is capable of infinite extension, and has an object of thought capable of infinite extension . . .

---

[1] In the text, § 185, after paṭhamaṃ jhānaṃ read . . . pe . . . pañcamaṃ jhānaṃ. So K. Cf. § 180. Again, after avikkhepo hoti supply . . . pe . . .

[190] . . . [*or*] where progress is painful, but intuition is quick, which is limited, and has a imited object of thought . . .

[191] . . . [*or*] . . . etc. [*Continue for* §§ 191–3 *as in* §§ 187–9.]

[194] . . . [*or*] where progress is easy, but intuition sluggish, which is limited,[1] and has a limited object of thought . . .

[195] . . . [*or*] . . . etc. [*Continue for* §§ 195–7 *as above.*]

[198] . . . [*or*] where progress is easy and intuition quick, which is limited, and has a limited object of thought . . .

[199] [*Continue for* §§ 199–201 *as above.*]

[202] [*These sixteen combinations are repeated in the case of the* 2*nd to the* 4*th Jhānas on the Fourfold System, and of the* 1*st to the* 5*th Jhānas on the Fivefold System.*]

[Here ends] the Sixteenfold Combination.

[2. The Remaining Seven Artifices *which may also be developed in* sixteenfold combination (a ṭ ṭ h a k a s i ṇ a ṃ s o ḷ a s a k k h a t t u k a ṃ).] [2]

---

[1] In the text supply p a r i t t a ṃ before p a r i t t ā r a m m a ṇ a ṃ.

[2] The first artifice for the induction of Jhāna having been that of earth-gazing (see above, *passim*). In the Sutta Piṭaka—viz. in the Mahā Sakuluḍāyi-Sutta (M. ii, p. 14), and in the Jhāna Vagga (A. i, 41)—ten kasiṇas are enumerated, those omitted in the Dhammasaṅgaṇi being the kasiṇas of consciousness (v i ñ ñ ā ṇ a) and space (ā k ā s a). The fact of the omission and the nature of the two omitted kasiṇas are commented on by Buddhaghosa (Asl. 186). He explains the omission of the former by its being identical with the second of the four Ā r u p p a j h ā n ā n i given in §§ 265–8, and that of the latter through its ambiguity. For either it amounts to the "yellow" kasiṇa (sun-lit space), or it amounts to the first Ā r u p p a j h ā n a

[203] Which are the states that are good?

When, that he may attain to the heavens of Form, he cultivates the way [thereto], aloof from sensuous desires, aloof from evil ideas, and so, by the artifice of

water . . .
fire . . .
air . . .
blue-black . . .
yellow . . .
red . . .
white . . .

enters into and abides in the First Jhāna . . . then the contact, etc., that arises—these . . . are states that are good.

[Here ends] the Sixteenfold Combination in the case of the seven remaining artifices for induction.

[II.

The Stations of Mastery [1] (abhibhāyatanāni).

1. "Forms as Limited" (rūpāni parittāni).

(*a* and *b*) Fourfold and Fivefold Jhāna.]

[204] Which are the states that are good?

(§ 265). The Ceylon tradition has ten kasiṇas also, but admits āloka (light) instead of viññāṇa. And it includes yet another quasi-kasiṇa in the shape of a bhūta-kasiṇa, or the four elements taken collectively, after each has been separately dwelt upon. See Yogāvacara's Manual, 1896, pp. 48–52.

[1] Eight "stations" or "positions of mastery" are given in the Mahā-parinibbāna-Sutta (pp. 28, 29; see SBE. xi, 49, 50; Dialogues, ii, 118; and in A. iv, 305), but the formulæ of the first four differ slightly from those in our text. The Cy. draws attention to this discrepancy (Asl. 189). In the Suttanta the æsthetic aspect of the objects perceived is taken into account in all four stations, the specific difference replacing it in two of them being the conscious dwelling on some part of one's own bodily frame or rūpaskandha. In the Dhammasangaṇi this consciousness is excluded from all the stations. To teach by way of its inclusion and exclusion is called "merely a *jeu d'esprit* in the Master's discourse" (desanā-vilāsa-mattam eva). See following note.

When, that he may attain to the heavens of Form, he cultivates the way [thereto], and, unconscious of any part of his corporeal self,[1] but seeing external objects to be limited, gets the mastery over them with the thought "I know, I see!"[2] and so, aloof from sensuous desires, aloof from evil ideas, enters into and abides in the First Jhāna, etc. . . . then the contact, etc., that arises—these . . . are states that are good.

[205] [*Repeat in the case of the 2nd to the 4th Jhāna on the Fourfold System, and of the 2nd to the 5th Jhāna on the Fivefold System.*]

[(*c*) *The Four Modes of Progress.*]

[206–10] *Repeat the four combinations of* progress *as* painful *or* easy, *and of* intuition *as* sluggish *or* quick *set out in* §§ 176–80, *substituting for* "earth-gazing" *the Mastery-formula just stated.*

[(*d*) The Two Objects of Thought.]

[211–13] *Repeat, substituting for* "earth-gazing" *the Mastery-formula,* § 181, *where the Jhāna* "is limited, and has a limited object of thought", *and* § 183, *where the Jhāna*

---

[1] Ajjhattaṃ arūpasaññī (=na rūpasaññī). This rendering is in accordance with Buddhaghosa's comments (Asl. 188, 189, 191). The student, either because he has tried and failed, or because he did not wish to try, has not induced Jhāna by way of fixing attention on his own hair or the rest. Cf. the Mahā Rāhulovāda-Sutta (M. i, 62), where the individual's rūpa-skandha is fully set forth with reference to the four elements, ajjhattikā paṭhavīdhātu, etc., beginning with "hair" and the rest. Cf. § 248 n.

[2] The external objects in question are contemplated on the kasiṇa system (Asl. 188). And just as a man of vigorous digestion bolts a spoonful of rice, so the aspirant after sublime truth swiftly and easily transcends the initial act of external perception when the object is insignificant, and brings forth the desiderated ecstasy (appanā).

"is capable of infinite extension, but has a limited object of thought".[1]

[(*e* = *c* and *d*) The Eightfold Combination (a ṭ ṭ h a k-k h a t t u k a ṃ.][2]

[214–21] *Repeat, with the same substitution,* §§ 186, 188, 190, 192, 194, 196, 198, *and* 200 *of the Sixteenfold Combination.*

[222] *Repeat these eight combinations in the case of each of the remaining Jhānas.*

[2. "Forms as limited and as beautiful or ugly"[3] (r ū p ā n i p a r i t t ā n i s u v a ṇ ṇ a - d u b b a ṇ ṇ ā n i).

(*a*) and (*b*)]

[223] Which are the states that are good?

When, that he may attain to the heavens of Form, he cultivates the way thereto, and, unconscious of any part of his corporeal self, but seeing external objects to be limited, and to be beautiful or ugly, gets the mastery over them with the thought, "I know, I see!" and so, aloof

---

[1] The "objects of thought" are here the kasiṇas essentially discerned to be "limited" or insignificant. Hence two, not four varieties; and hence eight, not sixteen combinations. The term a p p a m ā ṇ a ṃ connoting merely a *relative*, not an absolute infinitude, there is only a difference of degree in the depth, purifying efficacy, or what not, of the Jhāna attained to. The same illustrative figure is accordingly used, varied in degree. The *gourmand*, discontented with a small dish of rice, demands more and more. So the aspirant, aiming at perfect self-concentration, refuses to call that infinite which seems so (ibid.).

[2] So K.

[3] The general æsthetic designations of s u v a ṇ ṇ a ṃ and d u b b a ṇ ṇ a ṃ are in the Cy. paraphrased by p a r i s u d d h a ṃ and its negative. Just as a grasp of the limited nature of visible things was held to be due to much application of thought, and the notion of "infinite" to be a cure for dullness, so the beautiful and the ugly were medicine for enmity and lust respectively. The appropriateness of it all is discussed in the Visuddhi Magga (p. 101 f.; cf. Asl. 189).

from sensuous desires, aloof from evil ideas, enters into and abides in the First Jhāna, etc. . . . then the contact, etc., that arises—these . . . are states that are good.

[224] *Repeat in the case of each of the remaining Jhānas.*

Develop in eightfold combination.

[3. "Forms as infinite" (r ū p ā n i a p p a m ā ṇ ā n i).[1]

(*a*) and (*b*)]

[225] Which are the states that are good?

When, that he may attain to the heavens of Form, he cultivates the way thereto, and, unconscious of any part of his corporeal self, but seeing external objects to be infinite, gets the mastery over them with the thought, "I know, I see!" and so, aloof from sensuous desires, etc.

[*Continue as in* § 204.]

[226] *Repeat in the case of each of the remaining Jhānas.*

[(*c*) The Four Modes of Progress.]

[227–31] *Repeat* §§ 206–10, *substituting* "infinite" *for* "limited".

[(*d*) The Two Objects of Thought.]

[232–4] *Repeat, with the same substitution as in* (*c*), §§ 211–13.

[(*e* = *c* and *d*) The Eightfold Combination.]

[235–42] *Develop, with the same substitution as in* (*c*) *and* (*d*), *after the manner of* §§ 187, 189, *and so on to* § 201.

[243] *Repeat these eight combinations in the case of each of the remaining Jhānas.*

---

[1] See note on §§ 211–13. Taken in order, Buddhaghosa's comment there reproduced applies to that part of the text. According to the context, it might better apply here, where the external forms or kasiṇa-objects are now contemplated as "infinite". The reflection, however, applies to either passage.

[4. "Forms as infinite and as beautiful or ugly" (r ū p ā n i a p p a m ā ṇ ā n i s u v a ṇ ṇ a - d u b b a ṇ ṇ ā n i).[1]

(*a*) and (*b*)]

[244] *Repeat* § 223, *substituting* "infinite" *for* "limited".

[245] *Repeat in the case of each of the remaining Jhānas.*

Develop in eightfold combination.

[5. "Forms as indigo," etc. (r ū p ā n i n ī l ā n i).[2]

(*a*)]

[246] Which are the states that are good?

When, that he may attain to the heavens of Form, he cultivates the way thereto, and, unconscious of any part of his corporeal self, but seeing external objects which are indigo, indigo in colour, indigo in visible expanse,[3] indigo in luminousness, gets the mastery over them with the thought, "I know, I see!" and so, aloof from sensuous desires, etc.

[*Continue as in* § 204.]

*   *   *   *

---

[1] "By the mere laying to heart that 'it is beautiful', how is there deliverance?" Pṭs. ii, 39; cf. hereon, Asl. 191.

[2] It is well-known that it is as difficult to determine the range of colour indicated by n ī l a ṃ as to decide the colour-value of the word γλαυκός. Like the latter term, n ī l a ṃ may originally have referred more to lustre than to tinge, meaning darkly lustrous, jetty, or nigrescent. Any way, it is not plausible to render the term by "blue" when one is referred to human hair or bile (p i t t a ṃ) as instances of it in the human body. See note 2 to § 248. In Jāt. iii, 138, hair-dye or hair-wash is called n ī l i y a ṃ—much, perhaps, as we speak of "blacking" or "russet polish" for shoes. This implies that the colour called n ī l a ṃ was, if not the usual, at least the desiderated colour of human hair. In Jāt. vi, 126, it is applied to space (ā k ā s o). Elsewhere it is applied to clouds, hills, and trees. Possibly our own colour-parallels in these respects are a modern development. Cf. Havelock Ellis in *Contemporary Review*, vol. lxix, p. 727; *Bud. Psy.*, 49.

[3] N ī l a n i d a s s a n a ṃ, indicating, according to the Cy. (190), a uniform sheet of blue without break. The colours in this and following sections may reside in a flower, a piece of cloth, or some other basis.

[6–8. "Forms as yellow," etc. (r ū p ā n i p ī t ā n i).]

[247] *Repeat* § 246, *substituting for* "indigo, indigo in colour", etc., "yellow", "red", *and* "white" [1] *successively*.

Develop these Stations of Mastery in the Sixteenfold Combination.

[III.

The Three First Deliverances (t ī ṇ i v i m o k k h ā n i.[2]]

1.

[248] When, that he may attain to the heavens of Form, he cultivates the way thereto, and, conscious of his bodily form,[3] sees bodily forms, and so, aloof from sensuous desires,

---

[1] The remaining three English colour-names may match the Pali terms as loosely as in the previous case. Cf. SBE. xi, loc. cit. In the Sutta there translated instances of the colours are given, and, curiously enough, "white" is illustrated, not by milk, or the distant Himâlaya snows, but by the morning star—? lustrous.

[2] Followed by four more of the Eight Deliverances in the next chapter, §§ 265–68. The eighth alone is not given in the present work. See *Dialogues* ii, 119; A. iv, 306. According to the Cy. (190), the term "deliverance" (v i m o k k h a, or a d h i m u c c a n a ṃ) is used to denote the being set free from "adverse conditions" and their seductive fascinations, so that the attention is sustained with all the detachment and confidence that the child feels who is borne on his father's hip, his little limbs dangling, their clutch unneeded.

[3] R ū p ī. Judging by the Cy. (190), this is equivalent to a j j h a t t a ṃ r ū p a s a ñ ñ ī—that is, to the opposite of the term "unconscious of any part of his corporeal self", the attitude prescribed in the Stations of Mastery, *supra* § 204 *et seq.* The p a r i k a m m a ṃ selected is "one's own hair and the rest". If a n ī l a - p a r i k a m m a ṃ is sought, attention is fixed on the hair or bile (p i t t a ṃ) or the pupil of the eye. If the induction is to be by way of yellow, fat or skin may be taken; if red, flesh, blood, or the tongue, or the palms of the hands or feet, etc.; if white, the teeth, nails, or white of the eye. At the same time "he sees external bodily forms in the n ī l a or other kasiṇa *with the Jhāna-vision*" (j h ā n a c a k k h u n ā p a s s a t i).

How this dual effort of intense attention was effected I do not pretend to understand, but Buddhaghosa more than once refers us for a more detailed account to the Visuddhi Magga.

aloof from evil ideas, enters into and abides in the First Jhāna, etc. . . . then the contact, etc., which arises, these . . . are states that are good.

2.

[249] When, that he may attain to the heavens of Form, he cultivates the way thereto, and, unconscious of his corporeal self, sees external bodily forms, and so, aloof from sensuous desires, etc.

[*Continue as in preceding section.*]

3.

[250] When, that he may attain to the heavens of Form, he cultivates the way thereto, and, with the thought, "How fair it is!"[1] aloof from sensuous desires, etc.

[*Continue as in the first Deliverance.*]

These three Deliverances may also be developed in Sixteenfold Combination.

[IV.

The Four Jhānas of the Divine States (c a t t ā r i b r a h m a v i h ā r a j h ā n ā n i).[2]

1. Love (m e t t ā).

(*a*) Fourfold Jhāna.]

[251] Which are the states that are good?

When, that he may attain to the heavens of Form, he

---

[1] That is to say, says the Cy. (191), not the conscious acquirement of the ecstasy (a p p a n ā), but the consciousness of the perfection or purity of colour or lustre in the particular kasiṇa is here meant. (The reading should, of course, be s u b h a n t i .) And this æsthetic consciousness is declared by Buddhaghosa to quicken the sense of emancipation from morally adverse conditions analogously to that perception of moral beauty which may be felt in the Divine States of the following sections. According to the Paṭisambhidā-magga, here quoted, when, on pervading the whole world with heart of love, pity, etc., all feeling of aversion from living beings is rooted out, the student is struck with the glory of the idea, and works his deliverance.

[2] On these four great exercises, see Rhys Davids, SBE. xi, 201, n.; and on their emancipating efficacy, M. i, 38.

cultivates the way thereto, and so, aloof from sensuous desires, aloof from evil ideas, enters into and abides in the

---

Buddhaghosa again refers the reader to his Visuddhi Magga for a more detailed commentary (*vide* chap. ix, and cf. Hardy, *Eastern Monachism*, p. 243 *et seq.*). The four are set out here only under the "Suddhika" formulæ—that is, under heads (*a*) and (*b*). But (*c*), or the Modes of Progress, as well as (*d*) and (*e*), are understood to follow in each case (Asl. 192). The object of thought (ā r a m m a ṇ a ṃ) in this connexion will be "limited" if the student dwells in love, etc., on but a restricted number of beings; "infinite" if his heart embrace vast numbers.

The commentator has not a little to say in the present work, however, on the nature and mutual relations of the "states" (pp. 193–5), taken more or less verbatim from his (earlier) work, Visuddhi Magga. First, the characteristics of each are fully set forth, together with their false manifestation (v i p a t t i). Clinging (s i n e h a s a m b h a v o) is the v i p a t t i of love, the essential mark of which is the carrying on of beneficent conduct, etc. Tears and the like are less truly characteristic of pity than is the bearing and relieving the woes of others. Laughter and the like are less genuine expressions of sympathy (m u d i t ā, which is strictly *συγχαιροσύνη*, *Mitfreude*) than is appreciation of what others have achieved. And there is a condition of indifference or equanimity (u p e k k h ā) which is prompted by ignorance, and not by that insight into the karma of mankind which can avail to calm the passions.

He next designates the four antisocial attitudes which are to be extirpated by these ethical disciplines, taken in order—ill-will (v y ā p ā d o), cruelty (v i h e s ā), aversion (a r a t i), and passion (r ā g o)—and shows how each virtue has also a second vice opposed to it. This he terms its near enemy, as being less directly assailed by it than its ethical opposite, the latter resembling an enemy who has to lurk afar in the jungle and the hills. Love and vengeful conduct cannot coexist. To prevail in this respect, let love be developed fearlessly. But where love and its object have too much in common, love is threatened by lust. On this side let love be guarded well. Again, the near enemy to pity, more insidious than cruelty, is the self-pity pining for what one has not got or has lost—a low, profane melancholy. And the corresponding worldly happiness in what one has, or in consequence of obliviousness as to what one has lost, lies in wait to stifle appreciation of the good fortune of others. Lastly, there is the unintelligent indifference of the worldling who has not triumphed over limitations nor mastered cause and effect, being unable to transcend external things.

The remainder of his remarks are occupied with the necessary

First Jhāna (the first rapt meditation), wherein conception works and thought discursive, which is born of solitude, is full of joy and ease, and is accompanied by Love—then the contact, etc. . . . [*? continue as in* § 1] . . . the balance that arises—these . . . are states that are good.

[252] Which are the states that are good?

When, that he may attain to the heavens of Form, he cultivates the way thereto, suppressing the working of conception and of thought discursive, and so, by earth-gazing, enters into and abides in the Second Jhāna (the second rapt meditation), which is self-evolved, born of concentration, is full of joy and ease, in that, set free . . . the mind grows calm and sure, dwelling on high—and which is accompanied by Love—then the contact, etc.

[*Continue as in the foregoing.*]

[253] Which are the states that are good?

When, that he may attain to the heavens of Form, he cultivates the way [thereto], and further, through the waning of all passion for zest, holds himself indifferent, the while

---

ethical sequence in the four states, and the importance of observing method in their cultivation, and finally with their other technical appellation of Appamaññā, or Infinitudes. In this connexion he gives the touching illustration repeated in Hardy (op. cit. 249) of the mother and her four children. Her desire for the growth of the infant is as Mettā; for the recovery of the sick child as Karuṇā; for the maintenance of the gifts displayed by the youth as Muditā; while her care not to hinder the career of her grown-up son is as Upekkhā.

It may be remarked, by the way, that when Hardy, with a foreigner's want of muditā, calumniates the Buddhist mendicant (p. 250) as one who thinks about the virtues of solidarity without practising them, he quite forgets that these exercises are but preparations of the will for that ministering to the spiritual needs of others to which the recluse's life was largely devoted, and the importance of which the Western, in his zeal for material forms of charity, does not even now appreciate at its real value. And Buddhism did not believe in giving the rein to good impulses unregulated by intellectual control.

mindful and self-aware, he experiences in his sense-consciousness that ease whereof the Noble Ones declare: "He that is unbiassed and watchful dwelleth at ease"—and so, by earth-gazing, enters into and abides in the Third Jhāna, which is accompanied by Love [1]—then, etc.

[*Continue as in the foregoing.*]

(*b*) Fivefold Jhāna.

[254–7] *Repeat question and answers in* §§ 167, 168, 170, 172, *adding in each answer, as in the foregoing section,* "and which is accompanied by Love."

2. Pity (k a r u ṇ ā).

[258, 259] *Repeat question and answers in the preceding sections* (*a*) *and* (*b*), *but substituting in each case* "and which is accompanied by Pity" *for the clause on Love.*

3. Sympathy (m u d i t ā).

[260, 261] *Repeat question and answers in the preceding two sections, but substituting in each case* "and which is accompanied by Sympathy" *for the clause on Pity.*

4. Equanimity [2] (u p e k k h ā).

[262] When, that he may attain to the heavens of Form, he cultivates the way thereto, and, by the putting away of ease and by the putting away of ill, by the passing away of the gladness and of the sorrow he was feeling, he thus, by earth-gazing, enters into and abides in the Fourth Jhāna (the fourth rapt meditation) of that utter purity of mindfulness which comes of equanimity, where no ease is felt nor any ill, and which is accompanied by Equanimity [2]—then the contact, etc.

[*Continue as in* § 165.]

---

[1] Love necessarily involves gladness (s o m a n a s s a ṃ = c e t a s i k a ṃ s u k h a ṃ, § 10, n.), hence it cannot be cultivated by way of the Fourth—or, under (*b*), Fifth—Jhāna.

[2] Or indifference.

The Four Jhānas of the Divine States may be developed in Sixteen Combinations.

[V.

The Jhāna of Foul Things (a s u b h a - j h ā n a ṃ).]

[263] Which are the states that are good?

When, that he may attain to the heavens of Form, he cultivates the way thereto, and so, aloof from sensuous desires, aloof from evil ideas, enters into and abides in the First Jhāna, wherein, etc. . . . and which is accompanied by the idea of a bloated corpse [1] . . .

[*or*] [264] of a discoloured corpse . . .

[*or*] of a festering corpse . . .

[*or*] of a corpse with cracked skin . . .

[*or*] of a corpse gnawn and mangled . . .

[*or*] of a corpse cut to pieces . . .

[*or*] of a corpse mutilated and cut in pieces . . .

[*or*] of a bloody corpse . . .

[*or*] of a corpse infested with worms . . .

[*or*] of a skeleton . . .

then the contact . . . the balance which arises—these . . . are states that are good.[2]

---

[1] The formula of the First Jhāna is understood to be repeated in the case of each of the ten Asubhas, but of the First only. For, in the words of the Cy. (p. 199), " just as on a swiftly flowing river a boat can only be steadied by the power of the rudder, so from the weakness (d u b b a l a t t ā) of the idea (in this case) the mind can only be steadied in its abstraction by the power of applied thought (v i t a k k o)." And this activity is dispensed with after the First Jhāna.

[2] For a more detailed account of this peculiar form of moral discipline, the reader is again referred to the Visuddhi Magga (chap. vi). Hardy (*East. Mon.*), who quotes largely from the Sinhalese commentary on the Visuddhi Magga, may also be consulted (p. 247 *et seq.*); also *Psalms of the Brethren* (1913), pp. 123 f. In the Satipaṭṭhāna Sutta (D. 22. Cf. Warren, *Buddhism in Translation*, p. 353 *et seq.*; and MI. 58) a system of nine Asubha-meditations is set out in terms somewhat different. In S. v (pp. 129–31) five of the Asubhas, beginning with " the

The Jhāna of Foul Things may be developed in Sixteen Combinations.

[Here ends the Chapter on] Good in relation to the Universe of Form.

---

skeleton" meditation, are prescribed in connexion with the sambojjhangas of mindfulness and equanimity. And the same five are given in the Jhāna Vagga of A. i, 42 (cf. A. iii, 323). The ten here given are said in the Cy. (pp. 197–9) to be prescribed for such as were proved to be passionately affected by the beauty of the body—of the figure, skin, odour, firmness or continuity, plumpness, limbs and extremities, symmetry, adornment, identifying self with the body, or complacency in the possession of it (? kāye mamattaṃ; cf. SN. 951), and teeth respectively. A dead body is not essential to this kind of mind-culture, the Cy. citing the cases of those Theras who obtained the requisite Jhāna by the glimpse of a person's teeth, or by the sight of a rājah on his elephant. The essential procedure lay in getting a clear and courageous grasp of the transience of any living organism.

[CHAPTER III.

Good in relation to the Universe of the Formless (a r ū p ā v a c a r a - k u s a l a ṃ).

The Four Jhānas connected with Formless Existence (c a t t ā r i a r ū p a j j h ā n ā n i).[1]

1. The Sphere of Unbounded Space (ā k ā s ā n a ñ c ā y a t a n a ṃ).]

[265] Which are the states that are good?

When, that he may attain to the Formless heavens, he cultivates the way [thereto], and so, by passing wholly beyond all consciousness of form, by the dying out of the consciousness of sensory reaction,[2] by turning the attention

---

[1] These often appear in the Nikāyas as the fourth to the seventh of the Eight Vimokhas or Deliverances (cf. §§ 248–50; *Dialogues of the Buddha*, ii, 119 f.; A. iv, 306). They are treated of in the Visuddhi Magga (chap. iii), but here Buddhaghosa only makes comparison with the account of them given in the Vibhanga. In S. iii, 237, and frequently in M., they occur in immediate sequence to the four Jhānas without any collective title, and not as concomitants of the Fourth Jhāna. There, too, the formulæ also have this slight variation from those in the present work, that the conscious attainment of each stage of abstraction is expressed by a brief proposition of identification, e.g. a n a n t o ā k ā s o t i . . . n' a t t h i k i ñ c ī t i (It is boundless space! . . . There is nothing whatever!). The Cy. explains this (p. 204) as follows: It was the wish of the Buddha to carry out, as in previous procedure so in this, the study of the Four Objects of Thought [ā r a m m a ṇ ā n i; see above, *passim*, under (*d*)]. And the first of these is that one's object is "limited". But if the student, in attaining to an undifferentiated consciousness of unbounded space, *realize* its nature by the, so to speak, exclamatory thought, "It is boundless!" he cannot logically proceed to consider it as limited.

[2] The student is to withdraw all interest in and attention to the world of r ū p a, to cease so entirely to differentiate the *plenum* of external phenomena (including his own form) which impinge on his senses, that sensations cease, or resolve themselves into a homogeneous sense of extended vacuum. P a ṭ i g h o,

from any consciousness of the manifold,[1] he enters into and abides in that rapt meditation which is accompanied by the consciousness of a sphere of unbounded space—even the Fourth Jhāna, to gain which[2] all sense of ease has been put away, and all sense of ill has been put away, and there has been a dying out of the gladness and sorrow he was wont to feel—(the rapt meditation)

---

rendered by sensory reaction, is explained to be sight-perception, sound-perception, smell, taste, and touch-perception. "Thought is (here) not sustained by way of the five doors" (Asl. 201, 202). Hardest of all was it to abstract all attention from sounds. Āḷara Kāḷāma, one of Gotama's teachers, and proficient in these rapt states, at least so far as the sixth Vimokha (M. i, 164), was credited with the power of becoming so absorbed that he failed to see or hear hundreds of carts passing near him (D. ii, 130; Asl. 202). On the psycho-physiological use of paṭigho, see the theory of sense in the book on form, *infra*, § 597 *et seq.*

[1] Nānattasaññāṃ amanasikārā. On the latter term, see above, p. 5, n. 1. On nānattaṃ, see S. ii, 140 f.; also M. i, 3, where, in a series of concepts, it follows "unity" and precedes "the whole" (Neumann renders by *Vielheit*); also S. iv, 113, 114, where it is explained to refer to the various kinds of sensation, the corresponding viññāṇa, and the resulting feeling. In the Vibhanga, quoted by Buddhaghosa (p. 202), it is explained to mean cognition of the mutual diversity or dissimilarity (aññamaññaṃ asadisā) of nature in the eight kinds of good thoughts, the twelve bad thoughts (below, § 365), as well as in those ideas of good and bad results which are taken next to these. For cittāni, however, saññā is substituted, possibly limiting the application of the discernment of diversity to the sensuous basis of all those "thoughts". The context, nevertheless, seems to point to a certain general, abstract, "re-representative" import in saññā as here applied. It is said to be the consciousness of one who is occupied with manodhātu or with manoviññāṇadhātu—with, let us say, representative or with re-representative cognition—with ideas or with cognition of those ideas. The ideation in this case is about sensuous phenomena as manifold, and the abstract nature of it lies, of course, in considering their diversity as such.

[2] In the text the formula of the Fourth Jhāna remains unaltered (cf. § 165). But it is sandwiched between the cumbrous adjectival compounds referring to space and to disinterestedness. Hence some modification was necessary to avoid uncouthness of diction.

which is imbued with indifference, and where no ease is felt nor any ill, but only the perfect purity that comes of mindfulness and indifference—then the contact, etc. . . . [cf. § 165] the balance that arises, these . . . are states that are good.

[2. The Sphere of Infinite Consciousness (v i ñ ñ ā ṇ a ñ c ā-y a t a n a ṃ).] [1]

[266] Which are the states that are good?

When, that he may attain to the Formless heavens, he cultivates the way [thereto], and, having passed [2] wholly beyond the sphere of boundless space, enters into and abides in that rapt meditation which is accompanied by the consciousness of a sphere of infinite consciousness [3]—even the Fourth Jhāna, to gain which all sense of ease has been put away, etc.

[*Continue as in previous section.*]

[3. The Sphere of Nothingness (ā k i ñ c a ñ ñ ā y a t a-n a ṃ).]

[267] Which are the states that are good?

When, that he may attain to the Formless heavens, he cultivates the way thereto, and, having passed wholly beyond the sphere of infinite consciousness, enters into and abides in that rapt meditation which is accompanied by the consciousness of a sphere of nothingness—even the Fourth

---

[1] Strictly v i ñ ñ ā ṇ ā n a ñ c ā y a t a n a ṃ. The usually elided syllable (r ū ḷ h i - s a d d o) is noticed in the Cy. (205).

[2] K., here and in the two following replies, has the gerund s a m a t i k k a m m a, following the usage in the Nikāyas (see, e.g. D, MPS. 30; M. i, 174, 209; S. iii, 237, 238; A. iv, 306). Buddhaghosa apparently reads s a m a t i k k a m ā (205), as is the unvarying case in the first only of these four arūpajjhānas.

[3] The only explanation given of a term on which one would gladly have heard Buddhaghosa expatiate is, "There is no end for him in respect to that which has to be cogitated" (lit. minded; m a n a s i k ā t a b b a - v a s e n a) (Asl. 205). On the next stage (§ 267) he writes, nothingness is having nothing left, i.e. of the previous sphere, not even disruption remains.

Jhāna, to gain which all sense of ease has been put away, etc.

[*Continue as in* § 265.]

[4. The Sphere where there is neither Perception nor Non-perception (n e v a-s a ñ ñ ā-n ā s a ñ ñ ā y a t a n a ṃ).

[268] Which are the states that are good?

When, that he may attain to the Formless heavens, he cultivates the way thereto, and, having passed wholly beyond the sphere of nothingness, enters into and abides in that rapt meditation which is accompanied by the consciousness of a sphere where there is neither perception nor non-perception [1]—even the Fourth Jhāna, to gain which all sense of ease must have been put away, etc.

[*Continue as in* § 265.]

The Four Jhānas connected with Formless Existence may be developed in sixteen combinations.

---

[1] Buddhaghosa calls this mental state the cultivation of the functioning of the "subtle residuum of mental co-efficients," or synergies (s a n k h ā r ā v a s e s a - s u k h u m a - b h ā v a ṃ). In so far as perception (presumably understood as being wholly introspective) has become incapable of effective functioning (p ā ṭ u - s a ñ ñ ā - k i c c a ṃ), the state is non-perceptual. In so far as those faint, fine conscious reactions are maintained, the state is "not non-perceptual". This oscillation about a zero-point in consciousness is illustrated by the similes quoted (not from this Cy.) by Hardy (op. cit. 264), namely, of the bowl containing just so much oil as suffices for cleansing purposes, but not to be poured out; also of the little pool, sufficient to wet the feet, but too shallow for a bathe. Both oil and water exist, or do not exist, according to what action can be taken with respect to them. The Cy. adds that this liminal point obtains not only in s a ñ ñ ā, but also in feeling, thought, and contact (208). The study of the "threshold" of consciousness, and of the supra- and sub-liminal grades clustering about it, is familiar enough to the investigator in psychophysics. What is unfamiliar to us is the exploitation of the borderland of consciousness in the interests of ethical growth. Leibnitz might have found in the n e v a - s a ñ ñ ā - n ā s a ñ ñ ā y a t a n a ṃ, had he had opportunity, the inspiration for his theory of *petites perceptions*.

[CHAPTER IV.

Degrees of Efficacy in Good Consciousness of the Three Realms.

1. Good consciousness in the Universe of Sense (k ā m ā - v a c a r a k u s a l a ṃ).]

[269] Which are the states that are good?

When a good thought concerning the sensuous universe has arisen, which is (I) accompanied by gladness and associated with knowledge—a thought which is

of inferior, or
of medium, or
of superlative [efficacy],[1]

or the dominant influence in which is

desire, or
energy, or
[another] thought, or
investigation;[2]

---

[1] Efficacy is not in the text. The effective power or karma of all the foregoing thoughts and exercises to modify the individual's existence in one world or another for good seems to have been, for practical purposes, distinguished under three grades of excellence. So I gather, at least, from the comment on this curious section (pp. 211, 212): "'inferior' (h ī n a ṃ) must be understood to mean paltry in respect of heaping up." "Heaping up" is in later books almost always associated with karma. Meaning to toil, more specifically to dig up, pile up, it is used to express the metaphorical notion of ever accumulating merit or demerit constituting the individual's potentiality in the way of rebirth. Cf. Mil. 109; also below, [§ 1059], on "she who toils".

[2] For the Four Iddhipādas, see M. i, 103; A. iii, 82; S. v, 264–6, etc. The Cy. states that when anyone, in the act of accumulating, relinquishes desire or the rest, "that" is called inferior [in efficacy]; that when these four states are moderately or superlatively efficacious they are called accordingly; and that "when anyone has accumulated, having made desire (c h a n d o), i.e. the wishing-to-do, his sovereign, chief, and

or the dominant influence in which is
desire of inferior,
of medium, or
of superlative [efficacy];
or the dominant influence in which is
energy of inferior,
of medium, or
of superlative [efficacy];
or the dominant influence in which is
[another] thought of inferior
of medium, or
of superlative [efficacy];
or the dominant influence in which is
investigation of inferior,
of medium, or
of superlative [efficacy],[1]

---

leader", then the procedure is said to be under the dominant influence of desire. So for the other three.

It is to be regretted that the Cy. does not discuss the term vīmaṃsā (investigation), or the propriety of its position in this series of four. The word only occurs in the Iddhipāda formula; in the Nikāyas (except in the late Pṭs), it is defined in the Vibh., as is paññā, but is not given as its equivalent. It was quite possibly imported into the predominating Buddhist culture from another school of thought. There is a suggestion of dual symmetry about the series: as chando is to viriyaṃ (conation passing into action), so is cittaṃ (consciousness) to the discursive re-representative intellection of vīmamsā. I have rendered cittādhipateyyaṃ, not by "consciousness", but by the influence of *another* thought in accordance with the Cy. (213), where it is said to be an associated thought, or states associated with the original "good thought".

There is another brief comment on the adhipateyyas below, § 1034, n. 2.

[1] The tabulated form adopted in this and following replies is intended not only to facilitate a conspectus of the system, but also to indicate the elision in the Pali (expressed by . . . pe . . .) of the repetition of the unvarying framework of the reply before and after each tabulated term. The Roman numerals in this and the next reply refer to the original statement of the "Eight Main Types of Thought" in Chapter I. Apparently the sensuous

then the contact . . . the balance that rises—these . . . are states that are good.

[270] Which are the states that are good ?

When a good thought concerning the sensuous universe has arisen which is (II) accompanied by gladness, associated with knowledge, and instigated . . .
or (III) accompanied by gladness, and disconnected with knowledge . . .
or (IV) accompanied by gladness, disconnected with knowledge, and instigated . . .
or (V) accompanied by indifference, and associated with knowledge . . .
or (VI) accompanied by indifference, associated with knowledge, and instigated . . .
or (VII) accompanied by indifference, and disconnected with knowledge . . .
or (VIII) accompanied by indifference, disconnected with knowledge, and instigated—a thought which is of inferior . . .
or of medium . . .
or of superlative [efficacy] . . .
or the dominant influence in which is
desire, or
energy, or
another thought ;
or the dominant influence in which is
desire of inferior,
of medium, or
of superlative [efficacy] ;
or the dominant influence in which is
energy of inferior,
of medium, or
of superlative [efficacy] ;
or the dominant influence in which is

---

basis of the ā r a m m a ṇ a ṃ of each thought is not intended to be here rehearsed.

[another thought of inferior,
of medium, or
of superlative [efficacy];
then the contact . . . the balance that arises—these . . . are states that are good.[1]

2. Good in relation to the Universe of Form.

[271] Which are the states that are good?

When, that he may attain to the heavens of Form, he cultivates the way thereto, and, aloof from sensuous desires, aloof from evil ideas, by earth-gazing enters into and abides in the First Jhāna (the first rapt meditation) . . . which is
of inferior,
or of medium,
or of superlative [efficacy];
or the dominant influence in which is
desire, or
energy, or
a thought, or
investigation;
or the dominant influence in which is
desire . . . energy . . . a thought . . . investigation
of inferior,
of medium,
or of superlative [efficacy]—
then the contact . . . the balance that arises—these . . . are states that are good.

[272] *Repeat in the case of the other Jhānas, both of (a) and (b).*

---

[1] In accordance with the usual procedure in the Pali classics, when combining several subjects in one sentence, the final details apply only to the last subject in the series. Hence, after the case of "or (VIII)", etc., the "states" possibly arising refer only to VIII, the last of the "good thoughts". And hence "investigation" is omitted in connexion with Thought VIII, because presumably the latter is "disconnected with knowledge". And it would likewise have been omitted in connexion with Thoughts III, IV, and VII, but *not* in connexion with the others.

3. Good in relation to the Formless Universe.

[273] Which are the states that are good?

When, that he may attain to the Formless heavens, he cultivates the way thereto, and so, by passing wholly beyond all consciousness of form, by the dying out of consciousness of sensory reaction, by turning the attention from any consciousness of the manifold, he enters into and abides in that rapt meditation which is accompanied by the consciousness of a sphere of unbounded space—even into the Fourth Jhāna, to gain which all sense of ease has been put away, etc.—(the rapt meditation) where there is neither ill nor ease, but only the perfect purity that comes of mindfulness and indifference, and which is of

inferior . . .
medium . . .
or superlative [efficacy] . . .

or the dominant influence in which is

desire . . .
or energy . . .
or a thought . . .
or investigation . . .

or the dominant influence in which is

desire . . . energy . . . a thought . . . investigation
of inferior . . .
medium . . .
superlative [efficacy]—

then the contact . . . the balance that arises—these . . . are states that are good.

[274–6] *Here follow the three remaining* "Jhānas connected with Formless Existence", *each modified by the characteristics enumerated in the foregoing answer.* Cf. §§ 266–8.[1]

---

[1] In § 275 the text inadvertently omits majjhimaṃ . . . pe . . . paṇītaṃ . . . pe . . . before vīmaṃsādhipateyyaṃ.

[CHAPTER V.

Thought engaged upon the Higher Ideal (lokuttaraṃ cittaṃ).

I. THE FIRST PATH (paṭhamo maggo).[1]

The Twenty Great Methods (vīsati mahānayā).

1. *Rapt Meditation* (jhānaṃ).

(i) The Four Modes of Progress in Schemata (suddhika-paṭipadā).]

[277] Which are the states that are good?

When he cultivates the Jhāna of the Higher Ideal (the rapt meditation) whereby there is a going forth and onward, making for the undoing of rebirth[2]—and when, that he

[1] That is to say, the first stage of the way or course of life leading to Arahantship or Nirvana. In the answers, bhūmi (Stage) is substituted for Path. And the " First Bhūmi " is declared in the Cy. (pp. 214, 215) to be equivalent to the first-fruits (or fruition) of recluseship (cf. D. i, second sutta); in other words, to the fruit of sotāpatti, or of " conversion ", as it has been termed.

[2] The special kind of Jhāna which he who has turned his back on the three lower ideals of life in the worlds of sense, form, or the formless, and has set his face steadfastly toward Arahantship, must " practise, bring forth and develop ", is described by Buddhaghosa as being ekacittakkhaṇikaṃ appanā-jhānaṃ—ecstatic meditation on a concept induced by the momentary flash of a thought (cf. KV., pp. 458, 620)—and by the text itself as niyyānikaṃ apacayagāmiṃ. The former of these two last terms is thus commented upon: " It is a going forth (down from) the world, from the cycle of rebirth. Or, there is a going forth by means of it. The man who is filled with it, comprehending Ill, goes forth, putting away the uprising (of Ill), goes forth, realizing the cessation (of Ill) goes forth, cultivating the path (leading to that cessation) goes forth ". And the latter term: This is *not* like that heaping together and multiplying of rebirth effected by the good which belongs to the three worlds of being. *This* is even as if one man having heaped up a stockade eighteen cubits high, another should afterwards take a great hammer and set to work to pull down

may attain to the First Stage, he has put away views and opinions,[1] and so, aloof from sensuous desires, aloof from evil ideas, enters into and abides in the First Jhāna, wherein is thinking applied and sustained, which is born of solitude, is full of zest and ease, progress thereto being difficult and intuition sluggish—then there is contact, feeling, perception, volition, thought, application of mind, sustained application, zest, ease, self-collectedness, the faculties of faith, energy, mindfulness, concentration, insight, mind, happiness, life, and *the faculty of believing "I shall come to know the unknown"*,[2] right views, right intention, *right speech, right action, right livelihood*,[3] right endeavour, right mindfulness, right concentration; the powers of faith, energy, mindfulness, concentration, insight, conscientiousness, the fear of blame; disinterestedness, absence of hate, dullness, covetousness and malice, right views, conscientiousness, fear of blame, serenity, lightness, plasticity, facility, fitness and directness in both sense and thought, mindfulness, self-awareness, quiet, intuition, grasp and balance.

Now these—or whatever other incorporeal, causally induced

---

and demolish his work. For so it, too, sets about pulling down and demolishing that potency for rebirth heaped up by the three-world-good, *by bringing about a deficiency in the causes thereof.*

[1] Diṭṭhigatāni, lit. view-gone [things]. All traditions or speculations adhered to either without evidence or on insufficient evidence, such as are implied in the states called "theory of individuality, perplexity, and perversion in rule and ritual" (Asl. 214; *infra* §§ 1002–5).

[2] The italics show those constituents of consciousness wherein this Jhāna differs from that mentioned in § 160, the constituents of which are identical with those of the First Type of Good Thought, § 1.

[3] These three factors of the "Eightfold Path", which were not explicitly included in the Eight Types of Good Thoughts, were, according to the Cy., included implicitly in the "or-whatever-states". See above, p. 4, n. 2. Here the Cy. only remarks that, whereas these three are now "included in the Pali" because the Eightfold Path has Nirvana for its goal, "pity" and "sympathy" are not included because they have living beings for their object, and not Nirvana.

states there are on that occasion—these are states that are good.

[278–82] "Contact," "feeling," "perception," "volition," *and* "thought" *are described as in* §§ 2–6.

[283] What on that occasion is application of mind?

The discrimination, the application, which on that occasion is the disposing, the fixing, the focussing, the superposing of the mind, the best intention, "Path-component," "contained in the Path"[1]—this is the application that there then is.

[284] "Sustained thought" *is described as in* § 8.

[285] What on that occasion is zest?

The zest which on that occasion is joy, rejoicing at, rejoicing over, mirth, merriment, felicity, exultation, elation of mind, the zest which is a factor of enlightenment[2]—this is the zest that there then is.

[286] "Ease" *is described as in* § 10.

[287] What on that occasion is self-collectedness?

The stability, solidity, absorbed steadfastness of thought which on that occasion is the absence of distraction, balance, unperturbed mental procedure, quiet, the faculty and the power of concentration, the best concentration, the concentration which is a factor of enlightenment, a "Path-

---

[1] The Path being the "Eightfold Path", "application of mind" (vitakko) is reckoned as included in it, in virtue of its being approximately equivalent to "intention" (sankappo).

[2] Pīti-sambojjhango. The seven Sambojjhangas are enumerated in A. iv, 23; S. v, 110, 111. In Mil. 340 they are termed "the jewel of the seven-fold wisdom of the Arahats". On the state called sambodhi, see Rhys Davids, *Dialogues of the Buddha*, i, pp. 190–2. It is in the Cy. (217) described as the harmony of its seven constituent states, and as forming the opposite to the detrimental compound consisting of the accumulations of adhesion (līnaṃ) and excitement, indulgence in the pleasures and satiety of sensuality, and addiction to the speculations of Nihilism and Eternalism (below, § 1003). The verb bujjhati is thus paraphrased: He arises from the slumber of vice, or discerns the four Noble Truths, or realizes Nirvana.

component", "contained in the Path"—this is the application that there then is.

[288] "Faith" *is described as in* § 12.

[289] What on that occasion is the faculty of energy?

The mental inception of energy which there is on that occasion, the striving and the onward effort, the exertion and endeavour, the zeal and ardour, the vigour and fortitude, the state of unfaltering effort, the state of sustained desire, the state of unflinching endurance, the solid grip of the burden, energy, energy as faculty and as power, the best energy, the energy which is a factor of enlightenment, a Path-component, contained in the Path—this is the energy that there then is.

[290] What on that occasion is the faculty of mindfulness?

The mindfulness which on that occasion is recollecting, calling back to mind the mindfulness [1] which is remembering, bearing in mind, the opposite of superficiality and of obliviousness; mindfulness, mindfulness as faculty and as power, the best mindfulness, the mindfulness which is a factor of enlightenment, a Path-component, contained in the Path—this is the mindfulness that there then is.

[291] "Concentration" *is described in the same terms as* "self-collectedness", § 287.

[292] What on that occasion is the faculty of insight?

The insight which there is on that occasion is understanding, search, research, searching the Truth, discernment, discrimination, differentiation, erudition, proficiency, subtlety, criticism, reflection, analysis, breadth, sagacity, leading, insight, intelligence, incitement, insight as faculty and as power, as a sword, as a height, as light, as glory, as splendour, as a precious stone; the absence of dullness, searching the Truth, the best views, that searching the Truth which is a

---

[1] S a t i, repeated as in § 14, has dropped out of the printed text. K. repeats it.

factor in the Great Awakening,[1] a Path-component, contained in the Path—this is the insight that there then is.

[293–5] *The faculties of* "mind", "gladness", *and* "life" *are described as in* §§ 17–19.

[296] What on that occasion is the faculty of believing, "I shall come to know the unknown" (anaññātaññassāmītindriyaṃ)? [2]

The insight that makes for the realization of those Truths [3] that are unrealized, uncomprehended, anattained to, undiscerned, unknown—the insight that is understanding, search, research, searching the Truth, etc.

[*Continue as in* § 292.]

[297] What on that occasion are best views?

Answer as for "insight", § 292.

[298] "Best intention" *is described in the same terms as* "conception", § 283.

[299] What on that occasion is best speech (sammā-vācā)?

To renounce on that occasion, abstain, refrain, and feel

---

[1] Under the name of Dhammavicayo, searching the truth, or doctrine, or religion.

[2] According to Buddhaghosa (216), the inspiring sense of assurance that dawns upon the earnest, uncompromising student that he will come to know the doctrine of the great truths—that Ambrosial Way unknown in the cycle of worldly pursuits and consequences where the goal is not ambrosial—is to him as the upspringing of a new faculty or moral principle.

[3] Tesaṃ dhammānaṃ . . . sacchikiriyāya paññā, etc., which may more literally be rendered the insight (or understanding, etc.) of, for, or from, the realization of, etc. "Bringing right opposite the eyes" is the paraphrase (Asl. 218). The student while "in the First Path" learns the full import of those concise formulæ known as the Four Noble Truths, which the Buddha set forth in his first authoritative utterance. Previously he will have had mere second-hand knowledge of them; and as one coming to a dwelling out of his usual beat, and receiving fresh garland and raiment and food, realizes that he is encountering new experiences, so are these truths, while not known by him, spoken of as "unknown" (Asl. 218).

averse from the four errors of speech,[1] to leave them uncommitted and undone, to incur no guilt, nor to trespass nor transgress with respect to them, to destroy the causeway leading to them [2]—the best speech, a Path-component, contained in the Path—this is the best speech that there then is.

[300] What on that occasion is best action (sammā-kammanto)?

To renounce on that occasion, abstain, refrain, and feel averse from the three errors of conduct,[3] to leave them uncommitted and undone, to incur no guilt, nor to trespass nor transgress with respect to them, to destroy the causeway leading to them [2]—best conduct, a Path-component, contained in the Path—this is the best conduct that there then is.

[301] What on that occasion is best livelihood (sammā-ājīvo)?

To renounce on that occasion, abstain, refrain, and feel averse from the wrong modes of livelihood, to leave them unpractised and undone, to incur no guilt, nor to trespass nor transgress with respect to them, to destroy the causeway leading to them—best livelihood, a Path-component, contained in the Path—this is the best livelihood that there then is.

[302–4] "Best endeavour", "best mindfulness", "best concentration",[4] *are described as in* §§ 289–91.

[305–11] *The* "powers" *of* "faith", "energy," "mindfulness," "concentration," *and* "insight" *are described as in*

---

[1] That is, lying, slander, rude speech, and frivolous talk. See the Cuḷa Sīla, e.g. in D. i, 4.

[2] Setughāto, i.e. the cause or condition of evil speaking—namely lust, hate, and dullness (Asl. 219). The metaphor occurs in A. i, 220, 221, 261 ; ii, 145, 146 ; cf. setukāraka, S. i, 33, and KS. i, 46, n. 2.

[3] That is, murder (of *any* living thing), theft, and unchastity. D. i, 4.

[4] Samādhi, before sambojjhango, has dropped out of the printed text.

§§ 288–92; *those of* "conscientiousness" *and* "the fear of blame" *as in* §§ 30, 31.

[312–19] "Disinterestedness" *and* "the absence of hate" *are described as in* §§ 32, 33; "the absence of dullness" *as in* § 309 ("insight"); "the absence of covetousness" *and* "the absence of malice" *are described as in* §§ 35, 36; "conscientiousness" *and* "the fear of blame" *as in* §§ 38, 39; "best views" *as in* § 292 *or* 309 ("insight").

[320] What on that occasion is serenity of mental factors?

The serenity, the composure which there is on that occasion, the calming, the tranquillizing, the tranquillity of the skandhas of feeling, perception, and synergies, the serenity which is a factor of enlightenment—this is the serenity of mental factors that there then is.

[321] What on that occasion is serenity of consciousness?

The serenity, the composure which there is on that occasion, the calming, the tranquillizing, the tranquillity of the skandha of consciousness, the serenity which is a factor of enlightenment—this is the serenity of consciousness that there then is.

[322–31] *The remaining five attributes characterizing both mental factors and consciousness* "on that occasion": "buoyancy," "plasticity," etc.—*are described as in* §§ 42–51.

[332–7] "Mindfulness", "self-awareness", "quiet", "insight", "grasp", and "balance" *are described as in* §§ 290, 292 ("wisdom"), 291, 292, 289 ("energy") *and* 291 *respectively*.

These, or whatever other incorporeal, causally induced states there are on that occasion—these are states that are good.

[Summary.]

[337*a*] Now at that time
the skandhas are four,
the spheres are two,
the elements are two,
the nutriments are three,

the faculties are nine,
the Jhāna is fivefold,
the Path is eightfold,
the powers are seven,
the moral roots are three,

contact,
feeling,
perception,
volition,
thought,
} are each single [factors];

the skandhas of
feeling,
perception,
synergies
consciousness,
} are each single [factors];

the sphere of mind,
the faculty of mind,
the element of intellection,
the sphere of a [purely] mental state,
the element of a [purely] mental state,
} are each single [factors].

These, or whatever incorporeal, causally induced states there are on that occasion—these are states that are good.

* * * *

[*Here the questions and answers concerning the first two of the four skandhas enumerated are to be understood to follow as in* §§ 59–61.]

[338] What on that occasion is the skandha of synergies ?

Contact,
volition,[1]
applied thinking,

[1] The printed text has v e d a n ā instead of c e t a n ā, which is obviously wrong.

sustained thinking,
zest,
self-collectedness,
the faculties of
faith, concentration,
energy, insight,
mindfulness, life,
believing "I shall come to know the unknown";
the best views, the best livelihood,
the best intention, the best endeavour,
the best speech, the best mindfulness,
the best action, the best concentration;
the seven powers;[1]
disinterestedness,
the absence of
hate and dullness;
the absence of
covetousness and malice,
the best views;
conscientiousness, the fear of blame;
serenity, wieldiness,
buoyancy, fitness,
plasticity, directness
of mental factors and consciousness;
mindfulness and awareness;
quiet and insight;
grasp and balance.

These, or whatever other incorporeal, causally induced states there are on that occasion, exclusive of the skandhas of feeling, perception, and consciousness—these are the skandha of synergies.

* * * *

[*Questions on the remaining items in the* "Summary" *are understood to follow.*]

---

[1] These are set out in the original as in § 277.

[340] [1] Which are the states that are good?

When he cultivates the Jhāna of the Higher Ideal (the rapt meditation), whereby there is a going forth and onward, making for the undoing of rebirth—and when, that he may attain to the First Stage, he has put away views and opinions, and so, aloof from sensuous desires, aloof from evil ideas, enters into and abides in the First Jhāna . . . progress thereto being difficult, but intuition quick . . .

[*or*] [341] . . . progress thereto being easy, but intuition sluggish . . .

[*or*] [342] . . . progress thereto being easy and intuition quick—then the contact . . . the balance that arises—these . . . are states that are good.

[343] *Repeat the Four Modes in the case of the 2nd to the 4th Jhāna on the Fourfold System, and of the 1st to the 5th Jhāna on the Fivefold System.*

[Here end] the Modes of Progress in Schemata.

[(ii) The Section on Emptiness (suññataṃ).] [2]

(*a* and *b*)

[344] Which are the states that are good?

When he cultivates the Jhāna of the Higher Ideal (the

---

[1] The answer marked [339] in the text is merely a repetition of lokuttara-jhānaṃ as dukkhāpaṭipadaṃ dandhābhiññaṃ, i.e. of the first "Mode of Progress" given in [277]. I have therefore omitted it. No repetition is noticed in this connexion by the Cy. K. has no such repetition.

[2] Called in the Cy. (221) suññata-vāro, with the subsections suddhika-suññatā, or "Emptiness applied to the Jhāna-formula", i.e. the group marked (*a* and *b*), and suññata-paṭipadā, or "the Modes of Progress taken in connexion with Emptiness", i.e. the group marked (*c*). On suddhika see below, 138, n. 2.

On the technical term "emptiness", see above, § 121, and Rhys Davids, *Yogāvacara's Manual*, pp. xxvii, xxviii. Of the three "riddles" there discussed—"the empty, the aimless, and the signless"—only the first two are here prescribed for cultivation (cf. p. 138 f.). Buddhaghosa argues on the subject at some length (Asl. 221–5). He explains that the three terms are

rapt meditation), whereby there is a going forth and onward, making for the undoing of rebirth—and when, that he may attain to the First Stage, he has put away views and opinions, and so, aloof from sensuous desires, aloof from evil ideas, enters into and abides in the First Jhāna, wherein is application and sustaining of thought, which is born of solitude, is full of joy and ease, and which is EMPTY—then the contact . . . the balance that arises—these . . . are states that are good.

[345] *Repeat the 2nd to the 4th Jhānas on the Fourfold System, and the 1st to the 5th on the Fivefold System, with the addition in each case of the phrase* " and which is EMPTY ".

[Here ends] the " Emptiness " Section.

[(*c*) The Modes of Progress, with " Emptiness " as the Basis (suññata-mūlaka-paṭipadā).]

[346] Which are the states that are good ?

When he cultivates the Jhāna of the Higher Ideal . . . and when, that he may attain to the First Stage, he . . . enters into and abides in the First Jhāna . . . progress thereto being difficult and intuition sluggish, the method being the concept

---

so many names for the way to the Ideal (lokuttara-maggo), each throwing a special *aspect* of it into greater relief than the other two, while yet no advance can be made without all three concepts. The advent of the Path as a conscious ideal is especially characterized by insight into the fact that the sanskāras are *void* of a permanent soul, and of all that conduces to happiness. The virtue or quality of the Path, again, is wholly *empty* of lust, hate, and dullness. So also is its object, namely Nirvana. But the chief import of " empty " is said to relate to the fact first named—the nonentity of any substratum or soul in anything. The "aimless" (unaimed-at, unhankered-after, undesired), applies chiefly to the insight into dukkhaṃ, or the nature of pain or ill. All aspiration or hankering after sanskāras withers up under the penetration of such insight. By it, too, the path of the Ideal becomes revealed. The third " riddle ", the " signless "—i.e. the path conceived as free from the three signs of false tenets of Permanence, Sorrow, and Soul—comes up for meditation later (§§ 506, 511, etc.).

of EMPTINESS—then the contact . . . the balance that arises—these . . . are states that are good.

[347–9] *Repeat the same formula, substituting in succession the three remaining Modes of Progress* (§§ 176–9), *with the addition in each case of the phrase* " the method being the concept of EMPTINESS ".

[350] *Repeat the same formula, substituting in succession the remaining Jhānas on the Fourfold System and those on the Fivefold System, and applying in each case the Four Modes of Progress, with the additional phrase on* " Emptiness ".

[(ii) The Unaimed-at (a p p a ṇ i h i t a ṃ).

(*a* and *b*).][1]

[351] Which are the states that are good?

When he cultivates the Jhāna of the Higher Ideal . . . and when, that he may attain to the First Stage, he . . . enters into and abides in the First Jhāna . . . which is born of solitude, is full of zest and ease, which is AIMLESS—then the contact . . . the balance that arises—these . . . are states that are good.

[352] *Repeat the same formula, substituting the remaining three, and the five Jhānas in succession, with the addition in each case of the phrase* " and which is UNAIMED-AT ".

[(*c*) The Modes of Progress, with the Unaimed-at as the Basis (a p p a ṇ i h i t a - m ū l a k a - p a ṭ i p a d ā).]

[353] When he cultivates the Jhāna of the Higher Ideal . . . and when, that he may attain to the First Stage of it, he . . . enters into and abides in the First Jhāna . . . progress whereto is difficult and intuition sluggish, the method being the concept of the UNAIMED-AT—then the contact . . . the balance that arises—these . . . are states that are good.

[354–6] *Repeat the same formula, substituting in succession*

[1] As in the foregoing, the Cy. (ibid.) co-ordinates this, and the following section, with the two on " emptiness ", calling (*a* and *b*) s u d d h i k a - a p p a ṇ i h i t ā, and the next group a p p a ṇ i h i t a - p a ṭ i p a d ā.

the three remaining Modes of Progress, with the addition in each case of the phrase " the method being the concept of the UNAIMED-AT ".

[357] *Repeat the same formula, substituting in succession the remaining three, and the five Jhānas, and applying in each case the Four Modes of Progress, with the additional phrase on the* " Unaimed-at ".

[2–20. The Remaining Nineteen Great Methods.]

[358] Which are the states that are good ?

Here follow nineteen concepts, each of which can be substituted for " the Jhāna of the Higher Ideal " *in the preceding* 81 *answers* [§§ 277–357], *as a vehicle in training the mind for Arahantship. They are as follows* :—

2. The Path of the Higher Ideal.
3. The Advance in Mindfulness [1] toward the Higher Ideal.
4. The System of Best Efforts [2] toward the Higher Ideal.
5. The Series of Mystic Potencies [3] applied to the Higher Ideal.
6. The Faculty relating to the Higher Ideal.
7. The Power relating to the Higher Ideal.
8. The Awakening to the Higher Ideal.
9. The Truth of the Higher Ideal.
10. The Peace [4] of the Higher Ideal.
11. The Doctrine of the Higher Ideal.
12. The Skandha related to the Higher Ideal.
13. The Sphere of the Higher Ideal.
14. The Element of the Higher Ideal.
15. The Nutriment of the Higher Ideal.
16. Contact with the Higher Ideal.
17. Feeling relating to the Higher Ideal.
18. Perception relating to the Higher Ideal.

---

[1] Satipaṭṭhāna. M. i, 56.
[2] Sammappadhāna. See below, § 1367.
[3] Iddhipāda. See above, § 273 *et seq.*
[4] Samatho. See above, § 54.

19. Volition relating to the Higher Ideal.
20. Thought relating to the Higher Ideal.

[The Dominant Influences in the Modes of Progress (a d h i p a ṭ i).]

[359] Which are the states that are good?

When he cultivates the Jhāna of the Higher Ideal . . . and when, that he may attain to the First Stage, he . . . enters into and abides in the First Jhāna . . . progress whereto is painful and intuition sluggish, and the dominant influence in which is desire, energy, thought, or investigation, then the contact . . . the balance that arises—these are states that are good.

[360] *Repeat this formula in the case of the remaining three and five Jhānas.*

[361] *Repeat the foregoing* [§§ 359, 360] *in the case of each of the nineteen remaining* " Great Methods ".

[Here ends] the FIRST PATH.

II. THE SECOND PATH.

[362] Which are the states that are good?

When he cultivates the Jhāna of the Higher Ideal (the rapt meditation), whereby there is a going forth and onward, making for the undoing of rebirth—and when, that he may attain to the Second Stage, he has diminished the strength of sensual passions and of malice,[1] and so, aloof from sensuous desires, aloof from evil ideas, enters into and abides in the First Jhāna . . . progress whereto is difficult and intuition

---

[1] Cf. D. i, 156, and MPS. 16, 17. It is striking that here and in the following answer no diminution of m o h o (dullness) is included. Cf., however, below, § 1134. Ignorance (= dullness) is only really conquered in the Fourth Path. The diminution is described (Asl. 238) as coming to pass in two ways; vicious dispositions arise occasionally and no longer habitually, and when they do arise it is with an attenuated intensity. They are like the sparse blades of grass remaining in a newly mown field, and like a flimsy membrane or a fly's wing.

sluggish—then the contact . . . the faculty of knowledge made perfect[1] . . . the balance that arises—these . . . are states that are good.

* * * *

[Here ends] the SECOND PATH.

III. THE THIRD PATH.

[363] Which are the states that are good?

When he cultivates the Jhāna of the Higher Ideal (the rapt meditation) whereby there is a going forth and onward, making for the undoing of rebirth—and when, that he may attain to the THIRD STAGE he has put away the entire residuum of sensual passions and of malice,[2] and so aloof from sensuous desires, aloof from evil ideas, enters into and abides in the First Jhāna . . . progress whereto is difficult and intuition sluggish—then the contact . . . the faculty of knowledge made perfect . . . the balance that arises—these . . . are states that are good.

[Here ends] the THIRD PATH.

IV. THE FOURTH PATH.

[364] Which are the states that are good?

When he cultivates the Jhāna of the Higher Ideal (the rapt meditation) whereby there is a going forth and onward making for the undoing of rebirth, and when, that he may attain the FOURTH STAGE, he has put away absolutely and entirely all passion for Form, all passion for the Formless,

---

[1] Cf. § 296. The faith and hope of the Sotāpatti, or student, of the First Path, while struggling with the "known limitations" of his stage of knowledge (ñātamariyadaṃ, the Cy. calls them, p. 239), are now rewarded by his attainment, as a Sakadāgāmī, of that deepening philosophic insight into the full implication of the "Four Truths" termed aññā, or knowledge *par excellence*, and applied in Buddhist writings, only to evolving or evolved Arahantship. Cf. below, § 555.

[2] These, which the Cy., in connexion with the Second Path, termed collectively kilesā, are now referred to as saṃyojanāni. See § 1229 *et seq.* and § 1113 *et seq.*

all conceit, distraction, and ignorance, and so, aloof from sensuous desires, aloof from evil ideas, enters into and abides in the First Jhāna . . . progress whereto is difficult and intuition sluggish—then the contact . . . the faculty of knowledge made perfect . . . the balance that arises—these . . . are states that are good.

[364*a*] What on that occasion is the faculty of knowledge made perfect (a ñ ñ i n d r i y a ṃ)?

The insight that makes for the realization of those truths that have been realized, comprehended, attained to, discerned, and known—the insight that is understanding, search, research, searching the Truth, etc.

[*Continue as in* § 292.]

*   *   *   *

These, or whatever other incorporeal, causally induced states there are on that occasion, these are states that are good.

[Here ends] the FOURTH PATH.

[Here ends] Thought engaged upon the Higher Ideal.

[*PART II.—BAD STATES OF CONSCIOUSNESS.*

CHAPTER VI.

The Twelve Bad Thoughts (dvādasa akusalacittāni).]

I.

[365] Which are the states that are bad? [1]

When a bad thought has arisen, which is accompanied by gladness, and associated with views and opinions,[2] and has as its object a sight, a sound, a smell, a taste,[3] a touch, a [mental] state, or what not, then there is

contact,
feeling,
perception,
volition,
thought,
applied, *and*
sustained thought,
zest,
ease,
self-collectedness; [4]

the faculties of
energy,

---

[1] In this connexion those constituents of the twelve thoughts which in themselves are ethically neutral are to be understood as unchanged in the connotation assigned them in connexion with good thoughts. There being for bad thoughts no other sphere of existence save the sensuous universe, this is to be understood throughout (Asl. 247).

[2] Diṭṭhigata-sampayuttaṃ. Cf. p.75, n. 1, with §§ 381, 1003.

[3] Rasārammaṇaṃ vā is inadvertently omitted in the printed text.

[4] See following note.

concentration,[1]
mind,
gladness,
life ;
wrong views,
wrong intention,
wrong endeavour,
wrong concentration ;
the powers of
energy,
concentration,
unconscientiousness,
disregard of blame ;
lust, covetousness,
dullness,[2] wrong views,
unconscientiousness,
disregard of blame,
quiet,
grasp,[3]
balance.

---

[1] Concentration of mind is essential to the higher life of Buddhism ; nevertheless, so far is it from constituting excellence, that it is also an essential to effective evil-doing. If the mind be undistracted, says Buddhaghosa, the murderer's knife does not miss, the theft does not miscarry, and by a mind of single intent (lit. of one taste) evil conduct is carried out (Asl. 248). Cf. the Hebrew idiom rendered by " the heart being set "—to do good or evil (Eccles. viii, 11 ; Ps. lxxviii, 8).

[2] Hate (d o s o) and malice (v y ā p ā d o) do not find a place among the factors of Bad Thoughts (corresponding to the place occupied by their opposites in the Good Thoughts, § 1) till we come to the last four types of bad thoughts. Whereas these are accompanied by sorrow (d o m a n a s s a ṃ), the subject of the first and the following three types of thought is a cheerful sinner. Zest, ease, gladness, were held to be incompatible with hate.

[3] V i p a s s a n ā (intuition) has been erroneously included in the text. Moral intuition was as incompatible with immoral thoughts to the Buddhist as it was to Socrates and Plato. Hence, also, " insight " and " mindfulness " are excluded, as well as " faith ". The Cy. rules that the followers of heretical dogmas

Now, these—or whatever other incorporeal, causally induced states that there are on that occasion—these are states that are bad.[1]

[366–70] What on that occasion is contact . . . feeling . . . perception . . . volition . . . thought ?

Answers as in §§ 2–6 *respectively.*

[371] What on that occasion is applied thought ?

Answer as in § 7, *substituting* " wrong intention " (micchāsankappo) for " best intention ".

[372–4] What on that occasion is sustained thought . . . joy . . . ease ?

Answers as in §§ 8–10 *respectively.*

[375] What on that occasion is self-collectedness ?

Answer as in § 11, *substituting* " wrong concentration " *for* " best concentration ".

[376] What on that occasion is the faculty of energy ?

Answer as in § 13, *substituting* " wrong endeavour " *for* " best endeavour ".

[377] What on that occasion is the faculty of concentration ?

Answer as in § 375.

[378–80] What on that occasion is the faculty of mind . . . gladness . . . life ?

Answers as in §§ 17–19 *respectively.*

[381] What on that occasion are wrong views (micchādiṭṭhi) ?[2]

---

and mere opinion can have but a spurious faith in their teachers, can only be mindful of bad thoughts, and can only cultivate deceit and delusion. Nor can there possibly be that sixfold efficiency of sense and thought which is concomitant with good thoughts (§§ 40–51). Asl. 249.

[1] Kusalā in the text is, of course, a slip. There are, in all these Bad Thoughts, ten " whatever-other " states : desire, resolve, attention, conceit, envy (issā, or read icchā, longing), meanness, stolidity, torpor, distraction, worry (Asl. 250). See above, p. 5, n. 1.

[2] Micchādiṭṭhi is defined in the Cy. (p. 248) as ayathāvadassanaṃ, seeing things as they are not. (On diṭṭhi, see § 1030, n.) Sixty-two kinds of this perverted

The views which on that occasion are a walking in opinion, the jungle of opinion,[1] the wilderness of opinion,[2] the disorder of opinion,[3] the scuffling of opinion,[4] the fetter of opinion,[5] the grip[6] and tenacity[7] of it, the inclination towards it,[8] the being infected by it, a by-path, a wrong road, wrongness, sectarianism,[9] inverted grasp—these are the wrong views that there then are.

[382–4] What on that occasion is wrong intention . . . wrong endeavour . . . wrong concentration ?

Answers as in §§ 371, 376, 375 *respectively.*

---

vision, or ill-grounded speculation, are distinguished in the Brahmajāla Sutta (D. i), all of them being theories of existence, and are alluded to by the commentator (p. 252). Cf. Rhys Davids, *American Lectures*, p. 27 *et seq.*

[1] Because of the difficulty of getting out of it, as out of a grass, forest, or mountain jungle (Asl., ibid.).

[2] Because of the danger and fearsomeness of indulging in such opinions, as of a desert beset with robbers and snakes, barren of water or food (ibid.).

[3] Buddhaghosa does not derive this term from visūkaṃ (cf. *Dialogues*, i, 7, n. 2), but from visu-kāyikaṃ = antithetically constituted—i.e. to sammādiṭṭhi. Nevertheless, the text (PTS.) reads visū.

[4] The disorder and struggle through some being Annihilationists, some Eternalists, etc. (Asl. 253).

[5] See § 1113.

[6] The obsession by some object of thought, like the grip of a crocodile (Asl. 253).

[7] The text of the Cy. reads patiṭṭhāho for paṭiggāho. K., however, reads patiggāho.

[8] i.e. towards the fallacious opinion of Permanence, etc. (Asl. 253.)

[9] Titthāyatanaṃ. It is impossible to get an English equivalent for this metaphor, which literally means only a standing-place, but which is usually, in its first intention, associated with a shallow river-strand or fording-place, and, in its second, with sectarian speculative beliefs and the teaching of them. Buddhaghosa himself gives an alternative connotation: (*a*) "where the foolish, in the course of their gyrations (? i.e. saṃsāra) cross over"; (*b*) the region or home of sectarians (titthiyā). Cf. the use of the term in M. i, 483.

[385, 386] What on that occasion is the power of energy . . . the power of concentration ?

Answers as in §§ 383, 384 *respectively.*

[387] What on that occasion is the power of unconscientiousness (a h i r i k a b a l a ṃ) ?

The absence which there is on that occasion of any feeling of conscientious scruple when scruples ought to be felt, the absence of conscientious scruple at attaining to bad and evil tastes—this is the power of unconscientiousness that there then is.

[388] What on that occasion is the power of disregard of blame (a n o t t a p p a b a l a ṃ) ?

The absence which there is on that occasion of any sense of guilt where a sense of guilt ought to be felt, the absence[1] of a sense of guilt at attaining to bad and evil states—this is the power of disregard of blame that there then is.

[389] What on that occasion is lust ?

The lust, lusting, lustfulness which there is on that occasion, the infatuation, the feeling and being infatuated, the covetousness, the lust that is the root of badness—this is the lust that there then is.

[390] What on that occasion is dullness ?

The lack of knowledge, of vision, which there is on that occasion; the lack of co-ordination, of judgment, of enlightenment,[2] of penetration; the inability to comprehend, to grasp thoroughly; the inability to compare, to consider, to demonstrate; the folly, the childishness, the lack of intelligence; the dullness that is vagueness, obfuscation, ignorance, the Flood[3] of ignorance, the Bond of ignorance,

---

[1] N a has here dropped out of the printed text.

[2] S a m b o d h o. Cf. § 285.

[3] On ignorance as a Flood and as a Bond, see below, §§ 1151, 1151*a*.

Whereas the mark (l a k k h a ṇ a ṃ) of greed is the seizing on an object in idea, it is the essential property (r a s o) of dullness to cover up the real nature of that object, with the result

the bias of ignorance, the obsession of ignorance, the barrier of ignorance; the dullness that is the root of badness—this is the dullness that there then is.

[391–7] What on that occasion is covetousness . . . are wrong views . . . is unconscientiousness . . . disregard of blame . . . quiet . . . grasp . . . balance ?

Answers as in §§ 389, 381, 387, 388, 375, 376, *and, again,* 375 *respectively.*

Or whatever other incorporeal, causally induced states there are on that occasion—these are states that are bad.

[Summary.]

[397*a*] Now, on that occasion
the skandhas are four,
the spheres are two,
the elements are two,
the nutriments are three,
the faculties are five,
the Jhāna is fivefold,
the Path is fourfold,
the powers are four,
the causes are two,[1]
contact, } are each single [factors];
etc. } etc.

[*Continue as in* § 58.]

* * * *

[398] What on that occasion is the skandha of synergies?
Contact,
volition,
applied, and
sustained thought,
zest,
self-collectedness;

---

that the attention devoted to it is of a superficial nature (a y o n i s o). Asl. 249.

[1] Namely " lust " and " dullness ".

the faculties of
energy,
concentration,
life ;
wrong views,
wrong intention,
wrong endeavour,
wrong concentration ;
the powers of
energy,
concentration,
unconscientiousness,
disregard of blame ;
lust, covetousness,
dullness ; wrong views ;
unconscientiousness,
disregard of blame ;
quiet,
grasp,
balance.

These, or whatever other incorporeal, causally induced states there are on that occasion, exclusive of the skandhas of feeling, perception, and consciousness—these are the skandha of synergies.

[*Continue as in* § 58.]

* * * *

II.

[399] Which are the states that are bad ?

When a bad thought has arisen which is accompanied by gladness, is associated with views and opinions, and is instigated,[1] and which has as its object a sight . . . or what not, then there is contact . . . balance . . .

[*Continue as in First Thought,* § 365.]

[1] The Cy. instances the case of a young man who, being refused the hand of the daughter of some false doctrinaire on the

III.

[400] Which are the states that are bad?

When a bad thought has arisen which is accompanied by gladness and disconnected with views and opinions, and which has as its object a sight, a sound, a smell, a taste, a touch, or what not, then there is contact, etc.

[*Continue as in the first Bad Thought, but omitting the single, twice enumerated item* "wrong views".[1]]

[Summary.]

[400*a*] Now, at that time

the skandhas are four,
the spheres are two,
the elements are two,
the nutriments are three,
the faculties are five,
the Jhāna is fivefold,
the Path is threefold,
etc., etc.

[*Continue as in* § 58.]

* * * *

[401] What on that occasion is the skandha of synergies? *Answer as in* § 398, *omitting* "wrong views".

IV.

[402] Which are the states that are bad?

When a bad thought has arisen which is accompanied by gladness, is disconnected with views and opinions, and is

---

ground of his being of a different communion, is prompted by his affections to frequent the church of the girl's people and to adopt their views, thus gaining his reward (Asl. 255).

[1] Somanassindriyaṃ, bracketed in the text, must, of course, be included. The Cy. instances the frame of mind of those who are indulging in "worldly pleasures", such as public sports and dances, and at village festivals (naṭasamajjādīni). Cf. *Dialogues of the Buddha*, i, p. 7, n. 4.

instigated, and which has as its object a sight . . . or what not, then there is contact . . . balance . . .

[*Continue as in the Third Thought*, § 400.]

V.

[403] Which are the states that are bad ?

When a bad thought has arisen which is accompanied by indifference, and associated with views and opinions, and has as its object a sight, a sound, a smell, a taste, a touch, a [mental] state, or what not, then there is

contact, consciousness,
feeling, applied, and
perception, sustained thought,
volition, indifference,
self-collectedness ;
the faculties of
energy,
concentration,
mind ;
indifference,
life ;
wrong views,
wrong intention,
wrong endeavour,
wrong concentration ;
the powers of
energy,
concentration,
unconscientiousness,
disregard of blame ;
lust, covetousness,
dullness ; wrong views ;
unconscientiousness,
disregard of blame,
composure,

grasp,
balance.

These, or whatever other incorporeal, causally induced states there are on that occasion—these are states that are bad.

[404–7] *Questions and answers on* "contact", "feeling", "indifference", *and* "the faculty of indifference" *identical with those* in §§ 151–4.

*   *   *   *

[Summary.]

[407*a*] Now, at that time
the skandhas are four,
etc.,
the faculties are five,
the Jhāna is fourfold,[1]
the Path is fourfold,
etc.
[*Continue as in* § 58.]

*   *   *   *

[408] What on that occasion is the skandha of synergies?
Contact,
volition,
applied, and
sustained thought,
self-collectedness,
etc.

[*Continue as in* § 398, "joy" *having been omitted as incompatible with* "disinterestedness".]

*   *   *   *

VI.

[409] Which are the states that are bad?

When a bad thought has arisen which is accompanied by indifference, is associated with views and opinions, and

---

[1] Cf. § 154*a*.

is instigated, and which has as its object a sight . . . or what not, then there is contact, etc.

[*Continue as in Thought V.*]

* * * *

VII.

[410] Which are the states that are bad?

When a bad thought has arisen which is accompanied by indifference, and disconnected with views and opinions, and which has as its object a sight . . . or what not, then there is contact, etc.

[*Continue as in Thought V, omitting* "wrong views".]

* * * *

[Summary.]

[410*a*] Now, at that time
the skandhas are four,
etc.,
the faculties are five,
the Jhāna is fourfold,
the Path is threefold,
etc.

[*Continue as in* § 397*a.*]

* * * *

[411] What on that occasion is the skandha of synergies?

Answer as in § 398, *omitting both* "zest" *and* "wrong views".

* * * *

VIII.

[412] Which are the states that are bad?

Answer as in Thought VII, with the additional factor inserted, as in Thoughts II, IV, VI, of "is instigated".[1]

---

[1] The Cy. gives no illustrations of this or the three preceding types of thought.

IX.

[413] Which are the states that are bad ?

When a bad thought has arisen which is accompanied by sorrow and associated with repugnance,[1] and which has as its object a sight, a sound, a smell, a taste, a touch, a mental state, or what not, then there is

contact,
feeling,
perception,
volition,
consciousness,
thought,
applied, and
sustained thought,
distress,
self-collectedness ;
the faculties of
energy,
concentration,
mind,
sorrow,
life ;
wrong intention,
wrong endeavour,
wrong concentration ;
the powers of
energy,
concentration,
unconscientiousness,
disregard of blame ;
hate,
dullness ;
malice ;

---

[1] Paṭigho, used (§ 1060) to describe doso, and again (§ 597 *et seq.*) in connexion with sense-stimulation, as " reaction ".

unconscientiousness,
disregard of blame,
quiet,
grasp,
balance.

These, or whatever other incorporeal, causally induced states there are on that occasion—these are states that are bad.

[414] *The question and answer on* "contact", § 2.

[415] What on that occasion is feeling?

The mental pain, the mental distress (d u k k h a ṃ), which, on that occasion, is born of contact with the appropriate element of representative intellection; the painful, distressful sensation which is born of contact with thought; the painful, distressful feeling which is born of contact with thought—this is the distress that there then is.

[416, 417] What on that occasion is distress (d u k k h a ṃ) . . . the faculty of sorrow (d o m a n a s s i n d r i y a ṃ)? *Answers as for* "feeling" *in* § 415, omitting "with the appropriate element of representative intellection".

* * * *

[418] What on that occasion is hate?

The hate, hating, hatred, which on that occasion is a disordered temper, the getting upset,[1] opposition, hostility, churlishness,[2] abruptness,[3] disgust of heart—this is the hate that there then is.

---

[1] V y ā p a t t i, v y ā p a j j a n ā. Cf. § 1060, n. 5. Here the comment is p a k a t i b h ā v a v i j a h a n a ṭ ṭ h e n a = throwing off a normal state (Asl. 258). "Like gruel that has gone bad" (Sum. i, 211).

[2] C a ṇ ḍ i k k a ṃ. See JPTS., 1891, p. 17; PP. ii, 1 (= ii, 11). Smp. 297. Morris thinks c a ṇ ḍ i t t a ṃ is the right spelling. The Cy. in four passages spells with k k. K., by an oversight, has c a ṇ ḍ i t t a ṃ in the present passage, but k k in §§ 1060, 1314.

[3] A s u r o p o. Refers, according to the Cy. (258), to the broken utterance of a man in a rage.

[419] What on that occasion is malice?
Answer as for "hate".

* * * *

Or whatever other incorporeal, causally induced states there are on that occasion—these are states that are bad.

[Summary.]

[419*a*] Now, on that occasion
the skandhas are four,
etc.,
the faculties are five,
the Jhāna is fourfold,
the Path is threefold,
the powers are four,
the causes are two,[1]
etc.
[*Continue as in* §§ 58-61.]

* * * *

[420] What on that occasion is the skandha of synergies?
Contact,
volition,
applied, and
sustained thought,
self-collectedness;
the faculties of
energy,
concentration,
life;
wrong intention,
wrong endeavour,
wrong concentration;
the powers of
energy,
concentration,
unconscientiousness,

---

[1] Namely, d o s o and m o h o.

disregard of blame ;
hate,
dullness ;
malice ;
unconscientiousness,
disregard of blame,
quiet,
grasp,
balance.[1]

These, or whatever other incorporeal, causally induced states there are on that occasion, exclusive of the skandhas of feeling, perception and consciousness—these are the skandha of syntheses.

* * * *

X.

[421] Which are the states that are bad ?

When a bad thought has arisen which is accompanied by sorrow, is associated with repugnance, is instigated, and has as its object a sight . . . or what not, then there is contact, etc.

[*Continue as in Thought IX.*]

* * * *

XI.

[422] Which are the states that are bad ?

When a bad thought has arisen which is accompanied by indifference and associated with perplexity, and which has as its object a sight, a sound, a smell, a taste, a touch, a mental state, or what not, then there is

---

[1] It is not a little curious that such constituents as "self-collectedness", "quiet", and "balance" should not be found incompatible with hate as described above. "Concentration" is less incompatible, and it must be remembered that all three states are described in the same terms. Hence, if one stands, the others cannot fall. But see under Thoughts X and XII.

contact,
feeling,
perception,
volition,
consciousness,
applied, and
sustained thought,
indifference,
self-collectedness ;
the faculties of
energy, indifference,
mind, life ;
wrong intention,
wrong endeavour ;
the powers of
energy,
unconscientiousness,
disregard of blame ;
perplexity ;
dullness ;
unconscientiousness,
disregard of blame,
grasp.

These, or whatever other incorporeal, causally induced states there are on that occasion—these are states that are bad.

[423] What on that occasion is contact ?

The usual formula.

* * * *

[424] What on that occasion is self-collectedness ?

The persistence of thought which there is on that occasion [1] —this is the self-collectedness that there then is.

* * * *

[1] Buddhaghosa says on this passage (Asl. 259) : " Inasmuch as this weak form of thought has only the capacity of proceeding and persisting (p a v a t t i - ṭ h i t i m a t t a k a ṃ)," none of the other features of " self-collectedness " are here applied to it.

[425] What on that occasion is perplexity (vicikicchā)?[1]

The doubt, the hesitating, the dubiety, which on that

It is clear, therefore, that the "... pe ..." after ṭhiti in the text is a mistake. And cf. K. "Concentration", it will be noticed, as well as "quiet" and "balance", are entirely omitted.

[1] It is tempting to render vicikicchā by "doubt". It would not be incorrect to do so. The dual state of mind which is the etymological basis of *dou-bt* is shown in two of the terms selected to describe the word. Again, the objects of vicikicchā, as given in § 1004, are those to which the term "doubt", in its ethico-religious sense, might well be applied. But there are features in which the Buddhist attitude of vicikicchā does not coincide with doubt as usually understood in the West. Doubt is the contrary of belief, confidence, or faith. Now, the approximate equivalents of the latter—saddhā and pasādo—are not alluded to in the answer, as they might be, for the purpose of contrast. Again, though this by itself is also no adequate ground for not matching the two terms in question, the etymology of the words is very different. There is nothing of the dual, divided state of mind in the structure of vicikicchā as there is in that of "doubt". Cikit is the desiderative or frequentative of cit, to think; vi, the prefix, indicating either intensive or distracted thinking. Thus, the etymology of the Indian word lays stress on the dynamic rather than the static, on the stress of intellection rather than the suspense of inconclusiveness. When the term recurs (§ 1004), Buddhaghosa refers it to kiccho—to "the fatigue incurred through inability to come to a decision"—a position nearer, psychologically, to "perplexity" than to "doubt". It is quite true that, on etymological ground, neither is kankhā a match for our term "doubt". Kānks is to desire. The word would seem to give the emotional and volitional complement of the intellectual state implied in vicikicchā, the longing to escape into certainty and decision attendant on the anxious thinking. Kankhā, however, is not one of any important category of ethical terms, as is vicikicchā; besides, its secondary meaning—namely, of a matter *sub judice*, or of the state of mind connected therewith (see Jāt. i, 165; M. i, 147)—seems to have superseded the primary meaning, which is retained in ākankhati (cf. Ākankheyya Sutta, M. i, 33). Hence, it can be fairly well rendered by "doubt". I do not, then, pretend that "perplexity" is etymologically the equivalent of

occasion is puzzlement,[1] perplexity; distraction, standing at cross-roads;[2] collapse,[3] uncertainty of grasp; evasion, hesitation:[4] incapacity of grasping thoroughly,[5] stiffness of mind,[6] mental scarifying[7]—this is the perplexity that there then is.

*   *   *   *

---

v i c i k i c c h ā, but I use it (1) to guard against a too facile assimilation of the latter to the implications of "doubt" as used by us, and (2) to throw emphasis on the mortal "coil" and tangle of thought in one who, on whatever grounds, is sceptically disposed.

[1] V i m a t i, almost an exact parallel to v i c i k i c c h ā, connoting as it does either intense or distraught mind-action.

[2] D v e ḷ h a k a ṃ, d v e d h ā p a t h o. Here we get to the etymological idea in our own "doubt". The Cy. has, for the one, "to be swayed or shaken to and fro"; for the other, "as a path branching in two, this being an obstacle to attainment" (259).

[3] S a ṃ s a y o, the etymological equivalent of "collapse". To succumb to one's inability to be persistently carrying on such problems as, Is this permanent or impermanent? etc., says the Cy. (ibid.).

[4] Ā s a p p a n ā, p a r i s a p p a n ā. According to the Cy., these mean, respectively, "to relinquish" (or slip down from—o s a k k a t i; cf. Trenckner's *Miscellany*, p. 60), "an object of thought through inability to come to a decision", and "to slip (or run—s a p p a t i [*vide* s a r p]) about on all sides from inability to plunge in". Asl. 260.

[5] A p a r i y o g ā h a ṇ ā, employed to describe m o h o. See § 390.

[6] I should not have hesitated to adopt, for t h a m b h i t a t t a ṃ, c h a m b h i t a t t a ṃ (vacillation), the alternate reading in the Cy. (Asl. 260), were it not that the latter paraphrases the term by saying "the meaning is a condition of denseness (or rigidity, t h a d d h o). For when perplexity arises, one makes one's mind stiff (stubborn, dense, t h a d d h a ṃ)". K. also reads t h a m b h i t a t t a ṃ. Both terms, however, though opposed in connotation, are derived from the root s t a m b h, to prop; and both are used to describe the element of air, which, though it is vacillating, holds solids apart. See below, § 965. There is the further comment (Asl. ibid.) that, "in respect of certainty, inability to *carry on the idea* in the mind is meant." V i c i k i c c h ā, then, though it implies active racking of the brain, impedes

[Summary.]

[425a] Now, at that time
the skandhas are four,
etc.,
the faculties are four,
the Jhāna is fourfold,
the Path is twofold,
the powers are three,
the cause is one,[1]
etc.

[*Continue as in* § 58.]

* * * *

[426] What on that occasion is the skandha of synergies?
Contact,
volition,
applied, and
sustained thought,
self-collectedness;
the faculties of
energy,
life;
wrong intention,
wrong endeavour;
the powers of
energy,
unconscientiousness,
disregard of blame;
perplexity,

---

progress in effective thinking, and results in a mental condition akin to the denseness and apariyogāhanā of moho.

[7] Manovilekho. "When perplexity arises, seizing the object of thought, it scratches the mind, as it were" (ibid.). When the term is used to describe kukkuccaṃ, or worry (§ 1160), it is illustrated in the Cy. by the scaling of a copper pot with an awl (āraggaṃ). Asl. 384.

[1] Namely, moho.

dullness ;
unconscientiousness,
disregard of blame,
grasp.[1]

Or whatever other, etc.

[*Continue as in* § 420.]

* * * *

XII.

[427] Which are the states that are bad ?

When a bad thought has arisen which is accompanied by indifference and associated with distraction, and which has as its object a sight, a sound, a smell, a taste, a touch, a mental state, or what not, then there is

contact,
feeling,
perception,
volition,
consciousness,
applied, and
sustained thought,
indifference,
self-collectedness,
the faculties of
energy,
concentration,
mind,
indifference,
life ;
wrong intention,
wrong endeavour,
wrong concentration ;
the powers of
energy,
concentration,

[1] On the omission of " balance ", cf. below, § 429, n.

unconscientiousness,
disregard of blame ;
distraction ;
dullness ;
unconscientiousness,
disregard of blame,
quiet,
grasp,
balance.

These, or whatever other incorporeal, causally induced states there are on that occasion—these are states that are bad.

[428] *Usual question and answer on* " contact ".

* * * *

[429] What on that occasion is distraction (u d d h a c-c a ṃ) ?

The excitement of mind which on that occasion is disquietude, agitation of heart, turmoil of mind—this is the excitement that there then is.[1]

* * * *

---

[1] Y a ṃ c i t t a s s a u d d h a c c a ṃ a v ū p a s a m o, c e t a s o v i k k h e p o, b h a n t a t t a ṃ c i t t a s s a—i d a ṃ v u c c a t i u d d h a c c a ṃ. It seems clear that, whether or no u d-d h a c c a ṃ can elsewhere be rendered by terms indicative of a puffed-up state of mind (see Rhys Davids, *Buddhism*, p. 109 ; Warren, *Buddhism in Translations*, p. 365 ; Neumann, *Die Reden*, etc., I, *passim*), the specific meaning in this connexion (TATTHA k a t a m a ṃ u d d h a c c a ṃ) is the antithesis of v ū p a s a m o, and the equivalent of v i k k h e p o, both of which are expressions about the meaning of which there is little or no uncertainty. In Sanskrit, a u d d h a t y a is only found twice in later works, one of them Buddhist (v. Böthl. and Roth., s.v.), and there means wrestling, a word used by ourselves for certain agitated, perfervid mental states. That the term should be yoked with k u k k u c c a ṃ (worry) in the Nīvaraṇas (see §§ 1158–60 ; and cf. the cognate meaning in another allied pair, t h ī n a m i d d h a ṃ, §§ 1155–7) goes far to rob it of implications of vanity or self-righteousness. (In *Dialogues of the Buddha*, i, 82, the former pair are rendered " flurry and worry ".) Buddhaghosa gives

[429*a*] Now, at that time

the skandhas are four,

etc.,

the faculties are five,

---

little help; but he distinguishes uddhaccaṃ, as a struggling over *one* object of thought (ekārammaṇe vipphandati), from perplexity as a struggling over *divers* objects of thought. The Buddhists were apparently seeking for terms to describe a state of mind antithetical to that conveyed by the designation thīṇamiddhaṃ—stolidity and torpor. In the latter there is excessive stability—the immobility not of a finely adjusted balance of faculties and values, but of an inert mass. In the former (uddhacca-kukkuccaṃ) there is a want of equilibrium and adjustment. From some cause or another the individual is stirred up, *distrait*, excited; in American idiom, "rattled."

What I have rendered "turmoil" (bhantattaṃ; more literally, wavering rolling, staggering) Buddhaghosa calls vibhanti-bhāvo (*sic lege*), bhantayāna-bhantagon-ādīnaṃ viya (Asl. 260).

Whatever the exact meaning of uddhaccaṃ may be, there is enough to show that it is in great part antithetical to some of the other constituents enumerated under the Bad Thought in question—at least, when these are taken in their full intention. I refer to the approximately synonymous group: "self-collectedness," "concentration," "quiet," and "balance." The last, indeed (avikkhepo), is a contradiction in terms to the phrase which describes uddhaccaṃ as cetaso vikkhepo! The text actually omits it, but this is through mere inadvertence (cf. § 430). It is given in K., and the Cy. explicitly states (p. 260) that there are *twenty-eight* constituents enumerated, fourteen of them being described in terms of one or other of the other fourteen. (If the reader will compare § 427 with the corresponding descriptions given in §§ 2–57, he will prove this to be correct.) Nor is there a word to comment on, or explain away, any apparent incongruity in the inclusion. There is only a short discussion, alluded to already, on the relation of uddhaccaṃ and vicikicchā. Thoughts XI and XII, as departing from the symmetrical procedure of I to IX, are said to be miscellaneous items, and to be concerned with persistent attending to the idea (ārammaṇe pavaṭṭanaka-cittāni). And just as, if a round gem and a tetragonal gem be sent rolling down an inclined plane, the former's motion is uniform, while that of the latter is from one position of rest to another, so

the Jhāna is fourfold,
the Path is threefold,
the powers are four,
the cause is one,
etc.

[*Continue as in* § 58.]

*   *   *   *

[430] What on that occasion is the skandha of synergies?

Contact,
volition,
applied, and
sustained thought,
self-collectedness;
the faculties of
energy,
concentration,
life;
wrong intention,
wrong endeavour,
wrong concentration;
the powers of
energy,
concentration,

---

vicikicchā connotes a continual working of thought, while uddhaccaṃ works on one given basis at a time.

There being, then, as it would appear, this fairly close analogy between "perplexity" and "distraction", it is fair to assume that "self-collectedness" and its synonyms are to be understood in Thought XII as present in the feeble degree to which they, or at least the first of them, is present in Thought XI (see § 424, n.). The compilers were thus between two fires as to their logic. Either avikkhepo must go to admit of the use of vikkhepo—in which case the synonyms of avikkhepo (samādhi, etc.) must go too—or it and its synonyms must be retained with a highly attenuated import. Possibly, the subject was conceived as perturbed on some one point only, but calm as to things in general.

unconscientiousness,
disregard of blame ;
distraction ;
dullness ;
unconscientiousness,
disregard of blame,
quiet,
grasp,
balance.

Or whatever other, etc.

[*Continue as in* § 62.]

* * * *

[Here end] the Twelve Bad Thoughts.

[*PART III.—INDETERMINATE STATES OF CONSCIOUSNESS.*[1]

CHAPTER I.

On Effect, or Result (v i p ā k o).

A. Good Karma.

1. In the sensuous universe.

(*a*) The Five Modes of Cognition considered as effects of good (k u s a l a v i p ā k ā n i p a ñ c a - v i ñ ñ ā ṇ ā n i).]

(i.) [431] Which are the states that are indeterminate?

When, as the result of good karma[2] having been wrought, having been stored up in connexion with the sensuous universe, visual cognition has arisen, accompanied by indifference,[3] and having as its object something seen, then there is

contact, volition,
feeling, consciousness,
perception, indifference,
self-collectedness;
the faculties of
mind,
indifference,
life.

These, or whatever other[4] incorporeal, causally induced states there are on that occasion—these are states that are indeterminate.

---

[1] D h a m m ā a v y ā k a t ā. The term and its treatment are discussed in my Introduction. Cf. Vis. Magga, chap. xiv.

[2] K a m m a ṃ; literally, action, work, deed.

[3] In this and the two following sections (2 and 3) u p e k k h ā is apparently used as a psychological term only, without ethical implication, and signifies simply neutral feeling.

[4] There will be but one of these, viz. attention (Asl. 262).

[432] *Question and answer on* " contact " *as above, passim.*

[433] What on that occasion is feeling ?

The mental [condition], neither pleasant nor unpleasant, which on that occasion is born of contact with the appropriate element of visual cognition ; the sensation, born of contact with thought, which is neither easeful nor painful ; the feeling, born of contact with thought, which is neither easeful nor painful—this is the feeling that there then is.

[434] What on that occasion is perception ?

The perception, the perceiving, the state of having perceived, which on that occasion is born of contact with the appropriate element of visual cognition—this is the perception that there then is.

[435] What on that occasion is volition ?

The volition, the purpose, the purposefulness which on that occasion is born of contact with the appropriate element of visual cognition—this is the volition that there then is.

[436] What on that occasion is consciousness ?

The consciousness which on that occasion is mind, intelligence, heart, that which is clear, the sphere of mind, the faculty of mind, cognition, the skandha of consciousness, the appropriate element of visual cognition—this is the thought that there then is.

[437] What on that occasion is indifference ?

Answer as for " feeling ", § 436, *omitting the phrase* " which is born of contact with the appropriate element of visual cognition ".

[438] What on that occasion is self-collectedness ?

The persistence of thought[1] which there is on that occasion —this is the self-collectedness that there then is.

[439] What on that occasion is the faculty of mind ?

Answer as for " thought ", § 436.

[440] What on that occasion is the faculty of indifference ?

Answer as in § 437.

---

[1] In the text omit . . . p e . . . after ṭ h i t i, as in § 424, and for the same reason (Asl. 262).

[441] What on that occasion is the faculty of life ?

Answer as in § 19.

Or whatever other incorporeal, causally induced states there are on that occasion—these are the states that are indeterminate.

[Summary.]

[441*a*] Now, on that occasion
the skandhas are four,
the spheres are two,
the elements are two,
the nutriments are three,
the faculties are three,[1]
contact counts as a single factor,
etc.

[*Continue as in* § 58.]

the faculty of ideation counts as a single factor,
the element of visual cognition counts as a single factor,
the sphere of [mental] states counts as a single factor,
etc.

[*Continue as in* § 58.]

* * * *

[442] What on that occasion is the skandha of synergies ?

Contact,
volition,

---

[1] Jhāna and the Path, says the Cy. (262), are not included in the summary ; and why ? Jhāna at its extremity has applied thought (v i t a k k o), and the Path at its extremity has moral root (h e t u). Hence, it is not consistent to include Jhāna in a thought that has no conceptual activity, or the Path, when the thought is not causally effective.

This remark throws a little light on to the problem of indeterminate states. In v i t a k k o the mind is working towards an end, good or bad ; in the Path the first factor (right views) is synonymous with " absence of dullness ", which is the cause or root of good (§ 1054). Neither v i t a k k o nor a m o h o is, therefore, a possible constituent in a cognition which is inefficacious to produce good or bad karma.

self-collectedness,
the faculty of life,

or whatever other incorporeal, causally induced states there are on that occasion, exclusive of the skandhas of feeling, perception, and consciousness—these are the skandha of synergies.

*　　　*　　　*　　　*

(ii.–v.) [443] Which are the states that are indeterminate?

When, as the result of good karma having been wrought, having been stored up in connexion with the sensuous universe,

auditory cognition,
olfactory cognition, or
gustatory cognition

has arisen, accompanied by indifference, and having as its object

a sound,
a smell, or
a taste

respectively . . . or

cognition of body (touch)

has arisen, accompanied by ease, and having as its object

something tangible,[1]

---

[1] Or "a touch" (v. p. 2, n. 2). The view that the cognition of something tangible has a positive hedonic concomitant—pleasant or, if the karma be bad (§ 556), unpleasant—as compared with the neutral feeling attending other kinds of sense-cognition (under the given circumstances), is of psychological interest. And the comment it evokes is not less so. Touch, or body-sensibility, is, the Cy. explains (236), the one sense through which the four elements without and within the individual come into direct contact. Other cognition is secondary, inasmuch as the other senses are *derived* (u p ā d ā). They are as balls of cotton-wool striking wool on anvils. In touch there is, as it were, a hammer beating through the wool, and the reaction is stronger. Cf. this with the theory of sense below, §§ 592–632, Introd., p. lxiii. Nevertheless, the ease or the distress is so faintly marked that the cognition remains "indeterminate".

The constituent states, contact, etc., refer only to the last-

then there is

contact, volition,
feeling,[1] thought,
perception, ease,
self-collectedness;
the faculties of
mind,
ease,
life.

Now, these, or whatever other incorporeal, causally induced states there are on that occasion—these are states that are indeterminate.

[444] *Question and answer on* "contact" *as above, passim.*

[445] What on that occasion is feeling?

The bodily pleasure, the bodily ease, which on that occasion is born of the appropriate element of the cognition of body; the pleasurable, easeful sensation which is born of contact with the body; the pleasurable, easeful feeling which is born of contact with the body—this is the feeling that there then is.

[446] What on that occasion is perception?

The perception, the perceiving, the state of having perceived which on that occasion is born of contact with appropriate element of the cognition of body—this is the perception that there then is.

[447] What on that occasion is volition?

The volition, the purpose, the purposefulness, which on that occasion is born of contact with the appropriate element of the cognition of body—this is the volition that there then is.

[448] What on that occasion is consciousness?

The thought which on that occasion is intelligence, mind, heart, that which is clear; the sphere of mind, the faculty of mind, cognition, the skandha of consciousness, the appropriate

---

named species of cognition. In the case of the other four, "indifference" would have to be substituted for "ease".

[1] Vedanā has dropped out of the printed text.

element of the cognition of body—this is the thought that there then is.

[449] What on that occasion is ease ?

The bodily pleasure, the bodily ease which on that occasion is the pleasant, easeful sensation born of contact with the body ; the pleasant, easeful feeling born of contact with the body—this is the ease that there then is.

[450–3] What on that occasion is self-collectedness [1] . . . the faculty of mind [2] . . . of ease . . . of life ?

Answers as in §§ 438, 448, 449, *and* 441 *respectively.*

Or whatever other incorporeal, causally induced states there are on that occasion—these are states that are indeterminate.

[Summary.]

[453*a*] Now, on that occasion

the skandhas are four,

etc.

[*Continue as in* § 441*a*, *substituting* " the element of the cognition of body " *for* " the element of visual cognition ".]

* * * *

[454] What on that occasion is the skandha of synergies ?

Answer as in § 442.

* * * *

[(*b*) Good (karma) taking effect in mental life (kusalavipākā manodhātu).]

[455] Which are the states that are indeterminate ?

When, as the result of good karma having been wrought, having been stored up in connexion with the sensuous universe, the element of mind [3] has arisen, accompanied

---

[1] In § 450 omit . . . pe . . . in the text after ṭhiti.

[2] In § 451 supply kāya- before viññāṇadhātu. The state manindriyaṃ is, it is true, one not of sense-cognition, but it is occupied, under the given circumstances, with a kāya-viññāṇaṃ. The " door of mano " has as its object any, or all, of the objects of the five senses.

[3] Once more the Cy. points out (263) the significance of the affix -dhātu (element), as meaning the absence of entity

by indifference, and having as its object a sight, a sound, a smell, a taste, something tangible, or what not, then there is

contact,	consciousness,
feeling,	applied, and
perception,	sustained thought,
volition,	indifference,

self-collectedness ;
the faculties of
mind,
indifference,
life.

These, or whatever other[1] incorporeal, causally induced states there are on that occasion—these are states that are indeterminate.

[456] *Question and answer on* " contact " *as above, passim.*

[457] What on that occasion is feeling ?

The mental [condition], neither pleasant nor unpleasant, which on that occasion is born of contact with the appropriate element of mind ; the sensation, born of contact with thought, which is neither easeful nor painful ; the feeling, born of contact with thought, which is neither easeful nor painful—this is the feeling that there then is.

(n i s s a t t a), the " emptiness " or phenomenal character of the ideational faculty. Cf. above, p. 33, n. The characteristics of m a n o are here set out. See Introduction (Theory of Intellection). The theory of a *sensorium commune* here alluded to is practically identical with that adopted by Aristotle in the " De Sensu ". " The basis (or site, v a t t h u) of this kind of thought is a constant, namely, the heart ; the objects of the 'doors' (or of the idea-door) are not constants." Door and object may shift, but the " place " (ṭhānaṃ) is one, namely, the function of receiving (reading, e k a ṃ ; s a m p a ṭ i c c h a n a - k i c c a ṃ). On the heart-basis theory see S. Z. Aung in *Compendium,* 277 f.

The process of cognition is completed by m a n o v i ñ ñ ā - ṇ a d h ā t u (see below).

[1] These (Asl. 264) include two others, resolve and attention. Cf. above, p.4, n.2.

[458–60] What on that occasion is perception . . . volition . . . thought ?

Answers as in §§ 446–8, *substituting* " element of ideation " *for* " element of the cognition of body ".

[461] What on that occasion is applied thinking ?

The discrimination, the application which on that occasion is the disposing, the fixing, the focussing, the superposing of the mind [1]—this is the applied thinking that there then is.

[462] What on that occasion is sustained thought ?

The process, the sustained procedure, the progress and access [of the mind] which on that occasion is the continuous adjusting and directing of thought—this is the sustained thought that there then is.

[463–7] What on that occasion is indifference . . . self-collectedness . . . the faculty of mind . . . of indifference . . . of life ?

Answers as in §§ 437, 438, 460, 440,[2] 441 *respectively.*

[Summary.]

[467*a*] Now, on that occasion

the skandhas are four,
the spheres are two,
the elements are two,
the nutriments are three,
the faculties are three,
contact counts as a single factor,
etc.

[*Continue as in* § 58.]

the faculty of mind counts as a single factor,
the element of mind counts as a single factor,
etc.

*   *   *   *

---

[1] Inasmuch, says the Cy. (264), as this thought is neither good nor bad (in its effect), intention (k a p p o), either right or wrong, is not included in the connotation of its component v i t a k k o. Cf. §§ 7 and 371, also p. 116, n. 1.

[2] The references given in the text will prove, on examination, to be for the most part misleading.

[468] What on that occasion is the skandha of synergies?

Contact,	sustained thought,
volition,	self-collectedness,
applied, and	the faculty of life.

Or whatever other incorporeal, causally induced states there are on that occasion, exclusive of the skandhas of feeling, perception and consciousness—these are the skandha of synergies.

* * * *

(*c*) Good (karma) taking effect in representative intellection (kusala-vipākamanoviññāṇadhātu).

(i) *When accompanied by happiness.*

[469] Which are the states that are indeterminate?

When, as the result of good karma having been wrought, having been stored up in connexion with the sensuous universe, an element of representative cognition[1] has

[1] The function of the manoviññāṇadhātu is discussed in the Introduction (Theory of Intellection). As a resultant state, it is here said (Asl. 264), when "accompanied by gladness", to eventuate in two sets of circumstances: "Standing in the doors of the five senses, it accomplishes the task (or function, kiccaṃ) of inquiring (santīraṇa) as to that idea (or percept) which the element of mind, just expired, received on the expiry of that sense-cognition which constituted the result of good karma." Again: "When the action of the six doors (senses and mind) results in a more impressive idea, this becomes what is called retention (that-idea)," tad-ārammaṇaṃ, i.e. "the object of the apperception" (lit. javanaṃ). And the element of representative cognition is drawn away to fix itself on that object. So a vessel crossing a strong current avails to turn the latter aside for a moment from its natural course, which is a flowing downward. The normal flow of the consciousness is, so to speak, down the stream of the individual life (bhavaṇgam ev' otarati). And it is this normal functioning of the intellect which alone is here taken into account.

The further stage of apprehending immediately preceding any apperception (javanaṃ, cf. Sum. 194; Abh. S. iii, 3)—I allude to that of "determining" (or full assimilation, as we might say—votthappanaṃ)—is not here explicitly mentioned. But it is probably implied in the phrase santīraṇādi, "inquiring *and the rest.*" And it is discussed a few pages further on (Asl. 269, 272).

arisen, accompanied by gladness, and having as its object a sight, a sound, a smell, a taste, something tangible, the idea [of any of these], or what not, then there is

contact,	applied, and
feeling,	sustained thought,
perception,	zest,
volition,	ease,
consciousness,	self-collectedness ;

the faculties of
mind,
gladness,
life.

These, or whatever other, etc.

[*Continue as in* § 455.]

[470–82] *These thirteen constituent states are described as in* §§ 2–11 *and* 17–19, *with the exception of* "applied thinking" (v i t a k k o) *and* "self-collectedness" (c i t t a s s' e k a g g a t ā), *which are described with the restricted connotation used in* §§ 461, 464.

[Summary.]

[482*a*] *Identical with* § 467*a*, *but* "the element of representative cognition" (m a n o v i ñ ñ ā ṇ a d h ā t u) *must be substituted for* "the element of mind".[1]

*   *   *   *

[483] What on that occasion is the skandha of synergies ?

Contact,	sustained thought,
volition,	zest,
applied, and	self-collectedness ;

the faculty of life.

Or whatever incorporeal, causally induced states there are on that occasion, exclusive of the skandhas of feeling,

---

[1] The reference to [58] in the text is again incorrect, for there is to be no rehearsal of either Jhāna or Path. Cf. p. 116, n. 1, and Asl. 264.

perception, and consciousness—these are the skandha of synergies.

*　　*　　*　　*

(ii) *When accompanied by indifference.*

[484] Which are the states that are indeterminate?

When, as the result of good karma having been wrought, having been stored up in connexion with the sensuous universe, an element of representative cognition[1] has arisen, accompanied by indifference, and having as its object a sight, etc. (cf. above, § 469] . . . then there is

contact,	consciousness,
feeling,	applied, and
perception,	sustained thought,
volition,	indifference,

self-collectedness;

the faculties of

mind,
indifference,
life.

These, or whatever other, etc.

[*Continue as in* § 469.]

[485–96] *These thirteen states are described as in the*

[1] This sort of resultant cognition is said to take effect or occur on five sorts of occasions: (i) The conception of infirm offspring, viz. blind, deaf, imbecile or insane, hermaphrodite or neuter; (ii) the subconscious flux (b h a v a n g a ṃ); (iii) in the inquiry (s a n t ī r a ṇ a ṃ) respecting an idea where the object causes neither pleasure not pain; (iv) when the retention (t a d - ā r a m m a ṇ a ṃ) of absorbing impressiveness arises (cf. § 469, n.); (v) when death opens the way to renewed existence (c u t i). It will be seen that these five correspond to the first, second, tenth, thirteenth, and fourteenth occasion on which v i ñ ñ ā ṇ a s occur, according to the Visuddhi Magga (chap. xiv, see Warren's " Table of Contents ", JPTS., 1891–3, p. 130). It is possible that the absence of explanatory matter in our Cy. is due to the existence of a full treatment by Buddhaghosa in the former earlier work.

foregoing section (i), *except that the questions and answers on* "feeling" *and* "indifference", *as given in* §§ 152–4, *must be substituted for those on* "feeling", "zest", *and the* "faculty of gladness", *given in* §§ 471, 477, *and* 481. "Ease" *is omitted.*

[Summary.]

[496*a*] *Terms identical with those in* § 482*a*.

* * * *

[497] *The skandha of synergies is identical with the content stated in* § 483, *but with the omission of* "zest".

* * * *

[(*d*) The Eight Main Types of Results (a ṭ ṭ h a m a h ā- v i p ā k ā).]

[498] Which are the states that are indeterminate?

When, as the result of good karma having been wrought, having been stored up in connexion with the sensuous universe, an element of representative cognition has arisen,

(i) accompanied by gladness and associated with knowledge . . .

(ii) accompanied by gladness, associated with knowledge, and instigated . . .

(iii) accompanied by gladness and disconnected with knowledge . . .

(iv) accompanied by gladness, disconnected with knowledge, and instigated . . .

(v) accompanied by indifference and associated with knowledge . . .

(vi) accompanied by indifference, associated with knowledge, and instigated . . .

(vii) accompanied by indifference and disconnected with knowledge . . .

(viii) accompanied by indifference, disconnected with knowledge, and instigated, and having as its object a sight, a sound, a smell, a taste, something tangible, or what not, then there is contact[1] . . . balance. These, or whatever other incorporeal, causally induced states there are on that occasion—these are states that are indeterminate.

[498*a*] Disinterestedness, the root of the indeterminate . . . absence of hate, the root of the indeterminate . . . absence of dullness, the root of the indeterminate . . . these are states that are indeterminate.[2]

[2. In the universe of Form.]

[499] Which are the states that are indeterminate?

When, that he may attain to the heavens of Form, he cultivates the way [thereto], and aloof from sensuous desires, etc.,[3] enters into and abides in the First Jhāna . . . then there is contact, etc.[4] Now, these . . . are states that are good. But when, as the result of just this good karma having been wrought, having been stored up, in connexion with the universe of Form, he, aloof from sensuous desires, etc., enters into and abides in the First Jhāna . . . then there is contact, etc. And these . . . are states that are indeterminate.

---

[1] It is difficult in the present stage of knowledge respecting the Buddhist (academic) theory of the Indeterminate and of V i p ā k o to supply any safe reference for the elided states here supposed to be rehearsed. The following section (see note) seems to indicate that at least *three* more states than those enumerated in the kinds of indeterminates just discussed are to be included, namely, disinterestedness, the absence of hate and of dullness. But the Cy. is not at all lucid (pp. 265, 266), and breaks away into a long, rambling discussion on casuistical views respecting v i p ā k o.

[2] This highly elliptical paragraph, in which I have supplied the third " root ", inadvertently omitted in the text, but required by the context (see above, §§ 32–34; K., Asl. 267, 268), is presumably intended to show wherein the n i d d e s a, or descriptive exposition of certain of the constituent states of each of the Eight Types of Result, differ from those given in each of the corresponding Eight Types of Good Thoughts (§§ 1–159). Cf. §§ 576, 582.

[3] See § 160.

[4] Continue as in § 160.

[500 *Repeat, substituting the formulæ of the remaining Jhānas on the Fourfold System, and of all the Jhānas on the Fivefold System.*

[3. In the universe of the Formless.]

[501] Which are the states that are indeterminate?

When, that he may attain to the heavens of the Formless, he cultivates the way [thereto], and so, by passing wholly beyond all consciousness of form, by the dying out of the consciousness of sensory reaction, by turning the attention from any consciousness of the manifold, he enters into and abides in that frame of mind which is accompanied by the consciousness of a sphere of unbounded space—even the Fourth Jhāna, to gain which all sense of ease has been put away, etc. [*continue as in* § 265]—then the contact . . . the balance that arises, these . . . are states that are good.[1]

But when, as the result of just this good karma having been wrought, having been stored up in connexion with the universe of the Formless, he, by passing wholly beyond all consciousness of form, by the dying out of the consciousness of sensory reaction, by turning the attention from any consciousness of the manifold, enters into and abides in that rapt meditation which is accompanied by the consciousness of a sphere of unbounded space—even the Fourth Jhāna, to gain which all sense of ease has been put away, etc. [*continue as above*] . . . then the contact [2] . . . the balance that arises, these . . . are states that are indeterminate.

[502–4] *Here follow in succession the other three* "Jhānas connected with Formless Existence" (§§ 266–8), *namely*, "the Sphere of Infinite Consciousness," "the Sphere of Nothingness," *and* "the Sphere where there is neither

---

[1] In the printed text the . . . p e . . . here should be omitted, as is done in §§ 503, 504. Omit likewise in § 502.

[2] On the difficulty of determining which constituent dhammas are to be here understood, see § 498, n.

Perception nor Non-perception", *each having the Fourth Jhāna as its* "result", *as in the formula stated in* § 501.

[4. Result in the Higher Ideal (l o k u t t a r a - v i p ā k o).

I. The First Path.

The Twenty Great Methods.

1. *Rapt Meditation.*

(i) The Scheme with the Four Modes of Progress.[1]]

[505] Which are the states that are indeterminate?

When he cultivates the Jhāna of the Higher Ideal (the rapt meditation), whereby there is a going forth and onward, making for the undoing of rebirth, and when, that he may attain to the First Stage, he has put away views and opinions, and so, aloof from sensuous desires, aloof from evil ideas, he enters into and abides in the First Jhāna . . . [*continue as in* § 277] progress thereto being difficult and intuition sluggish—then there is contact . . . balance. Now these . . . are states that are good.

But when, as the result of just this good Jhāna having been wrought, having been cultivated[2] in pursuit of the Higher Ideal, he, aloof from sensuous desires, aloof from evil ideas, enters into and abides in the First Jhāna . . . progress whereto is painful, intuition wherein is sluggish, and which is EMPTINESS—then there is contact . . . the

---

[1] S u d d h i k a - p a ṭ i p a d ā. On the term s u d d h i k a, lit. pure-ish, cf. *Points of Controversy*, p. 14, with *The Expositor*, p. 248. In the former work "simply treated" should be treated as formula or schematically. It was only when revising the latter work that I grasped the meaning of the term when used methodologically. European philosophy with a similar use of "pure" (e.g. *reine Vernunft*) ought to have made this clear.

[2] The word "karma" and its *proprium*, "storing up" (u p a c i t a t t a ṃ), are now superseded respectively by l o k u t t a r a ṃ j h ā n a ṃ and cultivation or practice (b h ā v i - t a t t a ṃ) (Asl. 289).

faculty of knowledge made perfect[1] . . . balance. And these . . . are states that are indeterminate.

[506] Which are the states that are indeterminate?

When he cultivates the Jhāna of the High Ideal (the rapt meditation) whereby there is a going forth and onward, making for the undoing of rebirth, and when, that he may attain to the First Stage, he has put away views and opinions, and so, aloof from sensuous desires, aloof from evil ideas, he enters into and abides in the First Jhāna . . . (*continue as in* § 277) progress thereto being difficult and intuition sluggish—then there is contact . . . balance. Now these . . . are states that are good.

But when, as the result of just this good Jhāna having been wrought, having been cultivated, in pursuit of the Higher Ideal, he, aloof from sensuous desires, aloof from evil ideas, enters into and abides in the First Jhāna . . . progress whereto is painful, intuition wherein is sluggish, and which is the SIGNLESS[2] . . .

[*or*] [507] (*repeating all the foregoing*) which is the UNAIMED-AT[3]—then there is contact ... the faculty of knowledge made perfect . . . balance. And these . . . are states that are indeterminate.

[508] Which are the states that are indeterminate?

When he cultivates the Jhāna of the Higher Ideal (the rapt meditation), whereby there is a going forth and onward, making for the undoing of rebirth, and when, that he may attain to the First Stage, he has put away views and opinions,

---

[1] Cf. above, § 362. No comment is given on the development of this faculty, in the case of indeterminate states, *before* the First Path is left behind. But the reason is presumably that, in the quest of the Ideal, the *result* implies the attainment of a higher path, or, at least, of the "fruition" of the First Path. The faculty is not expressly stated in the corresponding passages of §§ 508, 509, either in the printed text or in K.; but there can, by the context, be no doubt that it is to be taken as read.

[2] See above, p. 83, n. 2. [3] Ibid.

and so, suppressing applied and sustained thought, enters into and abides in the Second Jhāna . . .

[*or*] . . . in the Third Jhāna . . .

[*or*] . . . in the Fourth Jhāna . . .

[*or*] . . . [*continue in the same way for fivefold Jhāna*] . . . progress whereto is painful and intuition sluggish, then this constitutes good (karma).[1]

But when, as the result [*of this or that Jhāna the corresponding Jhāna is attained*], progress whereto is painful, intuition wherein is sluggish,

and which is Emptiness,

the Signless,

[*or*] the Unaimed-at,

then the contact . . . the balance that arises—these . . . are states that are indeterminate.

[509] *Repeat the two foregoing sections, substituting in order the three remaining Modes of Progress:* "progress whereto is painful, but intuition quick," "progress whereto is easy, but intuition sluggish," *and* "progress whereto is easy, and intuition quick" (§§ 176–80).

[(ii) Emptiness schematized (suddhika-suññataṃ).][2]

[510] Which are the states that are indeterminate?

When he cultivates the Jhāna of the Higher Ideal (the rapt meditation), whereby there is a going forth and onward, making for the undoing of rebirth, and when, that he may attain to the First Stage, he has put away views and opinions, and so, aloof from sensuous desires, aloof from evil ideas, he enters into and abides in the First Jhāna . . . which is

---

[1] The compilers would appear, here and in certain subsequent answers, to have made an attempt at condensation otherwise than by the usual . . . pe . . . This is, I believe, a very rare instance.

[2] One would have expected this simpler schema to have preceded the foregoing (i), especially as (iii) is but (i) repeated. Very possibly the MSS. are corrupt.

EMPTINESS—then there is contact . . . balance. Now these . . . are states that are good.

But when, as the result of just this good Jhāna having been wrought, having been cultivated in pursuit of the Higher Ideal, he, aloof from sensuous desires, aloof from evil ideas, enters into and abides in the First Jhāna . . . which is EMPTINESS . . .

[*or*] [511] which is the SIGNLESS . . .

[*or*] [512] which is the UNAIMED-AT—then there is contact . . . balance. And these . . . are states that are indeterminate.

[513] *Repeat in the case of each of the remaining Jhānas on the Fourfold System and of all the Jhānas on the Fivefold System.*

[(iii) The Four Modes of Progress taken in connexion with the Notion of Emptiness (suññata[1]-paṭipadā).

The First Mode.]

[514] Which are the states that are indeterminate?

When he cultivates the Jhāna of the Higher Ideal (the rapt meditation), whereby there is a going forth and onward, making for the undoing of rebirth, and when, that he may attain to the First Stage, he has put away views and opinions, and so, aloof from sensuous desires, aloof from evil ideas, he enters into and abides in the First Jhāna . . . progress whereto is painful and intuition sluggish,

and which is EMPTINESS,

then there is contact . . . balance. Now these . . . are states that are good.

But when, as the result of just this good Jhāna having been wrought, having been cultivated, in pursuit of the Higher Ideal, he, aloof from sensuous desires, aloof from evil ideas, enters into and abides in the First Jhāna . . . progress whereto is painful and intuition sluggish,

---

[1] *Sic lege.*

and which is EMPTINESS . . .
. . . [*or*] [515] which is the SIGNLESS . . .
. . . [*or*] [516] which is the UNAIMED-AT,

then there is contact . . . balance. And these . . . are states that are indeterminate.

[517] *Repeat in the case of each of the remaining Jhānas on the Fourfold System, and of all the Jhānas on the Fivefold System.*

[*The Second, Third, and Fourth Modes.*]

[518] Which are the states that are indeterminate?

When he cultivates the Jhāna of the Higher Ideal (the rapt meditation), whereby there is a going forth and onward, making for the undoing of rebirth, and when, that he may attain to the First Stage, he has put away views and opinions, and so, aloof from sensuous desires, aloof from evil ideas, he enters into and abides in the First Jhāna . . .

—progress whereto is painful, but intuition quick,
and which is EMPTINESS . . .
—progress whereto is easy, but intuition sluggish,
and which is EMPTINESS . . .
—progress whereto is easy and intuition quick,
and which is EMPTINESS . . .

[*Repeat, substituting each of the remaining Jhānas in the case of each of the three Modes*] . . .
then these constitute good (karma).

But when, as the result [of this or that Jhāna in any of the three Modes], he enters into and abides in any of the Jhānas taken in order, which is in any of the three Modes,

and which is EMPTINESS . . .
. . . [*or*] which is the SIGNLESS . . .
. . . [*or*] which is the UNAIMED-AT,

then there is contact . . . balance. And these . . . are states that are indeterminate.

[(iv) The Notion of the UNAIMED-AT (suddhika-appaṇihitaṃ).][1]

[519] Which are the states that are indeterminate?

When he cultivates the Jhāna of the Higher Ideal (the rapt meditation), whereby there is a going forth and onward, making for the undoing of rebirth, and when, that he may attain to the First Stage, he has put away views and opinions, and so, aloof from sensuous desires, aloof from evil ideas, he enters into and abides in the First Jhāna . . .

which is the UNAIMED-AT,

then there is contact . . . balance. Now these . . . are states that are good.

But when, as the result of just this good Jhāna having been wrought, having been cultivated in pursuit of the Higher Ideal, he, aloof from sensuous desires, aloof from evil ideas, enters into and abides in the First Jhāna . . .

. . . which is the UNAIMED-AT . . .

. . . [*or*] [520] which is the SIGNLESS . . .

. . . [*or*] [521] which is EMPTINESS,

then there is contact . . . balance. And these . . . are states that are indeterminate.

[522] *Repeat in the case of each of the remaining Jhānas on the Fourfold System, and of all the Jhānas on the Fivefold System.*

[(v) The Four Modes of Progress taken in connexion with the Notion of the UNAIMED-AT (appaṇihita-paṭipadā).]

[523] Which are the states that are indeterminate?

When he cultivates the Jhāna of the Higher Ideal (the rapt meditation), whereby there is a going forth and onward, making for the undoing of rebirth, and when, that he may attain to the First Stage, he has put away views and opinions, and so, aloof from sensuous desires, aloof from evil ideas,

[1] The explanation why "the Signless" does not get as full "a turn" in these schemata as Emptiness and the Unaimed-at is presumably because of its middle position. Cf. p. 72, n.

enters into and abides in the First Jhāna . . . progress whereto is difficult and intuition sluggish,

and which is the UNAIMED-AT,

then there is contact . . . balance. Now these . . . are states that are good.

But when, as the result of just this good Jhāna having been wrought, having been cultivated in pursuit of the Higher Ideal, he, aloof from sensuous desires, aloof from evil ideas, enters into and abides in the First Jhāna . . . progress whereto is difficult and intuition sluggish,

and which is the UNAIMED-AT . . .

. . . [*or*] [524] which is the SIGNLESS . . .

. . . [*or*] [525] which is EMPTINESS,

then there is contact . . . balance. And these . . . are states that are indeterminate.

[526] Which are the states that are indeterminate?

When he cultivates the Jhāna of the Higher Ideal (the rapt meditation), whereby there is a going forth and onward, making for the undoing of rebirth, and when, that he may attain to the First Stage, he has put away views and opinions, and so, suppressing the working of applied and of sustained thought,[1] he enters into and abides in the Second Jhāna, or into [*any of the remaining Jhānas, both on the Fourfold and the Fivefold System*] . . .

progress whereto is difficult and intuition sluggish,

and which is the UNAIMED-AT,

then this constitutes good (karma).

But when, as the result [*of this or that Jhāna the corresponding Jhāna is attained*], progress whereto is difficult and intuition sluggish,

and which is the UNAIMED-AT,

[*or*] which is the SIGNLESS,[2]

---

[1] For v i v i c c e v a k ā m e h i read v i t a k k a v i c ā r ā n a ṃ v ū p a s a m ā.

[2] For a p p a ṇ i h i t a n ti v i p ā k o repeated, read a n i m i t t a n ti v i p ā k o.

[*or*] which is EMPTINESS,[1]

then there is contact . . . balance. And these . . . are states that are indeterminate.

[527] *The Second, Third, and Fourth Modes are now substituted in turn, as was done in* § 518.

[The Remaining Nineteen Great Methods.]

[528] Which are the states that are indeterminate ?

Here follow nineteen concepts, each of which can be substituted for " the Jhāna of the Higher Ideal " *in the preceding exercises* (§§ 505–28), *the exercise to which they are actually applied in this paragraph being the* " Scheme with the Modes of Progress " *given in* §§ 505–9. *These nineteen concepts are enumerated in* § 358.

[(vi) The scheme with the Modes of Progress taken in connexion with the Dominant Influence of Desire (chand-ādhipateyya-suddhika-paṭipadā).][2]

[529] Which are the states that are indeterminate ?

When he cultivates the Jhāna of the Higher Ideal (the rapt meditation), whereby there is a going forth and onward, making for the undoing of rebirth, and when, that he may attain to the First Stage, he has put away views and opinions, and so, aloof from sensuous desires, aloof from evil ideas, enters into and abides in the First Jhāna . . . progress whereto is difficult and intuition sluggish, and the dominant influence in which is Desire—then there is contact . . . balance. Now these . . . are states that are good.

But when, as the result of just this good Jhāna having been wrought, having been cultivated in pursuit of the Higher Ideal, he, aloof from sensuous desires, aloof from evil ideas, enters into and abides in the First Jhāna . . . progress whereto is difficult and intuition sluggish,

---

[1] Suññataṃ has been inadvertently omitted from the text.
[2] Omitted in K.

—which is EMPTINESS . . .
. . . [*or*] [530] which is the SIGNLESS[1] . . .
. . . [*or*] [531] which is the UNAIMED-AT,

and the dominant influence in which is Desire—then there is contact . . . balance. And these . . . are states that are indeterminate.

[532] *Repeat in the case of each of the remaining Jhānas on both systems.*

[533] *Repeat in the case of each of the three remaining* " Modes of Progress " *applied to each Jhāna.*

[(vii) The schematized Notion of Emptiness, and taken in connexion with Desire as the Dominant Influence (chandādhipateyyaṃ suddhika-suññataṃ).][2]

[534] Which are the states that are indeterminate?

When he cultivates the Jhāna of the Higher Ideal (the rapt meditation), whereby there is a going forth and onward, making for the undoing of rebirth, and when, that he may attain to the First Stage, he has put away views and opinions, and so, aloof from sensuous desires, aloof from evil ideas, enters into and abides in the First Jhāna . . . which is EMPTINESS, and the dominant influence in which is Desire—then there is contact . . . balance. Now these . . . are states that are good.

But when, as the result of just this good Jhāna having been wrought, having been cultivated in pursuit of the Higher Ideal, he, aloof from sensuous desires, aloof from evil ideas, enters into and abides in the First Jhāna . . .

which is EMPTINESS . . .
. . . [*or*] [535] which is the SIGNLESS . . .
. . . [*or*] [536] which is the UNAIMED-AT,

and the dominant influence in which is Desire—then there is contact . . . balance. And these . . . are states that are indeterminate.

---

[1] Read in the printed text animittaṃ for appanimittaṃ.

[2] Omitted in K.

[537] *Repeat in the case of each of the remaining Jhānas on both systems.*

(viii).[1]

[538] Which are the states that are indeterminate?

When he cultivates the Jhāna of the Higher Ideal (the rapt meditation), whereby there is a going forth and onward, making for the undoing of rebirth, and when, that he may attain to the First Stage, he has put away views and opinions, and so, aloof from sensuous desires, aloof from evil ideas, enters into and abides in the First Jhāna . . . progress whereto is difficult and intuition sluggish, which is EMPTINESS, and the dominant influence in which is Desire—then there is contact . . . balance. Now these . . . are states that are good.

But when, as the result of just this good Jhāna having been wrought, having been cultivated in pursuit of the Higher Ideal, he, aloof from sensuous desires, aloof from evil ideas, enters into and abides in the First Jhāna . . . progress whereto is difficult and intuition sluggish,

—which is EMPTINESS . . .

. . . [*or*] [539] which is the SIGNLESS[2] . . .

. . . [*or*] [540] which is the UNAIMED-AT,[3]

and the dominant influence in which is Desire—then there is contact . . . balance. And these . . . are states that are indeterminate.

[541] *Repeat in the case of each remaining Jhāna as passim.*

[542] *Repeat in the case of each of the three remaining* "Modes of Progress" *applied to each Jhāna.*

(ix).

[543–6] *This group is identical with group* vii [§§ 534–7], *except that the the concept, the* UNAIMED-AT, *takes the place of the concept* EMPTINESS, *and conversely.*

---

[1] No title is appended to this group, but it will be seen that it is a repetition of group vi (p. 135), with this additional feature, that the Jhāna which constitutes the Karma is EMPTY.

[2] Read a n i m i t t a ṃ for s u ñ ñ a t a ṃ.

[3] Omit l o k u t t a r o before p h a s s o

(x).

[547–51] *This group is identical with group* viii [§§ 538–42], *except that the concept, the* UNAIMED-AT, *takes the place of the concept* EMPTINESS, *and conversely.*

[The Remaining Nineteen Great Methods.[1]]

[552] Which are the states that are indeterminate ?

When he cultivates the Path of the Higher Ideal, the Advance in Mindfulness toward the Higher Ideal, the System of Right Efforts toward the Higher Ideal, etc. [*continue as in* § 358, *down to* " Thought relating to the High Ideal "], whereby there is a going forth and onward, making for the undoing of rebirth, and when, that he may attain to the First Stage, he has put away views and opinions, and so, aloof from sensuous desires, aloof from evil ideas, enters into and abides in the First Jhāna . . . progress whereto is difficult and intuition sluggish, and the dominant influence in which is Desire—then there is contact . . . balance. Now these . . . are states that are good.

But when, as the result of just this good Jhāna having been wrought, having been cultivated in pursuit of the Higher Ideal, he, aloof from sensuous desires, aloof from evil ideas, enters into and abides in the First Jhāna . . . progress whereto is difficult and intuition sluggish, which is

EMPTINESS,
or the SIGNLESS,
or the UNAIMED-AT,

and the dominant influence in which is

Desire,
or Energy,
or a Thought,
or Investigation,

then there is contact . . . balance. And these . . . are states that are indeterminate.

[Here ends] Result in the FIRST PATH.

---

[1] Cf. above, p. 135.

[II.—IV. The Remaining Three Paths. Cf. §§ 362–4*a*.]

[553] Which are the states that are indeterminate?

When he cultivates the Jhāna of the Higher Ideal (the rapt meditation), whereby there is a going forth and onward, making for the undoing of rebirth, and when, that he may attain to the Second Stage, he has diminished the strength of sensual passions and of malice [1] . . . [*or*] when, that he may attain to the Third Stage, he has put away the entire residuum of sensual passions and of malice . . . [or] when, that he may attain to the Fourth Stage, he has put away absolutely and entirely all passion for Form, all passion for the Formless, all conceit, excitement, and ignorance—and so, aloof from sensuous desires, aloof from evil ideas, enters into and abides in the First Jhāna . . . progress whereto is difficult and intuition sluggish, then there is contact . . . the faculty of knowledge made perfect [2] . . . balance. Now these . . . are states that are good.[3]

But when, as the result of just this good Jhāna having been wrought, having been cultivated in pursuit of the Higher Ideal, he, aloof from sensuous desires, aloof from evil ideas, enters into and abides in the First Jhāna . . . progress whereto is difficult and intuition sluggish, and which is Emptiness, then there is contact . . . the faculty of one whose knowledge is made perfect . . . balance. And these . . . are states that are indeterminate.

[554] *Question and answer on* "contact" *as above passim.*

---

[1] The passage which occurs here in the printed text, line 3 of the answer, viz. vivicc' eva . . . down to phasso hoti, seems to be a corrupt reading, presenting discrepancies with that symmetry both of construction and elision which usually marks Piṭaka compilation. K. omits the phrase.

[2] This term (aññindriyaṃ hoti) is omitted in K. It belongs, however, to the attainment of the Second Path (see above, p. 88, n. 2), and is only superseded by the intellectual climax of aññātāvindriya (§ 555). I do not think, therefore, that it is a wrong reading.

[3] Avyākatā here in the printed text should, of course, be kusalā.

[555] What on that occasion is the faculty of one who has come to know (a ñ ñ ā t ā v i n d r i y a ṃ)? [1]

The perfected knowledge, the science, the understanding of the doctrines of those whose knowledge is made perfect, their searching, research, searching the Truth; discernment, discrimination, differentiation; erudition, proficiency, subtlety; criticism, reflection, analysis; breadth, sagacity, leading; insight, intelligence, incitement; insight as faculty and as power; insight as a sword, as a height, as light, as glory, as splendour, as a precious stone; the absence of dullness, searching the Truth, right views, that searching the truth which is a factor in the Great Awakening; a Path-component, contained in the Path—this is on that occasion the faculty of one whose knowledge is made perfect.

* * * *

Or [2] whatever other incorporeal, causally induced states there are on that occasion, these are states that are indeterminate.

[Here ends] result in connexion with the Higher Ideal.

---

[1] Cf. Vibhanga, p. 124; Sam. Vin. (Cy.), p. 125. By Buddhaghosa (Asl. 291) it is defined as the distinctive "faculty of the a ñ ñ ā t ā v ī (lit. the holder of things known), of him who, in the philosophy of the Four Truths, has completed what was to be done". And the "doctrines" mentioned in the answer are defined as the associated or constituent doctrines "within" which the subject has attained proficiency, or which he has mastered inwardly (s a m p a y u t t a - d h a m m ā n a ṃ . . . ṭ h i t ā n a ṃ d h a m m ā n a ṃ a b b h a n t a r e).

Possibly, however, d h a m m ā n a ṃ refers to those intellectual states as mastered and controlled by the a ñ ñ ā t ā v i n, which are comprised in the answer.

[2] A v i k k h e p o h o t i . . . p e . . . as included in the printed text is omitted in K. It is, however, not incorrect, since a description of constituent states, beginning with "contact" and ending with "balance", similar to that given in §§ 278–337, and only differing by the substitution of "the faculty of one whose knowledge is made perfect" for "the faculty of believing that I shall come to know the Unknown", is here supposed to be fully rehearsed. As it stands, however, it is a little misleading.

[B--Bad Karma.[1]

(*a*) *The Five Modes of Sense-Cognition.*]

[556] Which are the states that are indeterminate?

When, as the result of bad karma having been wrought, having been stored up, visual cognition has arisen, accompanied by disinterestedness and having as its object a sight . . . auditory cognition has arisen, accompanied by disinterestedness and having as its object a sound . . . olfactory cognition has arisen, accompanied by disinterestedness and having as its object a smell . . . gustatory cognition has arisen, accompanied by disinterestedness and having as its object a taste . . . cognition of body has arisen, accompanied by distress and having as its object something tangible, then there is

contact, volition,
feeling, consciousness,
perception, distress,
self-collectedness;
the faculties of
mind,
distress,
life.[2]

Now these, or whatever other incorporeal, causally induced states there are on that occasion—these are states that are indeterminate.

---

[1] With section B, and its three subdivisions *a* to *c*, compare the co-ordinate results of good karma described above, §§ 431–68 and 484–97. Under B *happy* results are out of the question, the determining antecedents having been evil.

[2] Judging by the corresponding answer respecting good karma in § 443, the . . . p e . . . here appended in the printed text is erroneous. K. omits it.

This list and the following sections (557–60) apply to the last-named mode of sense-cognition, namely, that of body. In the case of the other modes, "disinterestedness" instead of "distress" would occasion to certain questions different answers.

[557] *Question and answer on* " contact " *as above passim.*

[558] What on that occasion is feeling ?

The bodily pain, the bodily distress which, on that occasion, is born of contact with the appropriate element of cognition of body ; the painful, distressful sensation which is born of contact with the body ; the painful, distressful feeling which is born of contact with the body—this is the feeling that there then is.

[559] What on that occasion is distress ?

The bodily pain, the bodily distress which, on that occasion, is the painful, distressful sensation born of contact with the body ; the painful, distressful feeling born of contact with the body—this is the distress that there then is.

[560] What on that occasion is the faculty of distress ?

Answer as in § 559.

* * * *

Or whatever other incorporeal, causally induced states there are on that occasion, these are states that are indeterminate.

[Summary.]

[560*a*] Now at that time
the skandhas are four,
the spheres are two,
the elements are two,
the nutriments are three,
the faculties are three,
contact,
etc.

[*Continue as in* § 58.]

the faculty of mind counts as a single factor,
the element of the cognition of body[1] counts as a single factor,

[1] For mano-viññāṇadhātu in the printed text read kāya-viññāṇadhātu.

the sphere of [mental] states counts as a single factor,
etc.

[*Continue as in* §§ 58–61.]

*   *   *   *

[561] What on that occasion is the skandha of synergies ?

Contact, sustained thought ;
volition, self-collectedness ;
applied, and the faculty of life.

Or whatever other incorporeal, causally induced states there are on that occasion, exclusive of the skandhas of feeling, perception, and consciousness—these are the skandha of synergies.

*   *   *   *

[*Continue as in* § 63, etc.]

[(*b*) *The Element of Ideation.*]

[562] Which are the states that are indeterminate ?

When, as the result of bad karma having been wrought, having been stored up, an element of ideation has arisen, accompanied by disinterestedness, and having as its object a sight, a sound, a smell, a taste, something tangible or what not, then there is

contact, consciousness,
feeling, applied, and
perception, sustained thought,
volition, indifference,
self-collectedness ;
the faculties of
mind,
indifference,
life.

Now these, or whatever other incorporeal, causally induced states there are on that occasion—these are states that are indeterminate.

*   *   *   *

[Summary.]

[562*a*] *This, including the description of the appropriate* skandha of synergies [563], *is identical with the corresponding Summary*, §§ 467*a*, 468.

[(*c*) *The Element of Representative Intellection.*]

[564] Which are the states that are indeterminate ?

When, as the result of bad karma having been wrought, having been stored up, an element of representative intellection has arisen, accompanied by indifference, and having as its object a sight, etc.,[1] or what not, then there is

contact,	consciousness,
feeling,	applied, and
perception,	sustained thought,
volition,	self-collectedness ;

the faculties of
mind,
indifference,
life.

Now these, or whatever other incorporeal, causally induced states there are on that occasion—these are states that are indeterminate.

* * * *

[*Continue as in* §§ 485–96.]

[Summary.]

[564*a*, 565] *This, including the description of the appropriate* skandha of synergies, *is identical with* §§ 496*a*, 497.

[Here end] the Indeterminates which are the result of Bad [Karma].

---

[1] Cf. § 562.

[CHAPTER II.

Inoperative consciousness.[1]

A. In connexion with the Sensuous Universe (kāmāvacara-kiriyā).

(*a*) *On occasion of Ideation.*]

[566] Which are the states that are indeterminate?

When a mental element which is inoperative has arisen,[2]

---

[1] I have borrowed for a title the term kiriya-cittaṃ from Asl. 293. The later (Burmese) form is kriyā-cittaṃ (see Abh. S., p. 2 *et seq.*; Bastian's *Buddhistische Psychologie*, Anhang). Kiriyā is discussed in my Introduction, p. c, f. The Cy. has the following on the term: "Kiriyā here means simply *doing* (karaṇa-mattaṃ). In all kiriyā-consciousness that in which the stage of javanaṃ is attained is like wind-snapped blossoms, but that in which that stage is not attained is like blossoms where the tree has been felled, barren of fruit. But when this or that is kept going in the performance of function, then there is 'doing' pure and simple. Hence the term kiriyā is used." Now, javanaṃ, according to Buddhaghosa (Sum. I, 195), is the effective outcome of an act of cognition, the stage when the mind or character of the percipient subject is modified (ethically) in one way or another. But in the species of indeterminate thoughts termed kiriyā there can be no practical outcome for good or bad, no karma can be set free. Hence the simile of the sterile blossoms. The Abh. S. (trs. in *Compendium*, p. 85 f.) gives also three species of non-causative kiriyā-thoughts as connected with the sensuous universe—reflection on sense-impressions, reflection on ideas, and the genesis of mirth (hasituppāda-cittaṃ). These correspond fairly well to the three given in the Dh. S., if the two modes of representative intellection be taken in inverted order.

[2] According to the Cy., the ideation which is kiriyā differs from the ideation which is *result* only in the mode of its arising (upattiṭṭhānaṃ). The latter arises immediately after the act of sense-cognition. The former arises while sensation is actually proceeding, while the organism is being turned towards the object (Asl. 293). Again (ibid.), that the consciousness is "neither good nor bad" means the absence of that cause of

which is neither good nor bad nor the result of karma, which is accompanied by indifference, and which has as its object a sight, a sound, a smell, a taste, something tangible, or what not, then there is

contact, consciousness,
feeling, applied, and
perception, sustained thought,
volition, indifference,
self-collectedness ; [1]
the faculties of
mind,
indifference,
life.

Now these, or whatever other incorporeal, causally induced states there are on that occasion—these are states that are indeterminate.

* * * *

[Summary.]

[566*a*] Now, at that time
the skandhas are four,
the spheres are two,
the elements are two,
the nutriments are three,
the faculties are three,
contact,
etc.

* * * *

---

good or of bad which is termed the root of the one or of the other ; it means the absence of those conditions of good or of bad which are termed considering things by way of their causes (yoniso-manasikārā), or not so considering them. "Nor the result of karma" means the absence of the generative condition (janakahetu), known as good or bad (as the case may be). Asl. 293. The marginal reading in the last sentence is obviously right.

[1] With its minimum connotation, i.e. as in § 438 and elsewhere (Asl. 293).

[567] *The* skandha of synergies (*as well as the remainder of the foregoing summary*) *is identical with the corresponding passages in* Chapter I, viz. §§ 467*a*, 468.

*　*　*　*

(*b*) *On occasion of Representative Intellection.*

1.

[568] Which are the states that are indeterminate ?

When an element of representative intellection which is inoperative has arisen, which is neither good nor bad nor the result of karma, which is accompanied by gladness,[1] and which has as its object a sight, a sound, a smell, a taste, something tangible, or what not, then there is

contact,	applied, and
feeling,	sustained thought,
perception,	zest,
volition,	ease,
consciousness,	self-collectedness ;

---

[1] The Cy. (p. 294) pronounces this species of thought not common to men, but peculiar to the arahant. " It is obtained in the six doors," e.g. when an arahant sees a spot (ṭ h ā n a ṃ) favourable to one of those prescribed spiritual wrestlings termed p a d h ā n ā n i [*sic lege* ; cf. below, § 1366, (v)], " by this thought he is gladdened." When he comes to a market-place, " hears the uproar of the bargaining, and thinks, ' I have done with all this thirst for gain,' by this thought he is gladdened. When he has made an offering of fragrant odours or flowers at the shrine, by this thought he is gladdened. When he is tasting the food he has received as ordained, and thinks, ' Verily I have carried out the doctrine incumbent upon me,' by this thought he is gladdened. When he is carrying out minor rules concerning the body, and thinks, ' I have fulfilled the rules concerning the door of the body,' by this thought he is gladdened. Such is this kind of intellection when obtained in connexion with the ' fivefold door '. In connexion with the door of *ideation*, it arises with reference to the past and the future." As, for instance, when the Buddha smiled at the recollection of occurrences in certain of his former births, or, again, when he foresaw this and that.

the faculties of

energy, mind,
concentration, gladness,
life.

Now these, or whatever other incorporeal, causally induced states there are on that occasion—these are states that are indeterminate.

[569] *Question and answer on* "contact" *as above passim.*

* * * *

[570] What on that occasion is self-collectedness?

The stability, solidity, absorbed steadfastness of thought which on that occasion is the absence of distraction, balance, imperturbed mental procedure, quiet, the faculty and the power of concentration [1]—this is the self-collectedness that there then is.

* * * *

[571] What on that occasion is the faculty of energy . . .
[572] of concentration?

Answers as in § 13 *and* § 570 *respectively.*

* * * *

[Summary.]

[572*a*] Now at that time
the skandhas are four,
the spheres are two,
the elements are two,
the nutriments are three,
the faculties are five,
contact,
etc.

[*Continue as in* § 482*a*.]

* * * *

[1] It might have been expected that this "power" as well as that of "energy" would have found a place in the enumeration of the constituent states. The Cy. (p. 295) explains that "concentration" and "energy" are not present in full strength. It follows that no "powers" are included in the summary.

[573] What on that occasion is the skandha of synergies?

Contact,
volition,
applied, and
sustained thought,
zest,
self-collectedness;
the faculties of
energy,
concentration,
life.

Or whatever other incorporeal, causally induced states there are on that occasion, exclusive of the skandhas of feeling, perception, and consciousness—these are the skandha of synergies.

* * * *

2.

[574] Which are the states that are indeterminate?

When an element of representative intellection which is inoperative has arisen which is neither good, nor bad, nor the result of karma, which is accompanied by indifference,[1] and which has as its object a sight, a sound, a smell, a taste, something tangible, or what not, then there is

contact, consciousness,
feeling, applied, and
perception, sustained thought,
volition, indifference,
self-collectedness;

---

[1] This kind of thought, unlike the last, is, says the Cy. (295), common to all intelligent (s a c i t t a k a) beings; in fact, there is none such who does not experience it. (The marginal reading is here evidently the more correct.) If it arise in connexion with the "five doors", it is an act of establishing; if in connexion with the door of ideation, it is an act of reflection. By it the six specific channels of cognition lay hold of their several objects.

the faculties of
energy, mind,
concentration, indifference,
life.

Now these, or whatever other incorporeal, causally induced states there are on that occasion—these are states that are indeterminate.

* * * *

[Summary.]

[574*a*] *Identical with* 572*a*.

* * * *

[575] *The* skandha of synergies *is identical with that in* § 573, *but* " zest " *must be omitted.*

* * * *

3.

[576] Which are the states that are indeterminate?

When an element of representative intellection which is inoperative has arisen that is neither good, nor bad, nor the result of karma—(I) [1] which is accompanied by gladness and associated with knowledge . . . (II) which is accompanied by gladness, associated with knowledge, and is instigated . . . (III) which is accompanied by gladness and disconnected with knowledge . . . (IV) which is accompanied by gladness, disconnected with knowledge, and is instigated . . . (V) which is accompanied by indifference and associated with knowledge . . . (VI) which is accompanied by indifference, associated with knowledge, and is instigated . . . (VII) which is accompanied by indifference and disconnected with knowledge . . . (VIII) which is accompanied by indifference, disconnected with knowledge, and is instigated—and which has as its object a sight, a sound, a smell, a taste, something tangible,

[1] The Latin numerals refer to the Eight Main Types of Thought set forth in the first 159 sections of this work. In this connexion, however, they are no longer effective as " good ", i.e. as producing good karma.

or what not—then there is contact . . . balance. Now these . . . are states that are indeterminate.

* * * *

[576a] That disinterestedness, the root of the indeterminate . . . that absence of hate, the root of the indeterminate . . . that absence of dullness, the root of the indeterminate . . . these are states that are indeterminate.[1]

* * * *

[B. In connexion with the Universe of Form (rūpāvacara-kiriyā).]

[577] Which are the states that are indeterminate?

When he cultivates rapt meditation in connexion with the universe of Form, which is inoperative, is neither good, nor bad, nor the result of karma, and which is concerned with easeful living under present conditions[2]—and so, aloof from sensuous desires, aloof from evil ideas, by earth-gazing, enters into and abides in the First Jhāna . . . then there is contact . . . balance. Now these . . . are states that are indeterminate.

[578] *Repeat in the case of each remaining Jhāna on the Fourfold, and of those on the Fivefold System.*

[C. In connexion with the Universe of the Formless (arūpāvacara-kiriyā).]

[579] Which are the states that are indeterminate?

When he cultivates rapt meditation in connexion with the universe of the Formless, which is inoperative, is neither good, nor bad, nor the result of karma, and is concerned with

---

[1] See above, § 498a.

[2] Diṭṭha-dhammasukha-vihāraṃ. In this individual existence (imasmiṃ attabhāve), explains the Cy. (296. On this term, cf. below, p. 159, n.3). In Sum. I, 121, the paraphrase runs, "that state of existence one happens to have got." Cf. *Dialogues of the Buddha*, i, 50, note. The passage there commented upon (D. I. 37.) is the heresy which holds that Jhāna constituted an equivalent for Nirvāna.

easeful living under present conditions—and when, by passing wholly beyond all consciousness of form, by the dying out of the consciousness of sensory reaction, by turning the attention from any consciousness of the manifold, he enters into and abides in that rapt meditation which is accompanied by the consciousness of a sphere of unbounded space—even the Fourth Jhāna, to gain which all sense of ease has been put away, etc. . . . then there is contact . . . balance. Now these . . . are states that are indeterminate.

[580–2] *Here follow, with the same opening formula as in the foregoing answer, the three remaining* " Jhānas connected with Formless Existence ". *See* §§ 266–8.[1]

[Here ends] the DIVISION ON THE UPRISING OF MIND.

---

[1] The PTS. text then appends a repetition of 576*a*, which is probably a gloss. In K. a footnote here draws attention to the apparent discrepancy in the fact that this passage, hitherto given under the universe of sense [§§ 498*a*, 576*a*], is here associated with the universe of the Formless. This, it adds, should be accepted, after due deliberation. Buddhaghosa makes no comment.

[BOOK II.

Material Form (rūpakaṇḍaṃ).

Introductory.]

[583] Which are the states that are indeterminate? [1]

The results of good and bad states taking effect in the universe of sense, in that of form, in that of the formless, or in [the life] which is Unincluded,[2] and as connected with the skandhas of feeling, perception, synergies, and consciousness; [3] as well as those inoperative states which are neither good, nor bad, nor the result of karma; all form, moreover; and [finally] Unconditioned Element [4]—these are states that are indeterminate.

---

[1] The subject of the Ethically Indeterminate has not been exhausted by the inquiry into Vipāko and Kiriyā. It includes two other species: Form (or External Phenomena) and Nirvāna (Uncompounded Element). (Asl. 296.) Hence it is that the following inquiry into "Material Form", as objective and subjective phenomenon, is led up to by a question connecting it with the foregoing inquiry into the uprising of mind, this being presented from the point of view of a-rūpino dhammā, or formless (incorporeal) states of consciousness.

[2] Apariyāpannā. This term, which is often employed in Book III, and which is intended to convey a sense of the "apartness" of the pursuit of the Highest from all lower aims, is dealt with below (§ 992).

[3] I follow, here as often as elsewhere, the punctuation of K. In this identical answer later on, however, K. is self-inconsistent, placing a colon before, and a comma after, the enumeration of the skandhas. See § 983. One or the other is probably an inadvertency through unfamiliarity with our methods of punctuation.

[4] Asankhatā ca dhātu. This term, which both Buddhaghosa and the original Atthakathā (see § 1376 in printed text of Dh. S.) identify with Nirvāna, occurs often in this connexion with its opposite "all form" (v. p. 155, n. 3) in Book III. I do not know whether this, so to speak, cosmological conception of the Ethical Ideal occurs in the older books of the

[584] In this connexion, what is "all form" (s a b b a ṃ r ū p a ṃ)?

The four great phenomena [1] and that form which is derived from the four great phenomena—this is what is called "all form".[2]

[584–94] *Here follows the Mātikā, or table of contents of the following analysis of Form, considered under quantitative categories—the usual Buddhist method. That is to say, Form is considered, first, under a number of single, uncorrelated qualities, then under dichotomized qualities, then under qualities which, taken singly, give inclusion, inclusion under the opposite, or exclusion from both; or which, taken in pairs, afford three combinations. We then get pairs of qualities taken together, affording* four *combinations. After that comes consideration of Form under more inductive classifications, e.g. the four elements and, fifthly, their derivatives, and so on, as given below.*

Piṭakas, or whether, indeed, the commentators have not laid upon the physical term more than it was intended to bear—a connotation that derives perhaps from the scholastic ages of Buddhism. For example, in §§ 1016–18 of the present work, to identify unconditioned element with Nirvāna, just after it has been opposed to the "topmost fruit of arahantship", would apparently land the compilers in a grave inconsistency. I have yet to meet with a passage in the first two Piṭakas which establishes the identification. In the Milinda-pañho giving the traditional doctrine of an age half-way between Piṭakas and Commentaries, we can see the theory of Nirvāna as the one a s a n k h a t a ṃ developing. See pp. 268 *et seq.* Cf. also KV. 317–30.

[1] M a h a b h u t ā n i, that is, the four elements, literally, the things-that-have-become, *die grossen Gewordenen*, *τά γιγνόμενα*—a far more scientific term than elements or *στοιχεῖα*. See further below, §§ 597, 647 *et seq.*

[2] The various implications of the term r ū p a ṃ, such as objective phenomena, concrete or compound, the object of the sense of sight, material existence without sensuous appetite, etc., are discussed in my Introduction (ii).

[CHAPTER I.

Exposition of [Material] Form under Single Concepts (e k a k a n i d d e s o).]

[595] All form is that which is
not root condition,
not the concomitant of a root condition,
disconnected with root-condition,[1]
causally related,[2]
conditioned,[3]
endowed with form,[4]
mundane,[5]
co-intoxicant,[6]
of the Fetters,[7]
of the Ties,
of the Floods,
of the Bonds,
of the Hindrances ;

---

[1] N a h e t u. On "root-condition", see under § 1053. The special connotation here is that "form", as such, is not the ground or "root", or psychical condition, of any moral or immoral result. (Asl. 303.) The two following terms are dealt with under §§ 1074, 1076.

[2] S a p p a c c a y a ṃ (cf. § 1083). The more general term including the more specific "root-condition".

[3] S a n k h a t a ṃ. This quality is involved in the preceding quality. See § 1085. See also above, p. 166, n. 1.

[4] R ū p i y a ṃ or r ū p a m e v a. The table of contents (§ 584) gives the former ; K. has here the latter. Either the one or the other has been omitted from the present section of the printed text. The Cy. gives the latter term—R ū p a m e v ā t i r ū p i n o d h a m m ā, etc. Asl. 304.

[5] L o k i y a ṃ ; the antithesis of l o k u t t a r a ṃ. Cf. § 1093.

[6] S ā s a v a ṃ. See § 1096 *et seq.*

[7] S a ṃ y o j a n i y a ṃ, etc. This and the four following terms are severally discussed in connexion with the ethical metaphors of Fetters and the rest. See § 1113 *et seq.*

infected,[1]
of the Graspings,[2]
belonging to the Vices,[3]
indeterminate,
void of mental objects,[4]
not a mental property,[5]
disconnected with thought,
neither moral result nor productive of it,[6]
not vicious yet belonging to the Vices,[7]
not applied and sustained thinking,[8]
not "applied, but only sustained thinking",
neither "applied nor sustained thinking",
not "accompanied by zest",
not "accompanied by ease",
not "accompanied by indifference",[9]
not something capable of being got rid of either by insight or by cultivation,
not that the cause of which may be got rid of either by insight or by cultivation,
neither tending to, nor away from, the accumulation involving rebirth,

---

[1] Parāmaṭṭhaṃ. See § 1174 *et seq.*
[2] Upādāniyaṃ. See § 990 and § 1213 *et seq.*
[3] Sankilesikaṃ. See § 993 and § 1229 *et seq.*
[4] Anārammaṇaṃ, the idea or mental object belonging, of course, to the arūpa-dhammo.
[5] Acetasikaṃ. See § 1022.
[6] See § 989.
[7] See § 994.
[8] Na savitakka-savicāraṃ. This and the two following technical terms mark off material form from the *mental* discipline of Jhāna. Jhāna may be practised for the sake of passing from a sensuous existence to the "universe of Form", but that is not the rūpa (material) here discussed. Cf. §§ 160, 168, 161, and 996–8.
[9] Cf. §§ 999–1001. These are all mental states, characterizing the other four skandhas, not the rūpakkhandho. Similarly, the four following doctrinal expressions are only applicable to mental and moral categories. Cf. §§ 1007–18.

belonging neither to studentship nor to that which is beyond studentship,
of small account,[1]
related to the universe of sense,
not related to the universe of form,[2]
nor to that of the formless,
included,
not of the Unincluded,[3]
not [something entailing] fixed [retribution],[4]
unavailing for (ethical) guidance,
apparent,[5]
cognizable by the six modes of cognition,
impermanent,[6]
subject to decay.

Such is the category of Form considered by way of single attributes.[7]

---

[1] Parittaṃ. See § 1019.

[2] Read na rūpāvacaraṃ.

[3] See p. **153**, n. 2.

[4] This and the following term belong to ethical, immaterial categories of thought. See §§ 1028–30 and 1291; also 1288, 1289, and 277.

[5] Uppannaṃ (lit. arisen) present (in consciousness). "For, strictly speaking, with reference to visual and other sense-cognition, they (*read* na hi tāni) do not cognize the past and future; that is the function of representative cognition (manoviññāṇaṃ)" (Asl. 304).

[6] Aniccaṃ, "inasmuch as, having fallen into this stream of sense-cognition, it ('form') has become mere flotsam, has become something gone, something that is not" (ibid.). This shows well the psychological standpoint of the later Buddhist tradition. Form is impermanent for the individual perceptive consciousness.

[7] The Cy. gives as the reason for there being no catechism on each of the foregoing attributes the fact that there is no correlated opposite, as in the next category, from which each term is to be differentiated (Asl. 303). This, in view of the procedure in Book I, is scarcely adequate. However, every term is examined in the sequel, as the foregoing notes will have indicated.

[CHAPTER II.

The Category of [Material] Form considered by way of dual attributes—positive and negative (duvidhena rūpa-sangaho).

" *There is [material] form which is derived.*"] [1]

[596] What is that [material] form which is derived?

The sphere [2] of

vision, smell,
hearing, taste,
body-sensibility; [3]

the sphere of

sights, odours,
sounds, tastes;
woman-faculty man-faculty,
life-faculty;

intimation
by act,
by speech;

the element of space;

---

[1] This and the following italicized headings are quoted from the table of contents, § 585, etc.—atthi rūpaṃ upādā, and, again, atthi rūpaṃ no upādā. The ablative resembles our idiom " *quâ* derived "—form as derived. In § 584 and in § 597, etc., the gerund upādāya is employed. Depending on, not released from, is the paraphrase (Asl. 300, 305). " Grounded in " were an approximate rendering, the literal meaning being " taking hold of ".

[2] Āyatanaṃ. The word means (see my Introduction) simply " field ", locus, range, *Gebiet*.

[3] Lit. body. The Upanishads use " skin ". Cf. our modern term " skin-sensibility ", in extension of " touch ", " tactile sense ". The corresponding objective " sphere of the tangible " is classed among things *un*derived. See § 647.

buoyancy,
plasticity,
wieldiness,
integration,
maintenance,
decay,
impermanence,
} of form.

solid nutriment.

[597] What is that [material] form which is the sphere of vision (c a k k h ā y a t a n a ṃ)?

The eye,[1] that is to say the sentient organ,[2] derived from the Great Phenomena, included in the self-state, nature of the self,[3] invisible and reacting[4]—by which eye, invisible and

---

[1] C a k k h u, which stands for vision, sense of sight and eye. "Eye," however, is always in the present work to be understood as the seeing faculty of visual sense, and not as the physical organ or "eye of flesh" (m a ṃ s a - c a k k h u). The Cy. gives a vivid detailed disquisition on the eye as psychophysical organ. Cf. *Expositor*, 402 f. The visual sentient organ (p a s ā - d a c a k k h u) was held to be in size of the measure of a louse's head. Cf. below, 190, n.2.

[2] P a s ā d o, not found prior to the Abhidhamma-Piṭaka. By selecting this term, continues the Cy., he (the Buddha) rejects the other (physical) eye. P a s ā d o, meaning literally clearness, brightness, serenity, faith, is used to denote the receptive reacting sense-agency. It is not easy to divine exactly how the Buddhists came to use the word in this connexion. It is used co-ordinately for all the other senses, hence the sensuous signification had nothing to do with the specific nature of sight (unless this was made the type of all other sensation). Taken causatively it may conceivably have meant either that which makes clear—a revealer, as it were (cf. Böthl. and Roth—p r a s ā d a n a), or that which gratifies or satisfies (*beruhigen*), both meanings emphasizing psychological *process*, rather than "product" or "seat".

[3] A t t a b h ā v a - p a r i y ā p a n n o. "The body and the five skandhas are here termed nature of the self, after the usage of foolish folk who say, 'This is myself'" (Asl. 308). Thus the usage of a t t a b h ā v o was considered to be a concession on the part of the Teacher to animistic phraseology.

[4] i.e. "impact and reaction are set up in the eye" (ibid.).

reacting, one [1] has seen, sees, will, or may see material shape that is visible and reacting—this that is sight, the sphere of sight, the element of vision, the faculty of vision, [this that is] "the world",[2] "a door", "an ocean", "lucent", "a field", "[physical] basis", "a guide", "guidance", the "hither shore", an "empty village"—this is that [material] shape which constitutes the sphere of vision.

[598] What is that [material] form which is the sphere of vision?

The eye, that is to say the sentient organ, derived from the four Great Phenomena, included in the self-state, invisible and reacting, and against which eye, invisible and reacting,

---

[1] Paraphrased by ayaṃ satto, any given individual (ibid.).

[2] This and the following similes will be quotations of metaphors applied to the senses in the Sutta Piṭaka. e.g. that of the "empty village" occurs in S. iv, 174—Suñño gamo ti kho, bhikkhave, channam ajjhattikānaṃ [?āyatanānam] adhivacanaṃ. That of a "door", which in the age of the Commentaries was the regular term for sense-organ, is, I believe, seldom used in the Sutta-Piṭaka, and then only as a poetical figure, not as a technical term. Cf. e.g. indriyesu guttadvāro (DI. 63, 250). Buddhaghosa simply paraphrases the various metaphors—"world," by reason of wasting and decay (S. iv, 52, 87); "door," by reason of customary resort; "ocean," by reason of its insatiableness (S. iv, 157); "lucent," by reason of its purity; "field," by reason of the springing up (growth) of contact, etc.; "base," by reason of its fixed seat; "guide," "guidance," by reason of its leading, showing a person agreements and differences; "hither shore," by reason of its being included in the "body of this life" (or individuality, sakkāyaṃ, S. iv, 175, 180); "empty village," because it is common to many, because there is no headman (i.e. Ego or soul. "Many" must mean the individual considered as an aggregate of constituents). The metaphors, it will be seen, are applied equally, with the sole exception of "guide" and "guidance", to each remaining sense. By the explanation of these two figures given in the Cy., they should have been left to stand for each sense. Buddhaghosa, however, is, of course, not responsible for the expressions used in the Piṭakas. Yet it is slightly disappointing that he makes no comment.

[material] shape that is visible and reacting, has impinged,[1] impinges, will, or may impinge—this that is sight, the sphere of sight, the constituent element of sight, etc. [*continue as in* § 597].

[599] What is that [material] form which is the sphere of vision ?

The eye, that is to say the sentient organ, derived from the four Great Phenomena, included in the self-state, invisible and reacting, which eye, invisible and reacting, has impinged, impinges, will, or may impinge on [material] shape [2] that is visible and impingeing—this that is sight, the sphere of sight, etc. [*continue as in* § 597].

[600] What is that [material] form which is the sphere of vision ?

The eye, that is to say the sentient organ, derived from the four Great Phenomena, included in the self-state, invisible and reacting, (i) depending on which eye, in consequence of some [visible] shape,[3] there has arisen, arises, will, or may arise

visual contact ; [4] . . .

(ii) and depending on which eye, in consequence of some [visible] shape, there has arisen, arises, will, or may arise—born of that visual contact—

a feeling . . .

[*or* iii] a perception . . .

[*or* iv] volition . . .

[*or* v] a visual cognition [5] . . .

---

[1] In this answer, according to the Cy. (p. 309), involuntary visual sensation is described, as when lightning flashes on the sight of one not looking for it.

[2] Here (Asl. 309) we have *voluntary* sense-impression described—the process in the case of one " who, by his own desire, seeking to look at some object, concentrates his vision ".

[3] Cakkhuṃ nissāya, rūpaṃ ārabbha.

[4] Here there should be in the text . . pe . . . as in the corresponding passage for the other four senses. Cf. n. 4. In K. it is also inadvertently omitted here.

[5] Cakkhuviññāṇaṃ here replaces the fourth mode of consciousness, cittaṃ, or thought, in the series invariably

[further, vi] depending on[1] which eye, and having a [visible] shape as its object, there has arisen, arises, will, or may arise visual contact,

(vii) and depending on which eye, and having a visible form as its object, there has arisen, arises, will, or may arise, born of that visual contact,

a feeling . . .
[*or* viii] a perception . . .
[*or* ix] volition . . .
[*or* x] visual cognition—

this that is sight, the sphere of sight, etc. [*continue as in* § 597].[2]

---

stated as aroused by " contact " in connexion with the Eight Types of Thought given in Book I, chap. i. Volition (cetanā) may stand for a train of ideas set going by the sensation having no special reference to the visible object as such. Visual cognition, on the other hand, would take special account of the thing seen. Or possibly the two are to be considered as corresponding approximately to process and product. Cf. what has been said above on both terms, p. 7, n. 1.

[1] Judging by the corresponding passages in §§ 604, 608, 612, 616, by K. and by the comments of Buddhaghosa, I find that the following passage has been erroneously omitted in the text before the words cakkhum p'etaṃ: . . . pe . . . yaṃ cakkhuṃ nissāya rūpārammaṇo cakkhusamphasso uppajji vā uppajjati vā uppajjissati vā uppajje vā, yam cakkhuṃ nissāya rūpārammaṇā cakkhusamphassajā vedanā . . . pe . . . saññā . . . pe . . . cetanā . . . pe . . . cakkhuviññāṇaṃ uppajji vā uppajjati vā uppajji vā uppajje vā. Cf. also § 620.

[2] According to the Cy. (310), this reply, when rehearsed in full, reveals ten distinct answers, each commencing with the refrain : " The eye, that is to say," etc., to " self, invisible and reacting ". They may be summarized and generalized thus : (i) Sense-impression or contact, as conditioned by sense-organ and sense-*stimulus*. (ii) Resultant feeling. (iii–v) Resultant intellectual states. (vi) Sense-impression or contact, as conditioned by sense-organ and idea of sense-*object*. (vii–x) Resultant states as in (ii-v). What was precisely the difference between the processes named as (i) and (vi) it is not yet easy to determine with certainty.

[601–4] What is that [material] form which is the sphere of hearing?

The ear, that is to say the sentient organ,[1] derived from the four Great Phenomena, forming part of the nature of the self, invisible and reacting,—

(*a*) by which ear, invisible and reacting, one has heard, hears, will, or may hear sound that is invisible and reacting;

(*b*) against which ear, invisible and reacting, sound that is invisible and reacting, has impinged, impinges, will, or may impinge;

(*c*) which ear, invisible and reacting, has impinged, impinges, will, or may impinge on sound that is invisible and reacting;

(*d*) depending on which ear, in consequence of a sound, there has arisen, arises, will, or may arise

auditory contact; . . .

and, depending on which ear, in consequence of a sound, there has arisen, arises, will, or may arise, born of that auditory contact,

a feeling . . .
[*or*] a perception . . .
[*or*] volition . . .
[*or*] auditory cognition;

[further] depending on which ear, and having a sound as its object, there has arisen, arises, will, or may arise

auditory contact,

and, depending on which ear, and having a sound as its object, there has arisen, arises, will, or may arise, born of that auditory contact,

a feeling . . .
[*or*] a perception . . .
[*or*] volition . . .
[*or*] auditory cognition;

---

[1] This, situated within the cavity of the aggregate organism of the ear, and well furnished with fine reddish hairs, is in shape like a little finger-stall (anguli-veṭhanaka). (Asl. 310.) Cf. Hardy, loc. cit.

this that is hearing, the sphere of hearing, the constituent element of hearing, the faculty of hearing, this that is "the world", "a door", "an ocean", "lucent", "a field", "a basis",[1] "the hither shore", "an empty village"—this is that [material] form which is the sphere of hearing.

[605–8] What is that [material] form which is the sphere of smell?

The nose, that is to say the sentient organ,[2] derived from the four Great Phenomena, forming part of the nature of the self, invisible and reacting,—

(*a*) by which nose, invisible and reacting, one has smelt, smells, will, or may smell odour that is invisible and reacting;

(*b*) against which nose, invisible and reacting, odour that is invisible and reacting, has impinged, impinges, will, or may impinge;—

(*c*) which nose, invisible and reacting, has impinged, impinges, will, or may impinge on odour that is invisible and reacting;

(*d*) depending on which nose, in consequence of an odour . . . depending on which nose, and having an odour as its object, there has arisen, arises, will, or may arise

olfactory contact,

and, depending on which nose, in consequence of an odour . . . depending on which nose, and having an odour as its object, there has arisen, arises, will or may arise, born of that olfactory contact,

a feeling . . .
[*or*] a perception . . .
[*or*] volition . . .
[*or*] olfactory cognition;

this that is smell, the sphere, the constituent element, the

---

[1] On the omission of "a guide", etc., see p. 160, n. 2.

[2] This is situated "inside the cavity of the aggregate nasal organism, in appearance like a goat's hoof". (Asl. 310.) Cf. Hardy, loc. cit. Probably the hoof is imagined as regarded from below.

faculty, of smell, this that is " the world ", etc. [*continue as in* § 604].

[609–12] What is that [material] form which is the sphere of taste ?

The tongue, that is to say the sentient organ,[1] derived from the four Great Phenomena, included in the self-state, invisible and reacting ;

(*a*) by which tongue, invisible and reacting, one has tasted, tastes, will, or may taste sapids that are invisible and reacting ;

(*b*) against which tongue, invisible and reacting, sapids that are invisible and reacting, have impinged, impinge, will, or may impinge ;

(*c*) which tongue, invisible and reacting, has impinged, impinges, will, or may impinge on sapids that are invisible and reacting ;

(*d*) depending on which tongue, in consequence of a sapid . . . depending on which tongue, and having a sapid as its object, there has arisen, arises, will, or may arise

gustatory contact,

and depending on which tongue, in consequence of a sapid . . . depending on which tongue, and having a sapid as its object, there has arisen, arises, will, or may arise, born of that gustatory contact,

a feeling . . .
[*or*] a perception . . .
[*or*] volition . . .
[*or*] gustatory cognition ;

this that is taste, the sphere, the constituent element, the faculty of taste, this that is " the world ", etc. [*continue as in* § 604].

---

[1] This is situated " above the middle of the aggregate gustatory organism, in appearance like the upper side of the leaf of a lotus ". (Asl. ibid.) Cf. Hardy, loc. cit. The palate apparently was not included in the gustatory apparatus.

[613–16] What is that [material] form which is the sphere of body[-sensibility] ?

The body, that is to say the sentient organ,[1] derived from the four Great Phenomena, included in the self-state, invisible and reacting ;

(*a*) by which body-sensibility, invisible and reacting, one has touched, touches, will, or may touch the tangible that is invisible and reacting ;

(*b*) against which body-sensibility, invisible and reacting, the tangible, which is invisible and reacting, has impinged, impinges, will, or may impinge ;

(*c*) which body-sensibility, invisible and reacting, has impinged, impinges, will, or may impinge on the tangible that is invisible and reacting ;

(*d*) depending on which body-sensibility, in consequence of something tangible . . . depending on which body-sensibility, and having something tangible as its object, there has arisen, arises, will, or may arise

tactile contact,[2]

---

[1] The sphere of k ā y o—so runs the comment (Asl. 311)—is diffused over the whole bodily form just as oil pervades an entire cotton rag. With the exception of this quality of relatively undifferentiated organ, the sense is co-ordinate with the other senses. To the objection that, if the sensitive surface be indeed so general it would convey confused impressions, it is counter-asserted that, if it were not so general, tactile impressions could not be adequately differentiated. Strictly speaking, the body-sense is both everywhere and not everywhere. *Not* everywhere to the extent of being in things *as* seen or *as* tasted. We cannot segregate and analyze sensations as we can grains of sand, and hence qualities are said to coalesce in the object. Nevertheless, each mode of sense conveys its specific messages.—Such seems to me the substance of what I have clothed to a slight extent in terms of Western psychology. The Commentary is, of course, tentative and groping, as elsewhere in its theory of sense ; yet it must not be forgotten that it was not till about fifty years ago that Ernst Weber's " Der Tastsinn und das Gemeingefühl " appeared, containing the positive results of a comparison of different skin-areas from the standpoint of their varying ability to convey clear or vague tactile impressions.

[2] Lit. body-contact.

and depending on which body-sensibility, in consequence of something tangible . . . depending on which body-sensibility, and having something tangible as its object, there has arisen, arises, will, or may arise, born of that tactile contact,

a feeling . . .
[*or*] a perception . . .
[*or*] volition . . .
[*or*] tactile cognition ;[1]

this that is body-sensibility, the sphere, constituent element, faculty of body-sensibility, this that is "the world", etc. [*continue as in* § 604].

[617] What is that [material] form which is the sphere of [visible] shape ?

The [material] form which, derived from the great principles, is visible under the appearance of colour and reacting[2]—is blue,[3] yellow, red,[4] white, black,[5] crimson,[6] bronze,[7] green-coloured,[8] of the hue of the mango-bud[9]; is

---

[1] Lit. cognition of body, so rendered in § 443 *seq.*

[2] S a p p a ṭ i g h a ṃ , here paraphrased as *producing* (j a n a k a ṃ) reaction and impact. Asl. 317.

[3] Compared to the u m m ā p u p p h a ṃ , or flax-blossom. Cf. my remark on n ī l a ṃ above, under § 246. Here the term is illustrated by an azure flower, such as we ourselves might quote as a type of blue. And yet even here the wide range and indefiniteness of the word find expression. For according to Böthl. and Roth, on the authority of Hemachandra, u m ā is applied to *night*.

[4] Like the blossom of *Pterospermum acerifolium* and *Pentapetro phœnicea* respectively (ibid.). I give these on Childers' authority.

[5] Like the morning star and charcoal respectively (ibid.).

[6] Like the reddish buds of the *Vitex negundo* and *kaṇavīra* trees (ibid.).

[7] H a r i , omitted in the text, but given in K. and the Cy. (ibid.). " Whereas, in the verse

H a r i t t a c a h e m a v a ṇ ṇ a ṃ k ā m a ṃ s u m u k h a p a k k a m ā ,

h a r i is spoken of as golden (s u v a ṇ ṇ a ṃ), by its being elsewhere taken in conjunction with coined gold (j ā t a r ū p a ṃ), it is here meant as dark (s ā m a ṃ) " (ibid.). Cf. Jāt. v, 216, s ā m ā t i s u v a ṇ ṇ a - s ā m ā .

[8] The colour of green grass (ibid.).

long, short,[1] big, little, circular, oval, square, hexagonal, octagonal, hekkaidecagonal; low, high, shady, glowing, light, dim, dull, frosty,[2] smoky, dusty; like in colour to the disc of moon,[3] sun, stars, a mirror,[4] a gem, a shell, a pearl, a cat's eye,[5] gold [6] or silver [7]; or whatever other shape there is which, derived from the four Great Phenomena, is visible and reacting—shape which, visible and reacting, one has seen, sees, will, or may see with the eye that is invisible and reacting—this which is visible shape, this which is the sphere of visible shape, the constituent element of visible shape—this is that form which is the sphere of visible shape.

[618] What is that [material] form which is the sphere of visible shape?

That [material] form which, derived from the Great Phenomena, is visible under the appearance of colour and reacting

---

[9] K. and the Cy. read a m b a n k u r a v a ṇ ṇ a ṃ.

[1] See my Introduction, on "long", "short", as only indirectly objects of sight. "The foregoing seven visibles are set forth without reference to any base (v a t t h u); the following according to common usage" (ibid.).

[2] Paraphrased as cloudy and as h i m a ṃ—which may be frosty, snowy, or dewy—respectively. As the allusion is only to lustre-contrast, the sparkle of hoar-frost is probably implied.

[3] The following terms, says the Cy. (ibid.), illustrate varieties of lustre. A little gratuitous astronomy is then thrown in. The orb of the moon, viz. the mansion of the moon-god, is 49 yojanas in extent, is made of gold, and roofed with silver. That of the sun is 50 yojanas, is made of gold and roofed with crystal. The constellations, the mansions of different gods, are 7, 8, or 10 yojanas in extent, and are made of the seven jewels. Between the moon below and the sun above is 1 yojana. The constellations take two years in their orbit. They and the sun go (*sic*) swiftly, the moon slowly. At times the moon leads, at times she is behind.

[4] Is of bronze (Asl. 318).

[5] Is not a gem; is the colour of the bamboo (ibid.).

[6] "The Master's colour" (ibid.).

[7] Under k a h ā p a ṇ a, i.e. silver coin, m ā s a k a s of copper, wood, and lac are to be included (ibid.). Quoted from Vin. iii, 228.

. . .[1] on which shape, visible and reacting, the eye, invisible and reacting, has impinged, impinges, will, or may impinge—this that is visible shape, etc. [*continue as in* § 617].

[619] What is that [material] form which is the sphere of visible shape?

That [material] form which, derived from the Great Phenomena, is visible under the appearance of colour and produces impact—which form, visible and producing impact, has impinged, impinges, will, or may impinge on the eye that is invisible and reacting—this which is visible form, etc. [*continue as in* § 617].

[620] What is that [material] form which is the sphere of visible shape?

That [material] form which, derived from the four Great Phenomena, is visible and produces impact—in consequence of which form, and depending on the eye, there has arisen, arises, will, or may arise

visual contact . . .

in consequence of which form and depending on the eye, there has arisen, arises, will, or may arise, born of that visual contact,

a feeling . . .
[*or*] a perception . . .
[*or*] volition . . .
[*or*] visual cognition . . .

[further] having which visible shape as its object,[2] and

[1] In this and the next two answers, according to K., the list of typical forms given in § 617 is to be rehearsed each time in full.

[2] In the printed text, for rūpārammaṇaṃ read rūpārammaṇo, and, two lines later, rūpārammaṇā. So for the other senses, § 624, etc. I follow the reading in K., making the word adjectival to cakkhusamphassajo, and then to vedanā, saññā, etc. Cf. the analogous passage in § 600 (in the passage I have restored to the text), in § 604, and so on. I confess I do not see what is gained by shifting cakkhuṃ nissāya, so that by K.'s reading it is sandwiched between adjective and noun, beyond the symmetry in

depending on the eye there has arisen, arises, will, or may arise

visual contact,

and, having which visible shape as its object, and depending on the eye, there has arisen, arises, will, or may arise

a feeling . . .
[*or*] a perception . . .
[*or*] volition . . .
[*or*] visual cognition . . .

this which is visible shape, the sphere, the constituent element of visible shape—this is that [material] form which is the sphere of visible shape.

[621] What is that [material] form which is the sphere of sound?

That sound which is derived from the four Great Phenomena, is invisible and reacting, such as the sound of drums, of tabors, of chank-shells, of tom-toms, of singing, of music;[1] clashing sounds,[2] manual sounds,[3] the noise of people,[4] the sound of the concussion of substances,[5] of wind,[6] of water,[7] sounds human and other than human, or whatever other sound[8] there is, derived from the Great Phenomena, invisible and reacting—such a sound, invisible and reacting, as, by

---

these sense-object answers, of giving precedence everywhere to the object. But this does not invalidate the reading in K. Ā r a m m a ṇ a ṃ is a term of mental procedure, not of bare sense-function, such as is indicated by the relation of r ū p a ṃ : c a k k h u .

[1] i.e. the sound of lutes and other stringed instruments (Asl. 319).

[2] e.g. of gongs and castanets (ibid.).

[3] i.e. of hand-clapping (ibid.).

[4] i.e. of a crowd when words and syllables have become indistinguishable (ibid.).

[5] i.e. of trees rubbing against each other, or of the knocking of blocks (ibid.). Vin. Texts, iii, 213, note.

[6] i.e. of wind as wind (ibid.).

[7] i.e. either of beaten or flowing water (ibid.).

[8] i.e. of splitting reeds, tearing cloth, and the like (ibid.).

the ear, invisible and reacting, one has heard, hears, will, or may hear . . .

[622] . . . and on which sound, invisible and reacting, the ear, invisible and reacting, has impinged, impinges, will, or may impinge . . .

[623] . . . which sound, invisible and reacting, has impinged, impinges, will, or may impinge on the ear that is invisible and reacting . . .

[624] . . . in consequence of which sound and depending on the ear, there has arisen, arises, will, or may arise

auditory contact . . .

. . . and [1] . . . born of that auditory contact,

a feeling . . .
[*or*] a perception . . .
[*or*] volition . . .
[*or*] auditory cognition . . .

. . . [further] having a sound as its object and depending on the ear, there has arisen, arises, will, or may arise,

auditory contact,

. . . and . . . born of that auditory contact,

a feeling . . .
[*or*] a perception . . .
[*or*] volition . . .
[*or*] auditory cognition ;

this that is sound, the sphere and constituent element of sound—this is that form which is the sphere of sound.

[625] What is that [material] form which is the sphere of odour ?

That odour which is derived from the four Great Phenomena, is invisible and produces impact, such as the odour of roots, sap, bark, leaves, flowers, fruit ; verminous odours, putrid odours, pleasant and unpleasant odours,[2] or

---

[1] Continue as for visible forms in § 620.

[2] Sugandho, duggandho—these, says Buddhaghosa, namely desired odour and undesired odour, exhaust all odour. He predicates the same good and bad tastes (sādu, asādu,

whatever other odour there is, derived from the four Great Phenomena, invisible and reacting; such an odour, invisible and reacting, as one has smelt, smells, will, or may smell with the nose, that is invisible and reacting . . .

[626] . . on which odour, invisible and reacting, the nose, invisible and reacting, has impinged, impinges, will, or may impinge . . .

[627] . . . such an odour, invisible and reacting, as has impinged, impinges, will, or may impinge on the nose, invisible and reacting . . .

[628] . . . in consequence of which odour and depending on the nose, there has arisen, arises, will, or may arise

olfactory contact . . .

and[1] . . . born of that olfactory contact,

a feeling . . .

[*or*] a perception . . .

[*or*] volition . . .

[*or*] olfactory cognition . . .

. . . [further] having an odour as its object and depending on the nose, there has arisen, arises, will, or may arise

olfactory contact,

---

§ 629). In § 648 we find, classed among the tangibles, pleasant contact and painful contact. But we do not find the commentator making the same comprehensive claim for hedonistic values in touches as in odours and tastes. Nor, as we have seen, does the text predicate anything hedonistically of sight or touch. This is interesting as bringing the psychology of Buddhism, with its acute if incipient intuition, in "touch" with our modern psychology. For we say that the more our knowledge of the external world is built up by a given sense, the more is that sense connected with *neutral* feeling. And it is precisely sight, touch, and hearing that give us most of that knowledge.

Aristotle remarks, with reference to the sense of smell only, that our never discriminating an odour without associating therewith an impression of something painful or pleasant, seems to reveal the imperfection of this sense in humans. Imperfect, i.e. in delicacy of discrimination, touch being herein the most perfect sense (*De. An.* II, ix).

[1] See § 624, note.

. . . and . . . born of that olfactory contact,
a feeling . . .
[*or*] a perception . . .
[*or*] volition . . .
[*or*] olfactory cognition;

this that is odour, the sphere and constituent element of odour—this is that [material] form which is the sphere of odours.

[629] What is that [material] form which is the sphere of taste?

That taste which is derived from the four Great Phenomena, is invisible and reacting, such as the taste of roots, stems, bark, leaves, flowers, fruits, of sour, sweet,[1] bitter,[2] pungent,[3] saline,[4] alkaline,[5] acrid,[6] astringent,[7] nice and nauseous sapids,[8] or whatever other taste there is, derived from the four Great Phenomena, invisible and reacting—such tastes, invisible and reacting, as with the tongue, invisible and reacting, one has tasted, tastes, will, or may taste . . .

[630] . . . against which taste, invisible and reacting, the tongue, invisible and impingeing, has impinged, impinges, will, or may impinge . . .

---

[1] Buttermilk (t a k k a m b i l a ṃ) is given as a typical sour sapid, ghee from cow's milk (g o s a p p i) as the type of a sweet sapid. But, adds the Cy., sweet added to astringent (k a s ā v a ṃ) and kept standing will lose all its sweetness, and so with raw sugar and alkaline substance. Ghee, however, kept standing, while it loses colour and smell, does not lose its taste. It therefore is the absolute sweet (e k a n t a-m a d h u r a ṃ) (Asl. 320).

[2] e.g. as nimb-tree fruit (ibid.).

[3] e.g. as ginger and pepper (ibid.).

[4] e.g. as sea-salt (ibid.).

[5] e.g. as the egg-plant (v ā t i n g a ṇ a k a ṭ ī r a ṃ), or as green palm sprouts (cocoanut cabbage) (ibid.).

[6] e.g. as the jujube, or the *Feronia elephantum*, etc. (ibid.).

[7] e.g. as the yellow myrobalan (h a r ī ṭ a k a ṃ). I am, as before, indebted to Childers' Dictionary for all this botanical knowledge.

[8] S ā d u a s ā d u. See § 625, n. 1.

[631] . . . a taste which, invisible and reacting, has impinged, impinges, will, or may impinge on the tongue, invisible and reacting . . .

[632] . . . in consequence of which taste and depending on the tongue, there has arisen, arises, will, or may arise

gustatory contact . . .

. . . and [1] . . . born of that gustatory contact,

a feeling . . .
[*or*] a perception . . .
[*or*] volition . . .
[*or*] gustatory cognition,

[further] having a taste as its object and depending on the tongue, there has arisen, arises, will, or may arise

gustatory contact,

. . . and . . . born of that gustatory contact,

a feeling . . .
[*or*] a perception . . .
[*or*] volition . . .
[*or*] gustatory cognition ;

this that is taste, the sphere and constituent element of taste—this is that form which is the sphere of taste.[2]

[633] What is that [material] form which is woman-faculty (itthindriyaṃ)?

That which is of the female, feminine in appearance, feminine in characteristics, in occupation, in deportment, feminine in condition and being—this is that [material] form which constitutes woman-faculty.[3]

---

[1] See § 624, note.

[2] For the sphere of the tangible, see below, § 648.

[3] Literally the indriyaṃ—the faculty, potentiality of the female. Under "appearance", which the Cy. (321) rules to be here the import of liṅgaṃ (= saṇṭhānaṃ, cf. Mil. 133, 134), he indicates the physical proportions in which the woman, generally speaking, differs from the man—smaller hands, feet, and face, upper trunk less broad, lower trunk broader. Characteristics (nimittaṃ) are that by which she is recognizable (sañjānanaṃ), both external bodily marks (no beard, e.g. nor tusks, which would seem to include certain

[634] What is that form which is man-faculty (p u r i s i n - d r i y a ṃ) ?

That which is of the male, masculine in appearance, masculine in characteristics, in occupation, in deportment, masculine in condition and being—this is that form which constitutes man-faculty.[1]

---

animals) and modes of dressing. Under " occupation " (k u t t a ṃ = k i r i y ā) there is an allusion to girls' distinctive amusements—playing with baskets, pestles [and mortars], and dolls (? literally, little daughters, d h ī t a l i k ā y a k ī ḷ a n t i), and weaving string with clay fibre (m a t t i k a - v ā k a ṃ), whatever that may be. Under " deportment ", the " undemonstrativeness " (a v i s a d a ṃ) in women's walking, standing, sitting, lying, and eating is specified, all these being done more mincingly, less assertively by women. If a man so deport himself, it is said of him, " He goes like a woman ! " The " condition and being " of the female, constituting her essential nature, are " born of karma, and take their source at conception ". The other female characteristics are evolved by her " potentiality " in the course of existence, just as the tree with all its appurtenances is evolved in time from the seed. This " indriya " is discernible, not by the eye, but by the mind (m a n o).

[1] The priority of place given to the female is a form of statement as characteristically Buddhist (not to say Indian) as that of saying " moon and sun ". Both no doubt have their source very deep in the history, or prehistory, of humanity. The Commentator gives the correlative opposites in describing male characteristics, down to the " swash-buckling and martial air ", which if a woman affect she is said to " go like a man ". Boys are said to occupy themselves with their characteristic games of playing at carriages and ploughs, and at making sand-banks round puddles and calling them reservoirs.

He then remarks that these sexual distinctions have been evolved during the course of life in primeval ages ; since when, originating by way of conception and, some of them, in the individual life, it happens that they get interchanged. He then quotes cases of hermaphroditism, said to have occurred in the members of the Order.

He is mindful also, as we might expect, to appreciate the sex to which he belongs, and makes a curious application to it of the doctrine of karma. " Of the two, the male sex-marks are superior (u t ṭ a m a ṃ), those of the female inferior (h ī n a ṃ). Therefore, the former disappear by means of a very bad karma,

[635] What is that [material] form which is life-faculty (j ī v i t i n d r i y a ṃ)?

The persistence of these corporeal states, their subsistence, their going on, their being kept going on, their progress, continuance, preservation, life, life as faculty—this is that [material] form which is life-faculty.[1]

[636] What is that [material] form which is bodily intimation (k ā y a v i ñ ñ a t t i)?

That tension, that intentness, that state of making the body[2] tense, in response to a thought, whether good, bad, or indeterminate, on the part of one who advances, or recedes, or fixes the gaze, or glances around, or retracts an arm, or stretches it forth—the intimation, the making known, the state of having made known—this is that [material] form which constitutes bodily intimation.[3]

---

while the latter are established by a karma indifferently good. The latter, on the other hand, disappear by means of a karma indifferently bad, while the former are established by means of a very good karma." Thus, both disappear by badness and are *acquired* by goodness."

Thus, our Commentator approximates more to Plato's position than to that of the typical religious celibate, finding woman not stronger to do evil, but rather the weaker in heaping up either good or evil.

[1] "What there is to say, has been laid already in connexion with the faculty of life as related to unmaterial (mental) states" (Asl. 323; see § 19).

[2] K ā y o is said to = s a r ī r a ṃ; possibly to distinguish it from k ā y o as used for "body-sensibility", or the tactile sense (Asl. 324), or again from sense-experience generally (p. 43, n. 3).

[3] K ā y a v i ñ ñ a t t i is analyzed in a somewhat rambling style by the Commentator. The gist of his remarks amounts, I gather, to the following: In any communication effected by bodily action—which includes communications from animals to men, and *vice versa*—that which is made known is one's condition (b h ā v o) at the time, one's self (s a y a ṃ), and one's intention (a d h i p p ā y o); in other words, the *how*, the *who* or *what*, and the *what for*. And this is wrought by a bodily suffusion (v i p p h a n d a n e n a).

[637] What is that [material] form which is intimation by language (v a c ī v i ñ ñ a t t i)?

That speech, voice, enunciation, utterance, noise, making noises, language as articulate speech, which expresses a thought whether good, bad, or indeterminate—this is called language. And that intimation, that making known, the state of having made known by language—this is that [material] form which constitutes intimation by language.[1]

[638] What is that [material] form which is the element of space (ā k ā s a - d h ā t u)?

That which is space and belongs to space, is sky and

He then classifies the kinds of thoughts which tend to "produce an intimation", no others having this tendency. They are :—

The eight good types of thought relating to the sensuous universe (§§ 1–159), and
the thought concerning super-knowledge (a b h i ñ ñ ā - c i t t a ṃ).
The twelve bad types of thought (§§ 365–430).
The eight main inoperative types of thought.
The two limited inoperative types of thought.
The one inoperative type of thought relating to the universe of form which has attained to super-knowledge,

making eleven types of indeterminate thought.

Finally he refers us to his theory of "doors" (d v ā r a - k a t h ā). See my Introduction. (Asl. 323–4.)

[1] V a c ī v i ñ ñ a t t i is dealt with *verbatim* as bodily intimation was, "vocal noise" being substituted for "bodily suffusion". "Making noises" is to be understood as making a noise in a variety of ways. "Articulate speech" (lit. broken-up speech) is no mere jangle (b h a ṅ g o), but is vocal utterance so divided as to serve for communication (Asl. 325).

It is interesting to note, in connexion with the problem as to whether communication or registration of thought is the historically prior function of language, that Buddhaghosa, for all his aptness to draw distinctions, does not make any allusion here to intimation by language forming only one of the functions of speech. Stil. more curious, as being more germane to this specific aspect of language, is it that he does not take into account the oral communication of the registered ideas of the race.

belongs to sky,[1] is vacuum and belongs to vacuum, and is not in contact[2] with the four Great Phenomena—this is that form which is the element of space.

[639] What is lightness of [material] form (r ū p a s s a l a h u t ā)?[3]

That lightness of form which is its capacity for changing easily, its freedom from sluggishness and inertia—this is lightness of [material] form.

[640] What is plasticity of [material] form?

That plasticity of form which is softness, smoothness, non-rigidity—this is plasticity of [material] form.

---

[1] Buddhaghosa's etymology (Asl. 325) derives ā k ā s o from "unscratched"—what may not be cut, or broken—which recalls Homer's ἀτρύγετος αἴθηρ and ἀτρυγετη θάλασσα as well as the ακάρπιστα πεδία of Eurïpides (Asl. 326). "Sky" he connects with striking—a g h a ṃ, a - g h a ṭ ṭ a n ī y a ṃ—what is not strikable. Â k ā s o, he continues, is that which delimitates, or sets bounds to forms, environing them and making them manifest. Through it, in forms thus bounded, we get the notions—hence above, hence below, hence across.

[2] A s a m p h u ṭ ṭ h a ṃ c a t ū h i m a h a b h ū t e h i. Although space is in this work treated of apart from the four elements, and does not, as a rule, count as a fifth element in the Piṭakas, yet, in the Mahā Rāhulovāda Sutta (M. i, 423), when Gotama is discoursing to his son of the distribution of the elements in the composition of the human body, he co-ordinates ā k ā s a d h ā t u with the four other dhātus, to all appearance as though it should rank as a fifth element. In the older Upanishads it is usually co-ordinated with the four elements, though not, as such, in a closed list. In the Taittirïya Up., however, it appears as the one immediate derivative from the Âtman; wind, fire, water, earth, plants, etc., proceeding, the first from ā k ā ç a, the rest, taken in order, from each other. The word a s a m p h u ṭ ṭ h a ṃ is paraphrased by n i j j a ṭ a k a ṃ (or n i s s a ṭ a ṃ), and may mean that space does not commingle with the four elements as they with each other.

"Belongs to" is, in the Pali, - g a t a ṃ.

[3] Cf. above, §§ 42–7, with this and the two following answers. Supremely well-dressed hide is given as an illustration of the placticity of matter (Asl. 326).

[641] What is wieldiness of [material] form?

That which is its serviceableness, its workable condition—this is wieldiness of [material] form.[1]

[642] What is integration (u p a c a y o) of [material] form?

That which is accumulation of form is [also] integration of [material] form [2]—this is integration of [material] form.

[643] What is subsistence of [material] form (r ū p a s s a s a n t a t i)?

That which is integration of form is the subsistence of form. This is subsistence of [material] form.

[644] What is decay of [material] form (r ū p a s s a j a r a t ā)?

That decay of form which is ageing, decrepitude, hoariness, wrinkles, the shrinkage in length of days, the hypermaturity of faculties—this is decay of [material] form.[3]

---

[1] Gold which is s u d d h a n t a (? s u d h a n t a, well-blown) is given as typically "wieldy" material (ibid.).

[2] Buddhaghosa evidently reads s o r ū p a s s a u p a c a y o here (for y o), and in the next section s ā r ū p a s s a (for y ā) (Asl. 327). This is only adopted by the text in §§ 732, 733. K. reads s o and s ā.

This and the following section formularize the coming into being of things. Integration is paraphrased (Asl. 327) as the cumulative effect of the spheres (ā y a t a n ā n a ṃ ā c a y o) as they are reproduced over and over again. The import of the term is v a ḍ ḍ h i, fullness of growth. Ā c a y o, or n i b b a t t i, is to u p a c a y o or v a ḍ ḍ h i as the welling up of water in a reservoir by a river's bank is to the brimming over of the water, while s a n t a t i or p a v a t t i (subsistence or persistence) is as the overflow and running of the water. All are expressions for the phenomenon of birth and growth (j ā t i r ū p a s s a).

[3] This is a stock formula, and occurs at M. i, 49; S. ii, 2 and 42. The Cy. points out (Asl. 328) that the three terms, "decrepitude", etc., show the phenomena that must take place in the lapse of time; the last two show the inference that is to be drawn from them. For just as a flood or a forest fire can be traced by the appearance of the grass and trees in its track, so can we infer respecting our life and faculties by the appearance of teeth, hair, and skin.

[645] What is impermanence of [material] form (r ū p a s s a a n i c c a t ā) ?

The destruction, disease, breaking-up, dissolution of form, the impermanence which is decline—this is impermanence of form.[1]

[646] What is bodily (solid) nutriment (k a b a ḷ i n k ā r o ā h ā r o) ? [2]

Boiled rice, sour gruel, flour, fish, flesh, milk, curds, butter, cheese, tila-oil, cane-syrup, or whatever else [3] there is in whatever region that by living beings may be eaten, chewed, swallowed, digested into the juice,[4] by which living beings are kept alive—this is bodily nutriment.

[All] this is [material] form which is derived.

[End of] the Section on Derivatives. First Portion for Recitation in the Division on [material] Form.

---

[1] This and the preceding section formularize the waning and passing away of things. Birth-and-growth, decay, and death are, by the Commentator, likened to three enemies of mankind, the first of whom leads him astray into a pit, the second of whom throws him down, and the third of whom cuts off his head (Asl. 329).

[2] Literally, morsel-made food. " Bodily " (or solid) suffices to distinguish it from the three immaterial nutriments. See p. 30.

[3] Under these come roots and fruits. Asl. 330.

[4] On this section, where " form " is considered under the aspect of sustaining growth, etc., the Commentator gives a brief dissertation where an adumbration of physiological truth is humorously illustrated. Whereas, he says (Asl. 330–2), food is here first set out in terms of its embodiment, in o j ā we have the evolved essence of it. Now whereas the former removes risk, the latter is a preservative. And the risk is this, that when no food is taken, the karma-born heat within feeds on the walls of the belly, making the owner cry out, " I am hungry : give me something to eat ! " and only setting his intestines free when it can get external food. The internal heat i likened to a shadow-demon, who, having got the entry into a man's shadow, bites his head when hungry so that he cries out. When other men come to help, the demon, quitting his hold, preys on them.

In the case of coarse food, e.g. kudrūsa grain, o j ā is said to be weak and sustains but a short time, while if a man drink

[*"There is [material] form which is not derived"* (n o u p ā d ā)].

[647] What is that [material] form which is not derived ?[1]

The sphere of the tangible, the fluid element—this is that [material] form which is not derived.

[648] What is that [material] form which is the sphere of the tangible (p h o ṭ ṭ h a b b ā y a t a n a ṃ) ?

The earthy (solid) element, the lambent (calorific) element, the gaseous (aerial) element[2]; the hard and the soft; the

---

ghee and the like he wants no other meal the whole day. Living beings are then classified in an order of increasing fineness in the food they live on, beginning with crocodiles, who, they say, swallow pebbles, continuing with peacocks, hyenas, and elephants, later with other birds, then with borderers, town-dwellers, kings, and ending with the Yāma and Paranimmitavasavatti gods, who enjoy food of supreme delicacy.

[1] "Just as derived form is derived in such and such a way and in no other, so, to say it is not derived is equivalent to saying it is not derivable." Asl. 333.

Possibly the form of negative here employed (n o u p ā d ā) is a technical mark of the relatively unethical nature of this aspect of r ū p a ṃ. A n u p ā d ā, on the other hand, is used with a philosophical import. Cf. D. i, 17 with M. i, 148—a n u p ā d ā v i m u t t o and a n u p ā d ā p a r i n i b b ā n a t t h a ṃ. See also below, §§ 1210 and 1213.

[2] In keeping with the general psychological standpoint of the present work, the things which are not derived from (have no foothold or support in) other things are considered under the aspect of sense-precepts. They are tangibles or intangibles. Element (d h ā t u) is now substituted for the collective term used above, namely, great phenomena or beings (m a h ā - b h ū t ā n i, § 584 *et seq.*). Both terms occur together in A. i, 222. The latter term may be used to denote great or wondrous derivatives of the four elements, great either physically or ethically, as when (Vin. ii, 240) the ocean and its "great creatures" serve to illustrate the Dhamma and those wondrous phenomena, the human beings who by way of it are seeking or have attained Nirvāna. Cf. Vism. 366 f. D h ā t u, on the other hand, as the Cy. with unflagging "mindfulness" once more points out, indicates absence of substratum or soul. Asl. 332.

On the essential characters of the four elements, see below, §§ 962–5, also the following note.

smooth and the rough; pleasant (easeful) contact, painful contact; the heavy and the light[1]—such a tangible, invisible and reacting,[2] as, with the body-sensibility, invisible and reacting, one has touched, touches, will or may touch . . .

---

[1] The first two and last of these four pairs are so many aspects or modes of the earth-element (Asl. 332), and are paraphrased respectively as rigid and non-rigid, polished and jagged (saw-like), weighty and non-weighty. These correspond almost exactly to our modern view of the modes of resistance, i.e. of *active* touch, or of skin-sensibility with a co-efficient of muscular sense. The Buddhist view lacks, as all but recent psychology has lacked, insight into the presence of the muscular factor; on the other hand, it is logically more symmetrical in giving "lightness" where Dr. Bain, e.g., gives "pressure"—another positive.

Pleasant contact is defined as a tangible which is desired on account of pleasant feeling; the opposite in the case of painful contact. Each of the three elements furnishes instances of either: In connexion with solidity there is the pleasant contact felt when a soft-palmed attendant is doing massage to one's feet, and the opposite when his hands are hard. From "caloric", or the flame-element, we may get the pleasure of a warming-pan in winter, or the reverse, if it is applied in summer. From the aerial element, we may get the pleasure of fanning in summer, or the discomfort of it in winter. Asl. 332, 333.

[2] The Cy. here discusses a point of attention in sense-perception which is interesting as adumbrating modern European theories respecting consciousness and subconsciousness (Asl. 333). In a concrete object of sense, the three modes of the tangible, i.e. the three elements (solid, hot, airy), may all of them be present. Now, do they all come "at one stroke" into the field of consciousness (ā p ā t h a ṃ)? They do. Thus come, do they impinge on the body-sense? They do. When it has thus made them a (mental) object, does cognition of body arise at one blow? It does not. Why? Thus: Mental objects are made either by deliberate sensing or by intrusion. (The latter term—u s s a d o—is more literally extrusion, or prominence, but either word shows that involuntary, as contrasted with voluntary, attention is meant.) Now, when one is deliberately testing the hardness or softness of a ball of boiled rice by pressure, heat and vapour are present, but it is the solid to which one gives attention. If hot water be tested by the hand, though there is solid and vaporous (matter), it is heat that occupies the attention. If one lets the breeze blow on the body at the window in hot weather, solid and heat

[649] . . . against which tangible, invisible, and reacting, the body-sensibility, invisible and reacting, has impinged, impinges, will, or may impinge . . .

[650] . . . such a tangible, invisible and reacting, as has impinged, impinges, will, or may impinge against the body-sensibility, invisible and reacting . . .

[651] . . . in consequence of which tangible and depending on the body-sensibility, there has arisen, arises, will or may arise

bodily contact . . .

and . . . born of that bodily contact,

a feeling . . .
[*or*] a perception . . .
[*or*] volition . . .
[*or*] cognition of body . . .

[further,] having a tangible as its object and depending on the body(-sensibility), there has arisen, arises, will or may arise

bodily contact . . .

and . . . born of that bodily contact,

a feeling . . .
[*or*] a perception . . .
[*or*] volition . . .
[*or*] cognition of body ;

this that is the tangible, the sphere and element of the

---

are present, but it is the aerial element that is attended to. Or take involuntary impressions: If you stumble, or knock your head against a tree, or bite on a pebble, heat and wind are present, but the intrusive object is *solid* matter. So analogously for walking on something hot, or being deafened by a hurricane. The three elements are not apprehended as such at the same instant. And with regard to the extended surface of the body-sentience, cognition of body arises only in that spot where the sentient surface is impinged upon, e.g. when a shoulder-wound is bathed (? dressed ; cf. Vin. ii, 115 and Transl.) with a quill, the kāya-pasādo of the shoulder is impinged upon, or intensified, and there cognition arises. And where the pasādo is most powerfully impressed, there cognition arises first.

tangible—this is that form which is the sphere of the tangible.[1]

[652] What is that [material] form which is the fluid (aqueous) element (ā p o d h ā t u) ?

That which is fluid and belongs to fluid, that which is viscid [2] and belongs to viscous, the cohesiveness of form [3] —this is that [material] form which is the fluid element.

[All] this is that form which is not derived.

---

[1] Buddhaghosa goes on, with reference to the senses generally, to give a psychological account of the passing from one group of sensations, or "object of thought", to another in terms not far removed from what would now be used to describe the "movement of attention" (Asl. 334). We pass from one object to another, (*a*) from deliberate inclination, or (*b*) from a sensation of preponderating impressiveness (a j j h ā s a y a t o v ā v i s a y ā d h i m a t t a t o v ā). E.g. (*a*) from saluting a shrine, a believer forms the intention of entering to do homage to a statue and contemplate the carvings and paintings. (*b*) While contemplating some vast tope, a man is struck by the sound of music, and is than affected by flowers and incense brought near.

[2] S i n e h o . Cf. the description with that of ā k ā s a d h ā t u , § 638.

[3] This is the aspect of the moist or liquid element in an object compact of several elements. The one essential "mark" of ā p o - d h ā t u is p a g g h a r a ṇ a ṃ , flowing. See § 963. But "cohesiveness of form means the cohering condition of some concrete in which there is superfluity of solid" (Asl. 335). For it is by the cohesive force of the fluid element that lumps of iron or what not are made rigid. Similarly in the case of stones, mountains, palms, tusks, horns, etc.

Hence Buddhaghosa passes on to discuss the mutually related spheres of the elements and their apparent approximations to each other, as in viscous things, e.g. or congealed liquid, or boiling water. Corrupt MSS., however, render parts of the disquisition hard to follow. His conclusion is that whereas the elements may vary in their condition as phenomena, their essential mark never alters, however latent it may be. And he quotes, as the A ṭ ṭ h ā n a p a r i k a p p a s u t t a , A. i, 222, that it is easier for the four elements to change their essential character than for the seeker of Nirvana (the Noble Student) to alter his high estate (Asl. 336).

[653] What is that [material] form [1] which is grasped at (u p ā d i ṇ ṇ a ṃ) ? [2]

The spheres of sight, hearing, smell, taste, body-sensibility, femininity, masculinity, life, or whatever form there exists through karma having been wrought, whether it be in the spheres of visible forms, odours, tastes, or the tangible; the element of space, the fluid element, the integration or the subsistence of [material] form, or bodily nutriment—this is that [material] form which is grasped at.

[654] What is that [material] form which is not grasped at ?

The sphere of sound, bodily and vocal intimation, lightness, plasticity and wieldiness of [material] form, its decay and impermanence, of whatever other [material] form exists which is not due to karma having been wrought, whether it be in the sphere of visible forms, smells, tastes, or the tangible; the element of space or that of fluidity; the integration or the subsistence of [material] form, or bodily nutriment—this is that [material] form which is not grasped at.

---

[1] Here follow the remaining pairs of correlated terms, making up the categories of form under the Dual Aspect.

[2] Literally, " which has been grasped at " or " laid hold of ". This and the cognate terms are discussed under the " Group on Grasping ", § 1213 *et seq*. It is disappointing to find that, with the exception of two items in the list of things " grasped at ", or come into being through the action of karma (the two phrases are approximately equivalent), the Cy. does not discuss the inclusion of any. One would have liked to hear e.g. why, of all sense-objects, sounds alone are " not grasped at " (cf. the heresy concerning sound as result [of karma, KV. 466], and why the elements of space and of fluidity may and may not be grasped at, or what they have to do with it in any way.

Concerning the two items above mentioned, how is it, asks the Cy. (337), " that 'decay and impermanence' are classed with respect of what is due, and what is not due to the performance of karma ? They are classed with what is not grasped at. That which has sprung from conditions other than karma is included under 'not due to the performance of karma . . .' And as these two forms arise neither from karma nor from form-producing conditions other than karma they are therefore not classified with reference to karma. How they are acquired will become evident later."

[655] What is that form which is both grasped at and favourable to grasping (u p ā d i ṇ ṇ' u p ā d ā n i y a ṃ)?

The spheres of the five senses, femininity, masculinity and life, or whatever other form exists through karma having been wrought, whether it be in the spheres of visible forms, odours, tastes or the tangible, in the elements of space or fluidity, in the integration or the subsistence of form, or in bodily nutriment—this is that form which is both grasped at and favourable to grasping.

[656] What is that [material] form which is not grasped at, but is favourable to grasping (a n u p ā d i ṇ ṇ' u p ā d ā n i y a ṃ)? [1]

The sphere of sounds, bodily and vocal intimation, the lightness, plasticity, wieldiness, decay and impermanence of form, or whatever other form exists which is not due to karma having been wrought, whether it be in the sphere of visible shapes,[2] smells, tastes, the tangible, in the element of space or of fluidity, in the integration, or the subsistence of form, or in bodily nutriment—this is that [material] form which is not grasped at but is favourable to grasping.

[657] What is that [material] form which is visible?

The sphere of visible shapes—this is that [material] form which is visible.

[658] What is that [material] form which is invisible?

The sphere of vision . . . and bodily nutriment—this is that [material] form which is invisible.[3]

---

[1] The privative prefixed to the first half of this dvandva-compound does not apply to the latter half. *All* form is u p ā d ā n i y a ṃ—see § 595 and cf. Dh.S. § 1538. Hence to get, as we do, a positive answer would, if u p ā d ā n i y a ṃ were to be taken negatively, be a very patent infringement of the law of contradiction. The distributed negative is given by a n u p ā d i ṇ ṇ ā n u p ā d ā n i y a ṃ as in § 992.

[2] I have elided s a d d ā y a t a n a ṃ, and, on the next line, inserted ā p o d h ā t u, as consistent with § 654. Cf. §§ 747, 750, and K.

[3] The answer in § 658 recurs with its elided passage very often, but it is not easy to point out the foregoing answer of

[659] What is that [material] form which reacts-and-impinges [1] (s a p p a ṭ i g h a ṃ)?

The spheres of vision, hearing, smell, taste, body-sensibility; the spheres of visible shapes, sounds, smells, tastes, tangibles—this is that [material] form which reacts-and-impinges.

[660] What is that [material] form which does not react-or-impinge?

Femininity . . . and bodily nutriment—this is that [material] form which does not react-or-impinge.

[661] What is that form which is faculty (i n d r i y a ṃ)?

The faculties (or personal potentialities) [2] of vision, hearing, smell, taste, body-sensibility, woman, man, life—this is that form which is faculty.

[662] What is that form which is not faculty?

The spheres of visible form . . . and bodily nutriment—this is that form which is not faculty.[3]

---

which it is an abbreviation. For §§ 653, 655, include "visible shape", "which is absurd". And they do not include "sound", which is invisible. I suggest that § 596 is referred to, with the implication that "the sphere of visible form" must be omitted. All the other terms in § 596, if understood as strictly abstract sensibility or sensation, or as abstract ideas, are inaccessible to sight. Even in "bodily nutriment" it is only the v a t t h u, or embodiment of the concept of nutriment, that is visible. And similarly, whereas one's bodily gestures are visible, the "intimation" given is a matter of inference, a mental construction.

[1] Both terms have been applied in the detailed theory of sense given in § 597 *et seq.*

[2] Keeping to § 596 as the norm for these abbreviated replies, we may assume that these two (§§ 659 and 660) divide out that answer between them. Impact and reaction, as here understood, belong exclusively to the sphere of sensation. The term p a ṭ i g h o has an emotional and moral significance elsewhere in this work, and means repulsion, repugnance. See § 1060.

[3] § 596 would seem to be divided also, and differently, by the i n d r i y a ṃ sections. What is n a i n d r i y a ṃ, not having δύναμις, are thus the five kinds of sense-objects, intimation, space, the three modes of form, and the course, of the evolving rebirth of form as represented in abstract idea.

[663] What is that [material] form which is Great Phenomenon (m a h ā b h ū t a ṃ)?

The sphere of the tangible and the element of fluidity—this is that [material] form which is Great Phenomenon.

[664] What is that [material] form which is not Great Phenomenon?

The sphere of vision . . . and bodily nutriment—this is that [material] form which is not Great Phenomenon.[1]

[665] What is that [material] form which is intimation (v i ñ ñ a t t i)?

Bodily and vocal intimation[2]—this is that [material] form which is intimation.

[666] What is that [material] form which is not intimation?

The sphere of vision . . . and bodily nutriment—this is that [material] form which is not intimation.

[667] What is that [material] form which is sprung from thought (c i t t a - s a m u ṭ ṭ h ā n a ṃ)?[3]

---

[1] This pair of relatives coincides with the first pair of attributes taken inversely: forms underived and derived (pp. 172–97).

[2] See above, §§ 636, 637. The abbreviated answer concerning the other relative will presumably be the entire list given in § 596, with the exception of the two modes of intimation.

[3] Cf. below, §§ 1195, 1196; above, § 636, n.; Comp. 162 (2). Here, after being silent over the last ten questions, the Cy. resumes its parable (p. 337). No *creation* of matter by mind is implied. The catechism merely refers to matter of some kind as brought into relation with an intelligent agent. And the purest instance of this is those groups of phenomena which are brought into play when the agent is expressing himself. The expression or intimation *itself*, it says, does not spring *directly* from mind, but it is said nevertheless to have its source in mind because those phenomena (of gesture and speech) on which the intimation depends are immediately prompted by mind, just as we say that old age and death "are" impermanence (in virtue of their forming part of the content of that idea). While there is mind, there is also expression of mind. But the concomitance stated in § 669 is not to be understood like that arising between thought and feeling and other mental processes. He is probably referring to the mental complex indicated above in § 1 and the like.

Bodily and vocal intimation, or whatever other [material] form exists that is born of mind, caused by mind, has its source in mind, whether it be in the sphere of visible shapes, sounds, odours, tastes or tangibles, in the spatial, or the fluid element, in the lightness, plasticity, wieldiness, integration or subsistence of form, or in bodily nutriment—this is that [material] form which is sprung from mind.

[668] What is that [material] form which is not sprung from mind?

The sphere of the five senses, femininity, masculinity and life, the decay and the impermanence of [material] form, or whatever other [material] form exists that is not born of mind, not caused by mind, does not have its source in mind, whether it be in the sphere of visible forms, sounds, odours, tastes, or tangibles, in the spatial or fluid element, in the lightness, plasticity, wieldiness, integration or subsistence of [material] form, or in bodily nutriment—this is that [material] form which is not sprung from mind.

[669] What is that [material] form which comes into being together with mind (citta-saha-bhū)?

[670] What is that [material] form which does not come into being together with mind?

Answers as in the preceding pair of relatives.

[671] What is that [material] form which is consecutive to mind (citt' ānuparivatti)?

[672] What is that [material] form which is not consecutive to mind?

Answers as in the preceding pair of relatives.

[673] What is that [material] form which belongs to the self (ajjhattikaṃ)? [1]

---

[1] See below, §§ 1044, 1045. It will already have been noted (p. 59, n. 1) that ajjhattaṃ, ajjhattikaṃ, does not run on all fours with our modern psychological term "subjective", or that which belongs to the *conscious experience* of the individual. It connotes anything belonging to an individual organism, physical or mental. Hence, too, the word "self" must here be understood in no narrow metaphysical,

The spheres of the five senses—this is that [material] form which belongs to the self.

[674] What is that [material] form which is external (to the self—b ā h i r a ṃ) ?

The sphere of the five kinds of sense-objects . . .[1] and bodily nutriment—this is that [material] form which is external (to the self).

[675] Which is that [material] form which is gross (o ḷ ā r i - k a ṃ) ?

The spheres of the five senses and of the five kinds of sense objects—this is that [material] form which is gross.

[676] Which is that [material] form which is subtle (s u k - h u m a ṃ) ?

Woman-faculty . . . and bodily nutriment—this is that [material] form which is subtle.[2]

---

or even psychological sense, but as equivalent to the concrete person or a t t a b h ā v o (see above, p. 175, n. 1). It is used in the sense of all but the last of the four constituents into which W. James divides the Self, viz. the material Self (body, clothes, family, home, property: the Buddhist would only admit the first item, I fancy), the social Self (recognition from others), and the spiritual Self (psychic faculties or dispositions). (*Principles of Psychology*, 1892, i, 292–6.) Only the fourth constituent, the "pure Ego", was rejected by Buddhism, as it was, twenty-two centuries later, by Hume. Cf., however, the apparently more "subjective" use in §§ 161 and 1207.

I have felt equal reluctance to foist the (relatively) modern counterpart "objective" on to b ā h i r a ṃ or b a h i d d h ā (see § 1045).

[1] Read in full, this should coincide with the latter part of § 596, beginning at "the spheres of visible shapes. . . ."

[2] The Cy., paraphrasing o ḷ ā r i k a ṃ by t h ū l a ṃ, explains that this has reference to the material embodiment of sense objects and to the fact of sensuous impact, s u k h u m a ṃ connoting the contrary. Under the latter class we have, according to my assumption (p. 186, n. 3; cf. Introd., liv), the indriyas of sex and life, intimation, space, the qualities, etc., of form, and the nutritive principle of food. The force of this effort at dichotomy is, to the modern Western mind, curious and not obvious. It is suggestive of tradition earlier than the date of the compiling of the Abhidhamma, as early

[677] What is that [material] form which is remote (d ū r e) ?

Woman-faculty . . . and bodily nutriment—this is that [material] form which is remote.

[678] What is that [material] form which is near (s a n - t i k e) ?

The spheres of the five senses and of the five kinds of sense-objects—this is that [material] form which is near.[1]

[*Basis* (v a t t h u).] [2]

[679] What is that [material] form which is the basis of visual contact cakkhusamphassassa vatthu) ?

---

as the earlier Upanishads—of a time when there was no definite antithesis between material and immaterial, extended and unextended. We have seen that the senses, though "invisible", were conceived as species of "[material] form"—nay, that the later Cy. preserved the tradition of their shape and size. And I incline to think that just as, in the older Upanishads, soul was a shadowy, impalpable, but "physical double of the physical body", and just as "when an early Greek philosopher speaks of τὸ ὄν he does not mean Being, but Body" (Burnet, *Early Greek Philosophy*, 27), so the items in the list divided out in these two answers are all *physical* "forms", whether patent, impressive, and pervading, or latent, fine, and mysterious.

[1] D ū r e, the Cy. explains, refers to that which on account of its being difficult to apprehend or discriminate cannot be discerned by way of the sensuous impact, whether it be literally far or near at hand. Conversely, s a n t i k e refers to things which are patent to sense, even though they may be distant. The content of each division agrees with that of the preceding division, and we see that, whereas the field of sense-preception is pronounced to be a relatively patent, as well as gross concern, the essence of sex, vitality, etc., down to the nutritive principle in food, is found to be as obscure, latent, or relatively inaccessible as it was subtle or minute. Asl. 337.

[2] From § 653 to § 961 the Commentator lapses into silence, dismissing the reader with the remark that in the exposition on "spheres", etc. (§§ 695–741), the method of treatment is more detailed than it was above, and, further, that the category of triplets (§ 742 *et seq.*) is easy to understand. To enable the reader to gather with more ease the drift of this part of the catechizing, I have inserted a few headings to indicate whenever there is a change in the *aspect* under which "form" is considered. Thus we have form considered under the aspect of the

The sphere of vision—this is that [material] form which is the basis of visual contact.

[680] What is that [material] form which is not the basis of visual contact?

The sphere of hearing . . .[1] and bodily nutriment—this is that [material] form which is not, etc.

[681] What is that [material] form which is the basis of

the feeling . . .
the perception . . .
the volition . . .
the visual cognition

which is born of visual contact?

The sphere of vision—this is that [material] form which is the basis of the . . . visual cognition[2] which is born of visual contact.

[682] What is that [material] form which is not the basis of the . . . visual cognition born of visual contact?

The sphere of hearing . . . and bodily nutriment—this

---

basis (v a t t h u) in the subjective procedure of coming-to-know, of the *object* so apprehended, and so forth.

In all the answers, where lacunæ occur, except where otherwise specified, the formula appears to be the answer of § 596, with one or more terms omitted, and with the occasional insertion of " the sphere of the tangible ", according to the sense required by each specific process of dichotomy.

[1] By referring to the standard answer, § 596, it will be seen that the negatives in the present answer include " visible shapes ", or the objects of the sense of vision. Now, v a t t h u means seat, embodiment, or what we might call physical basis. However, then, the process of sense-stimulation was ultimately conceived, the effective result was held to take place in the sense-organ (and heart). The sense-object was defined as the ā r a m m a ṇ a ṃ of the contact. See § 687.

[2] No hiatus appears, in either the English or Siamese edition of the text, between r ū p a ṃ and c a k k h u v i ñ ñ ā ṇ a s s a, but by the context the answer is, of course, understood to deal in turn with all four mental processes stated in the question. As usual, only the last term gets an explicit answer. All four processes must also be understood in the lacuna in § 682 and in § 686.

is that [material] form which is not the basis of the . . . visual cognition born of visual contact.

[683] What is that form which is the basis of

auditory . . .
olfactory . . .
gustatory . . .[1]
bodily

contact ?

The sphere of . . .[2] body-sensibility—this is that [material] form which is the basis of . . . bodily contact.

[684] What is that [material] form which is not the basis of . . . bodily contact ?

The sphere of vision . . . and bodily nutriment—this is that [material] form which is not the basis of . . . bodily contact.

[685] What is that [material] form which is the basis of

the feeling . . .
the perception . . .
the volition . . .
the . . . cognition of body

that is born of . . . bodily contact ?

The sphere . . . of body-sensibility—this is that [material] form which is the basis of the . . . cognition of body that is born of . . . bodily contact.

[686] What is that [material] form which is not the basis of the . . . cognition of body born of . . . bodily contact ?

The sphere of vision . . . and bodily nutriment—this is that [material] form which is not the basis of the . . . cognition of body born, etc.

[*Mental object or idea* (a r a m m a ṇ a ṃ).]

[687] What is that [material] form which is the object in visual contact ?

---

[1] J i v h ā s a m p h a s s a s s a has dropped out of the printed text.

[2] Here, of course, understand the spheres of hearing, smell, and taste, and in the three following lacunæ the corresponding forms of contact. Proceed similarly in the next two answers.

The sphere of visible forms—this is that [material] form which is the object in visual contact.

[688] What is that [material] form which is not the object in visual contact ?

The sphere of vision . . . and bodily nutriment [1]—this is that [material] form which is not, etc.

[689] What is that [material] form which is the object in

the feeling . . .
the perception . . .
the volition . . .
the visual cognition

that is born of visual contact ?

The sphere of visible shapes—this is that [material] form which is the object in . . . the visual cognition that is born of visual contact.

[690] What is that [material] form which is not [2] the object in the . . . visual cognition born of visual contact ?

The sphere of vision . . . and bodily nutriment—this is that [material] form which is not the object, etc.

[691] What is that [material] form which is the object in

auditory . . .
olfactory . . .
gustatory . . .
bodily

contact ?

The sphere of . . . the tangible—this is that [material] form which is the object in . . . bodily contact.

---

[1] i.e. as in § 596, omitting only "the sphere of visible shapes", and inserting, presumably, "the sphere of the tangible."

[2] The negative particle must be supplied in the printed text. The lacunæ in this and following sentences must be filled up analogously with those in the preceding group. Thus, in this question, the three other mental processes named in the preceding question are to be understood; the answer will be identical with that in § 596, excluding only "the sphere of visible shapes", but inserting "the sphere of the tangible". And so on.

[692] What is that [material] form which is not the object in . . . bodily contact ?

The sphere of vision . . . and bodily nutriment—this is that [material] form which is not the object in . . . bodily contact.

[693] What is that [material] form which is the object in
the feeling . . .
the perception . . .
the volition . . .
the . . . cognition of body
that is born of . . . bodily contact ?

The sphere of the tangible—this is that [material] form which is the object in the . . . cognition of body that is born of . . . bodily contact.

[694] What is that [material] form which is not the object in the . . . cognition of body that is born of bodily contact ?

The sphere of vision . . . and bodily nutriment[1]—this is that [material] form which is not the object, etc.

[*Sphere of sense* (ā y a t a n a ṃ).]

[695] What is that [material] form which is the sphere of vision ?

The eye, that is to say, the sentient organ which is derived from the four Great Phenomena . . . this that is " an empty village "—this is that [material] form which is the sphere of vision.[2]

---

[1] i.e. repeat § 596 (into which " the sphere of the tangible " does not enter).

[2] The replies given here and to the four questions condensed in § 697 are apparently intended to be those set out in sets of four expounding the current theory of sense-reaction, §§ 597–616. Similarly, for the replies to the questions on sense taken objectively (§§ 699, 701), see §§ 617–32, 648–51.

The contradictories seem to be described in all four answers, by a repetition of § 596, with the omission in each case of the specific item named in the question on the corresponding positive term, and, presumably, with the insertion of " the sphere of the tangible ".

[696] What is that [material] form which is not the sphere of vision ?

The sphere of hearing . . . and bodily nutriment—this is that [material] form which is not the sphere of vision.

[697] What is that [material] form which is the sphere of

hearing . . .
smell . . .
taste . . .
body-sensibility ?

The body, that is to say, the sentient organ which is derived from the four Great Phenomena . . . this that is "an empty village"—this is that [material] form which is the sphere of . . . body-sensibility.

[698] What is that [material] form which is not the sphere of . . . body-sensibility ?

The sphere of vision . . . and bodily nutriment—this is that [material] form which is not, etc.

[699] What is that [material] form which is the sphere of visible shapes ?

That form which, derived from the four Great Phenomena, is visible under the appearance of colour . . . this . . . which is the constituent element of visible form—this is that [material] form which is the sphere of visible forms.

[700] What is that [material] form which is not the sphere of visible shapes ?

The sphere of vision . . . and bodily nutriment—this is that [material] form which is not, etc.

[701] What is that [material] form which is the sphere of

sound,
odour,
taste,
the tangible ?

The earthy (solid) element . . . this that is the . . .

element of the tangible—this is that [material] form which is the sphere of the tangible.[1]

[702] What is that [material] form which is not the sphere of . . . the tangible ?

The sphere of vision . . . and bodily nutriment—this is that [material] form which is not, etc.

[*Element* (d h ā t u).]

[703] What is that [material] form which is the element of vision ?

The sphere of vision—this is that [material] form which is the element of vision.

[704] What is that [material] form which is not the element of vision ?

The sphere of hearing . . . and bodily nutriment [2]—this is that [material] form which is not the element of vision.

[705] What is that [material] form which is the element of visible shape ?

The sphere of visible shape—this is . . . the element of visible shape.

[706] What is that [material] form which is not the element of visible shape ?

The sphere of vision . . . and bodily nutriment—this is . . . not, etc.

[707] What is that [material] form which is the element of sound . . . of odour . . . of taste . . . of the tangible ?

The sphere of . . .[3] the tangible—this is . . . the element of the tangible.

[708] What is that [material] form which is not the element of the tangible ?

---

[1] In the printed text read r ū p a ṃ p h o ṭ ṭ a b b ā - y a t a n a ṃ. The answer is, of course, the last of the four several replies, the three first being understood.

[2] Here supply the answer in § 596, omitting the first term, and inserting " the sphere of the tangible ".

[3] Here, of course, supply the spheres of the other three senses.

The sphere of vision . . . and bodily nutriment—this is . . . not the element of the tangible.

[*Faculty* (i n d r i y a ṃ).]

[709] What is that [material] form which is the faculty of vision?

The eye, that is to say, the sentient organ which is derived from the four Great Phenomena . . . this that is "an empty village"[1]—this is . . . the faculty of vision.

[710] What is that [material] form which is not the faculty of vision?

The sphere of hearing . . . and bodily nutriment[2]—this is . . . not, etc.

[711] What is that [material] form which is the faculty of hearing . . . smell . . . taste . . . body-sensibility?

The . . .[3] body, that is to say, the sentient principle, which is derived from the four Great Phenomena . . . this that is "an empty village"—this is . . . the faculty of . . . body sensibility.

[712] What is that [material] body which is not the faculty of . . . body-sensibility?

The sphere of vision . . . and bodily nutriment—this is . . . not, etc.

[713] What is that [material] form which is woman-faculty?[4]

That which is of the female, feminine in appearance, characteristics, occupation, and deportment, feminine in condition and being—this is that form which is woman-faculty.

[713*a*] What is that [material] form which is not woman-faculty?

---

[1] For the full formula, see § 597.

[2] i.e. answer as in § 596, omitting the first item, and inserting "the sphere of the tangible".

[3] See §§ 601, 605, 609, 613.

[4] See §§ 633–5.

The sphere of vision . . . and bodily nutriment—this is . . . not, etc.[1]

[714] What is that [material] form which is man-faculty ?

That which is of the male, masculine in appearance, characteristics, occupation, and deportment, masculine in condition and being—this is that form which is man-faculty.

[715] What is that [material] form which is not man-faculty ?

Answer as in § 713*a*.[2]

[716] What is that [material] form which is (the faculty of) life ?

The persistence of these corporeal states, their subsistence, their going on, their being kept going on, their progress, continuance, preservation, life, life as faculty—this is . . . (the faculty of) life.

[717] What is that [material] form which is not (the faculty of) life ?

Answer as in § 713*a*.

[*Intimation* (v i ñ ñ a t t i).]

[718] What is that [material] form which is bodily intimation ?

Answer as in § 636.

[719] What is that [material] form which is not bodily intimation ?

The sphere of vision. . . . and bodily nutriment—this is . . . bodily intimation.

[720] What is that [material] form which is vocal intimation ?

Answer as in § 637.

---

[1] [713*a*] is inadvertently omitted in the printed text.

[2] §§ 713*a*, 715, and 717 are presumably identical with § 596, with the successive omission of the term excluded by each question, and with the insertion always of " the sphere of the tangible ".

[721] What is that [material] form which is not vocal intimation ?

The sphere of vision . . . and bodily nutriment—this is . . . not, etc.[1]

[Space and fluid.] [2]

[722] What is that [material] form which is the element of space ?

That which is space and belongs to space, is sky, belongs to sky, is vacuum, belongs to vacuum, and is not in contact with the four Great Phenomena—this is . . . the element of space.

[723] What is that [material] form which is not the element of space ?

Answer as § 721.

[724] What is that [material] form which is the element of fluidity ?

That which is fluid and belongs to fluid, that which is viscid and belongs to viscid, the cohesiveness of form—this is . . . the element of fluidity.

[725] What is that [material] form which is not the element of fluidity ?

Answer as in § 721.

[Modes of form.]

[726] What is that [material] form which is lightness of form ?

That lightness of form which is its capacity for changing easily, its freedom from sluggishness and inertia—this is . . . lightness of form.

[727] What is that [material] form which is not lightness of form ?

---

[1] Again, in these two negative categories, § 596 is presumably followed with corresponding omissions and insertions. See p. 191, n.2.

[2] Cf. with §§ 638, 652.

The sphere of vision . . . and bodily nutriment—this is . . . not lightness of form.

[728–31] *Questions on the other two modes of form* "plasticity" *and* "wieldiness" *are answered by the descriptions given in* §§ 640, 641. *The corresponding contradictory terms are described in the same terms as in* § 727, *viz.: as in* § 596, *with the omissions and insertion as indicated on p.* 216, *n.* 5.

[*Evolution of* (*material*) *form.*]

[732] What is that [material] form which is the integration of form?

That which is accumulation of [material] form is the integration of form—this is, etc.

[733] What is that [material] form which is not the integration of form?

The sphere of vision . . . and bodily nutriment—this is . . . not, etc.

[734–9] *Question on the* "subsistence", "decay", *and* "impermanence" *of form and their contradictories are answered analogously with those in the group on* "Modes of form", *the three positives being described as in* §§ 642–5.

[*Nutrition.*]

[740] What is that [material] form which is bodily nutriment?

This is answered as in § 646.

[741] What is that [material] form which is not bodily nutriment?

The sphere of vision . . . and the impermanence of form—this is . . . is not bodily nutriment.

Such are the Categories of [material] Form under Dual Aspects.

[End of] the Exposition of the Pairs.

[CHAPTER III.

Categories of Material Form under Triple Aspects. Exposition of the Triplets.] [1]

[742–4] What is that [material] form which is

(i) *personal* [2] *and derived?*

The spheres of the five senses.

(ii) *external and derived?*

The sphere of visible shapes . . . and bodily nutriment.[3]

(iii) *external and not derived?*

The sphere of the tangible and the fluid element.

[745–7] What is that [material] form which is

(i) *personal and grasped at?*

The spheres of the five senses.

(ii) *external and grasped at?*

Woman-faculty, man-faculty, life, or whatever other [material] form exists through karma having been wrought, whether it be in the spheres of visible shape, odour, taste, or the tangible, in the spatial or the fluid element, in the integration or subsistence of form, or in bodily nutriment.[4]

---

[1] To lighten the tedium to the reader of looking through this lengthy analysis of material form considered as of the self or of the not-self taken in combination with the presence or absence of some other attribute, I have attempted a mode of grouping the triplets. I have also curtailed each answer of that constant feature, the concluding affirmation, termed in the Cy. (p. 55) the a p p a n ā . Cf. preceding answers.

[2] A j j h a t t i k a ṃ . The word "personal" corresponds more strictly perhaps to p u g g a l i k a ṃ , but it is less cumbrous than "of", or "belonging to, the self", while it is, at the same time, not an incorrect rendering. See p. 189, n. 1.

[3] This presumably still refers to § 596, which these two first answers may be held to exhaust between them, without the insertion of "the sphere of the tangible", which comes under (iii). Cf. the preceding chapter.

[4] Cf. §§ 653, 654.

(iii) *external and not grasped at?*

The sphere of sound, bodily and vocal intimation, the lightness, plasticity, wieldiness, decay, and impermanence of form, or whatever other [material] form exists which is not due to karma having been wrought, whether it be in the spheres of visible form,[1] odour, taste, or the tangible, in the spatial or the fluid element, etc. [*continue as in* ii].

[748–50] What is that [material] form which is

(i) *personal and both grasped at and favourable to grasping?*

(ii) *external and both grasped at and favourable to grasping?*

(iii) *external and not grasped at, but favourable to grasping?*

The answers are identical with those in the preceding triplet, taken in order.[2]

[751–3] What is that form which is

(i) *personal and invisible?*

The spheres of the five senses.

(ii) *external and visible?*

The sphere of visible shape.

(iii) *external and invisible?*

The sphere of sound . . . and bodily nutriment.[3]

[754–6] What is that [material] form which is

(i) *personal and reacting?* [4]

The spheres of the five senses.

(ii) *external and reacting?*

The spheres of the five kinds of sense-objects.

---

[1] Saddāyatanaṃ, here repeated in the printed text, is omitted in K.

[2] In § 750 read kammassa before katattā.

[3] Fill up from § 596 as before.

[4] See p. 159, n.4, and p. 167, n.2.

(iii) *external and non-reacting?* [1]

Sex [2] . . . and bodily nutriment.

[757–9] What is that [material] form which is

(i) *personal and a faculty?*

The five faculties of sense.

(ii) *external and a faculty?*

Sex and vitality.

(iii) *external and not a faculty?*

The sphere of visible shape . . . and bodily nutriment.[3]

[760–2] What is that [material] form which is

(i) *personal and not one of the Great Phenomena?*

The spheres of the five senses.

(ii) *external and belonging to the Great Phenomena?*

The sphere of the tangible and the fluid element.[4]

(iii) *external and not one of the Great Phenomena?*

The spheres of the [other four kinds of sense-objects] [5] . . . and bodily nutriment.

[763–5] What is that [material] form which is

(i) *personal and not intimation?*

The spheres of the five senses.

(ii) *external and intimation?*

Bodily and vocal intimation.[6]

(iii) *external and not intimation?*

The spheres of the five kinds of sense-objects . . . and bodily nutriment.

[766–8] What is that [material] form which is

(i) *personal and sprung from mind?* [7]

The spheres of the five senses.

---

[1] For s a p p a ṭ i g h a ṃ read a p p a ṭ i g h a ṃ .

[2] This term is substituted as a convenient abbreviation for the indriyas of both sexes. Cf. § 596.

[3] Supply as before from § 596.

[4] See § 647 *et seq.*

[5] Actually "of visible shape . . ." See n. 1.

[6] See §§ 636, 637.

[7] See § 667 *et seq.*

(ii) *external and sprung from mind?*

Bodily and vocal intimation, or whatever other form exists which is born of mind, caused by mind, etc. [*continue as in* § 667].

(iii) *external and not sprung from mind?*

Sex-faculty, life-faculty, the decay and impermanence of form, or whatever other form exists which is not born of mind, caused by mind, etc. [*continue as in* § 668].

[769–71] What is that [material] form which is

(i) *personal and does not come into being together with mind?*

The spheres of the five senses.

(ii) *external and comes into being together with mind?*

Bodily and vocal intimation.

(iii) *external and does not come into being, etc.?*

The spheres of the five kinds of sense-objects . . . and bodily nutriment.

[772–4] What is that [material] form which is

(i) *personal and not consecutive to mind?*

(ii) *external and consecutive to mind?*

(iii) *external and not consecutive to mind?*

The answers are identical with those in the preceding triplet, taken in order.

[775–7] What is that [material] form which is

(i) *personal and gross?* [1]

The spheres of the five senses.

(ii) *external and gross?*

The spheres of the five kinds of sense-objects.

(iii) *external and subtle?*

Sex . . . and bodily nutriment.

[778–80] What is that form which is

(i) *personal and near?* [2]

The spheres of the five senses.

---

[1] See § 675 *et seq.*

[2] See § 677 *et seq.*

(ii) *external and remote?*

Sex . . . and bodily nutriment.

(iii) *external and near?*

The spheres of the five kinds of sense-objects.

[781–3] What is that form which is

(i) *external and not the basis of visual contact?*[1]

The spheres of the five kinds of sense-objects . . . and bodily nutriment.

(ii) *personal and the basis of visual contact?*

The sphere of vision.

(iii) *personal and not the basis of visual contact?*

The sphere of the other four senses.

[784–6] What is that form which is

(i) *external and not a basis of*
the feeling . . .
the perception . . .
the volition . . .
the visual cognition
that is born of visual contact?

(ii) *personal and a basis of the feeling*[2] *. . . the visual cognition that is born of visual contact?*

(iii) *personal and not a basis of the feeling . . . the visual cognition that is born of visual contact?*

Answers identical with those in the preceding triplet.

[787–9] What is that form which is

(i) *external and not a basis of*
auditory . . .
olfactory . . .
gustatory . . .
bodily contact?

The spheres of the five kinds of sense-objects . . . and bodily nutriment.

---

[1] See § 679 *et seq.*

[2] Concerning the lacunæ in this and the following sentences on "basis", cf. § 681 *et seq.* and notes.

(ii) *personal and a basis of . . . bodily contact?*

The spheres of the other four senses respectively.

(iii) *personal and not a basis of . . . bodily contact?*

The sphere of . . . vision, hearing, smell, taste.

[790–2] What is that form which is

(i) *external and not a basis of*

the feeling . . .
the perception . . .
the volition . . .
the . . . cognition of body

that is born of . . . bodily contact?

(ii) *personal and a basis of . . . the cognition of body that is born of bodily contact?*

(iii) *personal and not a basis of . . . the cognition of body that is born of bodily contact?*

Answers identical with those in the preceding triplet taken in order.

[793–5] What is that form which is

(i) *personal and not the object apprehended on occasion of visual contact?*

The spheres of the five senses.

(ii) *external and the object apprehended on occasion of visual contact?*

The sphere of visible form.

(iii) *external and not the object apprehended on occasion of visual contact?*

The spheres of the other four kinds of sense-objects . . . and bodily nutriment.

[796–8] What is that [material] form which is

(i) *personal and not the object of*

the feeling . . .
the perception . . .
the volition . . .
the visual cognition

that is born of visual contact?

(ii) *external and the object of . . . visual cognition?*

(iii) *extern il and not the object of . . . visual cognition?*

Answers identical with those in the preceding triplet, taken in order.

[799–801] What is that [material] form which is

(i) *personal and not the object apprehended on occasion of*

auditory . . .
olfactory . . .
gustatory . . .
bodily contact?

The spheres of the five senses.

(ii) *external and the object apprehended on occasion of . . . bodily contact?*

The sphere of the tangible.

(iii) *external and not the object apprehended on occasion of . . . bodily contact?*

The spheres of the five kinds of sense-objects . . . and bodily nutriment.

[802–4] What is that [material] form which is

(i) *personal and not the object of*

the feeling . . .
the perception . . .
the volition . . .
the . . . cognition of body

that is born of . . . bodily contact?

The spheres of the five senses.

(ii) *external and the object of the . . . cognition of body that is born of bodily contact?*

The sphere of . . . the tangible.

(iii) *external and not the object of the . . . cognition of body that is born, etc.*

The spheres of the other four kinds of sense-objects . . . and bodily nutriment.

[805–7] What is that [material] form which is

(i) *external and not the sphere of vision?*

The spheres of the five kinds of sense-objects . . . and bodily nutriment.

(ii) *personal and the sphere of vision?*

The eye, that is to say the sentient organ which is derived from the four Great Phenomena . . . this that is "an empty village"—this, etc.[1]

(iii) *personal and not the sphere of vision?*

The spheres of the other four senses.

[808–10] What is that [material] form which is

(i) *external and not the sphere of hearing, smell, taste, or body-sensibility?*

The spheres of the five kinds of sense-objects . . . and bodily nutriment.

(ii) *personal and the sphere of . . . body-sensibility?*

The body, that is to say the sentient organ, which is derived from the Great Phenomena . . . this that is "an empty village"—this, etc.

(iii) *personal and not the sphere of . . . body-sensibility?*

The spheres of the other four senses.

[811–13] What is that [material] form which is

(i) *personal and not the sphere of visible shape?*

The spheres of the five senses.

(ii) *external and the sphere of visible shape?*

That [material] form which, derived from the four Great Phenomena, is visible under the appearance of colour . . . this that is the element of visible shape—this, etc.[2]

(iii) *external and not the sphere of visible shape?*

The spheres of the other four kinds of sense-objects . . . and bodily nutriment.

---

[1] For this and similar answers in following triplets, see § 597 *et seq.*

[2] See § 617.

[814–16] What is that [material] form which is

(i) *personal and not the sphere of sound, or of odour, or of taste, or of the tangible?*

The spheres of the five senses.

(ii) *external and the sphere of . . . the tangible?*

The earthy (solid) element, etc. . . . this that is the constituent element of the tangible—this, etc.[1]

(iii) *external and not the sphere of . . . the tangible?*

The spheres of the other four kinds of sense-objects . . . and bodily nutriment.

[817–19] What is that [material] form which is

(i) *external and not the element of vision?*

The spheres of the five kinds of sense-objects . . . and bodily nutriment.

(ii) *personal and the element of vision?*

The sphere of vision.

(iii) *personal and not the element of vision?*

The other four senses.

[820–2] What is that [material] form which is

(i) *external and not the element of hearing, smell, taste, or body-sensibility?*

The spheres of the five kinds of sense-objects . . . and bodily nutriment.

(ii) *personal and the element of . . . body-sensibility?*

The sphere of . . . body-sensibility.

(iii) *personal and not the element of . . . body-sensibility?*

The spheres of the other four senses.

[823–5] What is that [material] form which is

(i) *personal and not the element of visible shape?*

The spheres of the five senses.

(ii) *external and the element of visible shape?*

The sphere of visible forms.

---

[1] See § 648.

(iii) *external and not the element of visible shape?*

The spheres of the other four kinds of sense-objects . . . and bodily nutriment.

[826–8] What is that [material] form which is

(i) *personal and not the element of sound, odour, taste, or the tangible?*

The spheres of the five senses.

(ii) *external and the element of . . . the tangible?*

The sphere of the tangible.

(iii) *external and not the element of . . . the tangible?*

The spheres of the five kinds of sense-objects . . . and bodily nutriment.

[829–31] What is that [material] form which is

(i) *external and not the faculty of vision?*

The spheres of the five kinds of sense-objects . . . and bodily nutriment.

(ii) *personal and the faculty of vision?*

The sphere of vision.

(iii) *personal and not the faculty of vision?*

The spheres of the other four senses.

[832–4] What is that [material] form which is

(i) *external and not the faculty of hearing, smell, taste, or body-sensibility?*

The spheres of the five kinds of sense-objects . . . and bodily nutriment.

(ii) *personal and the faculty of . . . body-sensibility?*

The body, that is to say the sentient organ which is derived from the four Great Phenomena . . . this that is "an empty village"—this, etc.

(iii) *personal and not the faculty of . . . body-sensibility?*

The spheres of the other four senses.

[835–7] What is that [material] form which is

(i) *personal and not the woman-faculty?*

The spheres of the five senses.

(ii) *external and woman-faculty?*

That which is of the female, female in appearance, etc. [*continue as in* § 633].

(iii) *external and not woman-faculty?*

The spheres of the five kinds of sense-objects . . . and bodily nutriment.

[838–40] What is that form which is

(i) *personal and not the man-faculty? etc.*

The questions and answers in this triplet are exactly analogous with those in the foregoing, § 634 *constituting the answer to* (ii).

[841–3] *This triplet is on* "life", *and is also exactly analogous with that on* "woman-faculty", § 635 *being substituted in* (ii).

[844–6] What is that form which is

(i) *personal and not bodily intimation?*

The spheres of the five senses.

(ii) *external and bodily intimation?*

That tension, intension, tense state of the body, etc. [*continue as in* § 636].

(iii) *external and not bodily intimation?*

The spheres of the five kinds of sense-objects . . . and bodily nutriment.

[847–9] *This triplet is on* "vocal intimation", *and similar to the foregoing,* §637 *being quoted as the answer to the second question.*

[850–76] *Here follow ten triplets on the presence or absence in form that is personal or external, of the ten following attributes—identical with those ending the categories according to Pairs* (§§ 722–41).

the element of space,	the integration of [material] form,
the element of fluidity,	the subsistence ,,
the lightness of [material] form	the decay ,,
	the impermanence ,,
the plasticity ,,	bodily nutriment.
the wieldiness ,,	

Questions and answers in each of these triplets are identical with those in the triplet last set out on " bodily intimation " (§§ 844–6), *the only varying elements being the specific kind of form inquired into and its definition in the second answer of each triplet. Thus the schema of the questions is*

(i) *personal and not* . . .
(ii) *external and* . . .
(iii) *external and not* . . .[1]

Such are the Categories of Form under Threefold Aspects.

[End of] the Exposition of Triplets.

---

[1] There are several omissions in the printed text, breaking into the symmetry of the triplets, viz.: question and answer (iii) on ā k ā s a d h ā t u (following § 851); question and answer (iii) on r ū p a s s a u p a c a y o (following § 865); question and answer (i) on r ū p a s s a s a n t a t i (following § 865). These, if duly inserted, would bring the number of questions (and answers) at the end of this chapter up to 879, instead of 876. Had the triplets been grouped as such, the omissions would not have been possible.

[Chapter IV.

Categories of [Material] Form under Fourfold Aspects.][1]

[Derivation—Work of Karma.]

[877–80] What is that [material] form which is

(i) *derived and grasped at?*

The spheres of the five senses; the faculties of sex and life, or whatever other form exists through karma having been wrought, whether it be in the sphere of visible forms,[2] odours, or tastes, the element of space, the integration or subsistence of [material] form, or bodily nutriment.

(ii) *derived and not grasped at?*

The sphere of sounds, bodily and vocal intimation, the lightness, plasticity, and wieldiness of [material] form, or whatever other [material] form exists which is not due to karma having been wrought, whether it be on the spheres of visible shapes, odours, or tastes, the element of space, the integration or subsistence of form, or bodily nutriment.

(iii) *underived and grasped at?*

[Material form] due to karma having been wrought, which is in the sphere of the tangible and the fluid element.

(iv) *underived and not grasped at?*

[Material form] not due to karma having been wrought, which is in the sphere of the tangible and the fluid element.

---

[1] The logical method in this division is familiar enough, namely (where capitals represent positive, and uncials, negative terms), AB, Ab, aB, ab. The former term in the pair combined is, with its negative, a relative constant, there being a series of only six, namely, the concept of form as derived, as the product of karma, as that which breeds karma (literally, is karma-*ish*, karmic, karm-*ous*), as impressing the senses, as faculty, and as one of the elements (i.e. the opposite of derived, conceived positively). The latter five of these six are in turn used as the relatively variable term, with the addition of three others: the concept of form with respect to grossness or delicacy, to distance, and to visibility.

[2] On sound and karma, see p. 185, n.2.

[Derivation—Production of Karma.]

[881–4] What is that [material] form which is

(i) *derived and both grasped at and favourable to grasping?*

(ii) *derived and not grasped at but favourable to grasping?* [1]

(iii) *underived and both grasped at and favourable, etc.?*

(iv) *underived and not grasped at but favourable, etc.?* [2]

The four answers are respectively identical with those in the preceding group.

[Derivation—Reaction.]

[885–8] What is that [material] form which is

(i) *derived and reacting?*

The spheres of the five senses, and of visible shape, sound, odour and taste.

(ii) *derived and non-reacting?*

Sex . . . and bodily nutriment.

(iii) *underived and reacting?*

The sphere of the tangible.

(iv) *underived and non-reacting?*

The fluid element.

[Derivation—Bulk.]

[889–92] What is that [material] form which is

(i) *derived and gross?*

(ii) *derived and subtle?*

(iii) *underived and gross?*

(iv) *underived and subtle?*

Answers respectively identical with those in the preceding group.

[Derivation—Proximity.]

[893–6] What is that [material] form which is

(i) *derived and remote?*

Sex . . . and bodily nutriment.

---

[1] See § 656, n. 1.

[2] Read n a before k a m m a s s a in the answer.

(ii) *derived and near?*

The spheres of the five senses, and those of visible shape, sound, odour and taste.

(iii) *underived and remote?*

The fluid element.

(iv) *underived and near?*

The sphere of the tangible.

[Work of Karma—Visibility.]

[897–900] What is that [material] form which is

(i) *grasped at and visible?*

The sphere of visible shape which is due to karma having been wrought.

(ii) *grasped at and invisible?*

The spheres of the five senses; sex and life, or whatever other [material] form exists through karma having been wrought, whether it be in the spheres of odour, taste, or the tangible, the elements of space or fluidity, the integration or subsistence of [material] form, or bodily nutriment.

(iii) *not grasped at*[1] *and visible?*

The sphere of visible shape which is not due to karma having been wrought.

(iv) *not grasped at and invisible?*

The sphere of sound, bodily and vocal intimation, the lightness, plasticity, wieldiness, the decay, or the impermanence of [material] form, or whatever other [material] form exists which is not due to karma having been wrought, whether it be in the spheres of odour, or of taste, or of the tangible, the elements of space, or of fluidity, the integration or subsistence of [material] form, or bodily nutriment.

[Work of Karma—Impact.]

[901–4] What is that [material] form which is

(i) *grasped at and reacting?*

The spheres of the five senses, or whatever other [material]

---

[1] In the printed text read anupādiṇṇaṃ.

form exists through karma having been wrought in the spheres of visible shape, odour, taste, or the tangible.

(ii) *grasped at and non-reacting?*

Sex or life, or whatever other [material] form exists through karma having been wrought in the elements of space or fluidity, in the integration, or subsistence of [material] form, or in bodily nutriment.

(iii) *not grasped at and reacting?*

The sphere of sound, or whatever other [material] form exists which is not due to karma having been wrought in the spheres of the other four kinds of sense-objects.

(iv) *not grasped at and non-reacting?*

Bodily and vocal intimation, the lightness, plasticity, wieldiness, decay, or impermanence of [material] form, or whatever other [material] form exists which is not due to karma having been wrought in the elements of space or fluidity, in the integration or subsistence of [material] form, or in bodily nutriment.

[Work of Karma—Great Phenomena.]

[905–8] What is that [material] form which is

(i) *grasped at and great phenomenon?*

The sphere of the tangible and the fluid element which are due to karma having been wrought.

(ii) *grasped at and not great phenomenon?*

The spheres of the five senses, sex, life, or whatever other [material] form exists through karma having been wrought, in the element of space, in the integration or subsistence of [material] form, or in bodily nutriment.

(iii) *not grasped at, but great phenomenon?*

The sphere of the tangible and the fluid element which are not due to karma having been wrought.

(iv) *not grasped at nor great phenomenon?*

The sphere of sound, bodily and vocal intimation, the lightness, plasticity, wieldiness, decay, and impermanence of form, or whatever other form exists which is not due to karma having been wrought, whether it be in the spheres of visible form, odour, or taste, in the element of space, in the integration or subsistence of form, or in bodily nutriment.

[Work of Karma—Bulk.]

[909–12] What is that form which is

(i) *grasped at and gross?*
(ii) *grasped at and subtle?*
(iii) *not grasped at and gross?*
(iv) *not grasped at and subtle?* [1]

Answers respectively identical with the four in the next preceding group but one (§§ 901–4).

[Work of Karma—Proximity.]

[913–16] What is that form which is

(i) *grasped at and remote?*
(ii) *grasped at and near?*
(iii) *not grasped at and remote?*
(iv) *not grasped at and near?*

Answers identical with those in the preceding group (*i.e. with those in* §§ 901–4), *but having the order of the first and second answers inverted, as well as that of the third and fourth.*

[917–36]

In the next five groups of four, form is considered as a combination of (*a*) "grasped at and favourable to grasping", *and either* "visible",[2] "reacting", "a great phenomenon", "gross" *or* "remote", *or the opposites of these five taken successively;* (*b*) "not grasped at, but favourable to grasping", *and the five above-named attributes and their opposites taken successively. Thus the questions are analogous to, and the answers identical with, those in the preceding five groups* (§§ 897–916).

---

[1] In the answer to this question the printed text has omitted to insert apodhātu. Cf. §§ 892 and 880.

[2] In the answer to the first question, § 917, read na before kammassa.

[Impact—Faculty.]

[937–40] What is that [material] form which is

(i) *reacting and faculty?*

The faculties of the five senses.

(ii) *reacting and not faculty?*

The five kinds of sense-objects.

(iii) *non-reacting and faculty?*

Sex and life.

(iv) *non-reacting and not faculty?*

Bodily and vocal intimation . . . and bodily nutriment.

[Impact—Great Phenomenon.]

[941–4] What is that [material] form which is

(i) *reacting and a great phenomenon?*

The sphere of the tangible.

(ii) *reacting and not a great phenomenon?*

The spheres of visible form, sound, odour, and taste.

(iii) *non-reacting and a great phenomenon?*

The fluid element.

(iv) *non-reacting and not a great phenomenon?*

Sex . . . and bodily nutriment.

[Faculty (Potentiality)—Bulk.]

[945–8] What is that [material] form which is

(i) *faculty and gross?*

The faculties of the five senses.

(ii) *faculty and subtle?*

Sex and life.

(iii) *non-faculty and gross?*

The spheres of the five kinds of sense-objects.

(iv) *non-faculty and subtle?*

Intimation . . . and bodily nutriment.

[Faculty (Potentiality)—Proximity.]

[949–52] What is that [material] form which is

(i) *faculty and remote?*

Sex and life.

(ii) *faculty and near?*

The faculties of the five senses.

(iii) *non-faculty and remote?*

Intimation . . . and bodily nutriment.

(iv) *non-faculty and near?*

The spheres of the five kinds of sense-objects.

[Great Phenomenon—Bulk.]

[953–6] What is that [material] form which is

(i) *a great phenomenon and gross?*

The sphere of the tangible.

(ii) *a great phenomenon and subtle?*

The fluid element.

(iii) *not a great phenomenon and gross?*

The spheres of the five senses and of visible form, sound, odour, and taste.

(iv) *not a great phenomenon and subtle?*

Sex . . . and bodily nutriment.

[Great Phenomenon—Proximity.]

[957–60] What is that [material] form which is

(i) *a great phenomenon and remote?*

The fluid element.

(ii) *a great phenomenon and near?*

The sphere of the tangible.

(iii) *not a great phenomenon and remote?*

Sex and life.

(iv) *not a great phenomenon and near?*

The spheres of the five senses and of visible form, sound, odour and taste.

[Form as Seen, Heard, Imagined, Understood.]

[961] (i) The sphere of visible shape is Form Seen,

(ii) The sphere of sound is Form Heard,

(iii) The sphere of odour, taste and the tangible is [Material] Form Imagined,[1]

(iv) All [material] form is Form Cognized by the mind.[2]

Such are the Categories of [Material] Form under Fourfold Aspects.

[End of] the Groups of Four.

---

[1] Or considered: m u t a ṃ. I am under the impression that the first three members of this group are survivals of an older tradition, belonging to an age when the five senses had not been co-ordinated by psychological analysis comparable to that effected by the earlier Buddhist school, and when m a n o and its function, expressed here (in part) by this old past participle, were more vaguely conceived. In the Prāçna Upanishad, e.g. which is probably older than the Abhidhamma, either the five senses are grouped as above under m a n a s, eye and ear, or the last two are alone held worthy to rank with the divine elements of life. If it be contended that the former interpretation is not plausible, it should be remembered that, in the (?) older Bṛihadārañyaka Upanishad (i, 5, 3), it is said that by m a n a s we know when we are *touched* from behind. It is as though the tradition were endeavouring to say, Smell, taste, touching, *without* the aid either of sight or of hearing, require a greater effort of inference, of mental construction, of imagination, to realize the external cause, or potential concrete mental percept, than either sight or hearing.

Buddhaghosa, who here resumes his parable (Asl. 338), paraphrases m u t a ṃ by m u n i t v ā j ā n i t a b b a ṭ ṭ h e n a: considered in the meaning of "is knowable"; and by p h u s i t v ā p i ñ ā ṇ u p p a t t i k ā r a ṇ a t o: by reason of the arising of knowledge when there has been contact.

[2] M a n a s ā v i ñ ñ ā t a ṃ, that is, m a n o v i ñ ñ ā ṇ e n a j ā n i t a b b a ṃ. Ibid.

[CHAPTER V.

The Category of [Material] Form under a Fivefold Aspect [pañcavidhena rūpasangaho).]

[962–6] What is that [material] form which is

(i) *earth-element* (paṭhavi-dhātu)? [1]

That which is hard, rough, hardness, rigidity, whether it be of the self,[2] or external, or grasped at,[3] or not grasped at.

(ii) *fluid-elcment* (āpodhātu)?

That which is fluid, belonging to fluid, viscid, belonging to what is viscid, the cohesiveness of form, whether it be of the self, or external, or grasped at, or not grasped at.[4]

---

[1] The essential mark (lakkhaṇaṃ) of the earth-element is given as "hardness" (kakkhaḷattaṃ, Asl. 332). This may very likely have conveyed to Buddhists what we understand by "solid", when the implication is density as opposed to what is liquid or gaseous, and I was tempted to use solidity in preference to hardness. But solidity is ambiguous, for it may mean the opposite of plane surface, and kakkhaḷattaṃ cannot be strained to mean that. Again, the opposite of hardness is neither liquid nor flat, but soft and pliant. Further, compare its use in describing gravel or stone-food in Mil. 67, where we should certainly use "hard". The other characteristics of paṭhavīdhātu are said to be establishing a fulcrum (or ποῦ στῶ, patiṭṭhānaṃ), and receiving (sampaṭicchanaṃ), viz. anything dumped upon it. Cf. M. i, 423; A. iv, 374.

[2] Ajjhattaṃ. See § 673, note, and § 742, note.

[3] In the Commentary, p. 338, where upādiṇṇaṃ is said to be na kammasamuṭṭhānaṃ eva, the negative particle must have crept in by some error, that which is upādiṇṇaṃ being essentially due to karma. See Dh. S., §§ 653, 654; Asl., pp. 46, 337 (§ 664), etc.; *Expositor*, 439, l. 17. Generally only body-matter (sarīraṭṭhakaṃ) is here referred to. For this, while it may, or may not, be upādiṇṇaṃ, is said to be wholly the issue of grasping when signifying that which is taken, laid hold of, infected.

[4] See § 652, note. The essential characteristics of āpodhātu are said to be flowing (paggharaṇaṃ), expansion or spreading (brūhanaṃ, cf. p. 12, n. 3; Mil. 313), and

(iii) *heat-element* (t e j o d h ā t u) ?[1]

That which is flame, belonging to flame, heat, belonging to heat, hot, belonging to what is hot, whether it be of the self, or, etc. [*continue as in preceding*].

(iv) *air-element* (v ā y o d h ā t u) ?

That which is air, belongs to air [the fluctuation], the inflation,[2] of form, whether it be of the self, or, etc.

(v) *derived ?*[3]

The spheres of the five senses . . . and solid nutriment.

Such is the Category of [Material] Form under a Fivefold Aspect.

[End of] the Group of Five.

---

congress (s a n g a h o, Asl., ibid.). The last term may possibly be an attempt to express what we term, loosely enough, by "water always finding its own level". The internal or personal ā p o is distributed as bile, phlegm, pus, blood, sweat, serum, tears, and so on. M. i, 42.

[1] Never a g g i (fire) in this connexion, in the Buddhist books. The essential characteristics are said to be (Asl., ibid.) heat, ripening, maturing (p a r i p ā c a n a ṃ), and softening. By the heat within food and drink are digested. M., loc. cit.

[2] The texts reads here both c h a m b h i t a t t a ṃ and t h a m b h i t a t t a ṃ, fluctuation (quaking) and inflation. The former term, however, is not elsewhere in the Atthasālinī applied to v ā y o ; the latter, with the intensive v i -, is declared to be the characteristic mark of v ā y o, other features of the element being onward movement (s a m u d ī r a n a ṃ) and away-leading force (a b h i n ī h ā r a ṃ)—*sic lege*. Cf. D. i, 76 ; M. i, 119 ; Asl. 332 . Now Buddhaghosa passes over c h a m - b h i t a t t a ṃ in silence, but explains t h a m b h i t a t t a ṃ. Again, though this is, of course, not conclusive, only the single term, t h a m b h i t a t t a ṃ r ū p a s s a, seems to be called for by the parallel, b a n d h a n a t t a ṃ r ū p a s s a (cohesiveness), in the description of fluidity. It is significant also that K. omits c h a m b h i t a t t a ṃ. On these grounds, taken together, I should be inclined to doubt the original inclusion of the term. The instance chosen to illustrate the inflating function characteristic of v ā y o is that of the sheaths or stems of lotuses and reeds, or bags "filled with air", or wind (v ā t a p u ṇ ṇ ā n i).

[3] "Derived" (u p ā d ā) is the opposite of (i) to (iv). See §§ 647, 648.

[CHAPTER VI.

The Category of [Material] Form under a Sixfold Aspect.]

[967]

(i) The sphere of visible shapes is [material] form cognizable by sight.

(ii) The sphere of sounds is [material] form cognizable by hearing.

(iii) The sphere of odours is [material] form cognizable by smell.

(iv) The sphere of tastes is [material] form cognizable by taste.

(v) The sphere of the tangible is [material] form cognizable by body-sensibility.

(vi) All [material] form is form cognizable by the mind.

Such is the Category of [Material] Form under a Sixfold Aspect.

[End of] the Group of Six.

[CHAPTER VII.

The Category of [Material] Form under a Sevenfold Aspect.]

[968]

(i) The sphere of visible shapes is [material] form cognizable by sight.

(ii) The sphere of sound is [material] form cognizable by hearing.

(iii) The sphere of odour is [material] form cognizable by smell.

(iv) The sphere of taste is [material] form cognizable by taste.

(v) The sphere of the tangible is [material] form cognizable by body-sensibility.

[969]

(vi) The spheres of visible shapes, sound, odour, taste, and the tangible are [material] form cognizable by the element of ideation.

(vii) All [material] form is form comprehensible by the element of representative intellection.

Such is the Category of [Material] Form under a Sevenfold Aspect.

[End of] the Group of Seven.

[Chapter VIII.

The Category of [Material] Form under an Eightfold Aspect.]

[970]

(i) The sphere of visible shapes is [material] form cognizable by the eye.

(ii) The sphere of sound is [material] form cognizable by the ear.

(iii) The sphere of odour is [material] form cognizable by the nose.

(iv) The sphere of taste is [material] form cognizable by the tongue.

(v) Pleasurable agreeable contact obtainable by touch is [material] form cognizable by the body.

(vi) Unpleasant disagreeable contact obtainable by touch is [material] form cognizable by the body.

(vii) The spheres of the five kinds of sense-objects are [material] form cognizable by ideation.

(viii) All [material] form is form comprehensible by representative intellection.

Such is the Category of [Material] Form under an Eightfold Aspect.

[End of] the Group of Eight.

[CHAPTER IX.

The Category of [Material] Form under a Ninefold Aspect.]

[971–3] What is that [material] form which is

(i) vision-faculty ?
(ii) hearing-faculty ?
(iii) smell-faculty ?
(iv) taste-faculty ?
(v) body-faculty ?
(vi) woman-faculty ?
(vii) man-faculty ?
(viii) life-faculty ?

The eight answers are those given in the original descriptions of the eight faculties or potentialities enumerated (§§ 597, 601, 605, 609, 613, 633–5).

(ix) What is that [material] form which is not faculty ?

The spheres of the five kinds of sense-objects . . .[1] and bodily nutriment.

Such is the Category of [Material] Form under a Ninefold Aspect.

[End of] the Group of Nine.

---

[1] That is to say, the *remainder* of § 596, but omitting, of course, the three "indriyas" of the sexes and life, and presumably inserting "the element of fluidity" (cf. p.186, n. 3).

[CHAPTER X.

The Category of [Material] Form under a Tenfold Aspect.]

[974, 975] *The first eight questions and answers are identical with the first eight in the preceding group.*

[976, 977] What is that [material] form which is

(ix) *not faculty but reacting?*

The spheres of the five kinds of sense-objects.

(x) *not faculty and non-reacting?*

Intimation . . . [1] and bodily nutriment.

Such is the Category of [Material] Form under a Tenfold Aspect.

[End of] the Group of Ten.

---

[1] That is to say, the remainder of § 596, beginning at bodily-intimation, and presumably inserting "the element of fluidity".

[CHAPTER XI.

The Category of [Material] Form under an Elevenfold Aspect.

[978, 979] What is that [material] form which is

(i) the vision-sphere ?
(ii) the hearing-sphere ?
(iii) the smell-sphere ?
(iv) the taste-sphere ?
(v) the body-sphere ?
(vi) the visible shape-sphere ?
(vii) the sound-sphere ?
(viii) the odour-sphere ?
(ix) the sapid-sphere ?
(x) the tangible-sphere ?

Answers as in §§ 597, 601, 605, 609, 613, 617, 621, 625, 629, 649 *respectively*.

[980]

(xi) What is that [material] form which is invisible, non-reacting, and included in the sphere of [mental] states ? [1]

Sex . . . and bodily nutriment.

Such is the Category of [Material] Form under an Elevenfold Aspect.

[End of] the Group of Eleven.

[End of] THE DIVISIONS OF FORM.

[End of] the Eighth Portion for Recitation.

---

[1] Dhammāyatana-pariyāpannaṃ. For the full content of the answer, see, as before, the last fourteen items in § 596.

[BOOK III.

THE DIVISION ENTITLED "THE DEPOSITION"[1]

(nikkhepa-kaṇḍaṃ).

PART I.

CHAPTER I.

The Group of Triplets (tikaṃ).]

[981] Which are the states that are good?

The three roots of good (karma),[2] to wit, absence of lust, absence of hate, absence of dullness; the skandhas of feeling, perception, activities and consciousness when they are associated with those three roots; whatever action, bodily, vocal and mental,[3] springs from those three roots.

[982] Which are the states that are bad?

The three roots of bad (karma), to wit, lust, hate, dullness; the vices that are united with them;[4] the skandhas of

---

[1] Or, following Mr. Maung Tin and the Burmese tradition, "The Summary." Nikkhepa is lit. a laying down, and, in the Suttas (e.g. S. iii, 26) is opposed to ādāna, laying hold of. In Mil. 356 it is the function of a balance; in Mil. 381 it is a grammatical term not easy to be sure about. Cf. *Expositor*, 9 and 446. Summary has already been commandeered for saṅgaha (pp. 24, 34, etc.) According to the Cy. (344, 345), the various classes into which the states of the moral consciousness were distinguished (dhamma-vibhāgo) are now to be set forth by a method which, in its greater conciseness, is a summarizing of the relatively more detailed exposition (vitthāra-desanaṃ) of Book I.

[2] By "root" is meant "cause, condition, bringing to pass, generating, originating, producing". And "since there is no such thing as good detached from a root", all good is hereby included. Asl. 344.

[3] Manokammaṃ, inadvertently omitted in the printed text. Cf. § 982 and *passim*.

[4] Tad-ekaṭṭhā ca kilesā. Ekaṭṭhaṃ is defined (Asl. 345) as located in one and the same *thought* by virtue of

feeling, perception, synergies and consciousness when these are associated with them ; whatever action, bodily, vocal and mental, springs from them.

[983] Which are the states that are indeterminate ?

The results of good and bad states taking effect in the worlds of sense, form, or the formless, or in the [life that is] Unincluded ;[1] the skandhas of feeling, perception, synergies and consciousness,[2] inoperative states,[3] moreover, which are neither good, nor bad, nor the results of karma ; lastly, all form and unconditioned element.[4]

[984] Which are the states that are associated with a feeling of ease ?

The skandhas of perception, activities and consciousness[5] (the feeling itself being excepted) are the states associated [with the consciousness arising] in pleasurable soil,[6] whether it belongs to the worlds of sense or of form, or to the life that is Unincluded.

---

a common origin, or in one and the same *person* by virtue of a common exclusion, to wit, here, of corrupt or faulty states. On vices (k i l e s ā), see § 1229 *et seq.*

[1] A p a r i y ā p a n n ā . See below, § 992, also § 583.

[2] To save much repetition throughout this division, *these* four skandhas are henceforward referred to as "the four skandhas".

[3] D h a m m ā k i r i y ā . Cf. § 566 *et seq.*

[4] In the printed text s a n k h a t ā should be a s a n k h a t ā .

[5] The skandha of feeling is in this case the predominating factor, and not reckoned as merely an associate, or sub-ordinate, adjunct in consciousness. (T a ṃ should be inserted before s a m p a y u t t o in the text.)

[6] S u k h a - b h ū m i y a ṃ . I have kept to the more literal rendering of b h ū m i here, in preference to some such term as "stage" (as in § 277 *et seq.*) or "source", because of the analogy drawn by the Cy. (p. 346) : just as by saying "This is a sugar-soil" or "a rice-land" we mean localities where these products thrive, so by s u k h a - b h ū m i , etc., we mean a thought (or state of mind, c i t t a ṃ), which is the place (or occasion, ṭ h ā ṇ a ṃ) for the uprising of ease (or pleasure).

[985] Which are the states that are associated with distressful feeling?

The skandhas of perception, synergies and consciousness (the feeling itself being excepted) are the states associated [with the consciousness arising] in a distressful soil belonging to the sensuous universe.

[986] Which are the states that are associated with feeling that is neither painful nor pleasant?

The skandhas of perception, synergies and consciousness (the feeling itself being excepted) are the states associated [with the consciousness arising] in a neutral soil, whether it belong to the worlds of sense, form, or the formless, or to the life that is Unincluded.

[987] Which are the states that are results?

The results of good and bad states which take effect in the worlds of sense, form and the formless, and in the life that is Unincluded; [in other words] the four skandhas.[1]

[988] Which are the states that involve resultant states? [2]

Good and bad states belonging to the worlds of sense, form and the formless, or to the life that is Unincluded; [in other words] the four skandhas.

---

[1] K. invariably places a colon before that enumeration of four or more skandhas which is part of the usual procedure in these triplets. There is nothing explicit in the Cy. to justify my interpretation by the parenthesis "in other words" of the somewhat amorphous construction of the answers thus punctuated. But I gather from its remarks that, in these concentrated replies, the skandha-list represents the preceding half of the answer, in which it occurs, *under another aspect*, viz. rāsaṭṭhena, or that of groups in consciousness. This is really the method followed in detail throughout Book I, but here in mere outline: first a reply in terms of dhammā, then the Summary (cf. p. 26), which is *mainly*, at least, in terms of skandha. Cf. e.g. §§ 431–41, 441*a*, 442. Also Asl. 152.

[2] Vipākadhamma-dhammā, paraphrased (Asl. 42) by vipāka-sabhāva-dhammā, states having a result-nature, or quality of result. See above, p. 114.

[989] Which are the states that neither are results nor have the quality of involving resultant states?

Those states concerning action which are neither good, nor bad, nor the results of ḳarma; all [material] form, moreover, and unconditioned element.

[990] Which are the states that are both grasped at and favourable to grasping? [1]

The co-Intoxicant [2] results of good and bad states taking effect in the worlds of sense, form or the formless; in other words, the four skandhas; such form, moreover, as is due to karma having been wrought.

[991] Which are the states that are not grasped at but are favourable to grasping?

Good and bad co-Intoxicant states taking effect in the worlds of sense, form, or the formless; in other words, the four skandhas; inoperative states, moreover, which are neither good, nor bad, nor the results of karma; as well as such form as is not due to karma having been wrought

[992] Which are the states that are neither grasped at nor favourable to grasping?

The Paths that are the Unincluded,[3] and the Fruits of the Paths,[4] and unconditioned element.

---

[1] See § 653 *et seq.*

[2] S ā s a v ā. See § 1096 *et seq.*

[3] See p. 153, n. 2. The term a p a r i y ā p a n n ā, when applied to d h a m m ā and used in an ethico-psychological sense, is described as here in terms of path, fruit, and uncompounded element. See § 1287. Its positive correlate is paraphrased, in Asl. 50, by "contained in the threefold cycle of existence" (i.e. the worlds of sense, form, etc.). I believe that a p a r i y ā p a n n a ṃ, with this lofty significance, does not occur in either of the older Piṭakas. But it appears in KV. 507, where it is declared a heresy to hold that any mere speculative opinion was of the Unincluded, and where the content of the latter concept is more amply set forth than in our manual.

[4] Read c a after m a g g a p h a l ā n i. The commentator vindicates the status of the arahant, here alluded to, as being free from all "grasping" as follows: Although the skandhas

[993] Which are the states that are vitiated and vicious ?[1]

The three roots of bad (karma), to wit, lust, hate, dullness ; the Corruptions that are united with them ; the four skandhas when these are associated with them ; whatever action, bodily, vocal and mental, springs from them.

[994] Which are the states that are not corrupt but baneful ?

Good and indeterminate co-Intoxicant states taking effect in the worlds of sense, form and the formless ; in other words, the *five*[2] skandhas.

[995] Which are the states that are neither corrupt nor baneful ?

The Paths that are the Unincluded, and the Fruits of the Path and unconditioned element.

[996] Which are the states associated with applied and sustained thought ?[3]

The four skandhas (applied and sustained thought itself excluded)[4] which are associated[5] [with the consciousness arising] in a soil favourable to applied and sustained thought, whether it belong to the world of Sense or of Form, or to the life that is Unincluded.

(the temporary being) of the arahant may become a cause of grasping to those who say, Our mother's brother, the Thera ! Our father's brother, the Thera ! yet there is no grasping, no perversion in the saint with regard to the Paths, the Fruits, and Nirvana. For just as there is no inducement to mosquitoes to alight on a ball of iron which has been heated all day, so these Things, by their excessive glory, do not attract the grasp of craving, pride, or false opinion.

[1] Or vitiating. See § 1229 (note) *et seq.*

[2] Beginning with the skandha of material form.

[3] See § 160. Part of the formula for the First Jhāna. The world, universe, or heaven of the Formless is omitted, being a "soil" where these mental processes could not grow. See § 265–8.

[4] They would else come under the skandha of synergies. See § 62, and p. 231, n. 5.

[5] Read t a ṃ before s a m p a y u t t o .

[997] Which are the states not so associated ? [1]

The four skandhas (sustained thought itself excluded) which are associated [with the consciousness arising] in a soil favourable not to applied, but only to sustained thought, whether it belong to the world of Form, or to the life that is Unincluded.

[998] Which are the states that are not associated with either applied or sustained thought ? [2]

The four skandhas which are associated [with the consciousness arising] in a soil not associated with either, whether it belong to the world of Sense, Form, or the Formless, or to the life that is Unincluded ; all [material] form, moreover, and unconditioned element.

[999] Which are the states that are accompanied by zest ?

The four skandhas (zest itself being excluded) which are associated [with the consciousness arising] in a soil yielding zest, whether it belong to the worlds of Sense or Form, or to the life that is Unincluded.

[1000] Which are the states that are accompanied by ease ?

The skandhas of [3] perception, synergies and consciousness (ease being excluded) which are associated [with the consciousness arising] in an ease-yielding soil, whether it belong to the worlds of Sense or Form, or to the life that is Unincluded.

[1001] Which are the states that are accompanied by indifference ?

The skandhas of perception, synergies and consciousness (indifference itself excluded) which are associated [with the consciousness arising] in a soil favourable to indifference, whether it belong to the worlds of Form or the Formless, or to the life that is Unincluded.

---

[1] See § 168 on Fivefold Jhāna.

[2] See § 162 *et seq.*

[3] "Zest" is not counted as a mode of feeling, but as a "synergy" (s a n k h ā r a) (see p. 9 , n. 4) ; "ease," however, and "indifference", being two of the three modes of feeling, this skandha ceases to be merely an associated state.

[1002] Which are the states that are to be put away by vision? [1]

The three Fetters,[2] to wit, the theory of individuality, perplexity, and perversion as to rule and ritual.

In this connexion

[1003] *What is the "theory of individuality"?* [3]

---

[1] D a s s a n a ṃ, lit., seeing or vision. In view of what *can* and can *not* be put away by "insight", it must be remembered that the term is here used in the technical sense it possesses for Buddhist ethics, and means the mental awakening, or intellectual conversion, by which one became a s o t ā p a t t i and entered the First Path—and no more. Asl. 356, 357; 43. It was the vehicle for breaking the three Fetters named here, and numbered as 4th, 5th, and 6th in the list of ten named later (§§ 1113, 1123, note). It represented a certain vantage-point for mind and heart, from which the Promised Land of Nirvana was caught sight of, and the fact of impermanence first discerned (see the standard passage on this and ñ ā ṇ a - d a s s a n a ṃ, D. i, 76), as well as the futility of Substantialist theories, and the impotence of a religion of rules and works. Confidence in the new methods sprang up with the wider vision. D a s s a n a ṃ was powerless to remove the cosmic processes of life and mind: the collocations of phenomena, the evolution of karma, the infinite mystery of the extra-sensuous (see § 1008 and note). On various ways of attaining this insight, see the interesting Kiṃsukā Sutta, S. iv, 191. Relatively to the higher standpoints to be gained it might rather, says Buddhaghosa, be called no-vision. For even as a man, bound on some mission to a king, if he saw the latter pass afar off on his elephant, would say, if questioned, that he had not seen him, he not having accomplished his mission, so the convert, though he have caught his first glimpse of Nirvana, yet because of all he has to do in the getting rid of evil, is said to have no vision. His knowledge consists in a contemplation of the Path (Asl. 43).

[2] On the Fetters, see § 1113 *et seq.*

[3] S a k k ā y a-d i ṭ ṭ h i, embodying one of the most dangerous of all delusions from the Buddhist point of view, is by the Cy. (p. 348) connected with k ā y o, the phenomenal compound of five skandhas, and either with s a t, in the sense of (noumenal) being, or with s a y a ṃ, one's own. Cf. SN., vv. 950, 951; Dhp., v. 367. The latter explanation —s v a k ā y a—is probably correct (*vide* E. Müller, *Pāli Grammar*, p. 19). "Individuality," then, stands for this skandha-complex, which we should now

When in this world[1] the ignorant,[2] average[3] man who

---

speak of as "body and soul" (or mind). Both term and theory are discussed by Dhammadinnā in M. i, 299 *et seq.* (See an article by the writer in JRAS., 1894, p. 324.) The fourth Upādāna, or "Grasping after a theory of soul", is described in identical terms. See § 1217.

Diṭṭhi, which is here rendered by "theory", and which might with equal propriety be translated by "speculation" or "views"—all four terms having a common etymological basis in the notion of seeing, or things seen—is in the answer rendered by "opinion", as fitting better that "mass of notions current among the mass of men" which in the case of the puthujjano does service for organized knowledge. Gotama might possibly have approved the Platonic description of δόξα as "something more dusky than knowledge, more luminous than ignorance". To translate by "heresy" or "delusion" has the disadvantage of necessitating the use of other terms in the case of the sound diṭṭhi, such as that described, in D. ii, 80 (*Dialogues*, ii, 85: "noble and saving insight"), as diṭṭhi ariyā niyyānikā. Cf. below, § 1366.

[1] Idha, a term, as the Cy. says, either of place, of the Sāsana, or of metric padding. Used in the first sense, and meaning occurrence in the world. Asl. 348.

[2] Assutavā, lit. one who has not "what is heard", i.e. not been taught, who through lack of investigation, inquiry, acquiring, in such matters as skandhas, elements, spheres, conditions, constituents, meditations, is without proper tradition and attainment. Ibid.

[3] Puthujjano, the "many folk", the common worldling. Buddhaghosa cites verses in his Dīgha Cy. (i, 59) distinguishing *l'homme sensuel moyen* as either blind or amiable; of these the former is here meant. In another quotation (ibid.) he is described as given to various common vices, governed by the individuality-theory, hanging on the lips of various ordinary preachers, immersed in every kind of rebirth; complicating life with various common complexities; carried away by divers vulgar currents; appeased by, or feverish with various low sources of gratification or of irritation; steeped in, greedy of, entangled in, infatuated with, involved in, sticking to, held fast and hampered by, the five low pleasures of sense; veiled, muffled, shrouded in, closed and cloaked and covered up by, the five low hindrances (§ 1152 *et seq.*); as absorbed among the countless folk in the past of low character and conduct opposed to noble doctrine; or, finally, as one separate and distinct from those noble folk who are given to virtue and learning.

perceives not the Noble Ones,[1] who comprehends not, nor is trained according to[2] the doctrine of the Noble Ones, who perceives not good men,[3] who comprehends not, nor is trained according to, the doctrine of good men, regards (1) the self as bodily shape,[4] or (2) as having bodily shape, or regards (3) bodily shape as being in the self, or (4) the self as being in bodily shape;[5] or regards (5) the self as feeling, or (6) as having feeling, or regards (7) feeling as being in the self, or (8) the self as being in feeling; or regards (9) the self as perception, or (10) as having perception, or regards (11) perception as being in the self, or (12) the self as being in perception; or regards (13) the self as synergies, or (14) as having synergies, or regards (15) synergies as being in the

---

[1] Ariyānaṃ adassāvī, referring either to the Buddhas, the Pacceka-buddhas and the disciples of the Buddhas, or to the Buddhas only. Buddhaghosa points out at some length that the inability to perceive, lit. see, holy persons is no mere visual shortcoming, but a lack of insight or of intelligent inference. The truly noble, as such, seen with the bodily, or with the "divine" eye, are not really seen. Their appearance (vaṇṇo) is apprehended, but not the area of their noble nature, even as gods and jackals, etc., see them and know them not. Even the personal attendant of a Thera may not discern the hero in his master, so hard is it without insight and understanding to discern the standpoint attained by the saints, or the conditions of true nobility. "What is to thee this vile body that thou seest, Vakkali? He who seeth the Doctrine, he it is who seeth Me!" S. iii, p. 120; Pss. of the Brethren, p. 198; Asl. 350.

[2] Avinīto. The Cy. enumerates, with examples, the five modes of the discipline (vinaya) of self-control, and of that of renunciation. These are given in Childers, s.v. vinayo.

[3] Sappurisā, meaning Pacceka-buddhas and the disciples of the Buddhas. (Asl. 349.)

[4] Or material form (rūpaṃ) as in Bk. II.

[5] These four "views" respecting the relation of each skandha to the central entity or attā are discussed in both Introductions. All, according to the Cy. (p. 354), are obstacles to the Paths, though not to heaven (maggā-varaṇā na saggā-varaṇā), and are overcome during progress through the First Path.

self, or (16) the self as being in synergies ; or regards (17) the self as consciousness, or (18) as having consciousness, or regards (19) consciousness as being in the self, or (20) the self as being in consciousness—then this kind of opinion, this walking in opinion, this jungle of opinion, wilderness of opinion, disorder of opinion, scuffling of opinion, this Fetter of opinion, the grip and tenacity of it, the inclination towards it, the being infected by it, this by-path, wrong road, wrongness, this sectarianism, this inverted grasp—this is called the theory of individuality.

[1004] *What is "perplexity"?*

To doubt, to be perplexed about, (1) the Master, to doubt, to be perplexed about, (2) the Doctrine, to doubt, to be perplexed about, (3) the Order, about (4) the Discipline, about (5) the past, the future, about both the past and the future, (6) as to whether there be an assignable cause[1] of states causally determined—it is this kind of doubt, this working of doubt, this dubiety, puzzlement, perplexity, distraction, standing at cross-roads ; collapse, uncertainty of grasp ; evasion, hesitation, in capacity of grasping thoroughly, stiffness of mind, mental scarifying, that is called perplexity.[2]

[1005] What is perversion as to rule and ritual ?

The theory, held by recluses and Brahmins outside our doctrine,[3] that holiness is got by rules of moral conduct,

---

[1] Ida-paccayatā.

[2] See § 425. The specific forms of doubt are thus commented on (Asl. 354, 355): (1) As to the Master's body: has it the thirty-two major bodily marks, or the eighty minor bodily marks of a Buddha, or, as to his qualities: is there omniscience with respect to things past, future, and present; (2) as to the adequacy of the Paths and their Fruits to lead indeed to the grand deathless Nirvāna; (3) as to whether those of the Order are indeed at various stages of the path to salvation, or have rightly won their way so far; (4) as to whether the Training is helpful; (5) as to whether evolution by way of skandhas, dhātus, and āyatanas has held in the past, or will hold in the future; (6) as to whether there is a twelve-graded cycle of causation, taking effect here and now or taking effect at all.

[3] Itobahiddhā.

that holiness is got by rites, that holiness is got by rules of moral conduct and by rites[1]—this kind of opinion, this walking in mere opinion, this jungle of opinion, this wilderness of opinion, this disorder of opinion, scuffling of opinion, Fetter of opinion, the grip and tenacity of it, the inclination towards it, the being infected by it, this by-path, wrong road, wrongness, this sectarianism, this inverted grasp—this is called the perversion as to rule and ritual.

[1006] These three Fetters, and the vices united with them,[2] and the four skandhas associated with them, as well as the action, bodily, vocal and mental, springing from them—these are the states which are to be put away by insight.

[1007] Which are the states that are to be put away by culture?[3]

---

[1] I have ventured to adopt a reading differing slightly from that both of the text and of K. The sense seems to demand it and the Cy. to imply it. The latter has: Sīlenā ti gosīlādinā. Vatenā ti govatādinā va (*sic lege*). Sīlabbatenā ti tadubhayena. Suddhī ti kilesasuddhi paramattha-suddhibhūtaṃ vā nibbānam eva. But it would not be in accordance with the methods of the Cy. to quote vatenā ti if suddhivatena stood in the text. (Asl. 355; cf. *Expositor*, 458, f.)

As to the terms gosīla, govataṃ, it is not clear what were the practices and mode of life followed in the "bovine morals", etc., of those who were called govattikā, or in the "canine (? Cynic) practices" of the kukkuravattikā. Both are named in M. i, 387. Cf. also D. iii, 5; Kh. P. Cy., p. 26.

Suddhi, it will be seen, is distinguished as, on the one hand, the mere renunciation of vices (see § 1229), on the other, perfect holiness or Nirvāna.

On sīlabbataparāmāso, see Rhys Davids' *American Lectures*, 146, and below, §§ 1174 f.

[2] On kilesā, cf. below, §§ 1229 f.

[3] Or practice, or development: bhāvanā, lit. the causative verbal noun from bhavati, to become; the collective name for the systematized effort in self-training of the disciple who, having attained "insight", leaves "the principles of the

Whatever lust, hate and dullness still remain, and any vices united with them; the four skandhas that are associated with them; whatever action, bodily, vocal or mental, springs from them.

[1008] Which are the states that are to be put away neither by vision nor by culture?

Good and indeterminate states relating to the worlds of Sense, Form or the Formless, or to the life that is Unincluded; the four skandhas; all [material] form, moreover, and unconditioned element.[1]

[1009] Which are the states the causes of which are to be put away by vision?[2]

The three Fetters, to wit, theory of individuality, perplexity, perversion as to rule and ritual.

In this connexion

[1010] What is "theory of individuality"? . . . [*continue as in* §§ 1003–5].[3]

---

doctrine" that he may "go on unto perfection" (Heb. vi, 1)—in other words, travel along the three higher Paths to Arahantship.

On the "powers of bhāvanā", see A. i, 52.

In A. i, 43, the "one thing needful" for the perfecting of bhāvanā is said to be kāyagata-sati, mindfulness in what concerns the body, or bodily action.

[1] Hence only akusalā dhammā, "bad states", can be put away by insight and culture. Nor can even these two avail in mutual independence, for see §§ 1258, 1260. The rest of one's karma goes on accumulating. The good and the indeterminate, the modes of matter, and Simple Element: these cannot cease for any individual until, according to Buddhaghosa, his abhisankhāra-viññāṇaṃ (Asl. 357), his constructing, storing consciousness, itself dies out with the extinction of his life as Arahant. See Sum. V. on the Kevaddha Sutta, D. i, 223; *Dialogues of the Buddha* i, 272 *et seq.*

[2] Pahatabba-āhetukā, "That is, the cause of them (hetu etesaṃ) is to be put away by insight." Asl. 43.

[3] Here the reading in the text is obviously corrupt. I follow that in K., viz.: Tattha katamā sakkāyadiṭṭhi? . . . pe . . . ayaṃ vuccati sakkāyadiṭṭhi — and so on.

[1010*a*] These three Fetters, and the vices united with them, and the four skandhas associated with them, as well as the action, bodily, vocal and mental, springing from them —these are the states the causes of which are to be put away by insight.

[1010*b*][1] The three Fetters:—theory of individuality, perplexity, perversion as to rule and ritual—are the *states* that are to be put away by insight. The lust, hate and dullness united with them are the *causes* that are to be put away by insight. And the vices united with them, the four skandhas associated with them, and the action, bodily, vocal and mental, springing from them, are the states *the causes of which* are to be put away by insight.

[1011] Which are the states the causes of which are to be put away by culture?

Whatever lust, hate and dullness still remain, these are *causes*[2] that are to be put away by culture. And the vices united with them, the four skandhas associated with them, and the action, bodily, vocal and mental, springing from them—these are *states the causes of which* are to be put away by culture.

[1012] Which are the states the causes of which are to be put away neither by vision, nor by cultivation?

The afore-mentioned states excepted, all other states, good, bad and indeterminate, relating to the worlds of Sense, Form and the Formless, and to the life that is Unincluded; in other words, the four skandhas; all [material] form, moreover, and unconditioned element.

---

[1] This paragraph, in which I again follow K., is not included in the text at all. Nevertheless, Buddhaghosa comments on it (p. 357).

[2] Here again I follow K. in reading p a h ā t a b b a - h e t ū for h e t u k ā . Buddhaghosa quotes the former reading (p. 358), as referring to the putting away of dullness accompanied by distraction.

[1013] Which are the states that make for the piling up [of rebirth]? [1]

Good and bad co-Intoxicant states relating to the worlds of Sense, Form and the Formless; [in other words], the four skandhas.

[1014] Which are the states that make for the undoing of rebirth?

The four Paths that are the Unincluded.

[1015] Which are the states that make neither for the piling up, nor for the undoing of rebirth?

The results of good and bad states taking effect in the worlds of Sense, Form or the Formless, or in the life that is Unincluded; [in other words], the four skandhas; inoperative states, moreover, which are neither good nor bad, nor the result of karma; all [material] form also and unconditioned element.

[1016] Which are the states that appertain to training? [2]

The four Paths that are the Unincluded and the three lowest Fruits of the life of the recluse.

[1017] Which are the states not appertaining to training?

The topmost fruit [3]—the fruit that is Arahantship.

[1018] Which are the states neither appertaining, nor not appertaining to training?

The afore-mentioned states excepted, all other states, good, bad and indeterminate, relating to the worlds of Sense,

---

[1] Apacayagāmino. On its opposite, see p. 74, n. 2. The latter is tantamount to going to Nirvana. The two processes are compared to the building up and pulling down of a wall. Asl. 44.

[2] Sekhā, i.e. (Asl. 44), springing up in the three, or in the seven courses of training (cf. Childers, s.v.). Asekhā implies that the student or probationer has perfected his studies and training and is become an adept, an Arahant. Cf. PP., p. 14. On the term "fruits of the life of the recluse", see the Sāmaññaphala Sutta, D. i, 47.

[3] Uparițțhimaṃ, a term used in PP. i, 42 *et seq.*, where it is applied to the "Fetters" which are put off *last*. Cf. below, § 1113, and p. 279. See also p. 153, n. 4.

Form and the Formless; all [material] form also and unconditioned element.

[1019] Which are the states that are limited? [1]

All states, good, bad and indeterminate, which relate to the universe of sense; in other words, the *five* skandhas.

[1020] Which are the states that are sublime? [2]

States, good, bad and indeterminate, which relate to the worlds of Form and the Formless; [in other words], the *four* skandhas.

[1021] Which are the states that are infinite? [3]

The Paths that are the Unincluded, and the Fruits of the Paths, and unconditioned element.

[1022] Which are the states that have limited objects of thought?

Conscious statesand their mental properties [4] which arise in connexion with limited matters.

[1023] Which are the states that have sublime [5] objects of thought?

Conscious states and their mental properties which arise in connexion with sublime matters.

[1024] Which are the states that have infinite objects of thought?

Those emotional, perceptual and active states, as well

---

[1] Parittaṃ, understood as involving intellectual and ethical, as well as physical insignificance—the connotation of the French term *borné*. The illustration chosen is that of a lump of cowdung! The essential quality is appānubhāvatā, i.e. of little importance or efficacy generally. Parittaṃ itself is ranked as an equivalent of the whole sphere of sense-experience. Asl. 44.

[2] Mahaggatā, i.e. in respect of "the ability to resist vice, of abundance of good result, of long duration", or of the attainment to a high pitch of will, energy, thought or wisdom. Ibid.

[3] Appamāṇā, or without measure. Asl. 45.

[4] On cittacetasikā dhammā, cf. §§ 1187–90, 1282, 1284, and *Compendium*, 94 f.

[5] See § 1021.

as those of mind and mental properties, which arise in connexion with infinite things.

[1025] Which are the states that are base?

The three roots of bad (karma)—greed, hate, dullness—the vices united with them; the four skandhas associated with them; the action, bodily, vocal and mental, springing from them.

[1026] Which are the states that are of medium worth?

Co-Intoxicant states, good, bad and indeterminate, relating to the worlds of Sense, Form and the Formless; [in other words], the four skandhas.

[1027] Which are the states that are excellent? [1]

The Paths that are the Unincluded, and the Fruits of the Paths, and unconditioned element.

[1028] Which are the states the wrongfulness of which is fixed as to its consequences? [2]

The five acts that have immediate results, and those wrong views that are fixed in their consequences.

---

[1] The three subjects of this triplet of inquiry—dhammā hīṇā, majjhimā, paṇītā—are paraphrased (Asl. 45) as lāmakā (of poor quality, cf. Vin. ii, 76), midway between this and the third quality, and supramundane or ideal (lokuttarā), respectively.

[2] Micchattaniyatā, thus explained by the Cy. (ibid.): "Wickedness" is that wrongful disposition which, in its desire for happiness, sees benefit in things baneful and persists in this perversion. "Fixed in its consequences" (lit. "reaching down to") means yielding a result immediately on the disintegration of the skandhas (i.e. after death). Cf. D. ii, 93: asmi . . . niyato—I am fixed or sure (as to my future); also *Points of Controversy*, 177, 185, 355, nn., and PP. 13: katamo ca puggalo niyato? The answer to this question is practically identical with those given in these sections. It is the *persons* (puggalā) who are decisively good and bad that are called ānantarakā (incurring immediate destiny good or bad) instead of the "acts" or the "Paths", as in the Dh.S.

These five acts, the Cy. says, refer to "matricide, etc.", as though the Abhithāṇas were here alluded to, whereas the

[1029] Which are the states the righteousness of which is fixed as to its consequences ? [1]

The four Paths that are the Unincluded.

[1030] Which are the states that do not entail fixed consequences ?

The afore-mentioned states excepted, all other states, good, bad, and indeterminate, relating to the worlds of Sense, Form and the Formless, or to the life that is Unincluded; in other words, the four skandhas; all [material] form, moreover, and unconditioned element.

---

five usually classed under this name appear to be murder, theft, impurity, lying, and intemperance. Cf. SN. 231; Kh. p. vi, 10; and below, §§ 1290, 1291. Compare the passage relating to l o h i t u p p ā d o, or the wounding of a Buddha, Vin. ii, 193, which is called an ā n a n t a r i k a - k a m m a ṃ. I venture to think that, in the Mil., p. 25, the phrase k o p a ñ c ā n a n t a r i y a k a m m a ṃ k a r o t i is not intended, as the translator infers, to sum up the five offences previously specified, but is an allusion to five others, of which matricide was one and l o h i t u p p ā d o another. It only remains to ascertain whether or not the other three coincide with any other three of the six A b h i t h ā ṇ a s.

As to the immediacy of their consequences, whereas, from the Devadatta incident in the Cullavagga, the outrages entailed at least some of their retribution in this life, it will have been seen that, according to Buddhaghosa, the effect is experienced immediately after the cessation of the present life. The Cy. goes on: In the case of these acts, it is impossible for any other conduct to push off the karma of any one of them, so as to obtain room for the realization of its own consequences. Asl. 358. The wrong views which are also n i y a t ā are specified in the Cy. as those held by the Anti-causationists (a h e t u k a - v ā d ā, D. i, 53; M. i, 407), those who denied the efficacy of action (a k i r i y a - v ā d ā, D. i, 52; M. i, 404, 405), and the Nihilists (n a t t h i k a - v ā d ā, or u c c h e d a - v ā d ā, D. i, 55; M. i, 401–3). These are past praying for; more literally rendered, not a hundred, nor yet a thousand Buddhas would be able to enlighten them. Ibid.

[1] The reading should be s a m m a t t a - n i y a t ā. Cf. Asl. 45; K.; KV. 609.

[1031] Which are the states that have the Path as their object of thought ? [1]

Conscious states and their mental properties which arise in connexion with the Noble Path.

[1032] Which are the states that are causally dependent upon the Path ? [2]

[Firstly] the four skandhas when associated with the stages of the Path as experienced by one who is conversant with the Path [3] (the stages themselves being excepted).

[Secondly (1033)] the four skandhas when associated with the right views—these being both Path and Cause—of one who is conversant with the Path (the right views themselves being excepted).

[Thirdly] the four skandhas when associated with the states of freedom from lust, hate and dullness peculiar to one who is conversant with the Path.

Now, these [last named] states are the " Path-causes " ; [4] the former (the skandhas) are those states which are causally dependent upon the Path.

---

[1] " ' Path ' means the quest of Nirvana, or the progress in the destruction of the vices." (Asl. 45.)

[2] " Maggahetuka, i.e. the cause of those (states) in the sense of conditioning them is the Eightfold Path." Asl. 45. Later (p. 359) the Cy. gives the purport of this triad as follows : " In the first formula the kind of causal conjunction of the skandhas, in their connexion with the Path by way of cause, in the sense of condition, is set forth. In the second, the kind of causal conjunction of the other parts of the Path with Right Views, which are a constituent of the Path and are reckoned as cause (amoho; cf. §§ 16, 34, 1054) ; and in the third, the kind of causal conjunction of Right Views with those causes that are operative in the Path, is set forth." Yet in the text it is the causal connexion of the four skandhas that is predicated about in all three formulæ. Does this implicate discrepant versions of the text ?

[3] Ariyamaggasamangissa maggangāni.

[4] In the printed text, after amoho read ime dhammā magga-hetū. Cf. Cy. 45 ; K. ; also above, § 1011.

[1034] Which are the causes that are Path-governed?[1]

[Firstly] those conscious states, and their mental properties, which in arising make the Noble Path their governor. [Secondly] the four skandhas when associated with the investigation carried on by one who is conversant with the Path, and who is cultivating a way wherein investigation is the dominant factor.[2]

[1035] Which are the states that "have arisen"?[3]

Those states that have been born, have become, have been gotten, created, re-created,[4] made manifest,—that have arisen, have come to pass, have happened, have supervened, have been caused to arise, are classed together among the things that have arisen, to wit, form, feeling, perception, synergies, consciousness.

[1036] Which are the states that have "not arisen"?

Those states that are unborn, have not become, have not

---

[1] M a g g ā d h i p a t i n o, i.e. the Path, having them (those states) under its control in the sense of maintaining them, is their governor. Asl. 45. Later (p. 359) we get supplementary remarks showing that the relation of governor (or sovereign) and governed, in this connexion, resembles that between Christ and the believer who brings "into captivity every thought to the obedience of Christ" (2 Cor. x, 5). All such thoughts or "states" are insignificant (p a r i t t ā) as compared with the one great object of devotion—the Path, the Fruit, Nirvana. Even to contemplate the progress of others in the Path, or to have seen the Tathāgata work a double miracle, is not precious to the student as is his own discernment and realization of what the Path means to *him*.

[2] The Cy. (p. 359) explains that the term shows a joint "supremacy" between the Path and an a d h i p a t e y y a ṃ to be only possible (cf. § 269) when the latter is either "investigation" or "energy". When the latter is "desire" or a "thought", then the Path yields its sway over the mind to the a d h i p a t e y y a ṃ. But when the student makes either of the former his governing influence, both it and the Path are his joint governors.

[3] U p p a n n ā, i.e. which from the moment they came into being, and for as long as they had distinguishable being, have come to pass and been sustained. Asl. 45.

[4] Read n i b b a t t ā, a b h i n i b b a t t ā.

been gotten, nor created, nor re-created, nor made manifest; that have not arisen nor come to pass; nor happened, nor supervened; that have not been caused to arise, that are classed together among the things that have not arisen, to wit, forms, feelings, perceptions, synergies, consciousness.

[1037] Which are the states that are bound to arise? [1]

The results of those good and bad states related to the worlds of Sense, Form and the Formless, or to the life that is Unincluded, the consequences of which are not yet matured,[2] to wit, the four skandhas and that form due to karma having been wrought which will arise.

[1038] Which are the states that are past?

Those states that are past are extinct, dissolved,[3] changed, terminated, exterminated; are past and classed among the things that are past; in other words, the five skandhas.

[1039] Which are the states that are future?

The states that are unborn, that have not become, not been gotten, nor created, nor re-created, nor made manifest; that have not arisen, nor come to pass, nor happened, nor supervened; that have not arrived, and are classed among the things that have not arrived.

[1040] Which are the things that are present?

Those states that have been born, have become, have

---

[1] Uppādino, i.e. "will certainly arise, from the fact that their efficient cause is in part completed" (Asl. 45). Later (pp. 360, 361) the potential happening of these resultant states is declared to be due to the enduring validity of their conditions (dhuvapaccayaṭṭhena), which cannot fail to produce their effects, even though 100,000 æons intervene. The gospel (lit. Path) of the future Buddha, Metteyya, is anuppanno, but his (or anyone's) fruition belongs to the uppādino-dhammā.

[2] Avipakkavipākānaṃ. Inserted in K., but, as is stated in that edition, not inserted in the Burmese or the European text.

[3] The printed text reads niruddhangatā; the Cy., niruddhā vigatā; K., niruddhā pariṇatā (not vipariṇatā).

been gotten, created, re-created,[1] made manifest; that have arisen, have come to pass, have supervened, have been caused to arise; that have arisen over against[2] and are classed among the things that have so arisen.

[1041–3] Which are the states that have the past . . . future . . . present as their object of thought?

Conscious states and their mental properties which arise in connexion with states that are past . . . future . . . present.[3]

[1044] Which are the states that are personal?[4]

Those states which, for this or that being, are of the self, self-referable, one's own,[5] individual, the issue of grasping; [in other words,] the five skandhas.

[1045] Which are the states that are external?

Those states which, for this or that other being,[6] for other individuals, are of the self, self-referable, their own, individual, grasped at;[7] [in other words,] the five skandhas.

[1046] Which are the states that are personal-external?

States which are both [personal and external].[8]

---

[1] Abhinibbattā is omitted in the printed text. Cf. § 1035; also K.

[2] Paccuppannā, the word rendered by "present" in the question. Cf. our "ob-vious", "ob-jective", "ob-ject", in its most general psychological sense, as something present to the subject of the mental "states".

[3] Cf. § 1022.

[4] On ajjhattā and bahiddhā, cf. §§ 742, 743. The Cy. distinguishes four varieties in the connotation of ajjhattaṃ, namely gocarajjhattaṃ, niyakajjhattaṃ, ajjhattajjhattaṃ and visayajjhattaṃ, two of which are identical with two of the three meanings cited by Childers. The specific meaning used here is said to be the second.

[5] For niyatā read niyakā.

[6] "That is, all beings except one's self." Asl. 361.

[7] Upādiṇṇā is omitted in the printed text.

[8] Tadubhayaṃ is the curt answer. It is to be regretted that Buddhaghosa's fertility in illustration was not applied to this species of dhammā. Incidentally one gathers that they

[1047–9] Which are the states that have an object of thought concerning the self . . . concerning that which is external [to the self] . . . concerning that which is " personal-external " ?

Conscious states and their mental properties,[1] which arise in connexion with states of the self . . . states that are external . . . states that are personal-external.

[1050] Which are the states that are both visible and reacting ? [2]

The sphere of visible shapes.

[1051] Which are the states that are invisible, but reacting ?

The spheres of the five senses and the spheres of sound, odour, taste, and the tangible.

[1052] Which are the states that are both invisible and non-reacting ?

The four skandhas ; that [material] form, moreover, which, being invisible and non-reacting, is yet included in the sphere of [mental] states ; [3] also unconditioned element.

[End of] the Triplets.

---

alternate between self-reference and reference to other selves. For whereas the d h a m m ā in the first and third questions are said to be either " limited " or " enlarged " (see §§ 1019–21), and those in the second are said to be " infinite ", states that are " infinite " are said " not to take as their object that which now relates to the external, now to the self." (Asl. 361, 362.)

[1] Cf. § 1022 *et seq.*

[2] See § 597 *et seq.*, § 657 *et seq.*

[3] See § 980.

[CHAPTER II.

The Group on Root Condition (h e t u - g o c c h a k a ṃ).][1]

I.

[1053] Which are the states that are root-conditions?

(A) The three root-conditions of good (karma).

(B) The three root-conditions of bad (karma).

---

[1] In connexion with the statement (§ 595) that form is "that which is not a root-condition (h e t u)," the Cy. distinguishes, as did Aristotle, four varieties of cause. The coincidence, however, scarcely extends beyond the number. H e t u is either (*a*), as such, condition (h e t u - h e t u); (*b*) as causal relation, or necessary antecedent "wherewithal" (p a c c a y a h e t u); (*c*) as ultimate or supreme (u t t a m a - h e t u); and (*d*) as an attribute held in common (s ā d h ā r a n a - h e t u). Asl. 303. These distinctions are shown to be applied as follows: (*a*) the trinity of threefold cause given in § 1053. Here the word is always paraphrased by "root", root, conversely, standing for productive agent in general (see the list in note to § 981), and, of course, for *moral* agency especially. (*b*) "I have declared, bhikkhu, that the four great phenomena are the causes, are the conditions of the material skandha (or body)." When the p a c c a y o is material, it may be said to coincide with Aristotle's second formal principle ἡ ὕλη καὶ τὸ ὑποκείμενον. Possibly p a c c a y o was this conception so generalized as to include the immaterial wherewithal requisite for the effect. Colebrooke, however (*Life and Essays*, ii, 419), said that the Bauddhas distinguish between h e t u as proximate cause and p r a t y a y a (p a c c a y o) as concurrent occasion. No such distinction appears in the Suttas. The distinction in Abhidhamma is that h e t u is a specific group of p a c c a y o, the genus. Cf. my Tikapaṭṭhāna (preface), part 7. (*c*) "When good (karma) takes effect, it is the object ultimately or supremely desired"—and the opposite, of course, in the case of bad karma. This may possibly approximate to Aristotle's final cause (τὸ οὗ ἕνεκα). (*d*) "As the essence of the elements of earth and water (solid and liquid) are the condition of sweet or not-sweet, so is ignorance the common base-element of the synergies (s a n s k ā r a s). In our present connexion the term is said to be used in its first-named meaning: root-condition. Cf. Duka, p. xii; Tikap. i, Foreword.

(C) The three, root-conditions of the indeterminate:—[these are]

The nine root-conditions operative in the sensuous universe.

The six root-conditions operative in the universe of Form.

The six root-conditions operative in the universe of the Formless.

(D) The six root-conditions operative in the life that is the Unincluded.

(A) In this connexion,

[1054] Which are the three causes of good karma?

Disinterestedness, absence of hate and dullness.

In this connexion,

[1055] *What is disinterestedness?*

The absence of greed, showing greed, greediness is the absence of lust, of lusting, of lustfulness; the absence of covetousness, that absence of greed which is the root of good (karma).[1]

[1056] What is the absence of hate?

The absence of hate, hating, hatred; love,[2] loving, loving disposition;[3] tender care, forbearance, considerateness;[4]

---

[1] Cf. § 32. The Pali terms coincide in both answers. In the following answer, the terms differ considerably from those in § 33.

[2] The printed text has m e t t a ṃ; the Cy. and K. read m e t t ī.

[3] "The mental condition of one who is possessed by love, who is unclinging." (Asl. 362.) Cf. *Expositor*, 467, n. 1: In B. ed. reads ayitassa for asitassa. I do not know the former term (= "is productive of"). But the love which is unclinging is just the cool benevolence encouraged by monastic religion.

[4] A n u d d ā, a n u d d ā y a n a, a n u d d ā y i t a t t a ṃ. The Cy. paraphrases by r a k k h a t i, showing the reference there is in these terms, usually rendered by "pity", "compassion", to the protective, shielding aspect of altruism and benevolence. Cf. its use in C. vii, 3, 13; S. ii, p. 218, where it is used to express that attitude of forbearance in the interests

seeking the [general] good,[1] compassion; the absence of malice, of malignity; that absence of hate which is the root of good (karma).[2]

[1057] What is the absence of dullness?

Knowledge about ill, about the uprising of ill, about the cessation of ill, and about the way leading to the cessation of ill; knowledge about the former things, about the latter things, about both taken together; knowledge about the assignable causation of causally determined states—even that kind of insight which is understanding, search, research, searching the Truth, etc. [*continue as in* § 34].

These are the three causes of good (karma).

(B) In this connexion,

[1058] Which are the three causes of bad (karma)?

Greed, hate, dullness.

In this connexion,

[1059] *What is greed?*

That which is

lust (r ā g o),
passion (s a r ā g o),[3]
seducing (a n u n a y o),[4]
compliance (a n u r o d h o),[5]

---

of the weaker brethren recommended by St. Paul to Roman and Corinthian adherents.

[1] H i t e s i t ā. See C. ix, 5, 7.

[2] By all these words (i.e. from "love" to "compassion"), concludes Buddhaghosa, the advance (u p a c ā r a) and conception (a p p a n ā) of love is described. Possibly the procedure in the induction of Jhāna was in his mind in using these technical terms. Cf. Rhys Davids, *Yogāvacara's Manual*, p. xi.

[3] "Meaning strong r ā g o." Asl. 362.

[4] This is opposed to p a ṭ i g h o or repugnance in Mil. 44; cf. 122 and 322. The comment (Asl. 362) — v i s a y e s u s a t t ā n a ṃ a n u n a y a n a t o—indicates that it is lust simulating mettā rather than involving dosa. Cf. p. 66, n.

[5] This is opposed to v i r o d h o, p a ṭ i v i r o d h o. See § 1060. The Cy. (ibid.) paraphrases by k ā m e t i. Cf. S. i, 111; KV. 485.

delighting in (n a n d ī),[1]
taking lustful delight in (n a n d ī - r ā g o),[1]
heart's passion (c i t t a s s a s a r ā g o),[2]
wanting (i c c h ā),
languishing (m u c c h ā),
gulping at, devouring (a j j h o s ā n a ṃ),[3]
cupidity (g e d h o),
voracity (p a l i g e d h o),
cleaving to (s a ṅ g o),
a slough (p a n k o),[4]
longing (e j ā),[5]
illusion (m ā y ā),[6]
genitrix (j a n i k ā),[7]
progenitrix (s a ñ j a n a n ī),

---

1 Buddhism consistently rejects the Vedic view of this word as a divine attribute.

2 Explained as qualifying the "infatuation" already named by emphasizing the reference to a mental state or psychosis, and not to any personal entity. Ibid.

3 "i.e. grasping by swallowing, by putting a complete end to." Asl. 363, 370. The term is probably formed from √ s ā, to bind (or to gain), and usually, by its context, signifies attachment. Cf. M. i, 109, 498; Mil. 74. Judging by the Commentary, however, there seems to be a homonym derived from the root a ç, to eat, similar to the parallel evolution of jhāyati, from √ d h y ā and √ k ṣ ā. Cf. Rhys Davids, *Dialogues of the Buddha*, i, 33, n. 2. The passage in A. i, 66, 67, is the only one at present known to me where the word, occurring as it does in co-ordination with terms of attachment and also of greed, may be rendered equally well in either sense.

4 Paraphrased by o s ī d a n a ṃ . Asl. 363.

5 Paraphrased by ā k a ḍ ḍ h a n a ṃ , used in the Dhp. Cy. (p. 412) to illustrate the magnetic power of the love of treasure and of family. Ibid.

6 Paraphrased by v a ñ c a n a ṃ . Ibid.

7 Because lust causes beings to be reborn on the Wheel (of life). So for the following epithet. As it is written :—
Taṇhā janeti purisaṃ, cittaṃ assa vidhāvati.

seamstress (s i b b a n ī),[1]
she who ensnares (j ā l i n ī),[2]
the flowing stream (s a r i t ā),[3]
she who is diffused (v i s a t t i k ā),[4]
the thread (s u t t a ṃ),[5]
diffusion (v i ṣ a t ā),[6]
she who urges (ā y ū h a n ī),[7]
the consort (d u t i y ā),[8]
aiming at (p a n i ḍ h i),[9]
she who leads to rebirth (b h a v a n e t t ī),[10]

---

[1] The Cy. explains that l o b h o sews, or joins beings to sorrow by way of rebirth, just as a tailor joins one piece of cloth to another. Ibid.

[2] She = t a ṇ h ā , by the diffusion of which the manifold web of the senses becomes as a net. Ibid.

Y a s s a j ā l i n ī v i s a t t i k ā
t a ṇ h ā n ' a t t h i k u h i ñ c i n e t a v e.
S. i, 107 ; = Dhp., v. 180.

[3] From the swift current of l o b h o , or else from its glutinous tenacity, according to the Commentator, who quotes :—

S a r i t ā n i s i n e h i t ā n i c a
s o m a n a s s ā n i b h a v a n t i j a n t u n o.
Dhp. v. 341.

[4] Or " poisonous ". See above, n. 2, and *Expositor*, 468, n. 4. Either rendering is sanctioned. Cf. n. 6.

[5] By reason of its chaining together destruction and misfortune as jars are arranged on a cord. Asl. 364.

[6] " In the sense of spreading out over sensuous objects." Ibid.

[7] " i.e. she causes beings to toil after (ā y ū h ā p e t i) this or that state." Ibid. On ā y ū h a t i , see JPTS., 1885, pp. 58, 59 ; 1886, pp. 155, 156 ; Mil. 108, 214.

[8] L o b h o (or t a ṇ h ā) is likened to a dear *alter ego*, or wife, or travelling companion. The idea is found is Sutta Nipāta, v. 740, quoted by the Cy. :—

T a n h ā d u t i y o p u r i s o d ī g h a ṃ a d d h ā n a ṃ s a ṃ- s ā r a ṃ
I t t h a b h ā v ' a ñ ñ a t h ā b h ā v a ṃ s a ṃ s ā r a ṃ n ā t i v a t- t a t ī t i.

[9] Cf. above, 92 f. " the unaimed at " (a p p a ṇ i h i t a ṃ).

[10] Cy. : B h a v a n e t t ī = the cord of existence. For by it beings are led, as cows by a cord bound about their necks, wherever they are wanted.

the forest (v a n a ṃ),
the jungle (v a n a t h o),[1]
intimacy (s a n t h a v o),[2]
fondness (s i n e h o),
affection (a p e k k h ā),[3]
connexion (p a ṭ i b a n d h u),[4]
appetite for (ā s ā),
hoping for (ā s i ṃ s a n ā),
anticipation (ā s i ṃ s i t a t t a ṃ),
appetite for visual shapes (r ū p ā s ā, etc.), for sounds, for odours, for tastes, for the tangible, for getting, for wealth, for children, for life,
mumbling (j a p p ā),[5] mumbling on, and over,
muttering,
murmuring,
self-indulgence (l o l u p p a ṃ),[6]
self-indulging,
intemperateness,
agitation (p u ñ c i k a t ā),[7]

---

[1] The impenetrable, impassable nature of tropical forest growth often serves to illustrate the dangers of l o b h o or t a ṇ h ā . Cf. Dh. p. 283, quoted in the Cy. Ibid.

[2] "Intimacy is of two kinds: it is either carnal (i.e. of t a ṇ h ā) or friendly. Here the former is meant." Asl. 365.

[3] "Ālayakaraṇavasena apekkhatī ti apekkhā. Ibid. The quotation in the Cy. on this word is from the Mahāsudassana Sutta, 229, with which cf. S. iii, 144.

[4] "As being constantly near to living beings there is no relative (or connexion) like t a ṇ h ā ." Asl. 365.

[5] The four following terms are all variants of j a p p ā . "Whenever anything is given to a greedy person, he will mutter, 'This is mine, this is mine! This has been given me by so-and-so!'" Asl. 365. K. repeats j a p p ā after a b h i j a p p a n ā. Cf. C. iv, 14, 26: s a k a ṇ ṇ a j a p p a k a ṃ .

[6] See Jāt. i, 340; iv, 306. Buddhaghosa derives this from l u m p a t i . Cf. Whitney's "Roots", etc., where it appears as the Intensive of l u p , but belonging in meaning to l u b h .

[7] The excitement or fluster produced by t a ṇ h ā is here, according to the Cy., likened to that shown by "dogs wagging

longing for the agreeable (s ā d u k a m y a t ā),[1]
incestuous passion (a d h a m m a r ā g o),[2]
lawless greed (v i s a m a l o b h o),
wish (n i k a n t i),
hungering for (n i k ā m a n ā),
entreating (p a t t h a n ā),
envying (p i h a n ā),
imploring (s a m p a t t h a n ā),[3]
craving for sensual indulgence (k ā m a t a ṇ h ā), for existence (b h a v a t a n h ā), for non-existence (v i b h a v a t a ṇ h ā), for[4] [material] form,[5] for immateriality, for annihilation, for visible shapes,[6] for sounds, for smells, for tastes, for the tangible, for mental states (d h a m m a t a ṇ h ā),
a flood (o g h o),
a yoke (y o g o),
a tie (g a n t h o),
grasping (u p ā d ā n a ṃ),
obstruction (ā v a r a ṇ a ṃ),
hindrance (n ī v a r a ṇ a ṃ),
covering (c h a d a n a ṃ),[7]
bondage (b a n d h a n a ṃ),[8]

---

their tails" (read s u n a k h ā) when seeking to find something. Ibid.

1 The Cy. and K. read s ā d h u.

2 For a mother, a mother's sister, etc. Asl. 366.

3 i.e. p a t t h a n ā intensified. Ibid.

4 i.e. for a state of annihilation. Ibid.

5 i.e. for a state of mere (s u d d h e) bodily shape. Ibid.

6 Before "craving for sounds" K. inserts r ū p a t a ṇ h ā for the second time, the r ū p ā n i craved for here being presumably "sights", "perceptions of sight", as distinguished from that supersensuous plane of being craved for under the former r ū p a t a ṇ h ā , and ranking next to the formless plane. The Cy., on the other hand, only notices between "craving for annihilation" and "craving for sounds", the word d i ṭ ṭ h i r ā g o , passion for speculation.

7 So Asl. and K. Cf. Sutta Nip. i, 5, 7.

8 i.e. "on the wheel" (of s a ṃ s ā r a). Asl. 366.

depravity (u p a k k i l e s o),
latent bias (a n u s a y o),[1]
obsession (p a r i y u ṭ ṭ h ā n a ṃ),[2]
a creeper (l a t ā),[3]
avarice (v e v i c c h a ṃ),[4]
root of ill,
source of ill (d u k k h a n i d ā n a ṃ),
production of ill (d u k k h a p p a b h a v o),
Māra's trap (m ā r a p ā s o),
Māra's fish-hook (m ā r a b a l i s a ṃ),
Māra's domain (m ā r a v i s a y o),
craving, the flux of craving for (s a n d a t a ṇ h ā),[5]
the fishing-net of (j ā l a ṃ t a ṇ h ā), the leash of (g a d d u l a t a ṇ h ā),[6]
the ocean (s a m u d d o),[7]
covetousness (a b h i j j h ā),[8]
greed as the root of evil—

this is what is called greed.

[1060] *What is hate?*

When annoyance springs up at the thought: he has done me harm, is doing, will do me harm; he has done harm, is doing harm, will do harm to someone dear and precious

---

[1] Anu+seti, to lie dormant.

[2] i.e. the heart becomes possessed by lust, as a road by highwaymen. Ibid. Cf. KV. xiv, 6.

[3] . . . l a t ā u b b h i j j ā t i ṭ ṭ h a t i. Dhp. 340. Quoted in the Cy. Greed or lust strangles its victim, as a creeper strangles a tree.

[4] See Sutta Nip. 1033. The Commentary, however, paraphrases the term as " multifarious wants ", V i e l h a b e r e i ; " v i v i d h ā n i v a t t h ū n i i c c h a t i." Ibid. Asl., p. 375, has a different explanation. Cf. SN. ii, s.v. v e v i c c h ā .

[5] N a n d a n a ṭ ṭ h e n a is in B. ed. s a n d a n a - . Asl. 367.

[6] Cf. Jāt. ii, 246; iii, 204. T a ṇ h ā drags its victims about as dogs are drawn by a leash (Asl. 367).

[7] The thirst of greed is hard to satiate. Ibid. Cf. above, p. 160, n.2.

[8] See § 391.

to me; he has conferred a benefit, is conferring, will confer a benefit on someone I dislike and object to; or when annoyance springs up groundlessly[1]:—all such vexation of spirit,[2] resentment, repugnance, hostility;[3] ill-temper, irritation, indignation;[4] hate, antipathy, abhorrence;[5] mental disorder,[6] detestation;[7] anger, fuming, wrath; hate, hating, hatred; disorder, getting upset, derangement; opposition, hostility;[8] churlishness, abruptness, disgust of heart—this is what is called hate.

[1061] *What is dullness?*

Lack of knowledge about Ill, lack of knowledge about the uprising of Ill, lack of knowledge about the cessation of Ill, lack of knowledge about the way leading to the cessation of Ill; lack of knowledge about the former things, about the latter things, and about both taken together; lack of knowledge about the assignable causation of causally determined states—even all that kind of lack of knowledge which is lack of insight, of understanding, of comprehension, of

---

[1] "Aṭṭhāne vā pana āghāto ti akāraṇe kopo. e.g. when one is vexed because it rains too much, or because it doesn't rain, or because the sun is too hot, or not hot enough, or because there is too much or too little wind, or because one cannot sweep away the Bo-tree-leaves, or because the wind prevents one from putting on one's robe, or because one has fallen over a tree-stump." Asl. 367.

[2] Cittassa āghāto. Āghāto is rendered above by annoyance. The two next terms are paṭighāto and paṭighaṃ. The latter is the word used to express action and reaction in sense-activity. § 597 *et seq.*

[3] Paṭivirodho. Cf. Mil. 203, 402.

[4] Kopo, pakopo, sampakopo.

[5] Padoso, sampadoso.

[6] Cittassa vyāpatti; paraphrased as a *bouleversement*, or cataclysm of mind. Vyāpatti is used for the wrecking of a ship in Jāt. iv, 107. Cf. above, § 418.

[7] Manopadoso. Cf. Jāt. iv, 29; M. i, 377, where it means apparently curse or execration—the original sense of "detesting".

[8] See § 418.

enlightenment, of penetration, of grasping, of sounding, of judging, of reflection, of perspicacity; unwisdom, childishness, unintelligence, the dullness that is stupidity, obtuseness, ignorance, a flood of ignorance, the yoke of ignorance, the latent bias of ignorance, the being obsessed by ignorance, the barrier of ignorance, the dullness that is the root of evil—this is called dullness.[1]

These are the three causes of bad [karma].

(C) In this connexion,

[1062] Which are the three causes of the indeterminate?

The absence of greed, hate and dullness [coming to pass] as the result of good states or as inoperative indeterminates.[2]

[1063] Which are the nine root-conditions operative in the sensuous universe (k ā m a v a c a r a h e t ū)?

The three roots of good [karma], the three roots of bad [karma], the three roots of indeterminate [states]—these are the nine.

[1064] Which are the six roots operative in the universe of Form?

The three roots of good [karma], the three roots of indeterminate [states]—these are the six.

[1065] Which are the six roots operative in the universe of the Formless?

The three roots of good [karma], the three roots of indeterminate [states]—these are the six.

[1066] Which are the six roots operative in the Unincluded?

The three roots of good [karma], the three roots of indeterminate [states]—these are the six.

In this connexion,

---

[1] According to Asl. 368, this is "thoroughly set out in the Commentary on the Vibhanga" (Sammoha-Vinodanī).

[2] K i r i y ā v y ā k a t e s u d h a m m e s u. See above, § 566 *et seq.* The Cy. here is silent.

[1067] Which are the three roots of good [karma]?

The absence of greed, hate and dullness.

In this connexion,

[1068–70] What is the absence of greed . . . of hate . . . of dullness?

Answers as in §§ 1055–7, *but omitting, in* § 1056, *from* "hatred" *to* "the absence of malice" *exclusively.*[1]

These are the three root conditions of good [karma].

(D) In this connexion,

[1071] Which are the three roots of indeterminate [states]?

The absence of greed, hate and dullness coming to pass as the effect of good states—these are the three.

These are the six root-conditions operative in the Unincluded.

These are the states which are root-conditions.

[1072] Which are the states that are not root-conditions?

Every state, good, bad and indeterminate, whether related to the worlds of Sense, of Form, of the Formless, or to the life that is Unincluded, except the states enumerated above; [in other words] the four skandhas; all [material] form also and unconditioned element.

[1073] Which are the states that have root-conditions as concomitants?[2]

---

[1] Adoso has been inadvertently omitted in the text.

[2] Sahetukā. The Cy. (p. 47) on this term has: Sampayogato pavattena saha hetunā ti sahetukā, and on the opposite (ahetukā): tath'eva pavatto n'atthi etesaṃ hetu ti. This may be rendered: "Sahetukā means proceeding together with a root, with a cause." And "ahetukā means, there is for them no such proceeding with a root". The *sustaining* of a cause in concomitance with a given state is so much harped upon by the Cy. that one is tempted to surmise that the mediæval controversy, known by the formula, *Cessante causâ cessat et effectus*, was not unfamiliar to Buddhist scholastics. Have we here the categorizing of certain states, for the maintenance of which, as effects, the continuance of the cause is required? In that case

Those states, [to wit] the four skandhas, which have as concomitant roots the states enumerated above.[1]

[1074] Which are the states that have not concomitant roots ?

Those states, [to wit] the four skandhas, all [material] form also, and unconditioned element, which have not as concomitant roots the states enumerated above.

[1075] Which are the states that are associated with a root-condition ? [2]

The states, [to wit] the four skandhas, which are associated with those states enumerated above.

[1076] Which are the states that are not associated with a root-condition ?

The states, [to wit] the four skandhas, all [material] form

---

the Buddhist would have agreed (see § 1075, n.) with a modern logician (J. S. Mill) that, in some cases only, " The continuance of the condition which produced an effect is necessary to the continuance of the effect." The coincidence, however, is extremely doubtful. The Pali even leaves it vague as to whether the concomitant cause is the cause of the state in question ; sometimes, indeed, this is evidently not the case. E.g. in § 1077, " dullness " is a hetu-dhammo, but not, therefore, the cause of the concomitant states, greed and hate. The compilers were, as usual, more interested in the psychology than in the logic of the matter, and were inquiring into the factors in cases of mental association.

[1] Tehi dhammehi, i.e. with one or other of the six roots of good or bad effects. Asl. 368.

[2] Hetu-sampayuttā. On the import of the term sampayutto, see p. 1, n. 4. This pair of opposites is further declared to be not different in meaning from the preceding pair (atthato nānattaṃ natthi), and the formulæ only differentiated for the purpose of adaptation to the various dispositions (ajjhāsayavasena) of the hearers. Asl. 48. This coincidence of meaning seems, however, to be applicable only in the sphere of hetu. In the next gocchaka, the attribute of āsavavippayuttā is allowed to be compatible with the attribute sāsavā, § 1111, and so for subsequent gocchakas.

also, and unconditioned element, which are not associated with the states enumerated above.

[1077] Which are the states that both are root-conditions and have such as their concomitants?

Greed with dullness is both. Dullness with greed is both. Hate with dullness is both. Dullness with hate is both.[1]

The absence of greed, the absence of hate, the absence of dullness—these also, taken one with the other, both are root-conditions and have such as their concomitants.

[1078] Which are the states that have root-conditions as their concomitants, but are not root-conditions?

The states, [to wit] the four skandhas, which have as their concomitant roots those states [enumerated above as roots], the latter states themselves excepted.

[1079] Which are the states that are both root-conditions and associated with such?

[1080] Which are the states that are associated with a root-condition, but are not such?

Answers identical with those in the foregoing pair.[2]

[1081] Which are the states that are not root-conditions, but have such as their concomitant?[3]

The states, [to wit] the four skandhas, which are not the root-conditions of those states enumerated above, but which have any of them as their concomitants.

[1082] Which are the states that are not root-conditions and have not such as their concomitants?

The states, [to wit] the four skandhas, all [material] form also, and unconditioned element, which neither are the root-conditions of those states enumerated above, nor have any of them as their concomitants.

---

[1] Dullness, when accompanied by perplexity and distraction (u d d h a c c a ṃ), is said to be a root-condition, but to have none as its concomitant. Asl. 368.

[2] Cf. § 1075, n. 2.

[3] Supplementary questions, says the Cy., dealing with the n a - h e t u states. Asl. 47.

[CHAPTER III.

The Short Intermediate Set of Pairs (c ū ḷ a n t a r a - d u k a ṃ).]

[1083] Which are the states that are causally related? [1]

The five skandhas, to wit, the skandhas of [material] form, feeling, perception, synergies and consciousness.

[1084] Which are the states that are not causally related?

"And unconditioned element." [2]

[1085] Which are the states that are conditioned? [3]

Those states which are causally related.

[1086] Which are the states that are unconditioned?

That state which is not causally related.

[1087] Which are the states that have visibility?

The sphere of [visible] shapes.

[1088] Which are the states that have no visibility?

The spheres of the senses and sense-objects; the four skandhas; that [material] form also which, being neither visible nor reacting, is included under [mental] states; [4] and unconditioned element.

[1089] Which are the states that react? [5]

The spheres of the senses and sense-objects.

[1090] Which are the states that are non-reacting?

The four skandhas; that [material] form also which, being

---

[1] S a p p a c c a y ā = a t t a n o n i p p h ā d a k e n a, s a h a p a c c a y e n a. Asl. 47. Cf. my foreword, Tikapaṭṭhāna.

[2] One would have expected the reading to be a s a n k h a t ā v a d h ā t u, instead of . . . c a d h ā t u, given both in the text and in K. The Cy. has a s a n k h a t a - d h ā t u ṃ s a n d h ā y a.

[3] S a n d h a t ā is defined as "made, come together by conditions". Asl. 47.

[4] See § 1052.

[5] S a p p a ṭ i g h ā. Cf. § 597 *et seq.*

neither visible nor reacting, is included under [mental] states; also unconditioned element.

[1091] Which are the states that have [material] form?[1]

The four great principles as well as the [material] form that is derived from the four great phenomena.[2]

[1092] Which are the states that have no material form?

The four skandhas, and unconditioned element.

[1093] Which are the states that are mundane?[3]

Co-Intoxicant[4] states, good, bad and indeterminate, relating to the worlds of Sense, of Form, or of the Formless, [to wit] the five skandhas.

[1094] Which are the states that are supra-mundane?

The Paths that are the Unincluded, and the Fruits of the Paths, and unconditioned element.

[1095] Which are the states that are cognizable in one way and not cognizable in another way?

States that are cognizable by sight are not cognizable by hearing; conversely, states that are cognizable by hearing are not cognizable by sight. States that are cognizable by sight are not cognizable by smell . . . by taste . . . by body-sensibility, and conversely.

States that are cognizable by hearing are not cognizable by smell . . . by taste . . . by body-sensibility . . . by sight, and conversely.

---

[1] R ū p i n o, i.e. they have a form which as such is devoid of discriminative consciousness (a v i n i b h o g a v a s e n a). Asl., p. 47, cf. p. 56; also Mil. 63; M. i, 293.

[2] Cf. § 597.

[3] L o k i y ā = bound down to, forming a part of, the circle (of existence), which for its dissolving and crumbling away (l u j j a n a p a l u j j a n a) is called l o k o. To have got beyond the world, to be a non-conforming feature in it—in it, but not of it—is to be l o k u t t a r o. Asl. 47, 48 (trs. transcendent).

[4] See § 1103.

So for states that are cognizable by smell, by taste, and by body-sensibility.[1]

[1] The Cy. meets the question, Why is there no couplet telling which states are cognizable or not cognizable by representative cognition or ideation (m a n o v i ñ ñ ā ṇ a ṃ)? by the answer: Such a distinction is quite valid, "is not not-there," but it is not stated explicitly, is left without specification (v a v a ṭ - ṭ h ā n a ṃ). "There is none of this when, for instance, we judge such and such things are not cognizable by visual intellection." See Asl. 369; *Expositor*, 474. Cf. Mil. 87, where this intellectual process is more clearly set forth.

[CHAPTER IV.

The Āsava Group (ā s a v a - g o c c h a k a ṃ).]

[1096] Which are the states that are Āsavas? [1]

The four Āsavas, [to wit] the Āsava of sensuality, the

---

[1] "Intoxicant" in the 1st edition. This was a *pis-aller* for ā s a v o, no adequate English equivalent being available (see Rhys Davids, *Dialogues*, i, p. 92, n. 3). The choice of it here has been determined by Buddhaghosa's comment. This is as follows: "Ā s a v ā means they flow on to. They are said to flow (*lege* s a v a n t i), to circulate about (p a v a t t a n t i) the senses and the mind. Or, they flow, in respect of mental states, right up to the [stage of] adoption (g o t r a b h u), as to space, right up to the highest planes of becoming—we mean, their range embraces both states and space, this keeping within being denoted by the prefix *ā*. The Āsavas, moreover, are like liquors (ā s a v ā), such as spirits, etc., in the sense of that which ferments in time. For, in the world, spirits, etc., which have fermented for a long period are called ā s a v a s. And if those spirits for this long storage are called ā s a v a s, these states deserve the name as well. For it is said: 'The ultimate point of ignorance, brethren, before which ignorance has not existed, is not manifest' [alluding to the āsava of ignorance]." Asl. 48; A. v, 113.

From this passage we gather that, to Buddhaghosa, the word ā s a v o, whatever other implications it may have had, typified mainly two notions, and these were *pervasion* and *fermentation of a very potent effect*. The former metaphor—that of a flowing in, upon, and over—occurs with a cognate verb in the standard description of the guarded avenues of sensation—a n v ā s (s) a v e y y u ṃ (e.g. D. i, 70). The latter notion appears in Subhūti's opening remark on the term ("Abhidhānappadī-pika-sūcī," s.v. *Asavo*): *māna-purisamadādayo yenāti*—that by which come "vain conceits", human madness [or infatuation], etc. No doubt the term also implied something that tainted, corrupted, defiled as it flowed. But there is no vague, weighty word in our religious idiom for Drug-flux; also Āsava is easily said. Let us Europeanize it!

Later (p. 369) the Cy. considers the Āsavas under numerical categories, according to the very usual Buddhist method. Thus, they are One, or undifferentiated, in virtue of their being, like liquor, long stored up. In the Vinaya they are treated of

Āsava of rebirth, the Āsava of speculative opinion, the Āsava of ignorance.

In this connexion

[1097] *What is the Āsava of sensuality?*

That sensual desire,[1] sensual passion, sensual delight, sensual craving, sensual fondness, sensual thirst, sensual fever, sensual languishing, sensual rapacity, which is excited by the pleasures of the senses[2]—this is called the Āsava of sensuality.

[1098] *What is the Āsava of rebirth?*

The desire, the passion for coming into being, delight in coming into being, craving, fondness for coming into being,

---

as Twofold: the Āsavas that have to be suppressed in this life and those that have to be eschewed in future lives (see V. iii, 21; V., pp. 143, 223). In S. iv, 256; v, 56, 189, they are distinguished under Three heads, diṭṭhāsava being omitted; see also v. M. i, 55; A. i, 167; iii, 414; and cf. D. i, 84. In the Mahāparinibbāna-sutta of the Dīgha Nikāya, however, all Four Āsavas are mentioned (pp. 84, 91). Hence follows one of three possible conclusions. Either Buddhaghosa is for once in error, or the edition of the Sutta last named needs correcting, or it is a later work, contemporary, it may be, with the Abhidhamma. In the passage on "Penetration" (A. iii, 410–17) they are treated of as leading to Five different forms of rebirth. In the Āhuneyya-sutta (A. iii, 387) they are treated of under Six methods for overcoming them. In the Sabbāsava-discourse (M. i, pp. 7–11) Seven methods are given.

[1] "Kāmachando ti kāmasankhāto chando na kattukamyatāchando na dhammachando." Asl. 370. This carefully drawn distinction between sensual desire and an ethically neutral state of bare conation, as well as the desire after the ideal, bears me out in the argument I ventured to put forward in JRAS., January, 1898, and which is rediscussed in my Introduction.

[2] Pañcakāmaguṇikorāgo kāmāsavo nāma (Asl. 369). The Cy. points out that to hanker after the mansions of the supreme gods or the wishing-trees of heaven or the craving for æsthetic luxuries (ābharaṇam) is not to be confounded with the Intoxicant of sensuality, since such desires are a step higher than the latter vice. But they are subsumed under the Tie of covetousness (§ 1136) and the Lust-cause (§ 1059). Asl. 371, 377.

the fever, the yearning, the hungering to come into being, which is felt concerning rebirths—this is called the Āsava of rebirth.[1]

[1099] *What is the Āsava of speculative opinion?* [2]

To hold that the world is eternal, or that it is not eternal,[3] infinite or finite;[4] that the living soul is the body, or that the living soul is a different thing from the body;[5] or that he who has won truth[6] exists after death, or does not exist after death, or both exists and does not exist after death, or neither exists nor does not exist after death—this kind of opinion, this walking in opinion, this jungle of opinion, wilderness of opinion, disorder of opinion, scuffling of opinion, the fetter of opinion, the grip and tenacity of it, the inclination towards it, the being infected by it, this by-path, wrong road, wrongness, this sectarianism, this shiftiness of grasp[7]—

---

[1] Literally, of becoming. "That which is called bhavāsavo is the hoping for re-becoming, the passion connate with the Eternalist speculation (v. following answer and § 1003, n. 3), the wish in Jhāna (jhānanikanti—*sic lege*), the passionate desire for re-births in the planes of Form and of Formlessness." Asl. 369.

[2] Diṭṭhāsavo, "i.e. the sixty-two theories." Ibid. See D. i, Brahmajāla Sutta.

[3] i.e. to hold that this five-skandha'd affair is permanent, fixed, a thing for all time—which is the Eternalist theory; or that it is annihilated, perishes—which is the Theory of Annihilation. Asl. 370, 371. Cf. §§ 1003, n. 3; 1315–16.

[4] Either of these theories is by the Cy. declared to be compatible with either of those in the preceding clause. And they are also said to be determined by the nature of the Jhāna practised by the adherent to one or the other. Asl. 371. See §§ 1317–18.

[5] i.e. that the life (or living soul) is, or is not, annihilated on the dissolution of the body. Ibid.

[6] Tathāgato—in the Cy., satto tathāgato nāma. Clearly, therefore, not a reference to the Buddha only. See R. Chalmers, "Tathāgata," JRAS., January, 1898, pp. 113–15. The four speculations about such a person's future existence are named respectively Eternalist, Annihilationist, Semi-eternalist, Eel-wriggling (amarāvikkhepikā). Ibid., see D. i, 3, §§ 58, 41, 59, 35.

[7] See under § 381.

this is called the Āsava of speculative opinion. Moreover, the Āsava of speculation includes all false theories.

[1100] *What is the Āsava of ignorance?* [1]

Answer as in § 1061 *for* " dullness ".

These are the states that are Āsavas.

[1102] [2] Which are the states that are not Āsavas?

Every state, good, bad and indeterminate,[3] which is not included in the foregoing, whether relating to the worlds of Sense, Form or the Formless, or to the life that is Unincluded, [to wit] the four skandhas; all [material] form also, and unconditioned element.

[1103] Which are the states that can have Āsavas? [4]

Good, bad and indeterminate states, whether relating to the worlds of Sense, Form, or the Formless; [in other words] the five skandhas.

[1104] Which are the states that can not have Āsavas?

The Paths that are the Unincluded, and the Fruits of the Paths, and unconditioned element.

[1105] Which are the states that are " associated with Āsavas "?

The states which are associated with those states,[5] [to wit] the four skandhas.

---

[1] In the text, after dukkhudaye aññāṇaṃ, supply dukkhanirodhe aññāṇaṃ.

[2] " § 1101 " is apparently an erroneous interpolation. See § 1104, where it appears again and in its right place.

[3] In the text read kusalākusalavyākatā.

[4] Sāsavā, i.e. states " proceeding along with Āsavas ", and which attānam ārammaṇaṃ katvā—" have made one's self their object." Asl. 48.

[5] Answers of this form, which frequently occur in these " Groups ", are not the mere repetitions of the question that they at first sight appear, but are, in logical idiom, analytic, or explicative propositions. The current term āsava-sampayuttā means or includes these four modes: kāmāsava-sampayuttā, bhavāsava-sampayuttā, and so on.

[1106] Which are the states that are " disconnected with Āsavas " ?

The states which are disconnected with those states, [to wit] the four skandhas ; all [material] form also, and unconditioned element.

[1107] Which are the states that are both Āsavas and can have Āsavas ?

The Āsavas themselves.[1]

[1108] Which are the states that can have Āsavas, but are not Āsavas ?

The states which have the foregoing states (§ 1096) as their concomitants ; that is to say, with the exception of the Āsavas, all states whatever, good, bad and indeterminate, which can have Āsavas, whether they relate to the worlds of Sense, of Form or of the Formless ; [in other words] the five skandhas.

[1109] Which are the states that are both Āsavas and associated with Āsavas ?

The Āsavas of sensuality together with that of ignorance, and conversely. The Āsava of rebirth together with that of ignorance, and conversely. The Āsava of speculative opinion together with that of ignorance, and conversely.

[1110] Which are the states that are associated with Āsavas but are not Āsavas ?

The states which are associated with the foregoing states (§ 1096)—the latter themselves excepted—[to wit] the four skandhas.

[1111] Which are the states that are disconnected with Āsavas but can have Āsavas ?

The states which are disconnected with those abovenamed states (§ 1096), but which, good, bad, or indeterminate, have them as concomitants, whether they belong to the worlds of Sense, of Form, or of the Formless, [to wit] the five skandhas.

---

[1] When mutually associated. Cf. the following pair of answers.

[1112] Which are the states that are disconnected with Āsavas and can not have Āsavas ?

The Paths that are the Unincluded and the Fruits of the Paths and uncompounded element.[1]

[1] In conclusion, the Cy. declares (p. 372) that the Āsava of speculative opinion is put away during one's progress through the first (s o t ā p a t t i) path, the Āsava of sensuality in the third (a n ā g ā m i) path, and the Āsava of birth and ignorance in the fourth (a r a h a t t a) path.

[CHAPTER V.

The Group of the Fetters (s a ṃ y o j a n a - g o c c h a k a ṃ).]

[1113] Which are the states that are Fetters?

The ten Fetters, to wit, the Fetter of

sensuality,
repulsion,
conceit,
speculative opinion,
perplexity,
perversion as to rule and ritual,
the passion for rebirth,
envy,
meanness,
ignorance.[1]

In this connexion,

[1114] *What is the Fetter of sensual passion?*

That sensual desire, sensual passion, sensual delight, sensual craving, sensual fondness, sensual fever, sensual languor, sensual rapacity, which is excited by the pleasures of the senses—this is called the Fetter of sensuality.[2]

---

[1] S a ṃ y o j a n ā n i "mean the things that bind, that fetter to the wheel of re-birth the individual for whom they exist". Asl. 48. This list differs in some items from the well-known d a s a s a ṃ y o j a n ā n i occurring so often in the Suttas, and enumerated in Childers. See Rhys Davids, *American Lectures*, 141 *et seq.* That that older category was known to Buddhaghosa may be gathered from his naming the first three in order as "states which are to be put away by insight", § 1002 *et seq.* He proffers, however, no comment on the two lists as such. In M. i, 360–3, *eight* states of mind are enumerated and severally designated as a Fetter and a Hindrance, but they are quite different from either category habitually understood by these two titles. Cf. also M. i, 432; A. ii, 238; Div.p. 533, 553.

[2] Cf. with § 1097. The single discrepancy is the omission in § 1114 of "sensual thirst" (k ā m a p i p ā s o), both in the PTS. text and in K.

[1115] *What is the Fetter of repulsion?* [1]

Answer as for " hate ", § 1060.

[1116] *What is the Fetter of conceit?* [2]

Conceit at the thought " I am the better man " ; conceit at the thought " I am as good [as they] " ; conceit at the thought " I am lowly "—all such sort of conceit, overweening conceitedness, loftiness, haughtiness, flaunting a flag, assumption, desire of the heart for self-advertisement—this is called conceit.

[1117] *What is the Fetter of speculative opinion?*

Answer as for the " Intoxicant of speculative opinion ",

---

[1] Paṭigha-saṃyojanaṃ, cf. §§ 413–21, trans. " reaction in sense ".

[2] Māno-saṃyojanaṃ—or pride. Conceit is etymologically more exact, though not so in any other respect. " Lowly " is hīno. Cf. §§ 269, *et seq.* 1025. " Loftiness and haughtiness " are uṇṇati, uṇṇamo. " [Flaunting] a flag " is simply dhajo, the metaphor implying the pretensions conveyed by raising a flag over one's self or property, but answering better to our metaphor of a " flourish of trumpets ". " Assumption " is sampaggāho. The Cy. (p. 372) hereon has ukkhipanaṭṭhena cittaṃ sampaggaṇhātī ti—to grasp in the sense of tossing (puffing up) the mind. Cf. sīsaṃ ukkhipitvā, quoted by Childers, and the Hebrew figures for arrogance, etc.—lifting up head, horn, heel, or one's self on high ; also paggāho, § 56. " Desire of the heart for self-advertisement " is ketukamyatā cittassa. I can only make sense of the Cy. hereon by altering the punctuation followed in the text. Thus : Ketu vuccati bahūsu dhajesu accuggatadhajo. Māno pi punappuna uppajjamāno aparāpare upādāya accuggataṭṭhena ketum viyāti ketu. Ketuṃ icchatī ti ketukamyatassa bhāvo ketukamyatā. Sā pana cittassa, na attano, tena vuttaṃ: ketukamyatā cittassā ti. " A flag hoisted above many flags is called a ketu (sign, or standard) ; cf. Rāmāyana i, 19, 16, quoted by Böthl. and Roth. By ketu is meant the conceit which, arising again and again, is like a signal in the sense of something set up on high. The state of ketu-desire, i.e. the wish for self-advertisement, is ketukamyatā. But this means [a state of] mind, not of a self-entity, therefore the phrase is desire of the mind [or heart] for self-advertisement."

§ 1099, *with this supplement*: And, with the exception of the "Fetter of perversion as to rule and ritual", all wrong views are included in the Fetter of speculative opinion.

[1118] *What is the Fetter of perplexity?*

Answer as for "perplexity", § 1004.

[1119] *What is the Fetter of perversion as to rule and ritual?*

Answer as for "perversion", etc., § 1005.

[1120] *What is the Fetter of the passion for rebirth?*

Answer as for the "Intoxicant of rebirth", § 1098.

[1121] *What is the Fetter of envy* (i s s ā s a ṃ y o j a n a ṃ)?

Envy, envying, enviousness—jealousy, the expression and mood of jealousy at the gifts, the hospitality, the respect, affection, reverence and worship accruing to others [1]—this is called the Fetter of envy.

[1122] *What is the Fetter of meanness* (m a c c h a r i-s a ṃ y o j a n a ṃ)?

The Five Meannesses, [to wit] meanness as regards dwelling, families, gifts, reputation, doctrine [2]—all this sort of mean-

---

[1] In other words, discontent and murmuring at the success of one's neighbour, and complacency when bad luck overtakes him (*S c h a d e n f r e u d e*). Asl. 373. Cf. PP. p. 19.

[2] Buddhaghosa is at some pains to distinguish genuine instances of want of magnanimity from such as are not. For example, it is m a c c h a r i y a ṃ when a bhikshu, enjoying the use of a lodging, grudges another a share of it, or when he grudges another intercourse with his own patrons and relatives, or gifts from the laity for his piety, or that he should enjoy a reputation for physical or moral attractiveness, or that he should win proficiency in the letter, or the spirit of doctrine. On the other hand, it is not m a c c h a r i y a ṃ to deprecate the arrival at one's lodging of quarrelsome persons and the like, or the introduction to one's own social circle of peace-breakers, or the gifts made to selfish, miserly brethren instead of to the virtuous. Nor is it ungenerous in every case to withhold instruction from an inquirer. Reserve may be employed out of regard either for the doctrine or for the inquirer. The latter may distort the imparted doctrine, or the doctrine may upset him. Nevertheless, it *is* an act of doctrinal illiberality to withhold the doctrine, if the inquirer is not a

ness, grudging, mean spirit, avarice and ignobleness,[1] niggardliness and want of generosity of heart[2]—this is called the Fetter of meanness.

[1123] *What is the Fetter of ignorance?*

Answer as for the Intoxicant of ignorance, § 1100.

These are the states that are Fetters.

[1124] Which are the states that are not Fetters?

Every state, good, bad and indeterminate, which is not included in the foregoing [ten] states, whether it relates to the worlds of Sense, or of Form, or of the Formless, or to the life that is Unincluded; [in other words] the four skandhas; all form also, and unconditioned element.

"weak brother", but one likely to prove hostile to "our Cause" (amhākaṃ samayaṃ bhindituṃ samattho).

There then follows a mythological paragraph on the unpleasant rebirths awaiting those who err with respect to any one of these five forms of meanness. Asl. 374, 375.

[1] Vevicchaṃ kadariyaṃ. These terms are characterized (Asl. 375, 376) as respectively the soft (mudu) and hard (thaddha) varieties of meanness (cf. Childers, s.v. thaddho). We might name them the negatively and the positively anti-social. For the former is the spirit that says, spreading itself over all its own gettings, "Mine be it, not another's!" (§ 1059). The latter (the anariyo) would even prevent another from giving to others.

[2] Kaṭukañcukatā aggahitattaṃ cittassa. There is doubt about the reading of the former term. K. has katakañcukatā, Buddhaghosa kaṭukañcukatā. The term is discussed by Morris, JPTS., 1887, p. 161. Buddhaghosa's remark is as follows (Asl. 376): "Kaṭukañcuko means that, on seeing a beggar, owing to one's styptic (kaṭuko) disposition, one's heart narrows or is bent (añcati—? $\sqrt{anh}$, or añc) and shrinks up." He then, in offering an alternative explanation, relapses into characteristic etymology, deriving kaṭukañcukatā from katacchugāho—spoon-helps. When your rice-pot is full to the brim, one can only take niggling helps with a bent-in spoon. And just as the heart of the niggard shrinks, so too is his body "bent back on itself, thrown back on itself, does not expand" (he quotes from Mil., p. 297). Similarly, aggahitattaṃ cittassa is a holding the heart fast, or back, preventing its expansion by way of gifts and service to others.

Which are the states that are

[1125] (*a*) *favourable to the Fetters?* [1]

Co-Intoxicant states, good, bad and indeterminate, relating to the worlds of Sense, Form, or the Formless; [in other words] the five skandhas.

[1126] (*b*) *unfavourable to the Fetters?*

The Paths that are the Unincluded and the Fruits of the Paths, and unconditioned element.

Which are the states that are

[1127] (*a*) *associated with the Fetters?*

[1128] (*b*) *disconnected with the Fetters?*

Answers identical with those given to corresponding questions respecting the "Āsavas". §§ 1105, 1106.

Which are the states that are

[1129] (*a*) *both Fetters and favourable to the Fetters?*

The Fetters themselves are both

[1130] (*b*) *favourable to the Fetters but not themselves Fetters.*

The states which are favourable to those [ten] states afore-named; that is to say, with the exception of the Fetters themselves, all co-Āsava states whatever, good, bad and indeterminate, whether relating to the worlds of Sense, Form or the Formless; [in other words] the five skandhas.

Which are the states that are

[1131] (*a*) *both Fetters and associated with Fetters?*

The Fetter of sensuality in conjunction with the Fetter of ignorance, *and conversely*, is both. *So is any one of the remaining eight Fetters* when in conjunction with the Fetter of ignorance, *and conversely.*

---

[1] Saṃyojaniyā. So the text and K. The Cy. reads saṃyojanīyā. But cf. ganthaniyā, oghaniyā, yoganiya, Asl. 49. The Cy. explains the term, which is literally fetter-ish, as that which benefits the Fetters by developing them, once their inception has begun. Asl. 48.

[1132] (*b*) *associated with the Fetters but not a Fetter?*

The states which are associated with those ten states afore-named, with the exception of the Fetters themselves; [in other words] the four skandhas.

Which are the states that are

[1133] (*a*) *disconnected with the Fetters yet favourable to them?*

The states which are disconnected with those aforementioned [ten] states, that is to say, good, bad and indeterminate states which are co-Āsava, whether they relate to the worlds of Sense, or of Form, or of the Formless; [in other words] the five skandhas.

[1134] (*b*) *disconnected with the Fetters and not favourable to them?*

The Paths that are the Unincluded and the Fruits of the Paths; all form also, and unconditioned element.[1]

---

[1] In quitting the subject of Fetters, the Cy. declares (pp. 376, 377) that the Fetters of sensuality and repulsion are put away during one's progress through the third (anāgāmi) path, the Fetter of conceit in the fourth (arahatta) path, the Fetters of speculative opinion, perplexity, and perversion as to rule and ritual, in the first (sotāpatti) path, the Fetter of the passion for rebirth in the fourth path, the Fetters of envy and meanness in the first path, the Fetter of ignorance in the fourth path. Hence the second path seems, according to Buddhaghosa, to constitute an interim in the breaking of Fetters.

The following tables show how far the Dh. S. and its Cy. agree with the authorities quoted in Childers, s.v. saṃyojanaṃ (cf. D. i, 156):—

Dh. S. and Asl.		*Childers.*
diṭṭhi vicikicchā sīlabbata-parāmāso	Removed by the First Path.	sakkāyadiṭṭhi vicikicchā sīlabbata-parāmāso
issā macchariyaṃ	Removed by the Second and Third Paths.	kāmarāgo paṭigho
kāmarāgo paṭigho	Removed by the Third Path.	

Dh. S. and Asl.		*Childers.*
		r ū p a r ā g o
m ā n o	Removed by	a r ū p a r ā g o
b h a v a r ā g o	the Fourth	m ā n o
a v i j j ā	Path.	u d d h a c c a ṃ
		a v i j j ā

On the work of the Fourth Path compare Dh. S., § 364, which is in agreement with the *right*-hand table. In the *first* edition (p. 452) of Dr. Oldenberg's *Buddha* attention was called to discrepancies in this connexion.

[CHAPTER VI.

The Group of the Ties (g a n t h a - g o c c h a k a ṃ).][1]

[1135] Which are the states that are Ties?

The four Ties, to wit, the bodily Tie of covetousness, the bodily Tie of ill-will, the bodily Tie of perversion as to rule and ritual, the bodily Tie of the disposition to dogmatize.

In this connexion,

[1136] *what is the bodily Tie of covetousness* (a b h i j j h ā k ā y a g a n t h o)?

Answer as for " lust ", § 1059.[2]

[1137] *what is the bodily Tie of ill-will* (v y ā p ā d o k ā y a g a n t h o)?

Answer as for " hate ", § 1060.

[1138] *what is the bodily Tie of perversion as to rule and ritual?*

Answer as in § 1005, *and*, § 1119, *for the Fetter so-called.*

[1139] *what is the bodily Tie of the disposition to dogmatize?* [3]

" 'The world is eternal!'—this is true, all else is false! 'The world is not eternal'—this is true, all else is false! 'The world is finite . . . is infinite'—this is true, all else is false! 'The living soul is the body . . . is a different thing from the body'—this is true, all else is false! 'He

---

[1] G a n t h o is defined as that which ties (or knots) or binds him for whom it exists on to the " circle " of re-birth. And the term k ā y a g a n t h o (body-tie) is used because the tying is effected through the body—that is, is got in conception and re-birth. Asl. 49, 377. The Ganthas are enumerated as in the present answer in S. iv, 59, and are frequently mentioned collectively, sometimes as Gandhas, throughout that volume. In the A. (ii, 24) I find only the general allusion s a b b a - g a n t h a - p a m o c a n o.

[2] See also p. 269, n.2.

[3] The sole comment on this species of spiritual hindrance is that it is the standpoint of those who have rejected the doctrines of the Omniscient. Asl. 377.

who has won truth exists after death . . . does not exist after death . . . both exists and does not exist after death . . . neither exists nor does not exist after death '—this is true, all else is false ! "—this kind of opinion, this walking in opinion, this jungle of opinion, wilderness of opinion, disorder of opinion, scuffling of opinion, this Fetter of opinion, the grip and tenacity of it, the inclination towards it, the being infected by it, this by-path, wrong road, wrongness, this sectarianism, this shiftiness of grasp—this is called the bodily Tie of the inclination to dogmatize.

And, excepting only the bodily Tie of perversion as to rule and ritual, all wrong views are included under the bodily Tie of the disposition to dogmatize.

These are the states which are Ties.

[1140] Which are the states that are not Ties ?

Every state, good, bad and indeterminate, which is not included in the foregoing [four] states, whether it relates to the worlds of Sense or of Form, or of the Formless, or to the life that is Unincluded ; [in other words] the four skandhas ; all form also, and unconditioned element.

Which are the states that

[1141] (*a*) *tend to become tied ?* [1]

Good, bad and indeterminate states, relating to the worlds of Sense, of Form, or of the Formless, which are co-Āsava ; [in other words] the five skandhas.

[1142] (*b*) *do not tend to become tied ?*

The Paths that are the Unincluded and the Fruits of the Paths, and unconditioned element.

Which are the states that are

[1143] (*a*) *associated with the Ties ?*

The states connected with those four afore-named states ; [in other words] the four skandhas.

---

[1] Ganthaniyā. Ārammaṇakaraṇavasena ganthehi ganthitabbā ti ganthaniyā. Asl. 49.

[1144] (*b*) *disconnected with the Ties?*

The states which are disconnected with those [four afore-named] states; [in other words] the four skandhas; all [material] form also, and unconditioned element.[1]

Which are the states that

[1145] (*a*) *are themselves Ties and tend to become tied?*

The Ties themselves are both

[1146] (*b*) *tend to become tied, but are not Ties?*

The states which tend to become tied by those [four afore-named] states, that is, every state, good, bad and indeterminate, which is not included in the latter, whether it relates to the worlds of Sense, of Form, or of the Formless; [in other words] the five skandhas.

Which are the states that are

[1147] (*a*) *Ties themselves, and associated with the Ties?*

The bodily Tie of perversion as to rule and ritual in conjunction with the bodily Tie of covetousness, *and conversely*, is both. The bodily Tie of the disposition to dogmatize in conjunction with the bodily Tie of covetousness, *and conversely*, is both.[2]

[1148] (*b*) *associated with the Ties but not Ties?*

The states which are associated with the four states afore-named (the Ties), the latter themselves excepted; [in other words] the four skandhas.

Which are the states that

[1149] (*a*) *are disconnected with the Ties, but tend to become tied?*

---

[1] Sabbañ ca rūpaṃ asankhatā ca dhātu is omitted in the text, but occurs in analogous passages (§§ 1124, 1167) and is given in K.

[2] It is not apparent to me why the Tie of ill-will (vyāpādo) is omitted from these combinations, both in the text and in K. Buddhaghosa makes no comment.

The states which are disconnected with the afore-named states, that is, good, bad and indeterminate states relating to the worlds of Sense, of Form, or of the Formless, which are co-Āsava ; [in other words], the five skandhas.

[1150] (*b*) *are disconnected with the Ties and do not tend to become tied ?*

The Paths that are the Unincluded and the Fruits of the Paths, and uncompounded element.

[CHAPTER VII.

The Group of the Floods (o g h a - g o c c h a k a ṃ).]

[1151] Which are the states that are Floods? . . . [*continue as in the* Group of Fetters.][1]

---

[1] This and the group in the next chapter are thus indicated to be taken as read, in both the text and K. By the table of contents, it can be seen that the same system of catechizing is followed as in the Groups of the Fetters and the Ties. In S. v, p. 59, may be seen the number and kind of "states" included under Floods or under Bonds, the contents of either group being identical with the four Āsavas. These are the Flood or Bond of sensuality (k ā m a), renewed existence (b h a v a), speculative opinion (d i ṭ ṭ h i) and ignorance (a v i j j ā). The Atthasālinī only remarks that the Floods are states so called because they sink him for whom they exist into s a ṃ s ā r a, while the Bonds, like the Ties, chain him to the Circle (p. 49). Also that the adjectives, o g h a n i y ā and y o g a n i y ā, analogous to g a n t h a n i y ā, stand for that which can be engulfed by Floods and enchained by Bonds respectively.

[CHAPTER VIII.

The Group of the Bonds (yoga-gocchakaṃ).]

[1151*a*] Which are the states that are Bonds?
. . . [*continue as in the* Group of Fetters].

[CHAPTER IX.

The Group of the Hindrances (nīvaraṇa-gocchakaṃ).]

[1152] Which are the states that are Hindrances?

The six Hindrances, to wit, the Hindrance of sensual desire, the Hindrance of ill will, the Hindrance of stolidity and torpor, the Hindrance of distraction and worry, the Hindrance of perplexity, the Hindrance of ignorance.[1]

In this connexion

[1153] *What is the Hindrance of sensual desire?*

Answer as for the "Intoxicant of sensuality", § 1097.[2]

[1154] *What is the Hindrance of ill will?*

Answer as for the "Tie of ill will", § 1137.

[1155] *What is the Hindrance of stolidity and torpor?*

First distinguish between stolidity and torpor.[3]

---

[1] In the Sutta Piṭaka, the Hindrances form a category of five, ignorance (avijjā) being excluded. See the description in D. i, 71–4, and cf. D. i, 246; M. i, 60, 144, 181, 269, 294, etc.; A. iii, 63; S. v, 60, 94–8. This discrepancy is not noticed by Buddhaghosa. See also § 1112, etc. The Hindrances are to be understood as states which muffle, enwrap, or trammel thought. States, again, which are nīvaraṇiyā are to be understood analogously to those which are saṃyojanīyā. Asl. 94.

[2] "Sensual thirst" is again omitted, as in the description of the corresponding Fetter, § 1114.

[3] It is interesting to note that whereas the text calls thīnaṃ (stolidity) a morbid state of the cittaṃ and middhaṃ a morbid state of the kāyo, Buddhaghosa, in his Cy. on the Dīgha Nikāya (Sum. 211), speaks of thīnaṃ as citta(gelaññaṃ, sickness or affection of the mind), and of middhaṃ as cetasikagelaññaṃ. The apparent inconsistency, however, will vanish if the predominantly psychological standpoint of the Dhamma Sangaṇi be kept in mind. By kāyo, as Buddhaghosa reminds us (Asl. 378; see above, p. 40, n. 3), is meant "the three skandhas" of feeling, perception, and synergies, that is

In this connexion,

[1156] *What is stolidity?*

That which is indisposition,[1] unwieldiness [2] of mind; adhering and cohering; clinging, cleaving to, stickiness; stolidity, that is, a stiffening, a rigidity of the mind [3]—this is called stolidity.

[1157] *What is torpor?* [4]

That which is indisposition and unwieldiness of sense, a shrouding, enveloping,[5] barricading within [6]; torpor that is sleep, drowsiness; sleep,[7] slumbering, somnolence—this is called torpor.

---

to say, the three through which we have subjective experience of bodily states objectively conceived. And cetasiko is the adjective corresponding to kāyo taken in this sense (§ 1022). Hence stolidity is confined to the viññāṇa-skandha, which = cittaṃ = (approximately) representative intellection, while torpor is a corresponding affection of mind on its presentative and emotional side.

[1] Akalyatā, equivalent to gilānabhāvo, Asl. 377.

[2] See § 47.

[3] "The (stolid) mind cannot be maintained in any required attitude or deportment. It is as inert as a bat hanging to a tree, or as molasses cleaving to a stick, or as a lump of butter too stiff for spreading" (Asl., ibid.). "Attached to" (līnaṃ) is paraphrased by avipphārikatāya paṭikuṭitaṃ, lit. bent back without expansion, where the notion, as conceived by the Commentator, has something akin to kaṭukañcukatā or niggardliness. See § 1122, n. 2.

[4] Middhaṃ, derived by the Cy. from medhati ($\sqrt{\text{med}}$, "be fat"); there is a cognate notion in our "torpor", cf. τέρπειν, to be sated, and $\sqrt{\text{tarp}}$.

[5] Onāho, pariyonāho. See Mil. 300; D. i, 246. In the latter work, the *ă* is short. In the Cy. (Asl. 378) the simile is "enveloping the senses (kāyo) as a cloud the sky". In Sum. i, 135, the latter of the two terms is applied to "covering" a drum.

[6] Anto-samorodho. The Cy. explains that, as men cannot get out of an invested city, so dhammā, blockaded by torpor, cannot get out by expansion or diffusion.

[7] There is no comment on this repetition of soppaṃ.

Now this is the stolidity and this is the torpor which are called " the Hindrance of stolidity and torpor ".[1]

[1159] What is the Hindrance of distraction and worry?

First distinguish between " distraction " and " worry ".

In this connexion,

[1160] *What is distraction?* [2]

That distraction of mind which is disquietude, agitation of heart, turmoil of mind—this is called distraction.

[1161] What is worry? [3]

Consciousness of what is lawful in something that is

[1] The Commentator, in his general remarks on this Hindrance, is at pains to point out that for the khīṇāsavo, or arahant, a periodical torpor or repose has ceased to engender bad karma. The Buddha allowed an after-dinner nap, for instance, at certain seasons (see M. i, 249), as not in itself conducive to a bemuddling of the mind. So powerful, however, is the hindrance to the non-adept, that its influence is not rooted out till the arahant Path is gained. The arahant is fain to rest his frail body (lit. his fingernail-kāyo), but to him it is as *un*moral an act as the folding up of leaves and blossoms at night. On overcoming torpor see A. iv, 86.

[2] See § 429.

[3] In its primary meaning kukkuccaṃ is fidgeting, bad deportment of hands and feet. See Jāt. i, 119; ii, 142; also Sum.V. i, 1, 2. Hence mental fidget, the worry of *scruple* (lit. " the little sharp stone in a man's shoe ". See Skeat's English Dictionary), the over-sensitive, over-scrupulous conscience. In the frequent cases of kukkuccaṃ, respecting the keeping of the rules of the Order, given in the Vinaya—" tassa kukkuccaṃ ahosi "—or kukkuccāyanto—no blame seems to have attached to the person in question. There was weakness in the anxiety felt by the non-robust conscience as to the letter of the law; on the other hand, there was loyalty to the Master's decrees. Even the great Sāriputta was not above such scruples, when, on falling ill at a rest-house, he declined to take food, in accordance with the 31st Pācittiya rule (Vin. iv, 70). But Buddhaghosa quotes this as an instance of praiseworthy scruple, to be distinguished, as " Vinaya-kukkuccaṃ ", from the after-flush of burning anguish (anutāpo) accompanying the consciousness of having done amiss, a feeling that is no longer possible for an arahant. Asl. 384. Cf. below, § 1304.

unlawful; consciousness of what is unlawful in something that is lawful; consciousness of what is immoral in something that is moral; consciousness of what is moral in something that is immoral [1]—all this sort of worry, fidgeting, over-scrupulousness, remorse of conscience, mental scarifying [2] —this is what is called worry.

Now this is the distraction and this is the worry which are what is called " the Hindrance of distraction and worry ".

[1162] *What is the Hindrance of ignorance?*

Answer as for " dullness ", § 1061.

[1163] Which are the states that are not Hindrances?

Every state, good, bad and indeterminate, which is not included in the foregoing [six] states, whether it relates to the worlds of Sense, of Form, or of the Formless, or to the life that is Unincluded; [in other words] the four skandhas; all form also, and unconditioned element.

Which are the states that are

[1164] (*a*) *favourable to the Hindrances?* [3]

States that have Āsavas, good, bad, and indeterminate, whether relating to the worlds of Sense, Form, or the Formless; [in other words] the five skandhas.

[1165] (*b*) *unfavourable to the Hindrances?*

The Paths that are the Unincluded and the Fruits of the Paths, and unconditioned element.

Which are the states that are

[1166] (*a*) *associated with the Hindrances?*

[1167] (*b*) *disconnected with the Hindrances?*

---

[1] Things lawful (k a p p i y a ṃ) and unlawful are explained as here referring merely to rules of routine in the Order, e.g. to kinds of food, the dinner-hour, etc. By things moral and immoral (a v a j j a ṃ , etc.) are meant acts of virtue and of vice. Asl. 383.

[2] See n. to § 425.

[3] N ī v a r a ṇ i y ā , to be understood as analogous to s a ṃ y o j a n ī y ā . Asl. 49.

Answers identical with those given to corresponding questions respecting the Āsavas, §§ 1105, 1106.

Which are the states that are

[1168] (*a*) *Hindrances themselves and favourable to the Hindrances?*

The Hindrances themselves are both.

[1169] (*b*) *favourable to the Hindrances, but not themselves Hindrances?*

The states which are favourable to the Hindrances aforenamed; that is to say, with the exception of the Hindrances, all states whatever that have Āsavas, good, bad, and indeterminate, whether they relate to the worlds of Sense, Form, or the Formless; [in other words] the five skandhas.

Which are the states that are

[1170] (*a*) *both themselves Hindrances and associated with Hindrances?*

The following pairs are both themselves Hindrances and associated with Hindrances: Sensual desire in conjunction with ignorance, *and conversely*. Ill-will in conjunction with ignorance, *and conversely*.

Stolidity and torpor,
Distraction,
Worry,
Perplexity, } *taken successively*, in conjunction with ignorance, *and conversely*.

Sensual desire,
Ill-will,
Stolidity and torpor,
Distraction,
Worry,
Perplexity, } *taken successively*, in conjunction with ignorance, *and conversely*.

[1171] (*b*) *associated with Hindrances, but not themselves Hindrances?*

The states which are associated with the [six aforementioned] states, the latter themselves being excepted; [in other words] the four skandhas.

Which are the states that are

[1172] (*a*) *disconnected with the Hindrances, but favourable to them?*

The states which are disconnected with those [six] states afore-named, that is to say, states that have Āsavas, good, bad, and indeterminate, whether they relate to the worlds or Sense, Form, or the Formless; [in other words] the five skandhas.

[1173] (*b*) *disconnected with the Hindrances and unfavourable to them?*

The Paths that are the Unincluded, and the Fruits of the Paths, and unconditioned element.[1]

---

[1] Worry and perplexity are discarded in the First Path; sensual desire and ill-will in the Third Path; stolidity, torpor, and ignorance in the Fourth. Asl. 384. Insight into the presence or absence of the (five) Hindrances is termed, in A. i, 272, m a n o s o c e y y a ṃ.

[CHAPTER X.

The Group on Perversion (p a r ā m ā s a - g o c c h a k a ṃ).][1]

[1174] Which are the states that are
The Contagion of speculative opinion?
In this connexion,

[1175] What is "perversion as speculative opinion"?

Answer as for the "Intoxicant of speculative opinion", *viz.*: "To hold that the world is eternal, or that it is not eternal," etc. (§ 1099).

[1176] Which are the states that are not perversion?

Answer as in the case of the "states that are not Hindrances" (§ 1163).[2]

[1177, 1178) Which are the states that are
(*a*) *perverted?*
(*b*) *unperverted?*

Answers as in the corresponding answers relating to the Hindrances (§§ 1164, 1165).

[1179, 1180] Which are the states that are
(*a*) *associated with perversion?*
(*b*) *disconnected with perversion?*

Answers as in the corresponding answers relating to the Hindrances (§§ 1166, 1167).

[1181, 1182] Which are the states that are
(*a*) *themselves perversions and perverted?*
Perversion itself is both.

---

[1] Or reversion. Cf. Mr. Maung Tin's translation of the Cy., p. 65: in the first edition of this work rendered contagion, infection. P a r ā m ā s a is, according to Buddhaghosa, employed to mean p a r a + ā + m a s a t i (Sk. mṛś), to touch—upon—as other, i.e. in a way inverse to the right way, wrong-minded procedure.

[2] Perversion is one and the same fault, but to agree with the questions is always referred to as plural. Asl. 385.

(*b*) *perverted but not perversions?*

The states which are infected by the states afore-named; that is to say, with the exception of the latter, all states whatever that have Āsavas, good, bad, and indeterminate, whether they relate to the worlds of Sense, Form, or the Formless; [in other words] the five shandhas.

[1183, 1184] Which are the states that are

(*a*) *disconnected with perversion yet perverted?*

(*b*) *disconnected with perversion and unperverted?*

Answers as in the corresponding sections on the Hindrances (§§ 1172, 1173).

[CHAPTER XI.

The Great Intermediate Set of Pairs (mahantara-dukaṃ).][1]

[1185, 1186] Which are the states that have

(a) *an object of thought?* [2]

The four skandhas.

(b) *no object of thought?*

All [material] form,[3] and unconditioned element.

[1187, 1188] Which are the states that are

(a) *of thoughts?* [4]

Sense-cognition, the element of ideation and the element of ideational cognition.

(b) *not of thoughts?*

The skandhas of feeling, perception, and synergies; all [material] form, moreover, and unconditioned element.

[1189, 1190] Which are the states that are

(a) *mental properties?* [5]

The skandhas of feeling, perception, and synergies.

(b) *not mental properties?*

Intellect and all [material] form and unconditioned element.

[1191, 1192] Which are the states that are

(a) *associated with thought?*

The skandhas of feeling, perception, and synergies.

(b) *disconnected with thought?*

All [material] form and unconditioned element.

---

[1] Cf. Chap. III of this book. The Cy. discusses the following compounds in dealing with the Mātikā (49 f.).

[2] Sārammaṇā.

[3] See p. 169: "void of idea." See KV. 404.

[4] Cittā. See § 1022.

[5] Cetasikā. See § 1022.

(Thought must not be described as associated or disconnected with itself.) [1]

[1193, 1194] Which are the states that are

(*a*) *conjoined with thought?* [2]

(*b*) *detached from thought?*

Answers as in §§ 1191, 1192, *respectively.*

(Thought must not be described as conjoined with, or detached from, itself.)

[1195, 1196] Which are the states that are

(*a*) *sprung from thought?* [3]

The skandhas of feeling, perception, and synergies; bodily and vocal intimation; or whatever other [material] form there be which is born of thought, caused by thought, sprung from thought, whether it be in the spheres of shapes, sounds, smells, tastes,[4] or the tangible, the elements of space or fluidity, the lightness, plasticity or wieldiness of [material] form, the integration or subsistence of [material] form, or bodily nutriment.

(*b*) *not sprung from thought?*

Thought; also every other kind of [material] form, and unconditioned element.

[1197, 1198] Which are the states that

(*a*) *come into being together with thought?* [5]

The skandhas of feeling, perception, and synergies; bodily and vocal intimation.

---

[1] This refinement in the Buddhist Logic of Terms is usually expressed by the brief parenthesis governed by ṭhapetvā, excepting. See e.g. § 984 *et seq.*

[2] Citta-saṃsaṭṭhā. "I.e. in a condition of continuity, immediate contiguity, with thought." Asl. 49. The contrary -visaṃsaṭṭhā = "not in the condition of continuity, immediate contiguity, with thought, although proceeding in unity with it." Ibid.

[3] Citta-samuṭṭhānā. Cf. § 667.

[4] Rasāyatanaṃ has been omitted in the text, apparently by inadvertence.

[5] Citta-sahabhuno.

(*b*) *do not come into being together with thought?*

Thought; also all other kinds of [material] form,[1] and unconditioned element.

[1199, 1200] Which are the states that are

(*a*) *consecutive to thought?* [2]

(*b*) *not consecutive to thought?*

Answers as in the two foregoing answers respectively.

[1201, 1202] Which are the states that are

(*a*) *conjoined with and sprung from thought?* [3]

The skandhas of feeling, perception, and synergies.

(*b*) *not conjoined with and sprung from thought?* [4]

Thought itself; all [material] form also, and unconditioned element.

[1203, 1204] Which are the states that

(*a*) *are conjoined with and sprung from, and that come into being together with, thought?*

(*b*) *are not such as are conjoined with and sprung from, and as come into being together with, thought?* [5]

Answers as in the two foregoing answers respectively.

[1205, 1206] Which are the states that are

(*a*) *conjoined with and sprung from and consecutive to thought?*

(*b*) *not conjoined with, sprung from and consecutive to thought?*

Answers as in the two foregoing answers.

---

[1] i.e. except the two modes of intimation, which are reckoned as "form". See § 596.

[2] Cittanuparivattinā.

[3] Citta-saṃsaṭṭha-samuṭṭhānā.

[4] The negative in the text is not distributed, and the compound of attributes qualifying "states" must be taken conjunctively. This is borne out by the answer. Cf. §§ 1196, 1198, also p. 204, n. 1.

Saha-bhuno is parsed as saha bhavanti, not bhūtā. Asl. 49.

[5] See n. 4 (above).

[1207, 1208] Which are the states that are

(a) *of the self?*

The spheres of the five senses and of ideation.

(b) *external?*

The spheres of the five objects of sense and of ideas.[1]

[1209, 1210] Which are the states that are

(a) *derived?*

The spheres of the five senses . . . and bodily nutriment.[2]

(b) *not derived?*

The four skandhas, the four great phenomena and unconditioned element.

[1211–12] Which are the states that are

(a) *grasped at?* [3]

Co-Intoxicant good and bad states, whether they relate to the worlds of Sense, of Form, or of the Formless ; [in other words] the four skandhas, and such [material] form as is due to karma having been wrought.

(b) *not grasped at?*

Good and bad states that have Āsavas, whether they relate to the worlds of Sense, of Form, or of the Formless ; [in other words] the four skandhas ; also such inoperative thoughts as are neither good, nor bad, nor the effects of karma ; the Paths, moreover, that are the Unincluded and the Fruits of the Paths, and unconditioned element.

---

[1] Dhammāyatanaṃ.
[2] Cf. § 596. [3] See M. i, 190.

[CHAPTER XII.

The Group on Grasping (u p ā d ā n a - g o c c h a k a ṃ).]

[1213] Which are the states that have the attribute of Grasping? [1]

---

[1] U p ā d ā n ā. This fundamental notion in Buddhist ethics is in the Cy. (pp. 450 and 385) paraphrased by the words "they take violently, i.e. they take hold with a strong grasp" (b h u s a ṃ ā d i y a n t i . . . d a ḷ h a g ā h a ṃ g a ṇ h a n t i), the prefix u p a being credited with augmentative import, as in other terms such as u p ā y ā s o and u p a k k u ṭ ṭ h o. This shows that, in so far as Buddhaghosa gives the traditional sense, the word, in the Buddhism of his day, connoted rather the dynamic force of "grasping" than the static condition of "attachment" (e.g. Warren, *Buddhism in Translations*, p. 189 *et seq.*) or "cleaving" (Hardy, *Manual*, 394). Nor does his comment ratify such renderings as "Hang" or "Lebenstrieb" (Neumann, *Die Reden Gotamo Buddhos*, pp. 104, 470). Fausböll's "seizures" (S. N. in SBE. x, p. 138) and Oldenberg's *Ergreifen* (*Buddha*, 3rd ed., 269), on the other hand, agree with Buddhaghosa.

The relation of the cognate term u p ā d ā n i y o to u p ā d ā n a ṃ (cf. §§ 655, 881, 1219) is most clearly set forth in S. iv, 89; there the special senses are termed u p ā d ā n i y ā d h a m m ā, and the passionate desire connected therewith the u p ā d ā n a ṃ. See also S. iv, 258. Buddhaghosa makes no comment on u p ā d ā n i y a ṃ when, as in § 1219, it is applied to d h a m m ā; but when it is a question of r ū p a ṃ . . . u p ā d ā n i y a ṃ (Dh. S., §§ 655, 881), he defines this as "*states* which are favourable to (h i t ā, lit. good for) the Graspings as objects by their being bound up with grasping; in other words, phenomena which are the conditions of the mental objects of grasping" (u p ā d ā n a s s a ā r a m m a ṇ a - p a c c a y a - b h ū t ā n i). Asl. 42.

In the same connexion, r ū p a ṃ u p ā d i ṇ ṇ a ṃ (Dh. S., § 653) is by Buddhaghosa defined as [states] which have been got, laid hold of, taken (g a h i t ā), by way of fruition—heaped up by karma having the property of craving. Ibid. None of the comments explains u p ā d ā n a ṃ in the sense of fuel, i.e. as the basis of rebirth (cf. S. iv, 399; ii, 85); each of the four Upādānas is paraphrased simply by to grasp at sense (k ā m a ṃ u p ā d i y a t i), at speculation, etc. As is usual in these compounds, the "of" is to be taken as meaning "which is".

The four Graspings:—the Grasping of sense-desires, the Grasping of speculative opinion, the Grasping of rule and ritual, the Grasping of a theory of the Self.

In this connexion,

[1214] *What is the Grasping of sense-desires?*

That sensual desire, sensual passion, sensual delight, sensual craving, sensual cleaving, sensual fever, sensual languishing, sensual rapacity, which is excited by the pleasures of the senses.[1]

[1215] *What is the Grasping of speculative opinion?*

"There is no such thing as alms, or sacrifice, or offering;[2] there is neither fruit, nor result of good, or of evil deeds; there is no such thing as this world, or the next;[3] there is no such thing as mother or father, or beings springing into birth without them;[4] there are in the world no recluses or brahmins who have reached the highest point, who have attained the height, who, having understood and realized by themselves alone both this world and the next, make known the same"[5]—all this sort of speculation, this walking in opinion, wilderness of opinion, puppet-show of opinion,

---

[1] See § 1114 and § 1097; also § 1153.

[2] The Cy. explains these negations as merely meaning that none of the three has an efficacy, any fruition. Asl. 385.

[3] Ignoring any deeper metaphysic that may have here been implied, the Cy. explains these negations as held by the inhabitant of another world respecting this, or by an inhabitant here below respecting another world. Ibid.

[4] Opapātikā, e.g. devas, also nerayikas and petas. The most literal rendering would be "reborner". Beings so born, continues the Cy., he assumes there are none; and that one's former lives have no efficacy over one's subsequent parentage.

[5] Buddhaghosa gives as typical forms of speculative grasping, "Both the soul (self) and the world are eternal." These he calls the purimadiṭṭhiṃ uttaradiṭṭhiṃ (*sic lege*), terms which, whether they mean "earlier and further heresies", or "Eastern and Northern views", or both, are equally interesting. The text, however, selects as a typical current speculation the views put forward by Ajita Kesakambali. See D. i, 55, and M. i, 402.

scuffling of opinion, this Fetter of opinion, the grip and tenacity of it, the inclination towards it, the being infected by it, this by-path, wrong road, wrongness, this "fording-place", this shiftiness of grasp[1]—this is what is called the Grasping after speculative opinion.

And with the exception of the Graspings of rule and ritual and soul theory, all wrong views are included in the Grasping of speculative opinion.

[1216] *What is the Grasping of rule and ritual?*

Answer as for "Perversion of mere rule and ritual", § 1005.[2]

[1217] *What is the Grasping of a theory of the Self?*

Answer as for the "Theory of individuality", § 1003.

[1218] Which are the states that are not Graspings?

All other states whatever, good, bad and indeterminate (except the foregoing), whether they relate to the worlds of Sense, or of Form, or of the Formless, or to the life that is Unincluded; [in other words] the four skandhas; all [material] form also and unconditioned element.

[1219] Which are the states that are favourable to Grasping?

States that have Āsavas, good, bad and indeterminate, whether they relate to the worlds of Sense, Form or the Formless; [in other words] the five skandhas.

[1220] Which are the states that are not favourable to Grasping?

The Paths that are the Unincluded, and the Fruits of the Paths; and unconditioned element.

[1221–4] Which are the states that are

(*a*) *associated with Grasping?*

(*b*) *disconnected with Grasping?*

(*c*) *Graspings and also favourable to Grasping?*

(*d*) *favourable to Grasping but not Graspings?*

---

[1] Cf. § 381.

[2] The "bovine morality and practices" noticed above (§ 1005, n. 3) are again instanced in the Cy. Ibid.

Answers exactly analogous to those given to corresponding questions in other Groups, e.g. §§ 1125, 1141, 1164.

[1225–8] Which are the states that are

(*a*) *both Graspings and associated with Grasping?*

The Grasping of speculation in conjunction with that of sense is both, *and conversely.*

So is each of the other two Graspings in conjunction with that of sense, *and conversely.*

(*b*) *associated with Grasping but not Graspings?*

(*c*) *disconnected with Grasping yet favourable to it?*

(*d*) *disconnected with Grasping and not favourable to it?*

Answers as in the Groups specified above, §§ 1125, 1141, 1164 et seq.[1]

---

[1] The First Path disposes of all forms of Grasping save the first, the extirpation of which is a task not finished till all the four Paths have been traversed. Asl. 386. Contrast with this §§ 1173 n., 1134 n., and 1112 n., where in every case "sense", "sensuality", and "sensual desire" are in the Cy. said to succumb in the Third or Anāgāmi's Path.

[CHAPTER XIII.

The Group on the Vices (k i l e s a - g o c c h a k a ṃ).]

[1229] Which are the states that are vicious ? [1]

The ten bases of vice, to wit

greed,	perplexity,
hate,	stolidity,
dullness,	distraction,
conceit,	unconscientiousness,
speculative opinion,	disregard of blame.

---

[1] On the term k i l e s a the Cy. is silent. It is true that the word lies as near to the Buddhist believer as "sin" to the Christian. As a rule, however, Buddhaghosa is too Socratic to accept familiar terms without examination. In this case he has confined his attention to the derivatives. Incidentally, however—in discussing the meaning of "good" (above, § 1 ; Asl. 62)—he makes spiritual health to consist in the absence of k i l e s a - disease, showing that k i l e s a was co-extensive with evil or the absence of moral good. Of the derivatives, only s a n k i - l i ṭ ṭ h a is made to convey the idea of impurity or foulness (see Childers, *s.v.* s a n k i l e s o), bad butter being so termed (Asl. 319). Elsewhere it is paraphrased as "possessed of s a n k i l e s o", while s a n k i l e s a (above, §§ 993–5 ; Asl. 42) is defined in close agreement with the description of s a n k l e ç a in Böthl. and Roth (*quälen, belästigen*) : "the meaning is to trouble, to torment," while the corresponding adjective is described as "deserving s a n k i l e s a by persistently making self the object of one's thoughts . . . the term being an equivalent for those things which are the conditions (or objects) of s a n k i l e s a". Vice or moral corruption is, however, I believe, approximately what this group of terms represents to modern Buddhists ; nor have I been able to select an English word adequate to render them in what seems to have been their first intention, viz. "torment" (caused by moral unsoundness). "Bases" or v a t t h ū n i are states so called because the vices dwell (v a s a n t i) in the (human) subject of them as immediate consequences (a n a n t a r a - p a c c a y ā) of those bases. Asl. 386.

[1230–7] In this connexion,

What is greed? . . . hate? . . . dullness? . . . conceit? . . . speculative opinion? . . . perplexity? . . . stolidity? . . . distraction? [1]

Answers as in §§ 1059–61, 1116–18, 1156, 1159.

[1238] *What is unconscientiousness?*

The absence of any feeling of conscientious scruple when scruples ought to be felt; the absence of conscientious scruple at attaining to bad and evil states.[2]

[1239] *What is disregard of blame?*

The absence of any sense of guilt where a sense of guilt ought to be felt, the absence of a sense of guilt at attaining to bad and evil states.

These are the states which are vices.

[1240] Which are the states that are not vices?

All other states whatever (i.e. all except the afore-named ten), good, bad and indeterminate, whether they relate to the worlds of Sense, Form or the Formless, or to the life that is Unincluded; [in other words] the four skandhas, all [material] form also and unconditioned element.

[1241, 1242] Which are the states that are

(*a*) *vicious?*

States that have Āsavas, good, bad and indeterminate, whether they relate to the worlds of Sense, of Form or of the Formless;[3] [in other words] the five skandhas.

(*b*) *not vicious?*

The Paths that are the Unincluded, and the Fruits of the Paths, and unconditioned element.

[1243, 1243*a*] Which are the states that are

(*a*) *vitiated?*

The three roots of bad (karma), to wit, greed, hate, dullness,

---

[1] In the answer, vūpasamo in the text should be avūpasamo.

[2] See §§ 387, 388.

[3] Aparīyāpannā should, of course, be omitted from the printed text.

as well as the vices united with them, the four skandhas associated with them, and the action, bodily, vocal and mental, springing from them.

(*b*) *not vitiated?*

Good and indeterminate states, whether they relate to the worlds of Sense, Form, or the Formless, or to the life that is Unincluded; [in other words] the four skandhas; all [material] form also, and unconditioned element.[1]

[1244–7] Which are the states that are

(*a*) *associated with the vices?*
(*b*) *disconnected with the vices?*
(*c*) *both vices and vicious?*
(*d*) *vicious but not themselves vices?*

Answers as in the corresponding pairs in the "Graspings", §§ 1221–4.

[1248, 1249] Which are the states that are

(*a*) *both vices and vitiated?*

The vices themselves.

(*b*) *vitiated but not themselves vices?*

The states which by those ten states are vitiated, the ten themselves excepted; [in other words] the four skandhas.

[1250–3] Which are the states that are

(*a*) *both vices and associated with vice?*

Greed, hate, conceit, speculative opinion, perplexity, stolidity, distraction, unconscientiousness, and disregard of blame *taken severally* in conjunction with dullness, and dullness in conjunction with *each of them.* Greed, also, in conjunction with distraction, *and conversely, and so for the remaining eight bases.* Greed, also, in conjunction with unconscientiousness, *and conversely, and so for the remaining eight.* Greed, also, in conjunction with disregard of blame, *and conversely, and so for the remaining eight.*[2]

---

[1] This section is omitted, apparently inadvertently, in the printed text. Cf. the Mātikā.

[2] It is not very obvious, nor is any explanation volunteered by the Cy., why just the 3rd, 8th, 9th, and 10th bases of vice are selected as the constant of two factors in this connexion.

(*b*) *associated with vices but not themselves vices?*[1]

{(*c*) *disconnected with vices but vicious?*
{(*d*) *disconnected with vices and not vicious?*

Answers to these three questions as in former groups. See §§ 1226–8, 1171–3, *etc.*[2]

---

[1] In the answer, supply ye dhammā after Tehi dhammehi.

[2] The First Path witnesses the overcoming of speculative opinion and perplexity, the Third Path disposes of hate, but it requires the Fourth Path to overcome the remaining seven. Asl. 387.

In the first edition kilesā was rendered as "Corruptions". "Vices" is not etymologically a better fit, but, as a stock term for wrong ways or states, it comes nearer *in usage* to kilesā. These stand, in all but the earliest Pali (kilesā is hard to find in Vinaya or Dhamma), for the lower, unregenerate side of the average man's nature.

[CHAPTER XIV.

The Supplementary Set of Pairs p i ṭ ṭ h i d u k a ṃ).]

[1254] Which are the states that are to be put away by vision ?

The Three Fetters, to wit: theory of individuality, perplexity and perversion as to rule and ritual.

[1255–7] *Identical with* §§ 1003–6.

[1258] Which are the states that are not to be put away by vision ?

All states whatever, good, bad and indeterminate, except the three afore-mentioned, whether they relate to the worlds of Sense, Form or the Formless, or to the life that is Unincluded; [in other words] the four skandhas; all [material] form also and unconditioned element.

[1259, 1260] Which are the states that are

(*a*) *to be put away by cultivation ?* [1]

All the remaining lust, hate and dullness as well as the vices united with them, the four skandhas associated with them, and the action, bodily, vocal and mental, springing from them.

(*b*) *not to be put away by cultivation ?*

Answer as for those states which are not to be put away by insight [§ 1258].

[1261] Which are the states the causes of which are to be put away by vision ?

The Three Fetters, to wit: theory of individuality, perplexity and perversion as to rule and ritual.

[1262–4] *Identical with* §§ 1003–6.

---

[1] On b h ā v a n ā, lit. causing, or making to be, cf. my *Bud. Psychology* (1914), p. 133 f. English has degenerated in this particular. We need our old weorthan, with a causative meaning. Will some poet introduce " werden " ?

[1265] Which are the states the causes of which are not to be put away by insight ?

Answer as for those " states which are not to be put away by insight ", § 1258.

[1266, 1267] Which are the states the causes of which are

(*a*) *to be put away by cultivation ?*

All the remaining lust, hate and dullness : these are the causes that are to be put away[1] by cultivation. And the vices united with them, the four skandhas associated with them, and the action, bodily, vocal and mental, springing from them, are the states the causes of which are to be put away by cultivation.

(*b*) *not to be put away by cultivation ?*

Answer as for the " states which are not to be put away by cultivation ", § 1260.

[1268–71] Which are the states

(*a*) " *with applied thinking* " ?

The four skandhas when associated with conception (the latter not being included) [which springs up] in a soil wherein is application of thought, either in the worlds of Sense or Form, or in the life that is Unincluded.[2]

(*b*) " *without applied thinking* " ?

The four skandhas when springing up in a soil void of applied thinking, either in the worlds of Sense, Form or the Formless, or in the life that is Unincluded ; applied thinking itself also, and all [material] form and unconditioned element.

(*c*) " *with sustained thinking* " ?

(*d*) " *without sustained thinking* " ?

Answers (*substituting* " sustained thinking " *for* " applied thinking ") *as in* §§ 1268, 1269, *respectively.*

---

[1] In the text, for p a h ā t a b b a - h e t u k ā (first occurrence) read p a h ā t a b b a - h e t ū .

[2] Cf. this and following pairs with §§ 996–8, and p. 231, n. 6. See also App. I, pp. 336, 337. In the text, a r ū p ā v a c a r e should be omitted, and a p a r i y ā p a n n e substituted for p a r i y ā p a n n e .

[1272–7] Which are the states that are

(*a*) *with zest?* [1]

(*b*) *without zest?*

(*c*) *accompanied by zest?*

(*d*) *unaccompanied by zest?*

(*e*) *accompanied by ease?*

(*f*) *unaccompanied by ease?*

Answers to each pair of questions analogous to those in §§ 1268, 1269, " zest " *or* " ease " *being substituted in due order for* " applied thinking ".

[1278, 1279] Which are the states that are

(*a*) *accompanied by indifference?*

The three skandhas of perception, synergies and consciousness,[2] when associated with indifference (the latter not being included), [which springs up] in a soil congenial to it, either in the worlds of Sense, Form or the Formless, or in the life that is Unincluded.

(*b*) *unaccompanied by indifference?*

The four skandhas [when springing up] in a soil uncongenial to indifference, either in the worlds of Sense or Form,[3] or in the life that is Unincluded; indifference itself also, and all [material] form and unconditioned element.

[1280–7] Which are the states that

(*a*) *relate (belong) to the universe of Sense?* [4]

Take from the waveless deep of woe beneath up to the

---

[1] Sappītikā. The term is used to qualify sukhaṃ, A. i, 81. How far, if at all, its connotation is distinguishable from that of pīti-sahāgatā (§ 1274) I cannot say.

In the answers to the positive terms arūpāvacare should be omitted from the printed text. Cf. § 265 *et seq.*

[2] Upekkhā (indifference) is a mode of vedanā or feeling, and is therefore not said to be associated with itself.

[3] In the printed text omit arūpāvacare.

[4] Kāmāvacarā. The avacaras are discussed in my Introduction (li). The text occurs also in Pṭs. i, 83. The Vbh. 86, placing other worlds in terms of vertical space, is not emphasized in pre-Abhidhamma Pali. You did not " climb the steep ascent of heaven " in the Suttas, as in later books

heaven above of the Parinimittavasavatti devas inclusive—then whatever has there its range, and is therein included, whether it be skandha, element or sphere [1]—form, feeling, perception, synergies, cognition : these are states that relate (belong) to the universe of Sense.

(*b*) *do not relate (belong) to the universe of Sense?*

The universe of Form, that of the Formless and the life that is Unincluded.

(*c*) *relate (belong) to the universe of Form?*

Take from the Brahma-world below up to the heaven above of the Akaniṭṭha gods inclusive—then whatever states, both of mind and mental properties, have therein their range and are therein included, whether they are states of one who has attained [Jhāna having potential good], or of one in whom [resultant Jhāna] has arisen, or of one living happily under present conditions.[2]

(*d*) *do not relate (belong) to the universe of Form?*

The universe of Sense, that of the Formless and the life that is Unincluded.

(*e*) *relate (belong) to the universe of the Formless?*

Take from the entrance among the denizens of " the sphere of infinite space " [3] as the lower limit, and up to the entrance above among the devas of " the sphere where there is neither perception nor non-perception "—then whatever states, both of mind and mental properties, have therein their range and

---

(cf. Mil. 82) or as in the cruder Christian ideas. You just happened there (uppajjati) or were manifested (pāturahosi).

[1] Khandha-dhātu-āyatanā (cf. K.). I take this to be an adjectival dvandva compound qualifying dhammā, but the five following terms, the skandhas, to be in apposition to dhammā.

[2] The three terms rendered by the last three periphrases are samāpannassa, uppannassa and diṭṭhadhamma-sukhavihārissa. The Cy. (p. 388) explains them as referring to kusala-jhānaṃ, vipāka-jhānaṃ and kiriyā-jhānaṃ. The subject is further dealt with in my Introduction (viii).

[3] See §§ 265–8.

are therein included, whether they are states of one who has attained [Jhāna having potential good], or of one in whom [resultant Jhāna] has arisen, or of one living happily under present conditions: these are states that relate (belong) to the universe of the Formless.

(*f*) *do not relate (belong) to the universe of the Formless?*

The universe of Sense,[1] that of Form, and the life that is Unincluded.

(*g*) *belong to the Included?*

States that have Āsavas, good, bad and indeterminate, whether they relate to the worlds of Sense, of Form or of the Formless; [in other words] the five skandhas.

(*h*) *belong to the Unincluded?*

The Paths, and the Fruit of the Paths, and unconditioned element.

[1288, 1289] Which are the states by which

(*a*) *there is a going away?* [2]

The four Paths that are the Unincluded.

(*b*) *there is no giving away?*

All states, good, bad and indeterminate, except those four, whether they relate to the worlds of Sense, Form or the Formless, or to the life that is Unincluded; [in other words] the four skandhas; all [material] form also, and unconditioned element.

---

[1] This is inadvertently omitted in the printed text.

[2] Niyyānikā. In § 277 *et seq.* the word has been rendered "whereby there is a going forth and onward", the Cy. leaving it somewhat vaguely defined, and the context, both in that connexion and this, showing that the expression imports rather the quest of the Ideal than its attainment. Here the Cy. is briefer and more emphatic (Asl. 50). The word is said to signify: "They, cutting off the root of rebirth and making Nirvana their object, go down (or on) from (niyyanti) that round of transmigration." The good states included under the opposite category will be those static stages of attainment in the upward progress termed the Fruits of the Paths.

[1290, 1291] Which are the states that are

(*a*) *fixed?*[1]

The five acts that have immediate results, and those wrong views that are fixed in their consequences; the four Paths also that are the Unincluded.

(*b*) *not fixed?*

Answer as in § 1289.

[1292, 1293] Which are the states that have

(*a*) *something beyond?*[2]

States that have Āsavas, good, bad and indeterminate, whether they relate to the worlds of Sense, of Form or of the Formless; in other words, the five skandhas.

(*b*) *no "beyond"?*

The four Paths that are the Unincluded, and the Fruits of the Paths, and unconditioned element.

[1294, 1295] Which are the states that are

(*a*) *harmful?*[3]

The three roots of bad (karma): greed, hate and dullness—and the Corruptions united with them; the four skandhas associated with them; the action, bodily, vocal and mental, springing from them.

---

[1] See §§ 1028–30.

[2] Sa-uttarā = capable of transcending, of rejecting self (or soul)—which is merely exegetical. Asl. 50. The term is applied to cittaṃ in D. i, 80. In the anuttarā dhammā this transcending has been accomplished. Anuttara is the ordinary term for uttermost, unparalleled, supreme.

[3] Saraṇā, "an equivalent for those passions, etc., overcome by which beings in divers ways incur weeping and misery" . . . "= together with fightings" (saharaṇehi). Asl. 50. "Dullness associated with lust is co-warring (saraṇo) with lust, or, associated with hate, is co-warring with hate." Asl. 388. One is reminded of the Christian parallel of "fleshly lusts which war against the soul" and of τῶν ἡδονῶν τῶν στρατευομένων ἐν τοῖς μελεσιν ʽυμῶν, although the concomitance in assault is in this case not emphasized. In the Therīgāthā Subhā turns the tables—"wars a good warfare"—by fighting against the sensual desires hostile to her progress (vv. 358, 360).

(*b*) *harmless ?*

Good, bad and indeterminate states, whether they relate to the worlds of Sense, Form or the Formless, or to the life that is Unincluded ; [in other words] the four skandhas ; all [material] form also, and unconditioned element.

[*PART II.*

The Suttanta Pairs of Terms (s u t t a n t i k a - d u k a ṃ).][1]

[1296, 1297] Which are the states that

(*a*) *partake of wisdom?* [2]

States which are the associates of wisdom.

(*b*) *partake of ignorance?* [3]

States which are the associates of ignorance.

[1298, 1299] Which are the states that have

(*a*) *the likeness of lightning?* [4]

Insight [5] into the three lowest of the Noble Paths.

---

[1] Buddhaghosa's exegesis is voluble over these pairs (Asl. 50–4, 497–518), but as to *why* they are incorporated here he is characteristically silent.

[2] V ī j j ā b h ā g i n o, i.e. "they (the d h a m m ā) partake (b h a j a n t i) of wisdom by way of association with it, they *versantur* (v a t t a n t i) as parts or divisions of wisdom" (Asl. 50). Of the eight modes of Buddhist v i j j ā, viz.: knowledge born of insight (v i p a s s a n ā ñ ā ṇ a ṃ), the potency (i d d h i) of the "mental image", and the six forms of intuition (a b h i ñ ñ ā)—the first only is here referred to (cf. D. i, p. 76 *et seq.*, and Childers, *s.vv.*). The reader will remember that v i j j ā is a term borrowed by Buddhist ethics from Brahmanic doctrine. Cf. the expression t i s s o v i j j ā, § 1366, (viii). It is equivalent to our "lore" and "wisdom" combined. Six states are in the Anguttara (iii, 334) said to be v i j j a - b h ā g i y ā.

[3] Ignorance respecting the Four Truths. Asl. 51.

[4] This and the following simile are gone into at some length (Asl. 388), as follows: Stage 1. The traveller sets out in the gloom. 2. He loses his way. 3. Lightning flashes out and illumines. 4. The road is made plain again. So to the "noble" disciple there is: (1) the inception of insight making for the first (second or third) Paths; (2) the obliteration of truth by darkness; (3) the glory of the Path is revealed; (4) the Four Truths are made plain. But in the thunderbolt of the might of Arahantship won we get the simile of (*a*) an all-penetrating power, (*b*) the mystery of its coming. Cf. that of the wind as applied to Regeneration, John iii, 8.

[5] P a ñ ñ ā, sometimes better rendered "wisdom". See § 16, and cf. n. 3.

(*b*) *the likeness of the thunderbolt?*

The science of the topmost Path, the Path of Arahantship.

[1300, 1301] Which are the states that are

(*a*) *foolish?* [1]

Unconscientiousness and disregard of blame. Besides, all bad states are foolish.

(*b*) *discreet?*

Conscientiousness and fear of blame. Besides, all good states are discreet.

[1302, 1303] Which are the states that are

(*a*) *dark?* [2]

Unconscientiousness and disregard of blame. Besides, all bad states are dark.

(*b*) *bright?*

Conscientiousness and fear of blame. Besides, all good states are bright.

[1304, 1305] Which are the states that

(*a*) *conduce to remorse?* [3]

Misconduct in act, word and thought. Besides, all bad states conduce to remorse.

(*b*) *do not conduce to remorse?*

Good conduct in act, word and thought. Besides, no good states conduce to remorse.

---

[1] Bālā, its opposite being paṇḍitā, which partakes of paññā. See § 16, where the substantival form, paṇḍiccaṃ, is rendered "erudition", and paraphrased (Asl. 147) as paṇḍitassa bhāvo, the state of a *wise* person, one who has discernment, discretion, one who has "chosen that good part" as contrasted with the "average sensual person" or foolish youth. With the answers cf. §§ 30, 31.

[2] On kaṇhā (or tamo) and sukkā (or joti), used with ethical significance, see M. i, 389; S. i, 93 f.; Dhp. 87; Mil. 200. (Cf. *Questions of King Milinda*, i, 284, n. 2.)

[3] Tapaniyā. Whereas we, in "remorse", bring into relief the "ayen*bite* of inwyt", the Buddhist term refers to the flush of heat when the deed ill done is realized as such.

[1306] Which are the states that are equivalent terms ? [1]

---

[1] This and the subjects of the two following questions are adhivacanā, nirutti and paññatti respectively. The three are said (Asl. 51) to "converge in meaning" (atthato ninnakaraṇā), though their form is diverse. In the phrase "An increaser of luck is an increaser of wealth" the terms are mutually delimitated. This is adhivacanaṃ. . . . In the phrase "They construct (or combine, abhisankharonti), brethren, and are therefore 'synergies' (sankhārā)", S. iii, 87, there is a statement, together with the cause, as in discourse (abhilāpā). . . . In the phrase "the application, disposing, superposing [of the mind]" (see above, § 7), something is set out on this wise or that; and this is paññatti.

It seems inferable from the foregoing that by adhivacanaṃ a simple equipollence of terms is to be effected. "Is" or "are", in translating, must be understood simply as =, and not as implying inclusion under a more general notion. The word occurs at every turn in the Cy., and has usually been rendered, in these footnotes, "equivalent to". Cf. a good instance in Jāt. i, 117; Div. 491.

The second example and the comment adumbrate what we mean by explanation. But in the absence of the context it is not easy to gather much respecting paññatti from the third passage cited. Coming to the answer common to all three questions, the Cy. instances as the things which are classed (sankhā), designated (samaññā), expressed, and current (vohāro), the names "I", "another", "a man", "cattle", "Tisso", "a bed", "a house", etc. *Name* is fourfold from the point of view of the grounds on which it is bestowed, viz. (1) given by general consent on a special occasion (sāmaññanāmaṃ), e.g. that of the first King Mahāsammato; (2) given because of a personal quality (guṇa-nāmaṃ), e.g. versed-in-the-Vinaya; (3) given because of a private wish or fancy (kittima-nāmaṃ), e.g. naming of an infant; (4) not given; of primeval origin; primordially fortuitous (opapātika-nāmaṃ), e.g. "moon", "earth", etc. See further § 1309, note, and cf. S. Z. Aung in Compendium, 4, 264.

Processes of nomenclature, etc. = adhivacanapathā, etc.

There is no being, no compound, concludes the Commentator, that is not somehow nameable. The very trees in desert and hill country will be named by country-folk. And if they admit to not knowing the name of any one kind, it will get the name of the

That which is an enumeration, that which is a designation, an expression, a current term, a name, a denomination, the assigning of a name, an interpretation, a distinctive mark of discourse on this or that state.

[1306*a*] All states are processes of equivalent nomenclature.

[1307] Which are the states that are explanations ?
Answer as in § 1306.
[1307*a*] All states are processes of explanation.

[1308] Which are the states that are expressions ?
Answer as in § 1306.
[1308*a*] All states are processes of expression.

In this connexion,
[1309] *What is name ?* [1]
The four skandhas and unconditioned element.

[1310] What is [material] form ?
The four great phenomena and the [material] form which is derived from them.[2]

" nameless ". Cf. our *os innominatum,* or the Pic Sans-nom, and the like.

" Distinctive mark " is v y a ñ j a n a ṃ .

[1] Here the Cy. makes use of its foregoing classification of name-kinds to show under which head to rank n ā m a when distinguished from r ū p a . N ā m a must, namely, be understood as o p a p ā t i k a - name, that is all its constituents must be understood. Feeling, e.g. when it arises, is not named on the grounds on which a new individual, or an " artificial kind " —table, etc.—might be named. " One has not to take a name for it, saying, ' Be thou called feeling ! ' The name has arisen together with it " (p. 392).

" Unconditioned element " is here spoken of again as Nirvana. Ibid. See above, § 583, n.

[2] Cf. § 584. The more concise form of question : t a t t h a k a t a m a ṃ . . . is now sustained till the end. Hitherto it has only been used to cross-question the student on the details of a given answer, on " name ", for instance, as part of the contents of the preceding answer. Hence the translation of t a t t h a by " in this connexion " (whatever the term in question may mean elsewhere). It is not clear, however, what is the force of t a t t h a

[1311] What is ignorance?

Answer as for "dullness", § 390 (*omitting* "on that occasion").[1]

[1312] What is the craving for rebirth?

Answer as for the "Fetter of the passion for rebirth", § 1120.

[1313] What is speculative opinion about rebirth?

Theories that both soul and world will come to be, etc.

[1314] What is speculative opinion about non-rebirth?

Theories that both soul and world will not come to be, etc.

[1315] What is the sort of speculation known as Eternalism?

That both soul and world are eternal, etc.

[1316] What is the sort of speculation known as Annihilation?

That both soul and world will be dissolved, etc.

[1317] What is the sort of speculation known as the Finite Theory . . . [1318] the Infinite Theory?

That both soul and world are finite . . . infinite, etc.

[1319] What is the sort of speculation known as the Theory of Origins . . . [1320] the Theory of the Hereafter?

Theories concerning the ultimate past . . . concerning futurity.

All this sort of opinion, walking in opinion, jungle of opinion, wilderness of opinion, disorder of opinion, scuffling of opinion, the Fetter of opinion, the grip and tenacity of it, the inclination towards it, the being infected by it, this by-path, wrong road, wrongness, this sectarianism, this

---

in these last fifty-seven questions, the greater part of the subjects not having occurred in the foregoing part of the manual.

[1] This pair of questions "is included to show" how the mass of views in the following pairs is "an upgrowth from the root of the Round of Rebirth". Asl. 392.

shiftiness of grasp—this is what is called speculative opinion about rebirth, and the rest.[1]

[1321] What is unconscientiousness ? . . . [1322] disregard of blame ?

Answers as for the ninth and tenth " bases of vice ", §§ 1238, 1239.

[1323] What is conscientiousness ?

The feeling of conscientiousness scruple when scruples ought to be felt, conscientious scruple at attaining to bad and evil states.

[1324] What is discretion ?

The sense of guilt where a sense of guilt ought to be felt, a sense of guilt at attaining to bad and evil states.[2]

[1325] What is contumacy ? [3]

The being surly, refractious, contumacious when that which is in accordance with the Norm has been said, contrariness, captiousness, want of regard, of consideration, of reverence, of deference.[4]

---

[1] This, the Diṭṭhi-formula (see §§ 381, 1099), is appended as well to each of the foregoing answers on speculative opinions. Of these, the first two (bhava and vibhava) are, in the Cy. (p. 392), connected with the next two respectively (cf. § 1099). All the eight are enumerated and discussed in the Brahmajāla Sutta. D. i, 13–40. The Cy. itself refers to this Sutta in connexion with the last two theories. See also *Dialogues of the Buddha*, i, 26, n. 3.

[2] See §§ 30, 31.

[3] Dovacassatā. For " surly " the Cy. (p. 393) and K. read dovacassāyaṃ.

[4] The first three terms in the answer are in the original simply different forms of the same abstract noun, viz.: dovacassāyaṃ, dovacassiyaṃ, dovacassatā. The fourth term is literally " taking the opposite side ". The fifth is literally " gratification in antagonism ". The last is described as due to a lack of the habit of placing others before one's self. Asl. 393. The term in question the Cy. finally dismisses with the remark that, if persisted in in the foregoing fashion, it involves

[1326] What is friendship with evil?

To follow after, to frequent the company of, and associate with [1] such persons as are unbelievers, immoral, uneducated, mean-spirited [2] and witless; [3] to resort to and consort with them, to be devoted to them, enthusiastic about them, [4] and entangled with them. [5]

[1327] What is suavity?

The being gentle, tractable, amenable [6] when that which is in accordance with the Norm has been said, the refraining from contradiction and from captiousness; the showing regard and consideration, [7] devotion and deference.

[1328] What is friendship with good?

To follow after, frequent the company of, and associate with, such persons as are believers, virtuous, well educated, generous and wise; to resort to and consort with them,

---

the four skandhas, especially that of syntheses. So for the complex generalizations in the following questions. They are not relatively simple states involving one skandha only. (The editing in the Cy. is here again very unfortunate.)

[1] Sevanā, nisevanā, saṃsevanā. The prefixes, according to the Cy., merely act as augmentatives.

[2] Maccharino; addicted to the five sorts of meanness. Asl. 394. See § 1122, note.

[3] Duppaññā.

[4] Bhajana, sambhajanā, bhatti, sambhatti; all meaning originally "forming a part of", "belonging to". But the two former are paraphrased by upasankamanā. In the sense of devotion bhatti (Sk. bhakti) does not, I believe, occur in the Nikāyas. Perhaps its oldest appearance with this import is in Jāt. v, 340—where the Cy. gives as equivalent sineho—and in the Svet. Upanishad 6, 23. But cf. Pss. of the Brethren, ver. 370, n. 4: bhattimā.

[5] Taṃ sampavaṇkatā (so K. and the Cy.), i.e. entanglement; lit. hooked along with them—with those persons, both in thought and deed. Asl. 394.

[6] Sovacassāyaṃ (*sic lege*), sovacassiyaṃ, sovacassatā.

[7] Ādariyaṃ, ādaratā; omitted in the text, but supplied in K. Cf. § 1325.

to be devoted to them, enthusiastic about them, mixed up with them.

[1329–32] What is skill in

(*a*) the Offences?
(*b*) restoration from the Offences?
(*c*) the Attainments?
(*d*) recovery from the Attainments?

That skill which is insight, understanding, search, research, etc.,[1] when applied to

(*a*) the Offences termed the Five Groups of Offences and the Seven Groups of Offences;[2]
(*b*) restoration from [the effects of] those Offences;[3]
(*c*) a case of Attainment[4] with applied and sustained

---

[1] The passage elided here and in the following sections is no doubt that in which insight (paññā) is described, § 16 and *passim*. On "skill" or "proficiency" (kusalatā), see Introduction viii, on "good".

[2] That is the group of "Āpatti's termed Pārājika, Sanghādisesa, Pācittiya, Pāṭidesanīya and Dukkaṭa offences, and the group which, besides these, includes Thullaccaya and Dubbhāsita offences. Asl. 394; cf. Vin. v, 91. The scientific procedure is described in the Cy. as insight into knowledge of their (respective) limits and of the ground (of the offence).

[3] Āpatti-vuṭṭhāna, or rising up from an offence. Buddhaghosa does not in this connexion explain the term, but in his Cy. on the passage, found in nearly identical words at Vin. iii, 112, and iv, 225 (which Cy. is found in Minayeff, Pāt. 69), he uses vuṭṭhāna as a general term covering all the three methods (parivāsa, mānatta, abbhāṇa) of expiation of, and release from, an offence committed by a member of the Order. Cf. Childers, *s.v.* sanghādiseso; Vin. v, 118. See also *infra*, § 1332.

[4] The Samāpattis, or various stages of self-concentration, include the Jhānas—as here—and other forms of samādhi, all pre-Buddhistic and all utilized in the body of Buddhist doctrine and culture. It is noteworthy that they are not here referred to as only eight in number—see Childers, *s.v.* (for that matter, neither do they find a place in the Aṭṭhaka-nipāta of the Anguttara). Neither is it clear that the three Samāpattis

thought, a case of Attainment with only sustained thought, a case of Attainment without either mode of thought;

(*d*) recovery from those Attainments.[1]

[1333] What is proficiency in the Elements?[2]

That proficiency which is insight, understanding, search, research, etc., when applied to the eighteen elements, viz.: sight, visible shape and visual cognition, hearing, sound and auditory cognition, smell, odour and olfactory cognition, taste, sapid object and gustatory cognition, body-sensibility, the tangible and tactile cognition, mind, mental object and representative cognition.

[1334] What is proficiency in attention?[3]

That proficiency in attention which is insight, understanding, etc., when applied to those elements.

---

quoted in the answer coincide in all respects with the first three stages of *five*-fold Jhāna. If they do, and if we are to assume that the term includes more than those three stages, then, by Subhūti's inclusion of four Vimokhas, this would give us *nine* samāpattis. Again, in M. i, 301, a *fifth* Vimokha—the last—is spoken of as a Samāpatti, this bringing the number up to ten, viz. fivefold rūpajhāna, the four Āruppas, and trance. Cf. M. i, 398–400.

[1] The kind of ability in emerging from (lit. rising out of -vuṭṭhāṇa; see *supra*, § 1330) one or another kind of samādhi is, by the Cy., specified as a predetermination of the time when the subject wished to arouse himself, and the carrying out of this act of will—a time stated in terms of the motions of celestial bodies. "When the moon, sun, constellations have gone to such and such a position, I shall awake." See, on this use of vuṭṭhāna, M. i, 302; A. iii, 311; S. iii, 270. On the modes of Jhāna here specified, see *supra*, § 160 *et seq.* Skill in the Attainment (samāpatti) itself is explained as the science of effecting discernment of the appanā or ecstatic concept (in Jhāna), as well as of the parikamma or preliminaries.

[2] Dhātuyo. The skill in this case is said to comprise acquisition, attention, hearing and remembering (instruction being entirely oral) and discrimination. Asl. 395.

[3] See p. 4, n. 2.

[1335] What is skill in the sphere [of sense]? [1]

That skill which is insight, understanding, etc., when applied to the twelve spheres, namely, sight and visible shape, hearing and sound, smell and odorous object, taste and sapid object, body-sensibility and the tangible, mind and mental object.[2]

[1336] What is skill in the causal law?

Insight, understanding, etc., when applied to the formula: "Karma comes to pass because of ignorance; consciousness comes to pass because of karma; name and shape come to pass because of consciousness; the sixfold sphere comes to pass because of name and shape; contact comes to pass because of the sixfold sphere, feeling because of contact, craving because of feeling, grasping because of craving, rebirth because of grasping, birth because of rebirth, old age and death, grief, lamentation, distress, sorrow and despair come to pass because of birth. Such is the uprising of this whole mass of Ill." [3]

[1337, 1338] What is skill in affirming . . . in negating [causal relation]?

Insight, understanding, etc., when applied to discerning that, in a given relation, certain states are . . . are not, the cause, the condition of certain other states.[4]

---

[1] See § 597 *et seq.*

[2] In the last three modes of ability six factors common to all are distinguished: acquisition, attention, hearing, comparison (lit. measuring), penetration, contemplation. Of these, all but the fifth are exercised on mundane objects of thought; penetration is concerned with supramundane matters; attention and comparison can be exercised about a mixture of both spheres of thought. Asl. 395. (To get this or any meaning out of the passage in question some emendation of the Cy. as edited has been necessary.)

[3] On this famous formula the Cy. merely remarks that "it will appear in the Vibhanga on the Paṭiccasamuppāda". Asl. 395. Cf. Cy. on the Vibhanga (PTS., 1923) and *Kindred Sayings*, ii (1922): "The Book on Cause."

[4] This species of skill (ṭhāṇakusalatā, aṭṭhāṇakusalatā) constituted one of the Ten Powers of the Buddha.

[1339] What is upright?

Uprightness, without deflexion, twist, crookedness.

[1340] What is soft?

That which is plasticity, gentleness, smoothness, pliancy, lowliness of heart.[1]

[1341] What is patience?

That patience which is long-suffering, compliance, absence of rudeness and abruptness, complacency of heart.[2]

[1342] What is loveableness? [3]

That which is the absence of excess in deed, in word, and in deed and word together.

Besides, all moral self-restraint is lovely.

[1343] What is amity? [4]

See M. i, 69. The Cy. (p. 395) takes for illustration sense-cognition as a series of specific results from specific processes; also cause and effect in the vegetable kingdom. It is of interest to note that hetū and paccayā are still used here in apposition, without being differentiated, just as they are in the Suttas. In the last Abhidhamma book (Paṭṭhāna) we see the differentiation.

[1] Ajjavo and maddavo, the terms in this and the foregoing question, are synonymous with uj(j)ukatā and mudutā, §§ 50, 51, 44, 45. The one additional term—the last—is paraphrased as "absence of conceit". Asl. 395. Cf. D. iii, 213 f.; A. i, 94 f. (in slightly different order).

[2] Patience (khantī) is one of the ten Pāramitās. Jāt. i, pp. 22, 23. See also A. iii, 254, 255. The last three synonyms are the opposites of the last three synonyms of "hate". See *supra*, §§ 418, 1060. Ajjavo, javano, maddavo, khantī, and soraccaṃ are, in A. iii, 248, given as the dhammā of a thoroughbred horse.

[3] Soraccaṃ, defined as "to be well on the hither side of wickedness", to avoid transgression in the three kinds in deed, in the four kinds in speech, and in one's mode of livelihood. See Rhys Davids, *Manual of Buddhism*, p. 142. The three transgressions of the mind are omitted, hence soraccaṃ applies apparently only to the self-expression of the individual. Asl. 396. On the word cf. *Kindred Sayings*, i, 217, n.*

[4] Sākhalyaṃ, paraphrased by sammodaka and mudu. Ibid. Cf. the usual formula for the exchange of courtesies on greeting, e.g. M. i, 16.

When all such speech as is insolent,[1] disagreeable, scabrous, harsh to others, vituperative to others, bordering upon anger, not conducive to concentration, is put away, and when all such speech as in innocuous,[2] pleasant to the ear,[3] affectionate, such as goes to the heart, is urbane,[4] sweet and acceptable to people generally—when speech of this sort is spoken—polished, friendly and gentle language—this is what is called amity.

[1344] What is courtesy ?

The two forms of courtesy : hospitality towards bodily needs and considerateness in matters of doctrine. When anyone shows courtesy it is in one or other of these two forms.[5]

---

[1] Aṇḍakā. This and the following terms occur in M. i, 286. See Morris's Notes, JPTS., 1884, 1886, 1889. Buddhaghosa's comment obviates the necessity either for Kern's hypothesis that the word, when applied to speech, should be read as kaṇḍaka, or for that of Morris, that it should be read as caṇḍaka. He says (Asl. 396) : Just as in a defective (sadose) tree bosses (aṇḍakāni : excrescences, warts) protrude, so through faultiness, by words of bragging and insolence, are swellings (aṇḍakā) produced.

"Disagreeable" (asātā) is omitted in M. i, 286. "Scabrous" = kakkasā = (Asl. ibid.) pūtikā. By a somewhat forced figure, such speech is compared to the disagreeable sensation in the ear (sotaṃ not kaṇṇā !) by the entrance of the crumbling pulverous tissue of a rotten tree. "Vituperative," etc. (parābhisajjanī) : as it were, a lurking branch of barbed thorns wounding the limbs and obstructing passage. Ibid.

[2] Innocuous = neḷā = niddosā. Asl. 397.

[3] i.e. by varied sweetness.

[4] Porī, i.e. town-conversation, either because it is full of good points (guṇa), or used by persons of breeding, or simply urban. For town-dwellers use fitting terms, calling a fatherly man father, and a brotherly man brother. Ibid.

[5] Paṭisanthāro, both āmisena and dhammena, is discussed at length by Buddhaghosa (Asl. 397–9). He takes, as usual, the etymology of the term—a spreading out or diffusion—and shows it as a covering or closing, through kindness and generosity, of the gap there may be between the having

[1345] What is it to have the door of the faculties unguarded?[1]

When a certain individual[2] sees an object with the eye[3] he is entranced with the general appearance, or in the details of it.[4] He does not set himself to restrain that which might give occasion for wicked states, covetous, dejected, to flow in over him, were he to dwell unrestrained as to the sense of sight. He keeps no watch over his faculty of sight, nor does he attain to mastery over it. And so in like manner when he hears a sound with the ear . . . smells an odour with the nose . . . tastes a sapid with the tongue . . . feels a tangible with the body . . . recognizes a mental object with the mind,

---

of the giver and the recipient of his attentions. Both are supposed to be members of the Order, and many of the hospitable and polite ministrations described occur in Vin. ii, 210, 211. See also Mil. 409.

[1] Aguttadvāratā. This and the contrary attitude in § 1347 constitute an important formula in Buddhist doctrine, and occur in D. i, 70; M. i, 180, 269, etc. It is also quoted KV. 426, 464.

[2] K. omits puggalo, given in the printed text. The latter omits it in the corresponding answer, § 1347.

[3] This is a passage naturally calling for psychological qualification from the Commentator (Asl. 399, 400). "'Eye' stands here for the total efficient cause (kāraṇa-vasena), namely, for that visual cognition which is the generally accepted shape- (or colour) seeing capacity. As the Ancients have said: The eye does not see shape, not being of the nature of mind (cittaṃ); the mind, not being of the nature of eye, does not see shape (the Cy. has here been wrongly punctuated). One sees with the sense-embodied mind impingeing on the "door-object" (dvārārammaṇe saṃghaṭṭanena pasādavatthukena cittena passati), that is, with the aggregate organism, or apparatus, as when we say, 'he shoots with the bow.'"

[4] On nimittagāhī and anuvyañjanagāhi, see notes relating precisely to this passage in D. i, 70; in *Dialogues of the Buddha*, i, 80. The former term is, in the Atthasālinī, defined as the act of one who, not content with simply beholding what is attractive and so forth, or what is characteristically female or male, grasps at it with passionate desire.

he is entranced with the general appearance and in the details of it. He does not set himself to restrain that which might give occasion for wicked states, covetous, dejected, to flow in over him, were he to dwell unrestrained as to the mental faculty. He keeps no watch over the mental faculty, nor does he attain to mastery over it. That these six faculties should be thus unguarded, untended, unwatched over, unrestrained, is what is called having the door of the faculties unguarded.

[1346] What is immoderation in diet ? [1]

When anyone, through carelessness and without judgment, takes food [2] for purposes of sport,[3] sensual excess, personal charm and adornment, his insatiableness, immoderation, and want of judgment are what is called immoderation in diet.

[1347] What is it to have the doors of the faculties guarded ?

When a certain individual sees an object with the eye he is not entranced with the general appearance or the details of it. He sets himself to restrain that which might give occasion for wicked states, covetous, dejected, to flow in over him, were he to dwell unrestrained as to the sense of sight. He keeps watch over this faculty of sight, and attains to mastery over it. And so, in like manner, when he hears a sound with the ear . . . smells an odour with the nose . . . tastes a sapid with the tongue . . . feels a tangible with the body . . . recognizes an idea with the mind, he is not entranced with the general appearance and the details of it. He sets himself to restrain that which might give occasion for wicked states, covetous, dejected, to flow in over him, were he to dwell

---

[1] Bhojane amattaññutā = a sustained indulging without reflection . . . the ignoring of measure or bounds therein. Asl. 402.

[2] Ahāraṃ, " both edible and potable." Asl. 401.

[3] Davāya, etc. That is to say, that he may be able to dance or do acrobatic feats, etc. Or like kings and courtiers who feed to swell their " pride of life " and manhood, etc. Asl. 402, 403.

unrestrained as to the mental faculty. He keeps watch over the mental faculty, and attains to mastery over it. That these six faculties should be thus guarded, tended, watched over, restrained, is what is called having the doors of the faculties guarded.

[1348] What is moderation in diet?

When anyone takes food with reflection and judgment, not for purposes of sport, excess, personal charm and attractions, but so as to suffice for the sustenance and preservation of the body, for allaying the pangs [of hunger] [1] and for aiding the practice of the higher life,[2] and thinking the while, " I shall subdue that which I have been feeling and shall cause no new feeling to arise,[3] and maintenance shall be mine, blamelessness also and comfort "—this content, moderation, judgment in diet is what is called moderation in diet.

[1349] What is forgetfulness? [4]

---

[1] Vihiṃsūparatiyā. Vihiṃsā = abhutta-paccayā uppajjanaka-khudā. Asl. 403.

[2] Brahmacariyānuggahāya.

[3] This formula (as Trenckner terms it, *Pali Misc.*, 74) of abstemious living occurs M. i, 355; S. iv, 104, 176, etc.; also Mil. 367. The comments in the Asl. reveal a more specific and less sublime interpretation of the vedanā in question than is taken by the translator of the last-named passage (Rhys Davids, *Questions of King Milinda*, ii, 231). According to the former, purāṇañ ca vedanaṃ is simply that due to one's not having dined, and navañ ca vedanaṃ to one's having dined too much, or to one's having dined. Asl. 403, 404. Psychologically, then, the ideal state of one relieved of the craving of appetite would seem to be, not the positive sensations of surfeit or of having well dined, but the relatively negative state of not-hungry, not-thirsty. Under " comfort " (phāsu-vihāro = bhojānisaṃso) gourmands, who fail to acquire the same, are described, with some gusto, under five current sobriquets—" Hold, waistcoat! " " Gyrator " (because unable to rise after eating), etc. Abstemious procedure is also categorized otherwise and in detail. Asl. 404.

[4] In this answer (describing muṭṭhasaccaṃ) the text requires some emendation. Anussati should be asati, and the privative *a* should, of course, be dropped in apilāpanatā, a-sammussanatā. K. reads (here

Unmindfulness, lapse of memory, non-recollection, non-remembrance, not bearing in mind, superficiality, oblivion.

[1350] What is lack of intelligence?

Answer as for " ignorance " *or* " dullness ", § 1311, etc.

[1351] What is mindfulness?

Answer as in § 14, *omitting* " on that occasion ".[1]

[1352] What is intelligence?

Answer as for " insight ", § 16. *And see* § 53.

[1353] What is the power [called] computation? [2]

Answer as for " insight ", § 16.

[1354] What is the power [called] cultivation?

That which is the pursuing, the cultivating, the multiplying of good states.

Moreover, the seven factors of Enlightenment [3] are the power of cultivation.

[1355] What is calm?

Answer as for " quiet ", §§ 11, 54.[4]

[1356] What is intuition? [5]

Answer as for " insight ", §§ 55, 16.

---

only) pamussanatā—not so the Cy.—and repeats asati after appaṭissati. See § 14 and footnote.

[1] K. reads for asammussanatā, appamussanatā. Cf. preceding note.

[2] Paṭisankhānabalaṃ. This is not included in any set of " powers " enumerated in the present work (cf. § 1, etc.), nor does it form part of paññābalaṃ (§ 29). However, it is included in the eight very different kinds of powers given in A. iv, 223, ranking as the specific balaṃ of the erudite or bahussuto. Cf. the use of paṭisankhā in Vin. i, 213. In the present connexion it seems, as a correlative term, to have superseded dassanaṃ (insight); see above, §§ 1002–12, 1251–67. Buddhaghosa's brief comment here is regrettably unenlightening. To what extent in *his* little world did the word stand for theory as compared with normative science, with philosophy, with Sānkhya?

[3] See §§ 285, 287, etc.

[4] In this and the following references the phrase " on that occasion " must be understood to be omitted.

[5] Vipassanā: the seeing things in various ways as impermanent, etc. Asl. 53.

[1357] What is "the mark of calm"? [1]

Answer as for "quiet", § 1357.

[1358] What is "the mark of grasp"?

Answer as for "grasp" *and* "energy", §§ 56, 13.

[1359] What is grasp?

Answer as for "the mark of grasp", § 1358.

[1360] What is balance?

Answer as for "balance", § 57.

[1361] What is moral failure? [2]

Excess in deed, excess in word, excess in both together. Moreover, all immorality is moral failure.

[1362] What is theoretic fallacy? [3]

"There is no such thing as alms, or sacrifice, or offering; there is neither fruit, nor result of good or evil deeds; there is no such thing as this world or the next; there is no such thing as mother, or father, or beings springing into birth without them; there are in the world no recluses or brahmins who have reached the highest point, who have attained the height, who, having understood and realized by themselves alone both this world and the next, make known the same"—all this sort of speculation . . . this is what is called theoretic fallacy. Moreover, all wrong views are theoretic fallacies.

[1363] What is moral achievement?

Absence of excess in deed, in word, and in deed and word together." [4]

[1364] What is achievement in view?

"There is such a thing as alms, sacrifice, and offering; . . . fruit, and the result of good and evil deeds; . . . this world and the next; mother, father, and beings springing into birth without them; . . . recluses and brahmins who have reached the highest, who have attained the height,

---

[1] Samatha-nimittaṃ.
[2] Sīlavipatti. Cf. §§ 1363, 1342.
[3] Diṭṭhivipatti. Cf. § 1215.
[4] Sīla-sampadā. Cf. § 1342.

who having understood and realized by themselves alone both this world and the other world, make known the same" —all this sort of science, understanding, etc.[1] . . . this is what is called progress in theory. Moreover, all best views are achievement in view.

[1365] What is purity in morals?

Absence of excess in deed, in word, and in deed and word together.[2]

[1366] What is purity in view?

Knowledge of the specific nature of Karma;[3] knowledge of the Truths in their due order; the knowledge of him who holds the Path; the knowledge of him who holds the Fruit of the Path.

(i)[4] The phrase "Now purity of view" is equivalent to

---

[1] Continue as in § 16.

[2] Cf. § 1363. Purity in view would seem to indicate perfection relative to achievement in view, while in moral matters a similar distinction does not apparently hold. The Cy. only explains this want of distinction by saying that in § 1363 the s ī l a of restraint of the Pātimokkha is alluded to, while in § 1365 v i s u d d h i - s ī l a is spoken of.

[3] K. reads here k a m m a s s a k a t a ṃ ñ ā ṇ a ṃ. Cf. the karma formula, M. iii, 203. Buddhaghosa, to judge by his exposition, reads k a m m a - s s a k a t a - ñ ā ṇ a ṃ (Asl. 406, 407) or - s s a k a t ā -, or - s s a k a t a ṃ ñ ā n a ṃ (Asl. 406). The corresponding adjective to this s a k a t ā or s a k a t a ṃ occurs in the passage quoted from the Sutta Piṭaka by Nāgasena (Mil. i, 45; cf. Rhys Davids' trans., i, 101, n. 1; also Asl. 66), namely, k a m m a s s a k ā (s a t t ā); i.e. according to the translator's view, "having each his own karma." On Buddhaghosa's curious statement that bad karma is not "one's own" (s a k a ṃ), see Asl. 406.

[4] With the foregoing question and answer the catechism proper of the "Dhamma Sangaṇi" comes to an end. There follow eleven sundry phrases or terms, not made the subject of any part of the catechism, and appended here in the phraseology of a commentary. They are severally either referred to some reply in the catechism, or briefly expounded, and are all culled from the Sutta Piṭaka as technicisms of Buddhist ethics. Buddhaghosa has nothing very enlightening on this fraction of ancient com-

that insight, understanding . . . right theory (views) [*described above*, § 16].

(ii) In the phrase " And as the struggle of him who holds certain views ",[1] " struggle " means that inception of energy etc. [*described above*, § 13].

(iii) The phrase " agitation " implies dread of birth, dread of old age, dread of sickness, dread of death.

(iv) The phrase " occasion of agitation " means birth, old age, sickness, death.

(v) The phrase " And the earnest struggle of him who is agitated " refers to [the four Right Struggles] :—When a bhikkhu brings forth the desire (*a*) that bad and wicked states which have not arisen should not arise, (*b*) that bad and wicked states which have arisen should be put away, (*c*) that good states which have not arisen should arise, (*d*) that good states which have arisen should stand firm, should not get confused, should be frequently practised, made to abound, cultivated, and perfected—then he uses endeavour, sets energy a-going, reaches forward in thought and struggles.[2]

(vi) The phrase " And discontent in good states " means the longing for higher achievement in one who is dissatisfied over the cultivation of good states.[3]

---

mentary included in the text, but promises an explanation of at least the division of the subject of " agitation " in the Commentary on the " Vibhanga ".

[1] Yathā diṭṭhissa ca padhānaṃ. It is just possible one should read Yathādiṭṭhissa; K., however, divides the two words. The Cy. merely remarks that the energy put forth is intelligent or scientific, and can be applied either to worldly or to higher things.

[2] See A. ii, 15, 16, 74. It will be seen that the four modes of will-culture described on p. 15 of A. ii, as the Sammappadhānāni (and quoted in the Dh. S.) are, on p. 74, termed respectively the Struggles for Self-control, for Renunciation, for Cultivation (or Development), and for Preservation. Yet on p. 16 a different connotation is given to each of these four terms.

[3] This and the next phrase (vii) occur consecutively in A. i, 50. The progress of sublime discontent in a pious individual

(vii) The phrase "And the not shrinking back in the struggle" means the thorough and persevering and unresting performance, the absence of stagnation, the unfaltering volition, the unflinching endurance,[1] the assiduous pursuit, exercise and repetition which attend the cultivation of good states.

(viii) The phrase "Wisdom" means the threefold wisdom, namely, (*a*) reminiscent knowledge of one's former births, (*b*) knowledge of the decease and renascence of beings, (*c*) the knowledge that makes an end of the Intoxicants.

(ix) The phrase "Emancipation" means the twofold emancipation, namely, (*a*) freedom of thought,[2] and (*b*) Nirvana.[3]

(x) The phrase "knowledge in making an end" means the knowledge he has who holds the Path.

(xi) The phrase "knowledge in origins" means the knowledge he has who holds the Fruit of the Path.

End of the Division entitled "The Deposition".

---

from giving small donations to the Order, then greater gifts, till he personally enters the Order and finally wins the goal of Arahantship, is briefly described, Asl. 407. The last attainment gives the winner the title of the Greatly Content.

[1] Cf. § 13.

[2] Cittassa adhimutti = vimutti (emancipation). D. i, 174.

[3] This is, I believe, the only passage in the original Manual where the word occurs. This is interesting in view of the fact that it occurs in what appears to be an appendix of original Commentary, and also that the term occurs so frequently in the old digest which follows in the text. See Appendix I. The Asl. remarks: "Nibbāna is freedom, because of the utter release from the kilesa's (the lower nature)," and gives the usual scholastic derivation: The gone-away (*niggataṃ*) jungle (*vānaṃ*), or, from that jungle.

APPENDIX I.

The Digest, or Condensed Paraphrase of Book III. (§§ 981–1295), entitled Division of Exposition, or the Elucidation (a t t h u d d h ā r o).

Immediately following the text of the Dhammasangaṇi itself is a supplement of some 230 questions and answers. The questions are verbatim those of the "Deposition" Division, or Book III., taken in order, but without the cross-questioning on the details of the various lists of ethical factors or defects, such as the varieties of cause (h e t u), or of the "Āsavas", etc. The answers are for the most part more tersely worded than those in Book III., and couched in language more or less different, including several terms that came into technical use after the earliest stage of Abhidhamma.

No distinctive title is assigned to this supplement in the Manual itself. It is probable that the final announcement "D h a m m a - s a n g a ṇ i - p p a k a r a ṇ i s a m a t t ā," refers, not to it, but to the entire work. In the "Atthasālinī", however (p. 409 *et seq.*), this section is pronounced to be commentary, not text, and is termed the A ṭ ṭ h a k a t h ā - k a ṇ ḍ a ṃ, or commentarial division; and in an earlier passage it was termed the fourth part (V i b h a t t i), comprising the a t t h u d d h ā r o (Asl. 6). The tradition, with characteristic myopia, dumps the work on Sāriputta: it was compiled by him with the object of making clearer the contents of the "N i k k h e p a - k a ṇ ḍ a ṃ" (Book III., i.e. virtually the whole Manual) to a pupil who could not otherwise understand it.

This being so, and the answers throwing no new light on to the subjects discussed, I have not thought it worth while to translate them. At the same time, it seemed advisable to sort out the specific, if not the individual, differences in diction, so that the reader may lose nothing that may prove of any value for the history either of the terms or of the concepts of Buddhism. I have also given translations of a few answers where the very difference in the terms used to obtain a virtually equivalent statement may prove helpful towards understanding the language of the Manual itself.

In respect of Pāli terms used, when there is need of referring collectively to the three modes, or worlds of all rebirth, as well as to that higher life of saintly aspiration which is not concerned with rebirth, these four are no longer distinctively spoken of as the avacaraṃ of this or that and the Unincluded, but are simply classed together as "the four bhūmis", the term used in the Paṭisambhidā (i, 83).

Again, "Nirvana" (nibbānaṃ) invariably replaces the term "unconditioned element". See Appendix II.

"Form" replaces "all form" (see § 983 *passim*), and "fruits of the life of the recluse" the word "fruits of the Paths". (See § 992 *passim.*[1]) The latter variation occurs but once in the Manual itself, viz., at § 1016.[2]

Frequent allusion is now made to those "types" of good and bad thoughts distinguished and analyzed by Book I. They are spoken of, not as cittāni, but as cittuppādā, or uprisings of consciousness, a term occurring only once in the Manual, viz., as a title. (See above, p. 164.)

The skandhas, so frequently adduced in Book III., are *never mentioned* (cf. Compendium ? 12th century, where citta-cetasikā replaces them).

The term "with Āsavas" (sāsavo) is no longer used except in the analysis of the Āsava Group.

The very frequent use of the ablative in -to (when the Manual would use a substantival adjective—for instance, kāmāvacara-kusalato instead of kāmāvacaraṃ kusalaṃ—betrays the later (commentarial) idiom.

---

[1] By an error, presumably in the MSS., the printed text has, in § 1597, jhānabalāni for sāmaññaphalāni. Cf. K.

[2] Printed above by an error as [1015].

The Manual itself uses this ablative, I believe, but twice, viz., in §§ 1062, 1071 : v i p ā k a t o = as, or by way of, result.

The term k i r i y ā, so seldom used in the Manual or in the Suttas, is now used extremely often.

* * * *

Taking now the three questions respecting (*a*) good, (*b*) bad, and (*c*) indeterminate states, with which Book III. (§§ 981–3, and for that matter the Manual itself) opens, we read the following concise replies, taken in order :—

" (*a*) Good in the four planes (b h u m m ī s u).
(*b*) The twelve uprisings of bad consciousness.
(*c*) Result in the four planes ; inoperative indeterminates [1] in the three planes ; [2] [material] form also and Nirvana."

Now, on referring to the analysis of the twelve Types of bad states (Book I., Part I., ch. ii), it will be seen that these cover the whole question, inasmuch as only one " plane "—that of sensuous existence—is involved. Good and indeterminate dhammas, on the other hand, involve all four planes, and cannot be answered simply in terms of the eight types of good consciousness (ch. i) in the one case, nor of genesis of consciousness in the other.

* * * *

The next triad of questions (§§ 1371 ff. ; cf. Book III., §§ 984–6) is answered in language which occurs at only one other passage in the whole work (§ 1268 *et seq.*), and which is of a vagueness that makes any equivalent rendering welcome.

" States associated with easeful feeling " :—

" The four uprisings of consciousness accompanied by gladness, which belong to good (karma) in the sensuous universe. The four, which belong to bad (karma). The six, which belong to the results of good (karma) in the sensuous universe,

---

[1] K i r i y ā v y ā k a t a ṃ . See Book I, Part II, ch. ii.
[2] i.e. excluding that of sense (see Book I, Part III, ch. ii).

as well as the five belonging to inoperative consciousness.[1] The threefold and fourfold[2] Jhāna relating to the worlds of Form whether it arise as good (karma), result (of good karma), or as a completed state. The threefold and fourfold Jhāna relating to the Higher Ideal, whether it arise as good (karma) or as result. The easeful feeling herewith arisen is not reckoned in."

"States associated with distressful feeling":—

"The two uprisings of consciousness which are accompanied by sorrow. Cognition of body, which is accompanied by distress. The distressful feeling herewith arisen is not reckoned in."

"States associated with neutral feeling":—

"The four uprisings of consciousness accompanied by indifference, which belong to good (karma) in the sensuous universe. The six, which belong to bad (karma). The ten which belong to the results of good (karma) in the sensuous universe.[3] The six, which belong to the results of bad (karma).[4] The six, which belong to inoperative consciousness.[5] The fourth Jhāna, relating to the worlds of Form, whether it arise as good (karma), result (of good karma), or as a completed state. The four Jhānas connected with Formless Existence,[6] whether they arise as good (karma), result (of good karma), or as completed states. The Fourth Jhāna relating to the Higher Ideal, whether it arise as good (karma), or as result (of good karma). The neutral feeling herewith arisen is not reckoned in.

"It is not proper to say that these three modes of feeling

---

[1] K. reads k ā m ā v a c a r a - k u s a l a s s a v i p ā k a t o c a k i r i y a t o c a p a ñ c a. But reference to §§ 469 and 568 shows that the analysis gives six and five respectively.

[2] Excluding the highest Jhāna, as transcending with "easeful feeling".

[3] Read k ā m ā v a c a r a - k u s a l a s s a.

[4] Four in § 556, one in § 562, one in § 564.

[5] Five in § 566, one in § 574.

[6] For a r ū p ā v a c a r ā read ā r u p p ā. Cf. p. 65 *et seq.*

are associated either with themselves, or with [material] form, or with Nirvana."

*   *   *   *

In §§ 1390 ff. the answers to questions §§ 1007–12 are (with the exception of that to 1009) more precise than those there given :—

"States which may be put away by insight" :—

"The four uprisings of consciousness which are associated with views and opinions, the uprising of consciousness which is accompanied by perplexity."

"States which may be put away by culture [1007]" :—

"The uprising of consciousness which is accompanied by distraction.

"The four uprisings of consciousness which are accompanied by greed, but disconnected with views and opinions, also the two uprisings of consciousness which are accompanied by sorrow: these states may be put away either by insight or by culture."

"States which may be put away neither by insight nor by culture" :—

"Good in the four planes; result in the four planes; inoperative indeterminates in three planes; [material] form also, and Nirvana."

States the root-conditions of which may be put away by insight, by culture, or by neither are described in the same terms. M o h o (dullness), however, when accompanied by distraction, can be put away by neither.

*   *   *   *

Questions 1022–4 are answered (§§ 1406–8) in quite other terms than those there used :—

(*a*) "States having limited objects of thought" :—

"All result of sensuous existence; ideation that is inoperative; representative cognition that is inoperative and having root-conditions,[1] and is accompanied by gladness."

---

[1] K i r i y ā - h e t u k ā m a n o v i ñ ñ ā ṇ a d h ā t u.

(*b*) " States having objects of thought of wider scope " :—

" The sphere of infinite consciousness ; the sphere where there is neither perception nor non-perception." (*Cf.* §§ 267, 268).

(*c*) " States having infinite objects of thought " :—

" The four Paths that are the Unincluded, and the four Fruits of the life of the recluse."

" The four uprisings of consciousness which are disconnected with knowledge and belong to good (karma) in the universe of Sense, also the four uprisings of consciousness disconnected with knowledge which are inoperative, and all bad (karma) : these states may be (*a*) or (*b*), but not (*c*), and may not be termed both (*a*) and (*b*).

" [Again] the four uprisings of consciousness which are associated with knowledge and belong to good (karma) in the universe of Sense, the four uprisings of inoperative consciousness which are associated with knowledge, the Fourth Jhāna relating to the universe of Form, whether it arise as good (karma), or as inoperative consciousness, and the representative cognition which is inoperative and free from root-conditions and is accompanied by indifference : these states may be (*a*), or (*b*), or (*c*), but it is not proper to call them (*a*) and (*b*) and (*c*).

" [Lastly] the threefold and fourfold Jhāna relating to the worlds of Form, whether it arise as good (karma), or as result, or as inoperative consciousness, the results of Fourth Jhāna, and the two first Jhānas connected with Formless existence, viz., the spheres of Infinite Space and of Infinite Nothingness : these states it is not proper to call (*a*) and (*b*) and (*c*).

"[Material] form and Nirvana are without objects of thought."

* * * *

One more group deserves quoting as giving answers not in terms of the subject inquired into. This is the two triads corresponding to §§ 1044–9. The commentarial chapter has the following :—

" The questions which are the states that are personal . . . external . . . personal-external seem to have fallen out, and we get instead a collective answer only :—

" With the exception of form which is not bound up with faculties,[1] and Nirvana, all states may be personal or external or personal-external. [Material] form which is not bound up with faculties, and Nirvana, are both external."

" States which have

(*a*) a personal object of thought,

(*b*) an external object of thought,

(*c*) a personal-external object of thought " :—

" (*a*) The sphere of infinite consciousness and the sphere where there is neither perception nor non-perception.

" (*b*) The threefold and fourfold Jhāna relating to the heavens of Form, whether it arise as good (karma), as result (of good karma), or as completed thought, also results of Fourth Jhāna, the sphere of infinite space, the four Paths that are the Unincluded and the four Fruits of the life of the recluse: these states have an external object of thought.

" Excepting form, states, good, bad and indeterminate relating to the sensuous universe, and the Fourth Jhāna relating to the worlds of Form, whether it arise as good

---

[1] Read, for M a n i n d r i y a ṃ , A n i n d r i y a - b a d d h a - r ū p a ñ c a . By an oversight this sentence and the next are printed in the text as if belonging to the previous triad. The import of the two sentences is probably simpler than it seems. It appears from Buddhaghosa's comment (*Expositor*, 533) that we must supply " one's own " before faculties. Those of another person are external to us.

(karma), or as completed thought: all these may be either (*a*), (*b*), or (*c*).

" But it is not proper to say that the sphere of nothingness is all three.

" Form and Nirvana are without objects of thought."

There is here a point of additional interest.

The second and fourth Āruppajjhānas are shown to have been conceived as exercises of pure introspection, and to be devoid of any implications of a World-Reason, or a macrocosmic Perception, let alone any of the " rapt soul " being caught up to other spheres.

APPENDIX II.

On that which is predicted about Unconditioned Element (asankhatā dhātu) in the Dhamma Sangaṇi.

Unconditioned Element is classed as the fourth and last species of the morally Indeterminate (avyākataṃ)—in other words, of that conduct or state of mind which is not productive of good or bad karma. But it alone, of those four, does not receive separate and systematic discussion, as is the case with the other three—Result, Inoperative Consciousness, and [Material] Form. The following predicates are elicited incidentally in the course of Book III., which discusses what may be called Applied Ethics. Again, whereas the word Nirvana (nibbānaṃ) is always substituted for asankhatā dhātu in the appended commentarial supplement to the original text, the term "unconditioned element" is not identified, in the Dhamma Sangaṇi, with the "topmost fruit" of the Paths, the arahatta-phalaṃ, which is one aspect of the state called Nirvana (*cf.* S. iv, 251, 252). The subject therefore seems to demand further inquiry. It is to facilitate this that the following results are appended, parallel more or less to the table on Form, pp. 168–71. *Cf.* note, p. 166.

Unconditioned element is

indeterminate	[983]
neither result nor productive of result	[989]
neither grasped at[1] nor favourable to grasping.[2]	[992]
neither vitiated nor vicious	[995]
"without applied or sustained thought"	[998][3]
to be put away neither by insight nor by culture	[1008]

[1] Given also in [1212]. [2] Given also in [1220].
[3] Given also in [1269], [1271].

something the root-conditions of which are to be put away neither by insight nor by culture [1012][1]
that which makes neither for the piling up nor for the undoing of re-birth [1015]
neither appertaining nor not appertaining to training [1017][2]
infinite [1021]
excellent [1027]
that which does not entail fixed consequences [1030][3]
invisible and non-reacting [1052][4]
not a root-condition [1072]
without root-conditions as concomitants [1074][5]
not associated with a root-condition [1076]
without material form [1092]
supra-mundane [1094]
not an Āsava [1102]
not having Āsavas [1104]
disconnected with the Āsavas [1106][6]
not a Fetter [1124]
unfavourable to the Fetters [1126]
disconnected with the Fetters [1128][7]
not a Tie [1141]
not that which tends to become tied [1142]
disconnected with the Ties [1144][8]
not a Hindrance [1163]
disconnected with an unfavourable to the Hindrances [1173]

---

[1] Given also in [1258] *et seq.*
[2] In the printed text [1018].
[3] Repeated in [1291].
[4] Repeated in [1088] and [1090].
[5] [1082] combines [1072] and [1074].
[6] [1112] repeats [1104] and [1106].
[7] [1134] repeats [1126] and [1128].
[8] [1150] repeats [1142] and [1144].

not a perversion [1176]
disconnected with perversion and unperverted [1184]
without concomitant object of thought [1186]
not mind [1188]
not mental property [1190]
disconnected with thought [1192]
detached from thought [1194]
not something coming into being together with thought [1198]
not consecutive to thought [1200]
not derived [1210]
without the attribute of Grasping [1218]
disconnected with Grasping, and not favouring it [1228]
without the attribute of vice [1240]
not vicious [1242]
not vitiated [1243*a*]
disconnected with the vices, and not vicious [1253]
without zest [1273]
unaccompanied by zest [1275]
unaccompanied by ease [1277]
unaccompanied by indifference [1279]
Unincluded [1287]
that by which there is no going away [1289]
something having no Beyond [1293]
not harmful [1295]

In the Cy. on the Dhātu-Kathā, nibbānaṃ (Nirvana) is always substituted for asankhato khandho.

THE END.

I.—GENERAL INDEX

The Arabic numbers refer not to pages but to sections, if not otherwise specified.

II.—PALI WORDS

Again, Arabic figures refer to sections, not pages, unless so specified.

The translation of the Commentary (PTS. 1920–1) has rendered the insertion of many commentarial terms, inserted in this Index in the 1st edition, no longer called for. A few are retained. But the multiplication of such insertions tends to blur the striking difference which exists between the slender psychological vocabulary of the Abhidhamma and the copious developments of the Commentarial (Buddhaghosan) age.